"Why are ⟨you⟩ ⟨⟩ ⟨so scared of⟩ **me?"** he asked. ⟨⟩ ⟨"It's not Noah⟩ or Connor."

She opened her mouth to protest, then stilled. He was right. *Shoot.* "I...don't know."

Frowning, he cocked his head. "Do you have something against having fun?"

"No." she laughed. "Fun is a good thing."

"And yet, you don't like me because I have fun."

"That's not true."

"Liar."

"I'm not lying." She shook her head, doing her best to be truthful without revealing too much. "I don't like you because you're dangerous."

He reeled back and stared at her. "Me, dangerous? No, darlin'. I'm a lover, not a fighter."

She blew out a breath. "And that's exactly why you're dangerous."

His brows disappeared under his hat. "Oh, now I'm really curious," he said. "Does that make me irresponsible, or irresistible?"

Tempting as hell.

"Both."

Heaven help her, a wicked gleam entered his eyes and turned them positively electric.

"So this is probably a bad idea." Placing his hands on either side of her head, he leaned in and inhaled near her ear.

What they're saying...

About Her Uniform Cowboy:

"Ms. Michaels pens a tale with pure heart and true grit! This story will hit so many readers close to home there is not one part of the plot that will feel foreign. No super models here, just true, down to earth servicemen and woman getting back to their place in the world. The characters and plot have a wonderful arc and the laughter, tears and emotional ride readers get to take on this journey will not disappoint."
—InD'tale Magazine, Crowned Heart of Excellence 4.5 Stars --Voted BEST COWBOY in a Book/Reader's Choice-LRC

About Her Unbridled Cowboy:

"I love Ms. Michaels' voice and she knows how to hook her readers in from the very beginning. I love how she develops her characters and makes them so believable that you feel as if these are real people you could become friends with. I highly recommend this second novel in the Harland County Series and I'm eagerly looking forward to book three and four. Don't pass this series up!"
—Night Owl Reviews, *Reviewer Top Pick*

About Her Fated Cowboy:

"As always, this author perfectly blended an amazing storyline, which contained characters you just can't help but fall in love with and she worked her magic in creating a masterpiece of the heart. I even enjoyed her sense of humor sprinkled throughout, which was placed in all the right places. This is one story I highly recommend and one author I just can't read enough from. Since this is the first book in the Harland County series, I'm eagerly looking forward to the next book."
—Night Owl Reviews, *Reviewer Top Pick*

Dear Reader,

Thank you for purchasing Her Forever Cowboy. This is the fourth book in my Harland County Series. *Unruly cowboys and the women who tame them.*

In this story, I've finally tackled Cole's good buddy and vice president, the charismatic ladies man.

Computer programmer, Kevin Dalton is as good-looking as he is smart. Extremely. The fun-loving cowboy loves women, but avoids relationships, and bottles up his feelings behind a joke and a smile. It takes a resilient 'cowboy tamer' to solve his code.

Shayla Ryan is the perfect fit for the puzzle-loving cowboy. On the run from her ex-con father, she's doing her best to keep her sister and daughter safe, and her body under control whenever the Casanova cowboy is around.

When they own up to the fact they have combustible chemistry, Kevin and Shayla attempt a 'just right now' arrangement that leads to a relationship. As they learn to open up, they learn to trust create a strong foundation for forever.

Another hot, heartfelt, sexy read, this story also includes some of the other characters in the series. I'm also creating a spin-off series-*Citizen Soldier Novels*-set in the Poconos of Pennsylvania, featuring Brandi's National Guard brothers briefly introduced in Her Uniform Cowboy.

Thanks for reading,

~Donna
www.donnamichaelsauthor.com

Also by Donna Michaels

Her Forever Cowboy

Harland County Series
Book Four: Kevin

By
Donna Michaels

HER FOREVER COWBOY

Harland County Series/Book FOUR: Kevin

ISBN-13: 978-1499767414
ISBN-10: 1499767412

Print edition June 2014
Book Four in Harland County Series

<u>Dedication</u>

To my street team, Donna Michaels' Minions, thank you for your continued support! To Harland County fans, I hope you enjoy the story of Cole's best friend Kevin, the brilliant, gorgeous Casanova cowboy who'd rather laugh and joke then open up and feel.

To my husband Michael, my family, and the HOODS. And to my cp JT Schultz, my mother, and my editor, Stacy, for their help and appreciation for this series.

Chapter One

Come to the pub, they said.

It'll be fun, they said.

"Fun my ass," Kevin Dalton grumbled, none too happy his friends failed to mention the sexy, redheaded she-devil would be at the Texas Republic with her killer lips and elbow to match.

When he'd first met the single mother a few months ago, he'd been fixated on her cute little girl smiling at him from over her mother's shoulder, and made the mistake of approaching from behind. He'd paid the price. The woman's elbow had been far from friendly to his lower extremities.

Swallowing a few choice words, and they were juicy, he slumped farther into the booth at the restaurant/bar owned by the Masters sisters. Or should he start referring to them as the McCall sisters? After all, Jordan and Kerri had married the McCall brothers this past year—Jordan to his good friend and boss, Cole, head of McCall Enterprises where Kevin was vice president and lead software engineer, and Kerri to the older, giant-sized cattle rancher, Connor.

Christmas this past week had been quite *Merry* with both McCall brothers married and his cousin Kade newly engaged. He was glad to see them all happy, he really was, but their perpetual smiles, coupled with the matchmaking glint now aimed at him from Mr. and Mrs. McCall and Mr. and Mrs. Masters were enough to sour his gut.

1

"What's with the face," Cole asked from across the table, brown gaze twinkling with undisguised joy. "Forget to wear your cup?"

Make that *ex*-good friend.

"Very funny." He didn't laugh, but he did groan as his buddy's older brother decided to settle into the booth next to him.

"Nah, he probably forgot to put on his big-boy underwear. Ain't that right, Dalton?" A lop-sided grin accompanied Connor McCall's jab to the ribs. "Quit being such a girl."

"Up yours, *Moose*." He didn't bother with the finger. A guy that big required a verbal reprimand if there was any hope of it sinking into the giant's thick skull.

"All right. Give my cousin a break." Kade Dalton, dressed in his Harland County Sheriff's uniform, sat next to Cole, gray eyes full of compassion and...*ah hell*, mirth. "You know Kevin doesn't have his *Man Card* yet."

"Bite me," he replied, tone sounding more aggravated than he actually felt.

He hardly ever got mad. Not his style. More of a lover not a fighter. His minor annoyance over the presence of the redhead in the bar had already passed. He was just having some fun with the guys. They loved attitude. And he had plenty.

He also loved his cousin. Although, he'd never admit anything sappy like that to the guys. That would constitute weeks of ribbing. *Yeah, no thanks*. Still, he was thrilled to see the weekend warrior so upbeat and positive.

For a while there, Kade had been just the opposite. His older cousin had needed an intervention to seek professional help regarding issues from a recent deployment with the Texas National Guard. It was truly great to see the guy happy. Of course, he knew the transformation wasn't all attributed to therapy. Hell no. Most of the credit went to his cousin's angel of a fiancée, Brandi Wyne. Too bad the beautiful designer from the north didn't have a sister.

Or two.

"Yeah, you're right." Connor nodded, eyeing him up. "He needs to earn it. Maybe once he takes off the girlie pants."

Kevin forced his lips to curve into a smile, and even managed a chuckle. Who was he trying to kid? It was funny. "You're just jealous because I'm better looking."

The cattle rancher's head jerked back with his smirk. "Yeah, right."

"Actually," his boss spoke up, lifting his beer. "We have to give 'ole blue eyes credit for those triplets I told you about from our Japan trip last year."

The Nakamura sisters...

Satisfaction spread warmth throughout Kevin's body and a matching smile across his lips. *Triplets. Japanese beauties*. Two items he'd crossed off his bucket list when he met them at the Software Development Expo where he represented McCall Enterprises. There to demonstrated his software design, he'd met the sisters later that night and had given them a private demonstration of his *hard*ware.

Kade nodded. "True. He does deserve credit."

"Yeah, I have to admit, that was very ambitious. Don't know how you managed that one, Kevin." Connor shook his head, small smile tugging a dimple to life.

"Nearly killed me," he admitted. Truth be told, he'd pulled a muscle in his groin. But hot damn, it had been so worth it. "Cowboys everywhere were relying on me to deliver. So I did."

"Three times?" Connor raised a brow.

He nodded. "I made damn sure each girl was satisfied before I crawled back to my room and passed out." Literally. With an icepack on his abused...muscle.

Laughter filled their booth and lightened the mood.

Kade lifted his beer and smiled. "To Kevin. Looks like he *did* earn that *Man Card*, after all."

The three laughing chuckleheads clinked mugs, but he didn't care. Hell no. Because *he* had the memory *and* the satisfaction of knowing he'd actually pleased the amorous sisters. A genuine smile crossed his lips and he sat a little taller. *Yeah*, he'd represented well. Real well.

"So, what seems to be the trouble with this one?" Cole nodded toward the line dancers tearing up the floor in front of a large, ten-foot spruce decorated in little cowboy boots, sea shells and twinkling lights.

Trouble? He frowned. "With what one?"

"You know *exactly* which one."

Yeah, he knew. They were referring to the spitfire with long auburn waves bouncing down her back as she kicked up her booted heels alongside Brandi. She was a natural. Perfect rhythm. Perfect sway. Perfect bounce. Too bad the perfect dancer was a perfect pain. Sure, he'd felt a connection, a damn strong connection, but he'd also felt her wrath. *No thank you.* Plenty of willing females out there. He did not need, nor want, to coax.

He took a pull on his beer, then nodded to the dancers. "Let's just say I know better than to bark at a dead tree."

Dark brows rose as his buddy turned to face the crowd. "She doesn't look all that dead to me. In fact, I'd say she looks quite...energetic."

4

She'd tasted even better.

Damn her.

"You've been avoiding the *dead tree* like the plague," his friend stated.

His head jerked back. "Bullshit. You're such an exaggerator, McCall."

"Not about this." Cole laughed. "You've avoided her here. Around town. My mom's Christmas party. Seriously, Kevin, what gives?"

A grinning Connor leaned close. "He's got an aversion to her elbow."

Damn straight. Kevin readily agreed with a nod. "Can you blame me? An elbow to the groin is not exactly a wonderful first meet."

He still couldn't believe she'd poled him. *Poled him.* And for no reason.

He'd been innocently walking toward Cole's wife Jordan, her sister, Kerri, and Brandi. The women were sitting at a picnic table eating ice cream at The Creamery, along with a redhead who was holding the cutest little baby girl he'd ever seen, when *wham!* The spitfire had elbowed his favorite body part and dropped him like a sack of cement.

"Sure left an impression, though." Cole snickered.

"Hell, yeah." He grimaced. "The fellas about-face whenever that woman's around. They cower and run for safety."

"You didn't seem all that put out when you two were *strawberry-sharing* a few weeks back," his buddy Cole reminded, grin widening, along with his death wish.

"Yeah, damn, that was some kiss." Connor nodded, dimple still glaring. "I thought the pub was going to catch fire."

"True, cuz." Kade scratched the bridge of his nose, a small smile tugging his lips. "You were kind of burning up the place."

The place?

Hell, he'd been ready to self combust. Burst into flames. Explode. One touch, one taste, and *bam*...his hunger for the prickly beauty intensified full throttle. A rarity. He'd pulled her close, and with their bodies lined up in perfect symmetry, which only intensified the damn heat, he'd proceeded to share the dessert and one hell of a memorable kiss. Delicious. Succulent. And it had nothing to do with the fruit. Absolutely nothing.

No. Sweet, juicy...hot, it was all her.

All Shayla Ryan.

Why did he have to feel this rare chemistry with the likes of her? The assistant who worked for his cousin's fiancée in Brandi's interior design company. A control freak who liked having things her way. Single mother of cute little Amelia, the twenty-one month old who readily jumped into his arms whenever they met, unlike her spitting image momma. Shayla was drop-dead gorgeous with curves to die for, silky red waves that brushed her mouth-watering chest, big blue eyes that could drop a man faster than her lethal elbow, and a sarcastic mouth to match.

A delectable mouth. A mouth that fueled his fantasies at night.

Still, she wasn't his type. Not that he ever really had one. No. Race, height, weight, none of that mattered. Even age didn't matter. Younger or older than him, Kevin didn't care as long as they were past the legal drinking age. He just plum loved women. Loved to make them happy. If an attraction existed and they were interested, then he was on board for some fun, whether it be sex or just hanging out. Because that was all it was for him. Fun. He wasn't looking for more, and made damn sure the woman knew that before moving forward.

Shayla wasn't about having fun, though. She had a baby. Responsibilities. Definitely not his type. He had no business sniffing around the beauty. So why his gaze settled on her swaying *badonk-a-donk*, and followed the seam in her tight jeans as it curved around her sweet ass…he had no idea. But he was hot. And hard. And pissed off at himself for his weakness where the redhead was concerned.

"Yeah, well, maybe we did burn up the place, but it's not going to happen again," he stated with a shake of his head. It wasn't. There were plenty of other *badonk-a-donks* that just wanted some fun.

A deep bark of laughter—in stereo—burst around him.

"You are so wrong, my friend," Cole said when he sobered, before tipping a pitcher to fill his mug. "That's how it starts."

"How what starts? An ulcer?" Because he certainly didn't need one of those.

"No." Connor snickered. "Getting sucked into the girl vortex."

A smile tugged Kevin's lips. "I like a girl's *vortex* very much."

"Not that, you horndog." His friend bumped his shoulder, nearly knocking him out of the booth. "The *girl* vortex. Her life. Her persona."

Wow. His brow rose as he stared at the giant. He had no idea Connor could pronounce big-boy words, let alone know the meaning. "Good for you, *Moose*. Vortex and persona. Two adult words in one breath. I'm so proud."

"It's not gonna work, pretty boy." Dimples glared. "You aren't gonna change the subject by picking a fight."

Damn, it was worth a try. Not that he wanted to fight the ogre, but it was better than talking about Shayla and that hot kiss.

"We're just trying to help you out, buddy," Cole said, leaning forward, pointing at himself then the other two guys. "Since the three of us were in denial a good sixty percent of the time in the beginning…"

"A hundred percent for me," Kade interrupted.

Connor raised a hand and snickered. "Hell, a hundred and fifty percent for me."

"That's because you're thick," Kevin told the grinning cattle rancher. "Kerri was sweet on you from the start, and you dropped the ball big time, big guy."

"Exactly why we're having this talk now, Mr. *Mensa*."

"Yeah, Kevin," Cole continued. "If any of us has a chance to get it right from the get go, it's you. You're the smartest, although I fear it's book smarts and not common sense smarts. At least not where women are concerned."

Seriously? He threw his head back and laughed. He'd been popular with the opposite sex since he was a teenager. No bragging. Just the truth.

"You're wrong, *bossman*," he felt obligated to protest, once he sobered. After all, he had a reputation to uphold. "I know more about women than the three of you put together."

The three of them laughed together. Then laughed some more.

It wasn't that funny.

"Excuse me, Kevin," a feminine voice interrupted. "Would you like to dance?"

Turning his head to view the owner of the sweet voice with even sweeter timing, he was pleasantly surprised to see the young woman he'd escorted to a sorority dinner earlier that year. Painfully shy and reserved, Nadine had needed a date for some spring shindig, and much to her dismay, her brother, a rodeo buddy of his, had asked him to escort her, no sex involved. Which was fine by Kevin. The sweetheart had felt more like a kid sister.

He watched as color flooded her cheeks, deepening the amber of her eyes, but she held his gaze and didn't look away. That was new. And good. The young woman was showing a confidence she'd lack in May.

"It would be my pleasure, Nadine," he replied, grasping her hand as he rose to his feet. He was more than ready to leave his chuckling knuckleheaded friends.

Leading her to the dance floor, he noted she'd blossomed quite a bit over the past half a year, trading in her sweats for designer jeans and a frilly blouse. Her brown hair was cut and styled, brushing her shoulders instead of pulled back with a scrunch thing on top of her head. He was happy to see the transformation and proud of her effort to come out of her shell.

"You look amazing."

Her blush deepened with her smile. "Thank you."

As they danced to an easy Texas two-step, he couldn't help but wonder what had caused the change, and why she was at the Texas Pub. "So, how've you been, darlin'?"

He knew she was a marketing major at Texas A&M, and smart as a whip. At the spring party, they'd danced a little, and he joked around until he'd gotten her to smile and loosen up enough to talk about her major. That's when he'd discovered they shared a love for puzzles of any kind. And video games. They'd played an RPG—roll playing game—for hours. It had been refreshing to be challenged. Unlike when he played against the MCalls. At least Kade could whip his ass in first person shooter games, although, he hadn't approached his cousin for a duel since his return from deployment. His gut had told him it wasn't a good idea.

"I've been good. Real good," Nadine replied. "I graduated this past semester and am starting a new job with McCall Enterprises this Monday."

He reeled back and grinned. "That's fantastic. Did you give Human Resources my name?"

She shook her head, a genuine smile curving her lips. "No. I wanted to get the job on my own. And I did." Pride and accomplishment sparkled in her eyes.

"Good for you," he said, continuing to lead the sweet girl around the floor, the smell of fresh pine a fragrant treat whenever they passed the decorated tree. "We're lucky to have you."

"Thanks, and thanks for believing in me and treating me like I wasn't invisible."

His heart twisted. Had people actually done that to her? *Cripes.* Sometimes society sucked. "You're more than welcome, darlin', but I didn't do anything but tell you what you already knew. You're beautiful, smart and funny, and I had a great time. Someday, some guy will be lucky to call you his own."

Pink returned to her cheeks and deepened with her shy smile. "He already has. I mean…I met a guy. We've been dating a few months, now." She motioned with her head toward a young cowboy semi-stewing near the bar.

Kevin brought them to a halt just as the music stopped. "Well good for you, but you probably shouldn't have asked me to dance." Lord knew he'd seen his share of jealous men over the years. That was the last thing he needed tonight.

She laughed. "It's all right. He knows about you."

Okay. He wasn't sure what to make of that statement. Not exactly the kind of threesome he was into. In fact, since the Nakamoras, he wasn't into multiple partners anymore. They'd cured him. Zapped him. Nearly killed him. Truth be told, age was catching up. He discovered it was much better to expend his energy on one lover. More rewarding for all concerned when he took his time and explored all his lover's merits.

"Thanks for believing in me, Kevin Dalton." The pretty marketing major lifted up on tip-toe and kissed his cheek. "I just wanted you to know girls like me sure could use a guy like you to make us realize that no matter what assets we posses, and don't posses, we all matter."

With that, she turned and sauntered to her cowboy who was now beaming with an ear-to-ear sappy grin. A smile pulled at Kevin's lips as a sense of pride and satisfaction puffed out his chest. Sweet kid. It was great to see her recognize she—

"Guess you can't win them all, cowboy."

His groin twitched. The fellas running for cover, no doubt.

Though he recognized that sexy voice, he'd already known the redhead was near before she even opened her delicious mouth. Every hair on his body had stood up and a prickling awareness spread down his spine as he stood talking to Nadine. He just chose to ignore it. Ignore her. Although, now that she'd spoken, he couldn't be rude. His momma had raised him better.

"Guess not," he said, turning to face the beautiful pain-in-*his*-ass. He didn't owe Shayla an explanation and wasn't about to give her one. "I'm surprised to see you down here kicking up your heels."

He knew mother and daughter resided with her sister in the apartment above the Texas Pub. She'd been there for months, but he'd rarely seen the woman downstairs, let alone dancing and, heaven forbid, having...*fun*.

She shrugged. "Not that it's any of your business, Romeo, but my sister is watching Amelia," she replied, chin out, shoulders back, scowl pinching the pleasantness from her face. "Caitlin insisted I join Brandi and Jordan and take some time for myself."

Her sister was a doll. Too bad it didn't run in the family.

"Well, good for you. I have to say you move quite graceful and fluent despite the pole up your...well, you know." He held the graphic words inside, but winked for effect.

A smirk tugged her pretty mouth. "Yeah, I know all right. And I know *you* ought to know all about...*poling.*"

Damn. The woman was mean. That remark had him resisting the urge to cover his favorite body part with both hands. The *fellas* literally twitched in fear.

What in the world happened to make the woman so damn ornery?

Granted, she'd lost her fiancé in the war last year, but that should make her sad, not physically and verbally abusive. Although, he seemed to be the only one on that end of the stick.

His gaze traveled down to the dragonfly on her boots and took a slow journey back up, lingering over the delectable, rounded flesh exposed by the V-neck of her navy T-shirt. *Freckles.* His blood heated. *Cute.* Just how many did she have? The urge to bend down and kiss each one was strong. *And stupid*. But, one thing was very obvious. Shayla may not like him, but her body sure as hell did. His wasn't the only one springing to life.

The urge to suck her pert nipples into his mouth hit him hard. He hadn't expected such a fierce tightening in his body. Still, that didn't stop him from carrying out his plan to teach the mean-mouthed woman a lesson.

He stepped closer, and hid a smile when she backed up into an empty table. Not so tough now. He followed, caging her with his body, enjoying the rise and fall of her chest as her soft curves brushed into him. The way her fiery gaze dropped to his mouth and she licked her lips. Yeah, he liked that. He liked that a lot.

But this wasn't about him. It was about putting the spitfire in her place.

What the hell was she thinking? *It's official, you've lost your mind, Shayla Ryan*. Why did she have to go and poke the tiger? Now he was in her face, in her space, all gorgeous six feet plus of male perfection with attitude. Exactly her type, and exactly what she did *not* need. But, oh yeah, she wanted. Oh boy, did she want the black-haired, blue-eyed cowboy with the five o'clock shadow covering his strong jaw. She wanted him bad.

And that ticked her off.

Instead of jamming her hands deep in her pockets, she wanted to run them up his tempting torso, over those incredible shoulders and into the hair curling slightly at the nape of his neck. But since that was a *want* and not a *need*, she just shoved them deeper into her jeans and grit her teeth when he reached out to twist a strand of her hair around his finger.

"True," he said, leaning close. "I do know about *poling*."

13

Ah, mercy, that man smelled great. Like a fresh rain in the woods, and male, very male. Even better than the decorated pine tree in the corner. But what he was selling, she wasn't buying. Been there, done that, wore a hole in the T-shirt. She no longer traveled that road. Amelia, her baby girl was her priority. No room in her life for a Casanova. No matter how damn tempting.

"You'd better move it or lose it, cowboy," she said, voice a little too breathy for him to take her threat serious.

And of course he didn't. He just grinned and moved closer.

Great, now the girls were perking up, happy with his nearness, even poking him periodically as her breathing increased. Damn them.

"Well now, here's the thing."

He tugged her hair until her gaze met his beautiful one. And his gaze *was* beautiful, with bright blue eyes framed by lashes so dark and thick he looked like a pirate.

"You're right, I do know all about...*poling,*" he admitted in a low, sexy drawl, releasing her hair to draw a line down her jaw to her mouth.

What was he doing? They were in public. People were watching. *Oh, look at that.* Apparently, she didn't care. She swayed closer. This was bad. She needed to stop him. Her whole body was trembling and tingling with awareness, especially her good parts. But if she removed her hands from her pockets, there was a great chance she would be yanking the tempting cowboy close and not pushing him away. And using her knee was out of the question. She was actually ashamed of what she'd done with her elbow when they'd first met. Although, no way in hell would she admit it.

"Trust me, darlin'," he continued, leaning down so close they shared a breath...or would've if she could remember how to breathe. "I guarantee when I *move* it, you'll *lose* it."

She nearly did.

Right there.

Lord have mercy. He had her wound so tight with barely a touch her quivering southern region was wet and ready to blow. Why was she so easy when it came to this cowboy? It was annoying as hell. If he made one more move, she was done.

With a knowing gleam in his mesmerizing eyes, he released her and stepped back. "It's a shame, really."

"W-what is?"

"That you're not my type."

With that jab, he twisted around and strode away, but not before she noted he saw her reach for the table to steady her swaying body, and he grinned.

He did not just do that...

Shayla knew she should let him go. Let the slick cowboy walk away all smug and arrogant. Keep to her rule where Kevin Dalton was concerned: avoid at all costs. But she always had a problem with *smug*, and hated *arrogant*. She could no more let the self-satisfying jerk get away with his comment than she could dance for the New York Ballet. Oh, she wanted to. *Badly*. But a flaw prevented her from doing either. An injury had killed her promising dance career, and her genetic code wouldn't allow the conceited cowboy to get away with his remark. Especially since it was a blatant lie.

Twisting on her *Justins'*, she marched straight to the Casanova, who was grinning from ear-to-perfect-damn-ear as he slid into the open-ended booth where the sheriff and the McCall brothers lounged.

Testosterone heaven.

Those men had it in spades. Her friends, Jordan and Kerri, were married to two of the handsome guys, and her boss, and friend, Brandi, was engaged to the gorgeous sheriff. *Lucky women.* How three such honorable and respected men of Harland County could socialize with a womanizing scoundrel like Kevin made absolutely no sense.

Well, except for the sheriff. The guys were cousins. Poor Kade, he had no choice. But the McCalls? *No accounting for taste.* She gave a mental shrug as she came to a halt at the Casanova's side of the table.

"Look, darlin'." Dalton held up a hand as he smiled sheepishly at her. "Surely I couldn't have made myself clearer?"

Clearer? Yeah, she was going to make things clear.

Holding onto her tongue because they had a full audience, complete with Jordan and Brandi who had joined their men. She cocked her head and stared down at the arrogant hunk. "Clearer on what?"

"You're just not my type," he repeated with a shrug of his broad shoulders and an apologetic expression on his damn face.

Several indrawn breaths mixed with a distinctive male chuckle and one murmured, "Ah hell." But Shayla paid them no mind. Instead, she leaned her hip against the corner of the booth, hooked a finger under the Casanova's chin and smiled. "Oh, I'm exactly your type, cowboy."

His brow disappeared under the dark hair covering his forehead. "Really? How do you figure?"

She leaned in, satisfaction warm in her veins when he glanced at her chest and clenched his jaw. A slight nudge of her finger had his gaze returning to hers before she answered, "Because I'm breathing."

With the table suddenly roaring with laughter, she patted his cheek then straightened. *There. Let him run that through one of his computer programs and think on it.*

To her surprise, the gorgeous cowboy threw his head back and laughed. A genuine laugh that lit his eyes electric blue, and zinged a strong round of awareness down her spine. *Shoot. Not good.* He was supposed to be mad. Arrogant. Defensive. Not laughing, and happy and friendly. She stepped back to steady her heartbeats. Stupid pulse.

"Good one, Shayla," Jordan complimented, perched at the end of the booth on her husband's lap.

"Yeah, well done." Cole nodded, drawing his wife's back against his chest as he smiled at Shayla. "You got any more?"

A smile tugged her lips. "Yeah, but it's time to call it a night." She nodded to Brandi and Jordan. "I had fun. Thanks."

It had been nice to leave her worries upstairs and take two hours off from reality. Really nice. She couldn't remember the last time she'd had the opportunity.

"I'm glad," her boss said from the other end of the table. "I'll see you in the morning."

Shayla nodded. Since Brandi only lived down the street, she'd fallen into the routine of walking to the designer's cottage where they'd go through the day's schedule over coffee.

"I'm getting ready to head back to the station. How about I walk you out?" Kade asked.

His offer didn't come as a surprise. The National Guardsman had a misguided sense of duty where she and

17

Amelia were concerned because her fiancé had died under his command in Iraq. But both soldiers had been doing their jobs. No one was to blame, although the sheriff apparently didn't see it that way. He shouldered all the blame, carried all the guilt, and stared at her with so much remorse darkening his eyes, at times her heart literally hurt.

It was wrong and unfounded, and last month, she'd risked a boatload of trouble by confiding in him the truth about her daughter. Bobby was not the biological father. That seemed to help a little, and bless him, Kade never turned her in for falsifying documents.

A real sweetheart. And gentleman. Tough to believe he was related to the self-centered Casanova regarding her with a lazy smile. The man didn't appear to have a care in the world. And why would he? He designed and played video games for a living. Kevin Dalton was a freaking billionaire with devastating good looks and life on easy street. If he wanted something, he went out and bought it. When he was tired of it, he threw it away. Shayla refused to ever become that '*it*.'

The cowboy's lack of responsibility astounded compared to his cousin Kade's.

Probably why she'd trusted the sheriff enough to confide in him even further when he had pressed about her guarded behavior. Kade was fair and just, and she felt it was in her daughter's best interest, as well as Caitlin's, to divulge a little of her past if they were going to stick around the area while her sister went to college. Sheriff Dalton and Deputy McCall were the only ones who knew Shayla's situation involving her deadbeat dad.

Fresh out of prison, Lyle Richardson was a threat. The ex-con was the reason she and her sister had changed their names, and moved around a lot. Never put down roots. Always looked over their shoulders, even while he'd been locked away.

Her thumb brushed over the dragonfly tattooed on the back of her wrist. A symbol of resilience in honor of her mother. Just touching the ink strengthened her perseverance to deal with her dad.

Lyle had a lot of sly, three-piece suited friends. The bastard had gotten wind that she'd come into some money when her fiancé had died, and she wouldn't put it past him to threaten her daughter to get it. Didn't matter that Amelia was his grandchild. Lyle Richardson didn't see people. He saw material objects. Meal tickets.

But Shayla was tired of moving around. So very tired. She didn't want to run anymore. She loved her apartment. Loved her new friends. For the first time, ever, she had a fulltime job with benefits, which was a miracle considering she didn't even have a high school diploma. And all of it gave her hope that, maybe...*just maybe*, she could make a stand and stay in Harland County.

Kade and Jordan had insisted it was possible.

The latter slid off her man's lap and joined her, waving a hand at the sheriff. "No need, Kade. Finish your coffee and enjoy a few extra minutes with your fiancée." Then the off-duty deputy draped an arm around her shoulders and chuckled. "Come on. I'll walk you to your apartment while Kevin catches his breath. I'd love to see that little sweetheart of yours anyway, if she's still awake."

Jordan and Kade were also the reason she had the wonderful, spacious, two-bedroom apartment above the restaurant. At first, Shayla had been leery of living over a bar with her baby, but the place was never rowdy, and the entrance to the upstairs was private and secure. Two things Kade had insisted on and the very things that helped her sleep easier at night.

"Okay. Goodnight, everyone," she said, nodding to the chorus of responses and ignoring the smiling cowboy to her right. She wanted out of there before things escalated. He was not going to ruin her otherwise wonderful night. She wouldn't allow it. *Dammit.* She worked hard and deserved a few hours of fun with the girls.

"Not his type my ass." Her friend laughed as they walked into the quiet kitchen to find Kerri McCall cleaning off the grill, the rest of the staff apparently dismissed for the night.

The pretty chef turned to them and smiled. "Hi, Shayla. Jordan. How was your night?"

"Great," she replied.

"Great? It was priceless," Jordan corrected with a grin. "She just put Kevin in his place."

Kerri stopped cleaning and twisted around, brown eyes wide and full of curiosity. "Oh, do tell. Please."

Reluctance tightened Shayla's chest. She wasn't one to relish the spotlight. She leaned against the counter and shrugged. "Not much to tell."

"She's being modest." Her deputy friend shook her head. "Kevin told her she wasn't his type."

Kerri's brows disappeared under her dark bangs. "What? Of course you are. You're breathing."

Shayla exchanged a look with Jordan before they burst out laughing.

"What'd I say?" The chef frowned, small smile tugging her lips.

Jordan sobered first. "That's *exactly* what Shayla told him."

Now Kerri was laughing. "Oh man," she said between giggles. "I wish I could've seen his face."

Jordan nodded. "Like I said, priceless."

"Well, be that as it may, I just hope he leaves me alone."

The deputy shook her head. "Oh, honey, that isn't going to happen."

"Why not?"

Chapter Two

The last thing Shayla needed was the devastatingly handsome cowboy going out of his way to tempt her. She was already on the cusp of giving into her attraction to the charismatic hunk.

"Because you're breathing," Kerri replied, before her hand flew to her mouth and she blushed.

Shayla chuckled and straightened from the counter. "Well, I'd better take my *breathing* self upstairs and relieve my sister." Caitlin was on holiday break from college, and although she appreciated her sister's offer to watch her daughter, she didn't want to take advantage.

"Okay." Jordan straightened, too. "See you later, Kerri."

They exited through the side door and into the cold winter night. That's when she realized she'd left her jean jacket back at the restaurant. What little brain cells she had these days seemed to disappear when that cowboy was around. *Oh well.* No way was she going back inside and risk round two with the charismatic temptation. Better to pop down in the morning when he wasn't around.

Admiring the clear sky and brilliance of the stars, Shayla shivered as they walked around the back to the stairs that led to a covered walkway. The crisp night air was a great neutralizer to her over-heated hormones. If Jordan noticed, she kept it to herself. Thank God.

The instant they stepped inside, warmth surrounded in a much welcomed hug, and by the time they reached the door at the end of the hallway, her shivers subsided.

Control was returning, and she was better, stronger…calmer.

Inserting her key in the lock, she turned to her escort. "You know, you really didn't have to walk me up here."

"I know," Jordan replied. "But your sister texted me and said she had a question."

A question…

Ah, crud. She knew what her sister was going to ask. A heaviness settled in Shayla's chest.

"Uh oh." Jordan cocked her head, gaze intense. "I can tell by the look on your face you know what your sister wants, and you're not crazy about it."

She sighed as she twisted her key. "Yeah, but, as much as I want to keep her safe, I have to let her live her own life."

"I know how that is." Her friend nodded, following her inside. "It was tough watching Kerri go off to culinary school in New York when she was eighteen."

Caitlin was a few years older, and her college was only thirty minutes away. But still, with their dad on the loose, Shayla was too uneasy about her sister being out of eyesight.

Walking down the small entrance hall, she could hear the TV on low, and when they rounded the corner the lights on the massive live spruce—compliments of Cole—twinkled brightly beneath plastic cartoon ornaments and tinsel garland, while her sister sat at the kitchen counter working on her laptop.

"Hi, Caitlin. Ah, looks like we missed Amelia," the deputy said, nodding to the baby monitor next to the computer, a disappointed frown on her face.

Her sister glanced up and smiled. "Hi, Jordan. Yeah, I put her down a half-hour ago. Sorry."

23

"No problem," their friend replied.

Caitlin glanced at her and frowned. "I was going to ask if you had a good time, Shayla, but since you returned without your jacket, I'll take that to be a 'no, I couldn't wait to leave.'"

Shayla laughed. "No, I had a good time. I just forgot my coat. That's all."

She did have a good time. Not counting the Casanova fiasco. That man was eye-candy best viewed from afar. And she knew better than to glance at the deputy. The woman's gaze already bore into her like a hot skewer, but Shayla wasn't in the mood for an assessment.

"Good. I'm glad. You deserve to have some fun," her sister stated, then turned her attention to Jordan. "I'm glad you're here. I wanted to ask your opinion on continuing to dorm."

Shayla's stomach clenched tight. They'd had this discussion already and it terrified her. But she'd agreed to let Caitlin run it by Jordan. Her sister deserved to have as much of a normal college experience as possible. It was bad enough the poor girl was a twenty-two-year old freshman, but it just hadn't been feasible for her sister to attend any college until this past year.

Having used some of her beneficiary money to legally change their names, Shayla then told her sister to pick a school of her choosing. Things were going fine. Her sister was excelling, enjoying her studies in her Veterinary Technician major and making new friends, thriving on a consistent routine. Something that had been foreign and missing from their lives for over four years.

Then they received word their dad was out and looking for them.

Caitlin had stuck out the semester at the freshman dorm, but Shayla had no intention of her sister going back. Attending college was fine, but by commuting. Not dorming. She needed to see her sister daily, to reassure herself Caitlin was all right.

If she had to get up an hour earlier to drop her sister off before work, then pick her up after work, she would. She could also purchase a car for her sister, although, the thought of Caitlin driving alone for that long stretch didn't sit well, either. Anything could happen. But, she'd wait to hear what the deputy had to say. Shayla didn't trust many people, but Jordan and Kade were an exception. The *only* exceptions when it came to her sister's welfare.

"What are the particulars?" Jordan switched to deputy mode as she sat across from her sister, gaze direct and alert.

Determined to stay out of the conversation unless pulled in, Shayla kept busy by cleaning off the counter, starting with the Rubik's cube she'd been working on for almost a year now. She placed the colorful square in a drawer and admitted the toy wasn't so much a game as it was a crutch, an *out,* something to occupy her mind when she needed a break from everyday pressures. Although, now, solving the cube was becoming more a matter of accomplishment. She was determined to succeed. A concept seeping into her life more and more.

With her sister now continuing her education, Shayla was toying with the idea of finishing hers. Getting her GED. Okay, she wasn't *toying* with the idea. She *was* getting her GED. Period. This spring.

Even though she wanted to stay in Harland County, she knew want and reality rarely met in the middle. Life was too unpredictable, and she'd learnt long ago to be prepared for anything. So she had to work fast. This time, if she was forced to leave, she was going to leave with a diploma, dammit. No more job *turnaways* because of her lack of education. Not that she wanted another job. She didn't. Shayla loved her job. Loved working for Brandi. Loved organizing, planning, coordinating work sites. Giving people a purpose. Watching her boss' visions come to life. *Helping* her boss' visions come to life.

But Shayla was a realist, and the reality was…her dad was going to show up and ruin everything. He always did. And if it wasn't him, it was one of his *friends*.

So, she already set things in motion. Discovered the nearest testing site was at the local community center through some career link program. They even had weekly classes and workshops to prepare for the test. Shayla was already signed up, had the pretesting out of the way, which showed what subjects she knew and those she needed to study. Math, some science and history, the parts of the courses she would've had in eleventh and twelfth grade. Brandi had insisted she take the morning classes since Jen, Kade's cousin, was already scheduled to watch Amelia at the Dalton's Shadow Rock Ranch on the days Mrs. Masters and Mrs. McCall weren't. Her boss didn't want her to have to struggle to find a sitter at night, even though it was only going to be a few weeks. Three, four tops.

"I'd be staying in an off-campus apartment already rented out by three other roommates," Caitlin informed.

Shayla brought her thoughts back to her sister's conversation as she threw junk mail in the garbage, loaded dirty dishes into the dishwasher, then put on a pot of coffee. Now, they just needed a snack.

Pulling out the last of the pumpkin roll with red and green tinted cream cheese Kerri had given them for the holidays, she vowed to only have one slice and part with the rest. As much as she hated to share the delicious, spicy dessert, her hips didn't need any more cushioning. Hell, she'd already eaten half the roll herself.

"The lease is in their names, so mine won't be on record," her sister continued. "And as far as the college knows, I'm still in my dorm, since freshmen aren't allowed to be off campus."

"How far is it from the university?"

"Only a block away."

She leaned back against the counter and watched Jordan. The deputy's gaze was serious as she tapped her jaw. Shayla could almost see the wheels turning behind the woman's dark eyes, but had no idea what it all meant. Her friend was tough to read.

"Security?"

Caitlin nodded, gaze open and hopeful. "Routine patrols that end right at the corner of the block."

Shayla knew all of this because she'd already grilled her sister with the same questions. Still, she didn't know if her reluctance was a product of years of being protective, or a real sense of danger. She just couldn't tell anymore.

Rubbing her temple, she sighed. God, she was tired.

Pouring out three mugs—the set a present given to her by Mr. and Mrs. McCall—she set them on a tray next to the sugar and creamer—given to her by Mr. and Mrs. Masters—then carried it all to the island where she settled onto the stool next to her sister.

"Thanks." Caitlin smiled.

Jordan's face lit up. "Mmm, Kerri's pumpkin roll. I kicked mine this morning."

"I can understand that," she said, and eying the snowmen on the blue mugs, relaxed a little as warmth seeped into her chest and eased some of the chill surrounding her heart.

It had been years since she'd received a gift from anyone other than her sister. The unexpected presents had touched her deeply, and Shayla knew, no matter where she resided in the future, she'd always remember her time in Harland County.

"I'll tell you what, Caitlin," Jordan said, setting her mug down. "How about we go to the university so I can actually take a look at the area and the set up? I know your sister would feel better, and so would I."

"Thanks. That would be great. I appreciate it." Her sister eagerly nodded. "When do you want to go?"

Jordan smiled. "Well, since tomorrow is New Year's Eve, how about we go on my next day off, which is Thursday, the second?" The deputy slanted her a look. "Sound good to you, Shayla?"

No. "Yes," she replied, the delicious roll turning to sawdust on her tongue.

"Perfect."

Hopefully. She hated to see her sister disappointed. The young woman deserved the moon. She'd been a rock, helping Shayla through the pregnancy and birth. Bobby's death. Their recent move, and watching Amelia two mornings last week while she had taken that pretesting.

"Speaking of perfect." Jordan smiled, mischief sparkling in her gaze, the deputy hat apparently off again. "What time are you arriving at the Dalton's New Year's Eve bash tomorrow?"

She wasn't.

Pushing crumbs around with her fork, she shook her head. "Yeah, about that…"

"Oh no, don't even try to weasel out of it, Shayla," Jordan warned. "I know for a fact Cody is looking forward to playing with Amelia. And like your sister said, you deserve to have some enjoyment. Both of you."

Enjoyment. When she thought of enjoyment, Kevin Dalton immediately came to mind. Which was stupid with a capital S. The kind of enjoyment that sexy cowboy oozed was the very kind Shayla had given up and no longer needed.

Liar, her body parts—the good ones—protested.

"I tell her that all the time." Caitlin frowned. "It's like she thinks because she's a mom now she's not allowed to let her hair down."

"Hey, *she* is right here," Shayla said, sitting straight and pointing to herself.

"Yeah, and *she* is going to the party tomorrow," her sister volleyed, touching her arm. "Look at how much fun we had at the McCall's Christmas party a few weeks ago. It was so nice of them to invite us, and even though you were the only one I knew, I didn't feel like an outsider. The McCalls, Masters and Daltons are really nice people. We're safe with them. I know we'll have fun."

"Yeah," Jordan said. "I'll be on duty, but I'm stopping in. Wouldn't miss the chance to ring in the New Year with my family and friends. And you shouldn't either."

Guilt hit Shayla's solar plexus with unmerciful force. She shifted in her seat and berated herself for allowing her concern over the stupid Casanova cowboy and his antics to keep Caitlin from enjoying a normal social event.

"All right. I'll try to put Amelia down for a second nap tomorrow, but I can't guarantee we'll be able to stay until midnight," she conceded, hating to deny her sister any bit of happiness.

"Sweet! Thanks." Caitlin leaned in to kiss her cheek. "We'll have fun. You'll see."

Fun...

That's what Shayla was afraid of.

An hour later, after Jordan left and her sister had gone to sleep, she sat on the couch with her Rubik's cube, hoping the puzzle would work its magic and calm her mind. It wasn't working. Between worrying about Caitlin and college, her dad and his greed, her upcoming classes and her run-in with the sexy Casanova downstairs, Shayla was too keyed up to sleep.

Or sit.

She rose to her feet and heaved a sigh. There was no other alternative. Well, actually, there was, but sex was out of the question. Heck, it had been out of the question for over two years now. Probably why she was so keyed up. Darn, sexy Dalton stirred her body, and now she had to deal with the fall out. Tossing her cube in the kitchen drawer, she heaved another long sigh, which rippled through her curtain of hair. It wasn't fair. The guy was probably off getting him some, while she was pent up with no one to...

A soft knock sounded at the door. Her heart immediately leapt in her throat.

Who in the...?

She glanced at the clock. Half-past eleven. Maybe the deputy forgot something. She hurried down the hall before the knocking got louder and woke up Amelia and Caitlin. Yeah, it was probably Jordan, after all, if it had been her father, he wouldn't have bothered to knock. He would've burst right in.

Holding her breath, she palmed the door and peered through the peephole Kade had installed.

Please let it be Jordan.

Blue jeans. Black Stetson. Blue-eyes…

It wasn't Jordan.

Holy heaven.

Her heart dropped to her knees then shot back to her chest where it raced out of control.

Kevin?

Opening the door before his third knock, she leaned against the doorframe, attempting to appear calm, when in truth, she needed the support. Her stupid legs were as shaky as her quivering stomach. "What do you need?"

Ah, hell, why did she have to go and ask that?

His brows arched, and amusement danced in his eyes as a slow smile spread across his handsome face.

"You know what I mean," she rushed to say before the cowboy managed to zap the rest of her strength with sexual innuendos.

Still smiling, he nodded and touched the brim of his hat. "Well now, I need a lot of things, darlin', but at the moment, I'm just here to bring you your coat as per Jordan's orders." He held up her jean jacket.

She was going to kill Jordan.

"Thanks," she said, swiping the coat from his hand, happy her voice hadn't wavered. "But I hope you weren't expecting me to invite you in. The others are asleep, and I'm heading to bed."

"No worries, darlin'."

"Good night." She nodded and turned to the door.

"But I have to admit, I am curious about something."

31

Don't do it. Don't take the bait. Step inside the apartment and shut the door. "Oh?" She turned around and stared at him instead. "Curious about what?"

"Maybe you should come out in the hall and shut the door so we don't wake anyone up," he suggested, reaching past her to close the door without waiting for her reply, his body much too close for comfort.

Clutching her coat, she walked a few feet away from him and leaned against the wall. "So, what's the problem?" The distance probably would've helped her to breathe easier if he hadn't followed.

"That's precisely what I'd like to know," he said, not making any sense.

Or was it her muddled brain? She couldn't seem to think clearly when he was around, especially when he was so close she could count his eyelashes. They were thick, and black.

Lucky bastard.

"Why are you always on the defensive around me?" he asked. "You're not like that with Kade or Cole or Connor."

She opened her mouth to protest, then stilled. He was right. *Shoot.* "I…don't know."

Frowning, he cocked his head. "Do you have something against having fun?"

"No." she laughed. "Fun is a good thing."

"And yet, you don't like me because I have fun."

"That's not true."

"Liar."

"I'm not lying." She shook her head, doing her best to be truthful without revealing too much. "I don't like you because you're dangerous."

He reeled back and stared at her. "Me, dangerous? No, darlin'. I'm a lover, not a fighter."

She blew out a breath. "And that's exactly why you're dangerous."

His brows disappeared under his hat. "Oh, now I'm really curious," he said. "Does that make me irresponsible, or irresistible?"

Tempting as hell.

"Both."

Heaven help her, a wicked gleam entered his eyes and turned them positively electric.

"So this is probably a bad idea." Placing his hands on either side of her head, he leaned in and inhaled near her ear.

Breath caught in her throat while goose bumps raced down her right side, perking her already perky nipples. "Yeah." It wasn't smart at all. And neither was she because he hadn't touched her. He was giving her the opportunity to protest. To move.

She didn't.

Yeah...stupid.

"And this," he said, against her neck, knocking his hat off, but he didn't stop, just continued to blaze a trail to her shoulder, giving her eyes a real good reason to roll back in her head.

"V-very bad." Her legs were about to buckle.

Push him away.

She needed to push him away. Now.

"Then I definitely shouldn't do this."

Thrusting his hand in her hair, he cupped the back of her head and kissed her full on the lips, and deep, very deep. That was it. She was done. To hell with pushing him away.

Shayla dropped the jacket, reached around his back and yanked him close, her perky nipples rejoicing at the contact with his hard, hot body. And he *was* hard and hot. All of him. A very impressive erection pressed *impressive*ly against her belly as his hips rocked against hers.

Someone moaned. Probably her. Didn't matter. He felt so damn good, plastering her against the wall, dipping and drinking as if he couldn't get enough. Or was that her? Again, it didn't matter. Her whole body was alive and on fire and wanted. It had been so very long since someone had wanted her. Not since that cowboy in Amarillo. Amelia's father.

Shoot.

Shayla drew back and sucked in air. "This…is…"

"Bad, I know," he said, breath ragged, gaze as dazed as she felt.

"It can't happen again."

He nodded.

"We're too…"

"Combustible," he correctly supplied.

"Exactly. We lead two different lives." She inhaled deeply. "You should go."

"I know."

He didn't move. Why didn't he move? She didn't have the strength, or willpower, to resist him if he initiated another killer kiss.

"You need to leave," she tried again.

Amusement chased away some of the haze from his gaze. "I will…as soon as you let go of me, darlin'."

"Oh." She released the lapel of his coat and belatedly pushed him away, fighting off a blush. *Idiot.* No time to be mortified. The best thing to defuse the situation was to leave. She walked back to her door and opened it, then glanced at him. "This can't happen again, Kevin. I have Amelia to think about."

She did not need another Casanova cowboy in her life, no matter how mind blowing the sex promised to be.

"I know," he repeated for the third time.

"Good." She stepped inside the apartment and closed the door without another word.

And without her coat.

Dammit.

Face heating beyond inferno, she opened the door to find the cowboy leaning against the frame, jacket dangling from his finger, a lopsided grin tugging his face to sexy.

Damn him.

She grabbed the coat, shut the door, then locked it. Not to keep him from coming in, but to keep her from going out.

"Pleasant dreams, Shayla," he said, door muffling his voice, but she still heard his damn chuckling.

It was going to be a long night.

"Well? What's the verdict, Jordan?"

Alex McCall waited with his wife, Leeann, and good friend, Nate Masters, as Nate's wife, Hannah, talked to her oldest daughter on the phone. Standing in a corner at the Dalton's, they eyed the door, watching guests arrive for the New Year's Eve party, but so far, not the one they'd hoped.

"Okay. Great." Hannah gave them a thumbs up, a smile easing the anxiety from her face. "I know you're on duty, but you are able to stop by, right? Your husband's here and looking a little bit lonely. Oh, that's good. Okay. Bye, honey."

His gaze automatically zeroed in on his youngest son. Cole was watching his brother and sister-in-law dancing, a wistful expression on his face. His son was a good man, and very supportive of his wife's career. Right now, Jordan was Kade's deputy. But the guardsman had already made it known he was not running for re-election in the spring, and had suggested to Cole's wife that she should run for Harland County Sheriff. *Don't that beat all?*

A smile tugged his lips. Alex had to agree. It was an excellent suggestion. His daughter-in-law was strong, tough, tenacious and fair. She'd certainly get his vote.

"Jordan said Shayla was definitely coming," Hannah informed, slipping her arm around her grinning husband. "Are we ready?"

He nodded with the rest of them.

"Well, my friend," Nate said, slapping him on the shoulder. "Over the last twenty-two months, we've managed to nudge our children toward their right match."

True—his boys with Nate's girls. "And fulfill half a promise we made to Sarah Dalton," he added.

"Yes," Nate agreed. "She would be very pleased with Brandi and very happy for Kade."

His gaze followed Nate's across the room to where their hosts were greeting arriving guests. The oldest Dalton stood next to his cousins with his arm around his new fiancée, and the most content expression on his face Alex had ever seen—and he'd known the boy since he was born. Then there was Brandi. She was all relaxed and happy, gazing adoringly up at Kade. The four of them had only played a small part in bringing those two love-birds together this year, but it warmed his heart to see the boy happy. He knew Sarah would feel the same.

Before their dear friend had passed on fifteen years ago, she had asked them to watch over her children, Kevin and Jennifer, and her beloved nephew Kade. And they had. As best they could. The kids were good. Didn't need much watching where their careers were concerned. In the beginning, they'd helped the Daltons out with college tuition, but the kids had long since graduated and insisted on paying them back.

"You've done right by the Daltons," Nate said. "Keeping an eye on them, helping when needed. Sarah and Hal would be pleased that Jen's an accountant and taking care of the books here at Shadow Rock while her husband manages the ranch."

He nodded. "Yeah. It was touch and go there for them in the beginning, but they managed to get it together. Jen and Brock have been married, what, three years now?"

"Four," his wife corrected.

"And they have cute little Cody," Hannah added.

Alex smiled, watching the young whipper-snapper sneaking a cookie off a table while the grownups were busy by the door. He got the biggest thrill when the little guy called him Grandpa McCall.

"Well, we've seen Cole and Connor finally wise up and marry your daughters," his wife told Hannah. "And now Kade is engaged to Brandi. His perfect match."

Drawing his pretty wife closer to his side, Alex smiled at her romanticism. But she was right. Brandi was perfect for that boy. Kade had seen too many deployments with the Texas National Guard. That last one had nearly done him in when he'd taken the death of one of his own, Shayla's fiancé, pretty hard. They'd all seen it. Thank God for Brandi. She was the only one to get through to him. The only one he'd listened to when things overwhelmed him. Now, he was seeing a therapist, no longer holding things in and on his way to healing. Alex was right proud of the boy.

"So, there's only one more left," Nate stated.

"The toughest," his wife added.

"Yep," Hannah agreed.

Alex nodded as the four of them stared at their target. Smiling, joking…" Kevin."

It was going to take more than one girl to rope the wild cowboy. The way the sparks flew off the vice president and the pretty single mother from north Texas, Alex was positive they'd found Kevin Dalton his woman. And with the loss of her fiancé, raising her daughter on her own, plus looking out for her younger sister, Shayla Ryan deserved her perfect match, too. The four of them would nudge when needed.

Starting tonight.

Of all nights for her daughter to not be tired, she had to pick this one. Shayla had hoped her baby girl would've conked out by ten since the little stinker hadn't settled down for a second nap that afternoon. But no. Here it was half-past and Amelia was still going strong.

Leaning against a wall in the Dalton's family room cleared of all furniture, she couldn't help but smile at Amelia and Cody. They were too cute, holding hands and jumping up and down while Brandi made her fiddle talk to a Charlie Daniels tune sung by a local band hired for the night. The little boy's cute, white dog, Ace, was by his side, jumping, too, tail wagging, letting out the occasional bark, to which her daughter giggled.

"Where does she get the energy?" Mrs. Masters asked, looking smart in a pretty, deep purple sweater and black slacks as she came to lounge next to her.

Shayla smiled and shrugged, trying not to feel frumpy in her jeans and boots, grateful for the silk, aqua blouse—a present from her sister. "Got me."

As it was, she was ready to call it a night. Sleep had pretty much eluded her last night, thanks to a certain Dalton. But, it wasn't just that. Since becoming a mother, she'd turn into a lightweight as far as burning the candle at both ends. Although, she hadn't had much need. She didn't date. Didn't go out with friends. Heck, until moving to Harland County this past summer, Shayla didn't really have friends. Except for Bobby, but he was gone. She never stayed in one place long enough to acquire them.

But she had them now. And her outing last night had shown Shayla what she'd been missing. Maybe her sister was right. She should make some time for fun. Mrs. McCall and Mrs. Masters offered to extend watching Amelia anytime at night, too. Okay, the sweet ladies had practically begged. Maybe she should take them up on that offer. Maybe she should…

"…dance," Mrs. Masters said.

Shayla blinked. "What was that? I'm sorry, I was in another world."

Her friend's mother chuckled. "It's okay. I often visit there, too."

The woman's smile was so friendly and welcoming Shayla couldn't help but smile back. Although in her fifties, Hannah Masters was still visually beautiful with lighter brown, shoulder-length hair, side-swept bangs and warm brown eyes. It wasn't a stretch to see where Jordan and Kerri got their good looks.

"I was saying you should go out there and dance," she repeated, nodding to the dance floor. "Caitlin told me you love to dance."

Dancing was her love, her heart, and it would've been her career, but one well-placed whack from her bastard of a father had put an end to those hopes years ago. Now, she had to settle for just dancing for fun.

Fun.

Exactly what she'd just told herself she was going to start doing. "All right. Maybe I'll go dance with Amelia."

"No." Mrs. Masters' silky hair swished as she shook her head. "Go dance with the grownups. I'll keep an eye on your little girl. Have some fun. Even your sister is out there."

And so she was. Shayla smiled. She'd been watching Caitlin kicking it up with several of the cowboys, Doctor Turner and even Kevin. Since going to college, her sister had really started to blossom. It was great to see her face devoid of fear and anxiety. She was too sweet and kind to bear such a mask.

Walking toward the floor, Shayla had to admit cowboys in south Texas could dance. Especially a certain blue-eyed Casanova. She'd watched the guy putting heel to floor with anyone and everyone, and damn, he had some moves. As always the case when the handsome cowboy crossed her mind, her insides fluttered. He was the reason she'd stayed by the wall. Bumping into the potent guy was too dangerous. That kiss last night was living proof.

She stopped halfway there. Yeah, maybe dancing with him on the floor wasn't such a good idea.

"There you are, Shayla," Kerri said, grabbing her by the arm. "Come on, let's dance. I didn't get a chance to join you guys the other night at the pub."

Before she knew it, the chef tugged her out onto the floor next to Caitlin. *Shoot.* Short of looking ignorant, there wasn't much she could do other than pick up the beat. So she did, and soon they were joined by Connor and Kade while Brandi finished her set. Laughing and grooving, Shayla didn't care that several cowboys had joined their group, and that Kevin was giving her the stink-eye.

Or was it directed at the cowboys.

She didn't know. Didn't care. Just danced and danced. She was supposed to have fun, dammit.

"It's good to see you enjoying yourself, Shayla," Cole said, joining their group. His wife was on duty and hadn't stopped in yet. "That first year can be tough. I'm glad you didn't close up and turn into an ass like I did."

Kerri had told her how her brother-in-law had been cold and guilt-ridden over his first wife's death, and that it had taken an understanding and...*pushy* Jordan to break him out of his funk. She didn't have that problem. Her engagement had been born out of necessity. Although she had loved Bobby, she hadn't been *in love* with him. Still, it did hurt to know she'd never see her friend again.

Turning to face Cole fully, she brought a smile to her lips and continued to dance. "I'm doing okay."

"If you ever need to talk, my ear is always open," he offered with a grin as he increased his pace.

Damn, he had good moves, too. What was in Harland County's soil? Or was it the water? She had yet to find one guy who didn't know how to dance. Granted, some were better than others, like the tall, laid-back cowboy, and a nameless blue-eyed devil. But still. Damn.

They had been kicking it up to a good beat when Cole stopped mid-dance. His back was to the door, but Shayla watched, fascinated at how he'd known the instant Jordan had entered the party.

"Thanks for the dance." He leaned down to kiss her cheek. "Excuse me," he said, then turned and strode straight for his grinning wife.

Unreal. "Did you see that?" She elbowed Caitlin.

"Yeah. That was something," her sister replied, while they both stood watching the couple unite.

She'd read about a connection like that in romance novels, but hadn't realized it was real. Envy and longing suddenly mixed to form a ball of need in her gut. What would it be like to have a guy 'feel' her that way? As soon as the thought entered her mind, her gaze was inexplicably drawn to the sexy, blue-eyed cowboy dancing nearby. He stilled. Didn't smile. Didn't frown. He just stared. So deep she swore he reached in and squeezed her heart.

"My sister and Cole have always been like that," Kerri said, stepping in front of her, breaking Kevin's spell, or whatever the hell he was doing.

Shayla blinked and nodded, mind only half-registering what her friend had said.

"I swear those two were cued into each other since the day she was born," Connor added, drawing Kerri closed to his side.

"Yes," his wife agreed. "I can't believe it's been a little over a year already since they got engaged."

Connor glanced down at Kerri and winked. "Would you believe it's been a year to the day that you stole my breath in this very house, and I haven't been able to catch it since?"

Shayla watched, smiling as Kerri lifted up on tip-toe and kissed the sweet cowboy's lips.

"Jeez, *McMoose*, what are you trying to do, make my guests puke?" Kevin asked, drawing up next to the big cowboy.

Connor smiled, and still gazing lovingly down at his wife, answered, "Actually, Dalton, I was only concerned with one of your guests."

Kevin's lips twitched into a full smile as he slapped the tall rancher's shoulder. "Well, all right then. Kerri certainly deserves to be happy. Although, why she's chosen the sorry likes of you is beyond me," he joked.

Connor nodded. "Me, too."

"Awe," Caitlin gushed. "You sure you don't have any other brothers, Connor?"

The cowboy laughed. "No. Sorry, darlin', but Brandi has four."

Yeah, and Shayla had met all of them through Skype. *Jeez*, they grew them handsome and built up in Pennsylvania.

"I have four what?" her boss asked, approaching their group now that she'd finished her set and put her fiddle away.

"Brothers," Kerri answered.

The designer laughed. "Oh, yeah. Guilty as charged. Why, who wants one?" A warm brown gaze settled on her.

Shayla held up her hands and laughed. "Wasn't me. Not that your brothers aren't drop-dead gorgeous."

Ben, with his delicious five o-clock shadow, keen green eyes and razor sharp wit, and then there were Keiffer, Mason and Ethan with the same chiseled good looks and yummy chocolate brown eyes. They were definitely what she called 'double-takers,' because you'd do a double-take if they walked by.

"It was me," Cailin admitted. "I'd asked Connor if he had another brother because those McCalls are just so sweet."

43

A grunt turned snort left Kevin, and Shayla couldn't help but grin. The guy was nothing if not entertaining. But she had to agree with her sister. Cole and Connor treated their women right. Just like Kade treated Brandi. With respect, and not afraid to show their feelings. It was refreshing as hell. The three of them restored a little bit of faith in Shayla that maybe there were some gems still out there.

"Like me. I can assure you, darlin'," Kevin said, stepping close to grasp Caitlin's hand and bring it to his lips. "We Dalton's aren't too shabby, either."

"True." Brandi smiled, leaning up to kiss her smiling fiancé's face.

"Conceited much?" The words left Shayla's mouth before she had the chance to swallow them down.

"Only a lot." Kade chuckled, drawing her boss in close.

Connor nodded. "Only every day of his life."

They all laughed, even the conceited man in question.

"Not *every* day, Moose," he said good-naturedly, releasing her sister's hand to fully face the older McCall. "I do take a day off once in awhile."

"Yeah," Cole said, returning with his deputy wife at his side. "Cut Kevin some slack, bro." The younger McCall stared at his brother, and if it weren't for the twinkle in his dark eyes, Shayla would've expected trouble. "He has to sleep sometime."

This was great. She didn't have to worry about giving the Casanova cowboy a hard time. His friends were happy to do it for her. A smile tugged her lips hard.

"So, are we going to stand around here taking jabs at Kevin or are we going to let him and Shayla get back to their dance?" the deputy asked, glancing at the group.

Wait…what?

She blinked at Jordan and shook her head. "We weren't dancing."

She really did need to kill that woman.

"Yeah, she probably couldn't keep up, anyway," the cowboy taunted, his blue eyes full of a challenge directed straight at her.

My ass, she wanted to say, but he'd no doubt have some smart-mouth rebuttal. And the last thing she needed was for him to be talking about her ass. It would plant all sorts of delicious…*unwanted*—not delicious—*unwanted* ideas in her head.

"Oh, you'd better be careful, Kevin," Caitlin warned. "My sister can out-dance just about anyone."

A chorus of 'oohs' went through the crowd, and Shayla realized all dancing had stopped, and all eyes were on them.

Shoot.

"I'm not afraid, darlin', cause your sister's too chicken."

Chicken my ass.

What she wouldn't give to wipe that self-serving grin off his handsome face.

Connor stepped forward. "Well now, I think there's only one way to prove it," the tall cowboy claimed. "A dance-off."

A what? *Ah, hell.*

"Great idea," Cole agreed. "Let's clear the floor and give them some room."

The floor cleared.

Dammit. This was getting out of hand. "Wait a minute. I didn't say…"

"See? Chicken," Kevin said, then proceeded to make chicken sounds.

That was it. Aggravation shot her adrenaline to high speed. She stepped to the smug bastard. "You want your ass handed to you, Dalton? Consider it handed to you," she said, poking his taut chest as she pushed him backwards across the floor. "You're going down."

A sexy-as-hell- grin tugged his mouth and his eyes smoldered. "I'd love to."

Every cell in her body woke up at once, while blood whooshed through her veins with an electrified tingle, pooling low in her belly and nearly buckling her legs. Damn him. An image of the gorgeous man, smiling wickedly up at her from between her legs had her whole body humming. It took all her energy not to reach out to him for support so she didn't make a fool out of herself and crumble at his feet.

Irony reared its smug head when the band began to play a lively Garth Brooks tune with *going down* in the title.

Bastard immediately started dancing while she stood there like a goof. *Oh, hell no.* A second later, she picked up the beat and jumped right in. Little did the guy know, she'd danced to that very song.

At regional's.

And won.

Didn't matter it was over a decade ago, her legs and muscles remembered the routine, every beat, every twist, every free spin, chasse, ball change and kick, and she was leaving the smug cowboy behind.

Until he grabbed her and began to… "Jitterbug?" she asked as his body moved perfectly with hers, side, side, rock step.

"I do it all, darlin'," he said between inside and outside turns. "Jitterbug. Tango. Waltz."

Wow. She smiled, beginning to enjoy herself. "Then let's get to it."

He twisted her back in and grinned. "Yes, ma'am'."

Shayla knew her leg was going to hurt like a bitch come morning, but she didn't care. She let it all out. Let her guard down.

And for the first time in over a decade… She. Had. Fun.

Hell yeah, the woman could dance.

Kevin knew the redhead had moves, but what she was doing was exquisite. Shayla Ryan was a natural. Combine her talent with his lessons and wow. He was pulling out all the stops, drawing on years of lessons from Mrs. Avery that he'd endured as a boy to please his mom. Now he was never happier because he could keep up with the girl. Barely at times, but he loved a challenge. He twisted her around and off his back, then rolled off hers as if in practiced precision.

Over the years, he'd had may dance partners, but never had he danced with someone so energetic, so knowledgeable, so damned in tuned to his body that she could anticipate his next move. *Pure poetry.*

"You're good, cowboy," she said as he pulled her in.

"Right back at you, darlin'," he replied before releasing her.

But instead of extending her hand for him to pull her back, she shook her head and sent him a wicked grin that shot a zing straight to his groin. *Hot damn*, she was up to something. A second later his jaw dropped.

The crazy woman walked up the damn wall and flipped back, landing on her feet, and without missing a beat, started to dance while the crowd cheered.

"You were saving that one, weren't you?" he asked, spinning her in an outside turn.

47

Donna Michaels

She grinned from ear to ear, barely out of breath. "You know it."

How could she not be out of breath? He was dragging his ass. But he never backed down from a challenge. And she looked so happy, so carefree. She was mesmerizing.

"What do you say we both give it a go?"

She reeled back slightly as they held hands and rock stepped off the balls of their feet. "You can wall-flip?"

He smiled. "What do you think?" He did it ten years ago at a bar in Tulsa. He'd landed it…mostly.

"That you're crazy…and you're on, cowboy. Let's do it."

She danced away from him, nodded then headed for the wall.

This was it. Do or die. And he wasn't about to die.

Kevin headed for the wall alongside the redheaded she-devil.

No guts, no glory.

With a running leap, he walked up the wall, then pushed off in a back-flip while the momentum was still strong and…

…landed the son-of-a-bitch.

Hell yeah! His right heel hurt like a bastard, but he kept going, not because the crowd was cheering, but because Shayla sent *him* his first genuine smile. *Ever.* It lit up her beautiful face, turning her eyes a sparkling, clear blue that stole his breath. His insides felt funny and his chest hurt, but he held her gaze.

God…he could stare into those eyes forever.

"I can't believe you did that," she said, voice a little breathless as he pulled her in with a turn.

"Me either." He laughed, then twirled her out then back in several times because he loved the feel of her body pressed against him.

Yeah, that made the pain radiating up his left leg worth it.

"You're crazy, Kevin Dalton. You know that?"

"So I've heard, darlin'," he said. "And you are damn good."

When the music stopped, he was still riding high on adrenaline and wanted nothing more than to continue to hold her body tight and bring his mouth down on hers for an encore of last night's kiss. The memory of her soft, seeking, demanding lips and her exquisite, spicy taste had haunted him all night. And the tantalizing rise and fall of her chest and the way her gaze dropped to his mouth didn't help his resolve to behave himself around the single mother.

But, despite what she thought, he wasn't a jerk.

He stepped back, grabbed her hand and raised it high in the air. "Here's your winner right here, folks. I concede defeat. Shayla Ryan can dance," he announced to his guests.

Shock widened her blue gaze and opened the mouth he was trying so hard not to notice. He lowered their hands as the crowed clapped and cheered, but just when he was about to pull away, she re-raised their hands.

"And I think it's only fair to call it a tie, because, cowboy, you're right. You are good," she stated, surprising the hell out of him.

With that adrenaline edging him on, he nearly yanked the woman in close so he could show her just how good he could be, but common sense reared its ugly head and he dropped her hand and smiled instead.

"Thank you, darlin'. I'd be happy to dance with you anytime."

And by dance he meant horizontal. No, no...he meant *vertical*. Definitely *vertical*. Good clean fun. Nothing that involved getting naked and horizontal.

She nodded, but didn't move. It was as if she was caught in this crazy vortex of need currently biting at his ass. God, she was making it tough for him to be a gentleman.

Her blue eyes blinked and he watched her drag in a breath. "I...ah...I should go check on Amelia."

Before he could respond, she twisted around and walked away. *Damn*, that woman had a great walk. He gave his head a shake, watched her another two beats, then turned and headed in the opposite direction—to the bar, receiving back slaps from his friends along the way.

"Nice moves, buddy," Cole told him.

"Yeah, well done, Kev," his cousin said.

Ah great, *McJollyRancher* was opening his mouth.

"Didn't know you had that in you, Dalton," Connor stated. "Thought for sure you'd go right through the wall."

It had been a concern, but thankfully, not a reality. "Me, too."

They laughed as he continued on his way, taking great care not to limp. Water first, because he was damn parched, then a stiff drink to take the edge off the pain in his foot.

He had half his whiskey finished when one of his cousin's National Guard buddies appeared at his side. "Hey, Jace."

"Kevin." Doc Turner nodded. "That was some fancy footwork."

He nodded back.

"So, how's the foot?"

He stilled, drink poised in mid air. "How the hell…?"

Jace smiled. "I'm a doctor. I know when a patient is hiding pain."

Kevin downed the rest of his JD and shrugged. "It's nothing. It'll pass."

"Sure it will." Jace snickered, looking completely unconvinced. "I'd be happy to look at it, but I already know your answer."

"No thanks."

The doc smiled. "Figured as much. Well, since you're walking on it, I'm betting it's not broken. I suggest to ice and wrap. I'd tell you to stay off it, but I know you're too ornery to listen."

He laughed. "True." Although, icing and wrapping sounded good. Like heaven good.

"And you might want to get that boot off now, while you can." The doc gestured to Kevin's aching foot. "I'd hate to see you have to cut through such fine leather."

He straightened. "What?" *Never.* No one was putting a blade near his Tony Lamas. Cupping the doc's shoulder, he nodded. "Thanks, Jace. See ya later."

Ignoring the pain was a hell of a lot easier when he wasn't walking. *Son-of-a-bitch*…now his foot *did* hurt when he stood. Sharp shards radiated through his whole foot with each step. Still, he managed not to limp through the crowd on the way to the bathroom where the household first aid supplies were stored.

Sweat trickled between his shoulder blades and broke out along his temple, but he didn't dare break his swagger. Last thing he needed was people making a fuss. With his hand on the knob of the bathroom door, he considered himself home free when it suddenly yanked

51

forward. Knocked off balance, he stumbled straight into the person coming out of the bathroom.

Shayla.

"Oh, Kevin, I'm sorry," she said in a damn sexy, breathless voice. "Are you all right?"

That was the first time she'd ever called him by his name. He kind of liked it. In fact, he liked it so much, he didn't dare tell her or she'd certainly never utter it again.

A heartbeat later, he realized they were clutching each other's arms in an attempt to steady the other. Their dance, and the way her body felt against him immediately came to mind. He cleared his throat and released her.

"Yeah. I'm fine, darlin'. Are you okay?"

She nodded, but…*shit*…her gaze narrowed as she searched his face. "What's wrong?"

"What do you mean?" He was determined to play it cool. Get her to leave, then take his boot off and wrap his damn foot.

Before he knew it, a blessedly cool hand ran across his forehead and temple, and he caught another whiff of her spicy, mango perfume.

"Jesus, cowboy." She drew her hand away as if burned. "You're sweating like a wh…" She stopped and cleared her throat. "You're just really sweating. Which is not normal." She drew him farther into the bathroom, closed the door, then leaned against it, arms folded across her generous chest, expression…not so generous. "Tell me what's going on. And don't say nothing."

"Oh, I think I saw this once. This is where you tell me to take everything off," he said in an attempt to throw her off the scent.

She snorted. "In your dreams, cowboy."

He cocked his head. "How'd you know?"

A myriad of emotions crossed her face at once, desire and longing mixed in there, then disappeared to leave her with a raised brow. "Nice try, but it's not going to work. Now, tell me, what did you do?"

He knew when to talk himself out of a paper bag and when to not even try. This was one of those *not-even-try* times. He hobbled past her to the linen closet and fished around for the ankle wrap and tape.

"You hurt yourself on that flip," she said, voice surprisingly more sympathetic than accusing.

"Yeah." He held up his stash. "Doc said to ice and wrap."

She smiled. Why was she smiling?

"I was just in here icing my knee," she confessed, pointing to a wet, crumpled napkin in the trash. "Sorry, I already tossed the ice."

Pain momentarily forgotten, he dropped his things on the counter to grab her arms, concern tightening his chest. "What happened? Sit down." He hoisted her up and set her next to the sink. *Cripes*, she weighted but a feather. "I'll go get Doc Turner."

Her hand snaked out to clamp around his forearm. "Wait. It's okay. Don't bother him. I'm fine," she insisted, her touch soft considering the firmness of her voice. "It's an old injury that flares up from time to time."

Kevin studied her face. It wasn't pinched. Her eyes were clear and bright.

"Really. I'm fine. You're the one who needs help." She squeezed his arm before releasing.

He immediately missed her warmth. What the hell was his problem? It was just a touch. Maybe the pain was affecting him more than he'd realized.

"What is it? Your knee? Foot? Ankle?" Shayla asked, half her body brushing his as she slid off the counter.

Right now, it was an entirely different body part that throbbed. *Hot damn*, he wondered briefly if he could hoist her back onto the counter and have her slip off again. Slowly.

Better yet...

Swallowing hard, he clenched his fists and fought the urge to lift her up so she could wrap those flexible legs around his hips while he pressed her against the door and kissed her long and deep. Very, very deep.

Not cool. He needed to keep his cool. Realizing she was still looking up at him, waiting for an answer, he cleared his throat. "Foot," he said, voice a bit tight.

Like his jeans.

"Well, let me help you. You can't wrap it without icing it first," she claimed, dropping to her knees.

All the fantasies he'd had of the redhead the past few months flashed before his eyes at the sight of her kneeling before him. She was so damn sexy looking up at him with those big blue eyes and parted lips. Every drop of blood in his body settled in his shorts. At once. He was so damn hard he could take on a steel beam. And win.

She glanced at his feet. "Which one?"

He opened his mouth, but nothing came out. Apparently, his dick still had control of his voice. He lifted his left foot instead.

She tried to tug off his boot. Wouldn't budge. Hurt like hell, though. Pain rocketed through his body and propelled his mouth open, but his voice remained hostage to his throbbing groin.

"All right, well, maybe it'll come off easier if you sit down," she said, rising to her feet. "There's not enough room in here, so where do you want to go? The couch in the living room?"

Hell no. The last thing he needed was others seeing him in this condition. And he wasn't talking about his stupid foot.

The threat of exposure helped him regain his voice. "No. Let's go to my room. It's just down the hall."

Chapter Three

Kevin just had this woman in his arms while they'd danced. He'd held her in his arms last night. She was curvy and soft and damned delicious. He knew this. But nothing had prepared him for the reaction his body had when Shayla crushed her breast into his side and slid her arm around his back to hug his waist.

It wasn't a fluke.

Heat skittered down his spine while his pulse literally jumped. Just like last night. The sensation, the feeling was real. This was all new, but holding a woman close certainly wasn't. It didn't make sense.

Must be the pain.

Yeah, the pain was definitely playing with his mind. But despite what Connor claimed, Kevin wasn't a wuss. He usually had a high tolerance of pain.

"Grab the wrap and tape," the redhead ordered as she led them to the door.

Kevin swiped the first aid stuff off the counter and wanted to tell her he could walk. He *should* tell her. That would stop the heat. But he couldn't.

Because *that* would stop the heat.

Apparently, he was a masochist. Who knew?

She opened the door, and at this point, her curves felt so damn good molded to his side he didn't care if anyone saw them. But they didn't as he directed the surprisingly helpful woman to his room at the end of the hall, allowing her to only take some of his weight. He was not an invalid, but he enjoyed every bit of her softness snuggled close.

Yeah, he was a jerk. But a happy one.

"Let's get you on the bed, then I'll fetch some ice," she said.

Before his brain had the chance to stumble over *the bed* scenario, she left him alone on the mattress with more than one ache in his body.

Which was plumb crazy.

He'd been with many women, and occasionally more than one at a time, so why did this cantankerous redhead get to him so bad? The whole night was nothing if not confusing.

"Okay," she said, returning a minute later with a clear bag of ice, brows knit together, gaze and stride full of purpose. "Now, where were we?"

A smile tugged at his lips. "Is this where you tell me to get naked?"

She stopped dead a foot away and blinked. "No, you goof, but hey, if it'll make you feel better, have at it."

The bag of ice hit him full force in the chest, but he caught it with ease before it fell to the floor. "Then, can you get naked?"

She dropped to her knees in front of him again, completely wiping his mind clear of all thoughts, leaving him a swollen tongue and an erection biting so hard into his zipper he saw stars.

"Why should I?" she asked, lifting his foot to rest against her boobs. Her very nice, rounded boobs. "You've already alluded that I've been naked in your dreams."

As he worked to remove his thick tongue from the roof of his mouth, he watched her gently but firmly tug the boot from his foot.

"There, that wasn't so bad, right?" She smiled triumphantly at him.

Donna Michaels

God, she looked so gorgeous, and so happy, he almost didn't have the heart to tell her it was the wrong boot. *Nah.* He had plenty of heart. "Wrong boot." And a boatload of wicked to go with it. "That'd be my other left."

She muttered under her breath, and if he'd been a timid man, he would've blushed. "You kiss your momma with that mouth?"

"Keep it up and I'll kiss your lips with my fist," she replied, yanking his other boot off none too gentle.

He yelped as pain radiated up his leg and stole his breath. "Jesus, lady, you're mean," he said through clenched teeth. "What'd you do? Break it clean off?"

"Ah, quit being such a baby."

Words of rebuttal died on his lips the second she shoved her hands up the leg of his jeans to remove his sock. Barely recovering from the incredible feel of her fingers on his flesh, the she-devil set his bare foot on her chest and gently stroked down to his ankle.

That's when he swallowed his tongue.

"Does this hurt?" A concerned blue gaze bore into his.

He shook his head. That actually felt good. Real good. *Too* good. So did the warm, soft cleavage pillowing his foot. He longed to replace it with his face so he could lick every freckle. Twice.

"Where does it hurt?"

She stroked different areas, and although several did hurt, he continued to shake his head because otherwise, she'd remove her fingers. He preferred to endure the pain while he tried to deduce why her touch was so different from other females. It was puzzling, and he was good at puzzles. But hell if he could figure out what caused the heated fission that passed between them.

58

Maybe the woman wasn't such a meanie after all.

She slapped the bag of ice on his ankle.

Wrong. "Dammit, woman," he ground out. "What's your problem?"

"You, ya big jerk," she huffed, but didn't move away. "I don't know what kind of game you're playing, but cut it out. I'm trying to help you, and it would be great to know exactly where to place the ice."

"Sorry," he said, but didn't mention the puzzle thing. "Right here is fine." He brushed her fingers and some of her chest as he repositioned the bag to cover the area that throbbed the most...on his foot. It would take a whole hell of a lot more than a few pieces of ice to reduce the swelling in his jeans. Nothing short of streaking through the Antarctic would work.

Her intake of breath trembled up his leg, and he wasn't sure if his touch or the ice caused the reaction. He stared into her fathomless eyes for a few beats and wondered briefly if his instability all stemmed from a roofie in the whiskey he'd downed. Being that he'd poured the Jack himself, he could rule out drugs.

Damn.

That meant he was *high* on this woman. Affected by her in some chemical way. Although he knew most things were possible with science, Kevin also knew a remedy wasn't probable. So, where exactly did that leave him?

With his body unreasonably turned on, and his frozen foot shoved in the redhead's mouthwatering cleavage.

"Damn, that's cold," he said, removing the ice.

"I know." She gently set his foot on the floor, and backed away before she rubbed her reddened chest where the ice had touched.

Shit. "I'm sorry, Shayla." He leaned forward to stroke the cold blotches. *Cripes*, she was soft. And silky…

A strangled sound came from her throat a second before she fell on her sweet ass and crab-crawled back a few feet. "No harm done. I'll live." She righted herself, then moved closer, picked up his discarded sock and wiped his foot dry. "Give me the wrap."

"Yes, ma'am." He handed her the bandage and smiled, but she didn't glance at him.

Damn. She was back in *she-bitch* mode with her guard up again. Having caught a few glimpses of her human side tonight, Kevin's curiosity was piqued. He watched as she deftly wrapped his foot.

"You're good at this. Was it because of your own injury?"

"Yes and no," she replied, gaze trained on her ministrations.

He tried again. "Don't tell me Caitlin was a tomboy."

"No." She laughed, and this time, glanced at him. "But there were quite a few rambunctious boys at the foster home."

Ah, hell. She'd been in foster care? For some reason, that thought tightened his chest. "I'm sorry." He was beginning to realize there were several layers to this woman, and a few, no doubt, attributed to her prickly demeanor.

She dropped her gaze and shrugged as she began to secure his bandage with tape. "It was only for a year."

"How old were you?"

Her fingers stopped for a second, then continued to tape his foot. "Sixteen," she replied without glancing up.

The sympathizer in him sprang to life, and his whole body shook with the need to take the woman in his arms and comfort her. Of course, that would go over like a lead balloon, and he'd more than likely get poled for his troubles. The fellas were definitely not in favor. He shoved his fingers in his back pockets to keep from reaching for her anyway.

"That had to be hard on you and Caitlin. She was what…?"

"Twelve," Shayla replied, still not making eye contact. "But, she was at a different home."

Christ. "They separated you?" He rubbed his chest as if that would ease the tightness squeezing the breath from his lungs.

"Yeah, but I'm glad. She was in a good home."

Which meant Shayla wasn't. Now his whole upper body hurt. And his mind latched onto something she'd said. "If you were sixteen when you entered foster care, and only there for a year, then you left at seventeen."

"Yes."

He frowned down at her. "I thought you had to stay in until eighteen?"

"You do," she replied, voice low and noncommittal as she shrugged. "I ran away."

To hell with it.

No longer caring about risking personal injury, Kevin hauled her onto his lap and crushed her close. "I'm sorry, darlin'," he said, burying his face in her hair before she had the chance to slug him. It was soft and silky and somehow stroking the strands calmed him down. He was definitely beginning to understand her prickly demeanor, and since she didn't push out of his arms or punch him in the face, he took that as a sign it was okay to continue to

61

stroke. "Kade's parents passed when he was eleven, but at least he had mine to take him in."

"He was lucky," she said, warm lips brushing his neck, sending a round of shivers down his spine. "When I was eighteen, I got custody of Caitlin, and she's been stuck with me ever since." The air cooled between them as she drew in a breath. "And I've no idea why I'm telling you this." All too soon, the spitfire scrambled from his lap and backed up a few feet away. "I think you can manage the rest on your own. I'd better go find my daughter before she wonders what happened to me."

The baffling beauty turned on her heel and strode from the room, leaving him there with a sockless foot, a ton of questions, and now, a third ache wracking his body. He glanced at the clock on his nightstand. Fourteen minutes to midnight. He removed his other sock, hobbled over to his cupboard and was surprised at how much the pain had subsided by simply wrapping his foot. All right, so it could also be because his mind was still mulling over the fact Shayla had been in a foster home. A bad one. And then on the streets.

But, she was fine now, his mind reasoned. Had a good job. Good apartment. Good life.

Nope.

Not thinking about it.

Not getting involved.

He eased on a clean pair of socks, slipped his feet into his Italian loafers, then rejoined the party. There was just enough time for a drink before he planned to snag the blonde who'd been flirting with him half the night and ring in the New Year with a kiss hot enough to make him forget about foster care, and a redhead who laughed when she danced, and had helped him even though he egged her on...and had the softest—

"There you are, Kevin," Kade said, approaching without his fiancée. "Take care of that foot?"

Really? A few of his favorite choice words rumbled up his throat. "She told you?"

Gray eyes narrowed on him. "She? She, who? Shayla?"

He refused to answer since Kade's tone sounded more confused than accusing. If he just kept his cool, maybe his cousin would put away the sheriff part of him for the night. After all, Kade wasn't on duty. Jordan was.

"No, she didn't say a word," the man eventually answered after staring him down to within an inch of his life.

Ah, hell. The sheriff persona did disappear, but now *Sgt. Hardass* took over. Kevin preferred to deal with Sheriff Kade Dalton. Not First Sergeant Kade Dalton. *Damn.*

"I know when my men are hiding something, and you definitely had that look fifteen minutes ago. But, we'll get to that."

Sgt. Hardass draped an arm around him, cupped his shoulder and led him...more like pushed, no...*propelled* him into their deserted kitchen. Once inside, *Sir-yes-sir* blocked the swinging door with his unmoving body, folded his arms across his chest and leveled him with another of his famous *don't-give-me-no-shit* looks.

"Now, let's talk about Shayla. Are you the reason I saw her coming from the hallway with her shirt wet? What the hell did you do?"

Kevin leaned back against the butcher block counter and sighed. He was going on thirty-one, vice president of a billion dollar company, turned industry leaders on their ears when he wrote new code, and yet, his cousin could still make him feel like a reckless teenager with just a stare. *What the hell?* He hadn't done anything wrong. No reason to feel guilty. And he didn't feel guilty. But he did...*feel*. And wasn't that just the problem?

"Talk to me, Kevin. I know you like everyone to think of you as a player, but I know you better. You have heart. You don't go around messing with people unless they want messing."

True. True. Unfortunately, *too* true. And *true*.

"Am I reading Shayla wrong? *Does* she want messing?"

"What?" He straightened from the counter and shook his head. "No. And I wasn't messing with her." Much...

Okay, maybe a little. But damn, she was so cute when she got angry. Except for her elbow. He shifted his stance as the *fellas* twitched. *No.* Her elbow was not cute at all.

"Then explain the wet shirt, and why she was coming out of your bedroom."

Shit. He'd hoped no one had seen that.

"It links back to my foot." No sense in denying since Kade had already called him out on it. "She was just helping me ice and wrap."

Sgt. Hardass cocked his head. "With her chest?"

"Well, yeah...actually. Sort of," he stammered, a small smile tugging his lips. "She's the one who shoved my foot there before applying the ice."

His cousin blew out a breath and nodded. "Okay, but it doesn't explain why she rushed from the hall as if her hair was on fire."

"Sorry, I don't have an answer for you, cuz." He lifted a shoulder and shook his head. "After wrapping my foot, she left my room in that very same manner."

Kade's gaze turned thoughtful as he rocked back on his heels. "I think I know why."

"Then, please, enlightened me," he begged. "Because I haven't got a clue."

"She likes you."

He reeled back. Then laughed. "Right. That's why she nearly tripped over her feet to get away from me."

"Yeah. She definitely likes you," Kade repeated, his tone returning to cousin mode. "But she doesn't want to."

Great. He really didn't need this knowledge. That made things worse, because he liked her, too, and he was having enough trouble dealing with that fact. He didn't want to *like* Shayla. He was happy just *lusting* the pretty redhead. No way did he want to bring *like* into the equation.

Kade stepped closer to place a hand on his shoulder and squeeze. "Don't mess with her, Kevin. She's had it rough. You can have your pick of women. Leave Shayla alone."

Nodding, he only half-heard his cousin's words, but knew he had to give some sort of reaction or Sgt. Hardass would return. "I don't plan on messing with her, but you'd better plan on getting back out before the clock strikes twelve or you'll have one unhappy fiancée."

"Shit." Kade's gaze shot to the clock on the microwave. "Two minutes. You're right. Let's get back in there."

Kevin fought a smile as he followed his cousin from the kitchen to rejoin the party. He knew the word *fiancée* would get Sgt. Hardass off his case. Okay, that was harsh. Kade was only trying to protect the single mother. He knew his cousin felt responsible for Shayla and her baby girl since her fiancé had been attached to Kade's unit and died during deployment last year.

An invisible band tightened across Kevin's chest. Shayla Ryan *had* been through a lot. Having Kade watch out for her was good. The poor thing didn't have anyone to turn to. Apparently, she'd been doing all the *looking out* and protecting since she was a teenager.

That didn't sit right with him. Kind of settled in his gut like a steel ball.

Re-entering the room, he noticed people started to break off in groups of two or more. Kade made a beeline for Brandi, who wrapped her arms around his cousin and managed to delete all traces of Sgt. Hardass from the party. *Good girl.*

His sister, Jen, leaned against her husband, Brock, while their son, Cody, laughed in his daddy's arms. Kevin whipped out his phone and quickly captured the Kodak moment.

"Excuse us, buddy," Cole said, moving past him to cage Jordan in the corner, or was that the other way around? A grin tugged his lips. One never knew with those two.

Same could be said for the other McCall brother who ushered Kerri into the laundry room, secret smiles on their faces. *Smart move.* The two could now ring in the New Year in private.

It did his heart good to see his family and friends so happy and content. Lord knew it had certainly been far from it a few years back. This had been a great year, and tonight was going to be even better. He surveyed the room, searching for the willing blonde. *Bingo.* One buxom beauty winking at him straight ahead...and four smiling faces on her right, all glancing expectantly from him to Shayla.

Ah, hell.

The older Masters and McCalls were in matchmaker mode again. Wasn't going to work. Not this time. No way were they going to successfully get him and the beautiful spitfire together. Kade had been right to warn him off. But it was unnecessary. Kevin didn't want to mess with the woman. He didn't do *permanent*, and that's what she needed.

Leaving the single mother alone was definitely in everyone's best interest.

So why the hell were his feet turning him away from the smiling, willing Dolly Parton look-a-like and carrying him straight to the blinking redhead with the sweet, smiling baby girl lifting her arms toward him?

Hell if he knew, but he caught the little bouncing angel and pulled her into his chest, enjoying her happy gurgle and the way she smelled like baby powder. The tiny sweetheart filled an invisible hole he didn't like to talk or think about.

"Where are you going, pumpkin?" he asked as the cutie pounded on his face with her hands. She certainly was a feisty one. Just like her momma.

"Sorry. She has a mind of her own," Shayla said, making to take the child from him.

"No, let her be. It's okay," he insisted, dropping his free arm around the woman's shoulders and drew her close.

Kevin knew he should heed Kade's warning. Let the woman be. Stay out of her life. But at that moment, he wasn't in control. His over stimulated body was in control, and his need and want were exactly the same for once. To taste the gorgeous redhead again. He'd worry about consequences tomorrow. Kevin was exactly where he wanted to be at the moment—closing the distance to Shayla's incredible lips.

And as the crowd counted backward...*three...two...one...* and called out *Happy*

New Year, Amelia grabbed his face with sticky hands and gave him a wet, sloppy kiss.

Something inside Kevin's chest clicked. Puzzle piece fit against puzzle piece. Which was crazy and made absolutely no sense, and yet...he could not deny one blatant fact.

That was the best damned *ring in the New Year* kiss he'd ever received.

Chapter Four

Two days into the New Year and Shayla was just as confused as she had been at the Dalton's party, watching the sexy-as-sin cowboy turn to putty in her daughter's hands. It should've made her laugh and tease the heck out of the Casanova. But, instead, her chest hurt from a heart inflated beyond measure...and reason.

Attraction to Kevin she understood. Drooling over his incredible body and good looks...she understood. But this affinity—this connection—made no friggin' sense. It was bad. *Real* bad. He was a rich playboy, just like Amelia's father, with no responsibilities other than to pleasure himself.

She sucked in a breath. Bad word choice. *Damn.*

Heat pooled low in her belly so strong and fast, she was grateful to be seated next to her sleeping daughter in the back of Jordan's car on the way to Caitlin's college. *Stupid body.* It was all Kevin Dalton's fault. Stinkin' cowboy wasn't even present and he managed to zap the strength from her legs.

"You okay?" her sister asked, twisting around in the front seat to stare at her.

Ah, hell. Did I moan?

Rubbing her temple, she silently wished her boss hadn't decided to wait until next week to start a new design job. Too much down time was causing her mind to wander to unsafe territory. She dropped her hand and sighed. "Just a little dizzy."

A lie. Sort of. She did have a slight headache. Lack of sleep does that to a person. Her reaction to the executive cowboy didn't only play havoc with her pulse, it interrupted her sleep as well.

Her sister's keen gaze narrowed as she chewed her lower lip. "You aren't sleeping much, are you?"

"You do look a little pale, Shayla," Jordan said, meeting her gaze in the rearview mirror.

Before she could respond, Caitlin reached back and squeezed her arm.

"I'm sorry, sis. I'll just stay with you and commute. I don't want to worry you. It's no big deal."

"Whoa." She covered her sister's hand and stared into a troubled gaze. *Dammit.* Caitlin thought her lack of sleep was her fault. *If only.* "No. Absolutely not. Jordan's taking us to check out the housing as planned."

Once again, she met her friend's gaze in the mirror and the woman nodded.

"But—" Caitlin began to protest.

"No." She squeezed her sister's arm. "No buts. We agreed to do whatever it is Jordan advises. That hasn't changed. Okay?"

Caitlin continued to stare at her, concern still clouding her pretty blue eyes. "I just hate that I'm causing you to worry. You've done so much for me already."

Was she kidding? There were times Shayla had barely provided more than a ramen soup meal…for days on end. And although she'd been so proud of their first apartment, it had only been a step above a flea-bitten mess. Thinking about the past and remembering the guilt she'd felt over taking her sister from a safe house with three squares a day to basically starve in a hovel was something she was still working on.

"I haven't done squat, but you're too sweet to say." She patted her sister's hand and sighed. "I'm sorry, Caitlin."

Her sibling drew back with a frown. "For what?"

"This should be your final year of college, not your first."

"Oh, Shayla, not that again. I told you, I'm so grateful to be going. Plus, my gosh, you're paying for all of it. Do you know how lucky I am? You're the best sister ever."

She snorted.

Again, *she* wasn't doing squat. Tuition was courtesy of Bobby, thanks to putting her down as his beneficiary and giving her power of attorney over his things while he'd been deployed. Other than their name change and Caitlin's college, Shayla planned to save the rest of the death benefit for Amelia's future. Bobby would've been happy.

Caitlin frowned. Hard. "I mean it. Even when you ran away from your foster home and went to live across town with Bobby, you still managed to come see me and attend every basketball game I was in, all throughout middle school."

Although Jordan's gaze snapped back to hers, and Shayla would've preferred to hold this conversation in private, she trusted her friend enough to reply to Caitlin.

"There was no way I would've missed them, sis."

Her mother had been around to attend Shayla's dance recitals, before her...*accident*, and she knew how great it had felt to have family at events. Caitlin wasn't going to go without. And her sister wasn't ever going to know that she and Bobby had been living in an abandoned building until they both managed to scrape up enough money doing odd jobs to buy an old trailer.

He'd been her first lover and a dear friend, but she had to be living on her own, in a decent place, with a steady income in order to gain custody of her sister the minute Shayla turned eighteen. Nothing had mattered more to her than Caitlin. She loved Bobby, but as a friend, and she knew he'd felt the same, so after only a few nights together, they'd both agreed to go back to a platonic relationship and not complicated it with sex.

"You made my chorus recitals, and art shows, birthdays. Snuck over on all the holidays," her sister continued to sing her praises. "Then when you got custody of me, you managed to keep me in that very same school district so I didn't have to start over."

Bobby had even helped her with that. He'd joined the Guard, and when he came back from basic training, he'd handed her all his pays so she could rent a two bedroom apartment. It took her a year, but she managed to pay him back with interest. One of her prouder moments.

He didn't want it, of course, but she'd insisted, and since he'd been dating a nice girl at the time, Shayla had been able to convince him to take the girl on a vacation. It was just too bad things hadn't worked out between him and that girl…and that she and her sister had to move from that nice apartment because of her father's goons.

The day after Caitlin's graduation, they'd hit the road, and they'd been running ever since. But no place was safe. She'd discovered that last spring when her paroled father paid her a visit and tried to extort money from her by threatening his granddaughter. Thankfully, it had been in a public place and she'd already mapped out escape routes in her head. A practice she deployed in every town they'd lived in. Even Harland County.

"So, no more lip about how you're sorry you didn't provide for me, Shayla. Because you did," Caitlin stated with a nod, bringing her back to the present.

"Yeah, but we—"

"No buts, remember?"

Stubborn woman cut her off. A smile tugged Shayla's lips. "College has made you bossy."

Caitlin laughed.

Jordan snickered. "I'd say it runs in the family."

Now Shayla laughed.

"True." Her sister smiled, glancing from Jordan to her. "So, it's time you start letting *me* take care of me, and you concentrate on my beautiful little niece."

As if on cue, Amelia began to stir from her car-induced nap.

"Well said." Jordan sniffed. "Sisters are the greatest."

Caitlin reached back to squeeze Shayla's hand. "And mine's my best friend."

Now *she* needed a tissue. "Ditto, kiddo."

Two hours later, they settled into a corner table at a restaurant across from the university after having explored the whole area, including the trek to the charming, two-story traditional where her sister hoped to stay.

Locked up tight, due to the holiday break, the house appeared to be safe from the outside. Jordan had walked the perimeter a few times, jotting in a notepad, for which they were now about to discuss.

Shayla had barely removed Amelia's coat and hooked her into a high chair when her sister leaned closer to the table and stared eagerly at Jordan.

"So? What's the verdict?"

The deputy chuckled. "Excited much?"

"Yeah, a little," Caitlin replied with a smile. "It's just that I'd really like to stay in that house with my...friends."

Had Amelia's babbling distorted her hearing, or did her sister just hesitate over that last word?

Jordan glanced at her notes, then closed the book and split her glance between them. "Short version. Everything looks good, but I'd really like to see the inside of the house to be one hundred percent certain."

Shayla nodded. "Me, too." A measure of relief and anxiety settled in her gut.

"I thought so." Caitlin smiled. "One of the roommates should be stopping by here with the key within the hour."

"Super," their friend exclaimed as she picked up a menu. "What'd you say we eat while we wait for our tour guide?"

They had just finished their lunch, and she was wiping applesauce off her daughter's face when her sister suddenly rose to her feet.

"Here's my roommate now."

Neat and clean and friendly, the roommate appeared very nice...and very male...and very, *very* affectionate toward her sister as he pulled Caitlin close and kissed her soundly on the lips.

Well, hell.

Shayla's stomach knotted tighter than the fist her daughter was using to tug on her hair. Things were starting to make a lot of sense. She glanced at Jordan. A ghost of a smile appeared on her friend's face.

Yeah, a *man*. Who knew?

No wonder her sister was so hell-bent to dorm and not commute. The guy was cute, and exuded a confidence born from years of responsibility. Going by his short brown hair and clean-shaven jaw, he almost appeared military.

"This is, Greg Mitchum," Caitlin introduced as Shayla removed Amelia from the highchair and stood.

Of course it is.

"Greg, this is Jordan."

Shayla watched as he shook her friend's hand, holding eye-contact the whole time. Good. So far he didn't appear shady, or homicidal.

"Ma'am," he said with a nod. "You're the deputy of Harland County, right?"

Jordan's brow rose. "Why, yes I am."

"Soon to be Sheriff," Caitlin chimed in. "Well, after she wins the spring election, of course."

"Best of luck to you, ma'am. From what I hear, you're a shoe in," he said, then turned to face her. "You must be Shayla. It's nice to finally meet you." His hand was warm and firm as they shook. Again, he held eye contact, and his gaze was open and sincere. "I'm sure you're more than a little surprised."

She couldn't stop the snort. "That's the understatement of the decade."

Amelia chose that moment to throw her sippy-cup. It bounced off of Greg and landed by his boot. Apparently, she didn't want to be left out of the introductions.

"Sorry about that," she said, taking the cup he'd retrieved from the floor.

He smiled. "No problem." Then he turned to the squirming little terror. "Hello, Amelia. You are even cuter in person."

Jordan took the cup from her hand.

"Thanks," she said, then switched Amelia to rest on her other hip. "She's in rare form today."

"Then what'd you say we head to the house and you can grill me there?" handsome, clean-cut Greg suggested with a grin.

Caitlin slipped an arm around his waist. "Great idea. Did you park here or walk?"

"Parked."

"Then I'll go with you, and we'll meet them back at the house." Her sister glanced her way. "Is that okay with you?"

No. She had a ton of questions. "Yeah, sure. We'll follow in Jordan's car."

A few minutes later, after paying the bill and buckling the protesting Amelia in her carseat, Shayla climbed in the front of Jordan's vehicle and sighed. *Damn*, that was a workout. Who needed Pilates when you had a toddler around?

"Okay, we're good to go," she told her friend sitting in the driver's seat with a gadget in one hand and a sippycup in the other. "Oh, I'm sorry, Jordan. Give me that."

"No, it's okay. I was using it to run Greg's print." The deputy held up the strange gadget and smiled.

*Oh my God, she didn't...*Shayla grinned. "I knew there was a reason I loved having you as a friend."

"You mean it wasn't my witty personality?"

"That's just a bonus."

They were both smiling as they turned their attention to the thumb print and photo on the screen of Greg in an Air Force uniform.

"I knew he was military," she said.

"Yes, and he has no priors." The deputy pushed a few buttons and more info appeared. "He's an engineering major. Father is an aerospace engineer.

Mom's a lawyer. Younger sister is a sophomore at this college, staying in the house, too."

Shayla sat back in her seat and sighed. It was all good news, and yet…she still worried.

"It's okay to worry. She's your sister." Jordan laid a hand on hers and squeezed.

Apparently the woman could read minds, too.

"The worrying never stops."

"I know." She removed her hand from under her friend's to fish a soft picture book from the diaper bag and reached over the seat to hand it to her fussing daughter. "I also know she needs to live her own life, but…"

"It's hard," Jordan finished. "I agree. It was tough letting Kerri move to New York with her male friend to attend culinary school, but as you said, they have to live their own life. And make their own mistakes."

She nodded again.

"Are you worried for Caitlin's safety from your dad, or heartache from Greg?" her friend asked as she started the car.

"Both."

Jordan nodded and pulled out of the parking lot. "The safety part we can work on, but the Greg part is out of our hands."

That was the problem. Shayla hated not being able to protect her sister. And even if the guy turned out to be nice, there was the added worry that her father and his goons would harm Greg and the other roommates, too.

"We just need to make sure the place is safe. I don't want any of them to get hurt."

"Will do," Jordan assured. "Now, tell me how you feel about Mr. *Airforce*. He did seem genuinely happy to see Caitlin."

"Yeah." She smirked, remembering the heated kiss. "I thought he was going to swallow her tongue."

Jordan laughed. "I hate to break it to you, but that's how you and Kevin looked at my sister's shower/bachelorette party a few months back."

Air funneled into Shayla's lungs so fast she coughed. *Shoot.* Now heat was settling low in her belly as the memory of that incredible, hot, decadent kiss washed clean over her. "Damn, I was trying to forget."

"Honey, one never forgets a kiss a like that."

Not when one kept reminding you. Or when the memory appeared in the deep, dark, lonely hours of the night. Or after kissing him a second time the other night.

"But I want to forget him." They had no future, so she really was trying to put the Casanova cowboy out of her mind. Without much luck. Even the memory of him was stubborn.

"Let me guess, the kiss, the touches, that incredible dance all haunts you, right?"

Shayla stared at her friend. "Yeah…how did…"

Pulling in the driveway behind Greg's vehicle, Jordan's smile turned wistful as she parked the car. "When I was sixteen, we moved to California, and I tried for years to forget Cole and the way he made me feel. I wanted so badly to believe everyone when they told me it was just a crush and I'd get over him."

"But…?"

"It was more than that. I knew it was. I *always* knew, but fate just never seemed to be on our side."

"Until last year."

A full-blown grin spread across her friend's face. "Until last year. Well, actually, it'll be two years this April," Jordan corrected, her expression becoming sad and troubled. "God, he was such a mess. So guilt-ridden over his first wife's death. He was a complete bastard."

Shayla reeled back having a hard time picturing the kind and generous man anything but.

The smile returned to Jordan's face. "I know it's hard to believe because he's back to his old self. The guy I hated to leave all those years ago."

"Well, I'm really glad things have worked out for you both," Shayla said, meaning every word.

"Me, too, but the point I was trying to make before I got off the beaten path was that just because you *want* to forget Kevin and the way he makes you feel, doesn't mean you *can*."

"Great." Her sigh filled the car. "I'll just have to avoid the guy as much as possible, I guess."

Jordan snickered. "It won't matter. I'm sorry, hun. You can try, but if Kevin makes you feel how Cole makes me feel, then that won't help one bit. In fact, it'll probably make it worse."

"Gee, thanks for not blowing smoke up my ass."

"You're welcome. Anytime." Jordan winked, then touched Shayla's arm. "Seriously, though, I've been in the *I-don't-want-to-be-obsessed-with-him* boots you're wearing, so if you ever need to talk, you know where to find me."

"Thanks, that's sweet. But, I'll be fine. It's just a physical thing. The guy is too irresponsible for me to let into Amelia's life."

"Kevin? Irresponsible?" Jordan threw her head back and laughed, and soon Amelia was joining in.

Shayla glanced at her happy daughter and smiled. "Yeah, I'm not knocking him. It's just that we live in two different worlds. He's rich and irresponsible, and I'm not."

79

"Shayla, trust me, don't let his dreamboat good looks or fun-loving, smart mouth persona fool you. Kevin Dalton never shirks his responsibilities."

Blinking at her friend, she couldn't stop her mouth from dropping open and chin from touching her chest. "You sure you're not talking about his cousin Kade?"

Kade Dalton was a responsible human being. Sheriff, First Sergeant, horse whisperer of sorts who worked with neglected and abused horses. Very responsible.

Kevin?

Nope. Not seeing it.

"Yes, I'm sure I'm talking about Kevin, although Kade is very similar."

She shook her head back and forth. Her friend was definitely delusional. "Sorry, I don't see it."

"Look, after his father died in an accident on the ranch, Kevin became so focused on keeping the ranch afloat and taking care of his invalid mother, he didn't make time for fun."

Her heart squeezed in her chest. He hadn't had the ideal childhood she'd mistakenly thought. It was a shame, but still, the man was a player and she did not want to know why.

"I'm sorry he had it rough," she said, and meant it, but had to stop her friend from revealing any more of the hot cowboy's past. The less she knew about the guy, the better. Much easier to remain unmoved by the sexy man if he was just a fun-seeking Don Juan. "My baby girl means too much to me to allow her to get attached to the guy just so he can leave and break her heart."

Jordan cocked her head. "Are you sure you're not talking about you?"

Again, she reeled back. "Me? No. I never had a guy leave me."

"What about Bobby?"

Shoot. Her friend was in deputy mode again, brown gaze slightly narrowed and glued to her face. Kade and Caitlin were the only ones who knew the truth about her relationship with her late fiancé. Even though she trusted Jordan, Shayla didn't enlighten her friend. She just wasn't comfortable opening up to people.

"He didn't leave me. Not intentionally."

Jordan smiled. "Good, I'm glad you realize that."

"I do, and I also realize Caitlin and Greg are waiting for us to get out of the car and start our tour." She motioned to the couple staring at them from the wide-front porch.

"Okay, then let's do this." With a smile and a nod, Jordan got out of the car.

"*Do-dis,*" her daughter repeated as she tossed her book on the floor.

It *was* time to *do-dis*, to put Kevin to bed…*ah hell*, she did not need that visual…put *aside* the discussion about Kevin, and concentrate on her sister's safety.

Damn, but that brain hiccup set her pulse fluttering out of control, and heat throughout her body. She opened the door and welcomed the winter breeze on her flushed skin.

The discussion Jordan had initiated was meant to be helpful, but it wasn't. Guilt settled like a ten pound weight across her shoulders for not confiding the truth about Bobby to her friend. Then there was her Kevin conundrum.

After removing her daughter from the car seat, Shayla rubbed her temple in a feeble attempt to get rid of

Donna Michaels

the increased pounding. It was turning into one of those days.

The way the wind blew in from the Gulf, cold and unforgiving, verified spring was still a good three months away. Damn. Kevin loved a warm day in winter. Made the season more bearable, and wearing a suit not as cold. He shivered under his overcoat. Too bad today wasn't one of those days. Jeans were better suited for these conditions, but failed to meet McCall Enterprises' dress code.

Maybe he could get the *bossman* to relax the code.

Shifting his weight to his uninjured foot, he approached the weathered wooden screen door and made a mental note to add painting to the list of spring chores he intended to do for his former elementary school teacher.

Before work every Thursday morning for the past five years, Kevin stopped in to check on the octogenarian. Standing on the woman's porch, he couldn't help but remember similar winter days in his childhood. Except back then, he'd been next to his mom, grumbling about having to take dance lessons—not hefting a twenty-five pound bag of cat food on his shoulder.

He knocked on the door and stood back, a slight smile tugging his lips as he waited for his old dance teacher to answer. Yeah, Mrs. Avery would've been right proud at how well her lessons had prepared him for the likes of one Shayla Ryan.

"You're such a nice young man, Kevin. You didn't forget me." The white-haired woman in a bright pink floral robe smiled and opened the door wide to let him in.

82

He leaned down to kiss her cheek as he entered. "I could never forget you, Mrs. Avery. You were my favorite teacher."

"You only say that because I gave you straight A's in English."

"Which I earned," he remarked, walking past Davey and Crockett, her two big Maine Coon cats lounging like kings on their own wing-back chairs.

At the sound of the bag rustling on his shoulder, the cats sparked to life, jumping off their thrones to follow him into the kitchen.

"True. Never could understand how such a fine-looking boy was also blessed with a beautiful brain and great rhythm."

"My grandmother used to say I was charmed."

"Hogwash. Touched is more like it. I knew your grandmother. She liked to spin a good yarn."

He laughed as he set the bag down in the pantry, making sure Davy and Crockett were in the kitchen before he shut the pantry door. She still had her wicked sense-of-humor. One of the reasons they got on so well. "Ah, now you're just sweet talking me," he teased, receiving a snort in response.

"You wish," she muttered good-naturedly, going through the ritual of burning him a bagel hard enough to crack a molar, then adding some kind of homemade salsa marmalade hot enough to peel paint.

Perfect for his warm weather chore list. He made a mental note to ask for some when he fixed her front door in the spring. It would certainly take less time than scraping, but he feared the old wood would disintegrate, or worse. Catch fire.

The sweet lady was an exceptional English teacher and a wonderful dance instructor, but her cooking skills had never improved over the twenty some years he'd known her. Considering all the meals he'd eaten that she'd prepared, the Thursday-bagels-of-death included, Kevin was surprised his gallbladder hadn't exploded by now.

A sudden, sharp stinging traveled up his legs at mach speed. He whipped open his coat to find two gray and white, meowing furballs clinging to his pants. Correction, clinging to his shredded flesh via thin claws sharp enough to slice through steel.

Swallowing down several curses, he unhooked himself from their talons, held them by the scruff of their necks and did a *son-of-a-bitch-that-stings* dance in the middle of the teacher's kitchen, all while she had her back to him.

He knew better than to rant. His younger self had tasted more than enough bars of soap in that very kitchen during his youth. Silence was his friend, and cats where Mrs. Avery's pride and joy.

"So, who are the newbies?" he managed to ask when the stinging subsided enough for him to not sound like a eunuch.

"Oh…" she turned around, a big smile lighting up her face, making her appear decades younger. "That's Daniel and Boone. Aren't they just darlin'?"

"Yeah." Now that they weren't imbedded in his legs.

He set *Freddy* and *Krueger* down by their water, then filled the food dish because Davy and Crockett were sitting there giving him the evil eye since, heaven forbid, they could see the bottom of the bowl. *Yeah*, those twenty pound cats were about to wither away. One gust of that Gulf breeze and those two were goners. Cracking a smile, he wondered if the pampered felines knew how lucky they were. They'd hit the *forever home* lottery with his former teacher.

He certainly appreciated having her in his life. Especially after his mom had passed from her long struggle with cancer. Mrs. Avery had stepped in, along with her quilting buddies, and made sure that he, Jen and Kade had square meals, clean clothes and a clean house in those first weeks. She'd always been more of a surrogate grandmother than former teacher or friend. He considered her family.

While *Grams* prepared the breakfast he would soon consume with an antacid chaser, he took out her trash and recyclables, removed his coat, changed the water bottle on the cooler, updated her computer, then washed his hands. He knew better than to sit at her table otherwise.

"So," she said after they'd eaten in silence for several minutes. "Do you have something to tell me?"

In an attempt to soften his mouthful of five-alarm charred bagel, and avoid chipping a tooth, he took a big gulp of cold milk and contemplated what she could possibly mean. Work was same old same old—write computer code, create computer software, wow peers, receive award, shove award in drawer and start over, with one or two seminars and exhibitions tossed in, like the one he was attending in Dallas tomorrow. No big news.

As for his personal life, there was no big news there either. He took pains to keep it that way. So, why did his mind conjured up the spitfire redhead with the softest touch this side of heaven, and her sweet little girl?

Because he had a cerebral error. He really needed to upgrade the filter on his brain, then defrag his *mind-*

palace. And just for extra precaution, delete all cookies related to that tempting single mother.

He swallowed down his soggy breakfast rock without gagging, or choking, then cleared his throat. "No, I don't think so. I already told you last Thursday that Kade got engaged, right?"

"Yes," she replied. "I'm glad for him. What a nice, respectable young man. He deserves to be happy. Always helping others. It's high time someone takes care of him, and Brandi is a dear, sweet girl."

"You know Brandi?"

"Yes, we often run into each other at The Creamery when I go there to buy cream for my babies. They just love old man Fosters' the best. Did you know his niece Holly is arriving from Denver this week to help with business while he goes in for that hip replacement?"

"No."

Good thing his mind understood plinko, because the way she jumped from subject to subject could leave some staring into space, or with a killer migraine.

"Well, she is. Nice girl. Business major. But don't go trying to change the subject, you rascal." She shook a boney finger at him. "I want to talk about you and that dancer."

Due to improper soaking, the last piece of bagel scraped the back of his throat, possibly taking a chunk out of his esophagus and a piece of his larynx on the way down. He'd barely gotten the milk into his mouth when she'd pulled the subject of Shayla out of her as-stonishing white hair.

"Come on. Fess up." His former teacher smiled bright. "I've seen Youtube videos of the two of you dancing."

While hacking up a lung, Kevin contemplated what had surprised him more. The fact the *eighty-years-young* woman knew about his dance with Shayla, or that she knew about Youtube.

Both.

He cleared his throat and stared across the table at the shrewd lady staring right back. He'd start with the safer of the two subjects. "You know about Youtube?"

A slim shoulder lifted then fell. "Sure. I've known about it and used it for years.

"Used it?" he asked, eyebrows raised as much as his interest.

"I have my own account to post educational quilting videos, and some funny cat stuff," she replied. "And you know I love to watch dancing. That's how I came across your New Year's Eve Dance Off."

He groaned. "Connor." That son-of-a—

"No. Not exactly." Mrs. Avery shook her head and laughed. "It was his father, your former boss, Alex."

"Mr. McCall?" *Damn*, he didn't see that one coming. "Why would he..."

She shrugged. "No idea, but I'm glad he did. You weren't even going to tell me about it, were you?"

"It was no big deal," he said, rubbing his injured foot under the table.

"Bull hockey," she exclaimed with a huff of breath. "That dance was magical and exactly what our charity needs to represent us in the Harland County Spring-Dance-a-Thon Fundraiser this April."

Kevin stilled. *Shit*. He didn't like where this was heading. His gaze shot to the back door. Could he make it outside before she uttered what he knew was about to come out of her mouth?

A very bad idea.

"I want you to enter."

Yep, bad idea.

"With your pretty, redheaded girlfriend."

A *very* bad idea. He should've raced out the door while he'd had the chance.

"Not sure that's smart, Mrs. Avery."

"Why not? It's obvious the two of you are sweet on each other. And you certainly both know how to dance."

Sweet on each other? He held in a snort. More like avoided each other so they didn't rip off each other's heads...or clothes to do an entirely different type of dance. Naked.

"It'll be fun, and you like fun, Kevin. Plus, it's all to benefit underprivileged children. Foster children. You always help out charities my quilting circle supports." She blinked at him, her shoulders drooping while her eyes lost some of their luster. "I was counting on you."

Damn, she was shrewd, playing the guilt card. Woman knew perfectly well he'd cave. She was right. He always helped out, usually with a hefty donation and manning a station at whatever venue the older women concocted.

Kevin blew out a long breath. He was such a sucker. "What do you need me to do?"

Her face miraculously brightened. "Exactly what you did in that video, dance with your girlfriend. What's her name?"

"Shayla, but she's not my girlfriend, Mrs. Avery. In fact, I don't really know her too well."

"Shayla," the older woman repeated, her expression softening as she tried it on her tongue a few times. "What a pretty name for such a pretty girl. And I wouldn't worry about knowing her because that'll change once you two start practicing. I'll expect you here Tuesday's and Thursday's, starting next week at six-thirty pm sharp."

Ah, hell. What did he get himself into? A rock the size of Gibraltar settled in his stomach.

Or was that the bagel?

He shifted in his seat and cocked his head. "Why so soon?"

"You need to get conditioned. A dance-a-thon is eighty-percent stamina."

Stamina? Hell, he had that in spades, especially when it came to dancing in the *sheets*.

"You two need to dance well and last the whole night so you can raise good money for the children. Breaks my heart that most of them go without some of the simple things other children take for granted, like coats and shoes and school supplies."

No child should go without. "Why don't you just let me donate the money?"

"That's sweet. You're always generous to our causes, but winning this will also raise awareness of the children's needs. There will be several charities represented in the dance-a-thon, but only the winning one will get coverage in three prestigious magazines and two nationwide newspapers," she explained. "The exposure will be priceless."

Wow. He whistled while, nodding. "That is great. Kind of a shame all of the charities couldn't have the exposure."

Mrs. Avery nodded. "I know. That's why we have to make sure we win, and with you dancing, especially with Shayla, we can't lose."

But *he* could lose—his ever-loving mind.

Being so close to the sexy single-mother, touching her, rubbing against her...*ah hell*, his body was already heating just thinking about it. He was in trouble. Big trouble.

Starting this weekend. Once he returned from the Dallas seminar, he was going to have to stop by her place and convince the stubborn woman to be his partner. His *dance* partner. No sheets involved.

His groin tightened.

Yeah. This was going to be hard…in more ways than one.

Chapter Five

Thursday morning, Alex sat across from his pretty wife in their kitchen, enjoying one of their cook's prize winning steak and egg breakfast burritos. For over thirty-five years now, Emma never disappointed. The McCall household was lucky to have her.

"This is first rate, Emma," he told her with a wink before enjoying another bite.

"Thank you, Mr. McCall," the robust woman replied, face beaming her pleasure. "I made yours with extra steak, and Mrs. McCall's with extra green peppers."

Leeann opened her mouth to reply, but the ringing of her cell phone stopped whatever she had been about to say. Her gaze bounced from her phone to their cook, then him. "It's Mrs. Avery."

Emma's intake of breath echoed around them. "I hope she has good news. That Kevin can be just as stubborn as your boys."

"I hear ya," he said, watching his wife answer the call.

"Hello, Mrs. Avery. How'd things go? Oh, that's wonderful. Thank you so much for your help." She gave him and their cook a thumbs up. "I knew it would. Super. Please keep us informed. All right. Good-bye."

"Hot damn, it worked." He slapped the table and grinned. They needed to tread carefully with Kevin and Shayla. Keep their distance. Do some nudging from afar. "Emma, did I ever tell you I have a brilliant wife?" he asked, never taking his gaze off his beautiful, Leeann, whose sparkling brown eyes still played havoc with his pulse.

"No," the cook answered, smile evident in her voice. "But I've known that for years."

Laughing, he rose to his feet to embrace his approaching wife. "Your idea to use the Harland County Dance-a-Thon as a way to force those two to spend time together was genius." He pulled her petite body in close and kissed the top of her head. The gray strands peppering into her light brown hair only added to her beauty. He was one lucky son-of-a-gun.

Her arms reached around him and held tight while her laughter rippled through him. "Well, after the way those two danced together at the Dalton's party, and Emma told me Mrs. Avery's quilting circle was looking for someone to represent them in the upcoming fundraiser, it really was a no-brainer."

"Thank goodness Mrs. Masters videotaped the dance." The cook crossed her arms over her chest and rocked back on her heels. "I wonder what made her do it."

His wife drew back and laughed. "Intuition. Hannah told me she just had this inkling that something spectacular was about to happen, so she pulled out her phone and hit record just before the music started."

"Lucky for us, and for the Youtube universe," he added with a smile.

Leeann patted his not-as-trim-as-it-used-to-be stomach and grinned up at him. "Yeah, your idea to upload it to the internet wasn't too shabby either, hun."

His smile broadened. "Seemed a shame to waste all that great footage." Those two sure did dance fluid, as if they'd rehearsed for days.

"All in all, I'd say we did well," his wife stated, reaching for her phone on the table. "I should call Hannah and let her know it worked."

Emma nodded. "Yes, those two have a good start."

Alex's *intuition* told him it was going to take more than a dance-a-thon to bring the stubborn couple together. But he kept that information to himself. His grinning wife and their cook looked too happy. He hated to burst their bubble. He'd just have to get with Nate and go over their contingency plan again.

After three successful matchups, the five of them knew to plan for the unexpected. Adding a sixth, Mrs. Avery, upped the odds in their favor. He wasn't going to leave anything to chance. Cole, Connor and Kade were all pleased with the way the matchmaking had turned out. Surely Kevin would feel the same a few months down the road.

The last thing Kevin wanted to do after driving over four hours from Dallas on a miserable, gray, rainy winter day was to break it to Shayla that he'd sort of committed them to the whole dance-a-thon thing.

And that practice began next week.

He knew from Kade that Brandi started a new design job on Monday, which meant Shayla would be back to work, too. Not exactly the best time to start dance lessons, but he wouldn't let Mrs. Avery down. Or the children. No way.

Pulling into the parking lot of the Texas Republic, he wasn't surprised to find the place hopping. It was half-past eight on a Friday night. The pub was always packed on the last day of the work week. Hell, most Friday's he was one of the *packees*. But not tonight. He drove around back and parked near the stairs that led to Kerri's old apartment.

He was beat.

Turning off the ignition, he heaved a sigh and shifted his body to pocket the keys in his Armani suit. He'd been in such a hurry to get on the road, he hadn't even taken the time to change into the jeans he'd packed for traveling. Comfort was key, but not today. Today, making good time was key. He'd settled for just tossing his jacket on the seat. It was the start of a weekend, and he'd known traffic would be a bear. And it had been, but now he was back in Harland County, and away from the rat race.

As soon as he got this confrontation with the *red-manian she-devil* out of the way, he was looking forward to driving the final five-point-two miles to Shadow Rock Ranch and crashing in his own bed for a good eight hours.

Despite having stayed in a five-star hotel in Dallas for the seminar, he gave the mattress a one star for sleep deprivation. The bed had been too soft and kept him from getting any decent sleep. Waking up almost every hour to switch positions, lying there willing himself to fall back sucked. All the tossing and turning was catching up to him now.

He opened the door and yawned again. Yeah, the date with his pillow couldn't come fast enough. As he climbed the stairs, walked down the hall and reached the apartment door, he thought about the spiel he'd come up with on his drive back. Hopefully, the redhead would buy it.

He knocked on her door. She would. He'd make sure of it.

A minute went by. No answer. Maybe she was putting the baby down or in the bathroom. Maybe she was in the tub.

The visual sparked a heat through his body strong enough to combat the winter chill.

Shaking his head, he knocked again. Still no answer. Which was odd, because he'd parked next to Shayla's SUV, and noticed a light on in her apartment when he'd pulled in.

Irritation pricked at his shoulder blades. Was she seriously not answering on purpose? *Ah, hell*, he was too tired to deal with that crap. He knocked one last time. Hard.

The locks on the door clicked, and a second later a pale, shivering, *zombie* Shayla opened the door, holding her daughter. For a brief moment, he thought about stepping back to safeguard his brain, but she stepped back instead, eyes widening before settling into a scowl.

"It's you. Go away," she said in a voice so low and weak he got the impression it was an effort to speak.

But not for her daughter. "*Hiyee*," Amelia said, lunging for him.

At least one female was happy to see him.

Catching the tot with one hand, he ushered her mom farther into the apartment with the other, then shut the door with his injured foot. *Dammit*. "Jesus, Shayla, you look like hell." And felt it, too. Her skin was on fire.

She looked like she wanted to snort but didn't have the strength. "Thanks, now go away."

He risked flogging by taking her elbow and ushering her into the living room which looked like an F5 had hit. Pillows and toys and wrappers covered the floor while cups and plates covered the coffee table. When he turned to view the kitchen, he found more of the same.

The condition of the apartment was a testament to how awful she must have felt. For a neat freak and organizing fanatic, no way would she ever allow the place to get this out of control.

"Where's your sister?" he asked.

"School. She left this morning."

Damn. He set Amelia on the couch with one cushion and handed her some picture books he'd seen her carrying everywhere. Thankfully, the cutie settled back and babbled as she turned the pages.

He straightened and studied the woman. Face pale, dark circle under her sunken eyes, she looked like death. "Why'd you let her go if you felt like this?"

"Because I didn't feel like this at the time." She teetered and reached for the wall for support. "I—I…" Her voice trailed off as her hand shot to her mouth and she rushed for the bathroom.

Ah, hell. He followed her. The poor thing looked ready to drop. He found her kneeling in front of the toilet.

"Go a-w-ay."

"Can't." The helper in him kicked in and took over. He and his bed were going to be kept apart for another night. At the moment, what he needed didn't matter. The poor single mother had no one to help her. She was taking care of her child when she should be resting in bed. He reached for her hair and held it back while she finished being sick.

"I'm sorry," she said as she slowly stood, still teetering. "I had hoped I was done doing that."

"No worries, darlin'."

He scooped her up after she rinsed her mouth, then headed down the hall to the master bedroom he'd helped move Kerri into almost a year ago. Kevin assumed it was the room Shayla now used.

"What are you doing?" Warm breath hit his neck as she tried to raise her head to stare at him.

"Taking you to bed." *Damn*, okay…he hadn't meant that as it sounded, but now that he'd heard it the wrong way his body responded with some heat of its own.

She made a noise, possibly a snort. "Out of luck, cowboy. Barely have strength to breath."

A smile tugged his lips. "No worries, darlin'." He set her on the edge of the bed in order to pull the covers down. "I'll take a rain check."Another weak attempt at a snort met his ears.

He picked her up and laid her down on the pillow, happy she was in sweats and a T-shirt so he didn't have to remove any clothes. Even sick, she would be too damn tempting for his mind to forget.

He pulled the covers up to her neck and she closed her eyes and sighed. And shivered. He felt her forehead with the back of his wrist.

Damn. She was burning up.

"I know this is a stupid question, Shayla, but have you taken any medicine for this fever?"

"No. Can't keep down."

Exactly what he'd figured. "Does anything besides your stomach hurt?"

"Yes," she replied, eyes still closed. "Head is pounding."

"Okay." Dehydration. "I'll be right back."

On his way through the living room, he checked on Amelia who was babbling to her stuffed bear, while pointing to her story book. God, she was so cute, his chest hurt just looking at her. Smiling, he strode into the open kitchen and gathered ice cubes, a bowl, butter knife and cup, then proceeded to crack each cube with the back of the knife until the cup was full. If he could get the fever down, then Amelia's mommy could take some pills.

Another quick glance at the busy little girl now standing in front of the couch with her back to him, found her reading to the bear. He snuck right by, made a quick stop into the bathroom to wet a washcloth, then he carried both offerings to the foolish woman trying to get out of bed.

"What do you think you're doing?" He set the cup and cloth on the nightstand and pushed the protesting mother back down.

"Need to care for my daughter."

"I'll take care of her. And you," he said, smiling at her raised brows.

"You?"

"Yes, me." He nodded. "I've taken care of sick people before." He'd had a lot of practice with his mother before she'd passed. "And I've watched my nephew Cody many nights. So stop worrying, and just concentrate on getting better. I promise, I'll take care of Amelia. She'll be fine. Here." He held the cup up to her mouth. "Try to suck on some ice. You're dehydrated. It's not helping your headache."

To his surprise, she complied, gaze glued to him the whole time. When she finally leaned back, he placed the wash cloth on her forehead and she hissed.

"Cold."

"It's room temperature. You're just that hot." He snickered. *Truer words.*

She nodded. "Maybe just a quick nap, then you can leave."

Not hardly.

"Okay," he said to appease the stubborn woman. He just needed her to fall asleep, then the exhaustion would take over and her nap would turn into hours, maybe even the whole night.

His gaze fell to her hand as she settled against the pillows. *Hot damn. A tattoo.* He quirked a smile. She was full of surprises. The tiny, green dragonfly inked on the back of her wrist no doubt held meaning.

He straightened. None of his business. *Nope. Not getting involved.* He was just helping the woman since she had no one else. That was all. Nothing more.

He stood vigil a few minutes; satisfied the sick mother was going to stay in bed, he turned on his heel and strode from the room. A quick call to Jace confirmed they were on track, and Kevin promised if more symptoms arose, he'd call the doctor back.

One redhead down. One to go.

The tougher one.

Kevin spent the next fifteen minutes cleaning up…with Amelia's help. Little darlin' jumped right in when she saw what he was doing. Of course, she found it all a game and he had to rescue the phonebook, a vase, an ereader and one of her mother's shoes from the trash.

An overzealous helper who deserved a treat. "Come here, pumpkin."

He sat on the couch, crossed his leg, then settled her on his uninjured foot and bounced her up and down. His nephew had loved 'horsie' at Amelia's age, and so did she. The cutie cackled and laughed as he held her hands and bounced her for a full minute.

"You like horsie," he said, smiling into her happy face.

"Horsie," she said, and laughed some more. "Horsie. Horsie!" The little bugger got louder and louder.

Kevin winced and stopped bouncing. He wanted to occupy her, not wake up her mother. Now the little redheaded she-devil's face began to pucker. The resemblance was uncanny.

"More!" She bounced herself on his foot and started to cry. Then made to throw herself backward, but he held on tight.

Damn. He'd forgotten about that part. Cody had done the same thing when Kevin had stopped before his nephew was ready.

Plan B.

"Want to go bye-bye?" He just realized he hadn't eaten in almost six hours. His stomach growled in confirmation.

"Horsie!"

"No, horsie right now. Horsie broken."

"No! Horsie!"

"How about we go downstairs and see Kerri?"

"Kerri?" The little girl's tears stopped in their tracks and she blinked at him. "Kerri! Jordan!"

Thank the Lord. "Yes, Kerri and Jordan." If the deputy wasn't on duty. He'd worry about that later. "Let's get you changed, and your coat on, then go downstairs."

"Kerri! Jordan!"

She clapped while he changed her diaper, and he was grateful to find what he needed in her diaper bag near the couch. He hadn't wanted to go into Shayla's room where he'd noticed Amelia's crib and changing table in the far corner. Now, he just hoped her coat was in the hall closet.

Knowing how smart and perceptive children could be at that age, Kevin decided to let her help him. "Where's your coat, Amelia?"

"Coat. Bye-bye," she babbled, running to the closet by the door.

"Smarty pants." He winked down at her.

"Pantz," she repeated with a giggle.

He helped her into her aqua coat with little mermaids on the front and back, then picked up the bundle of energy.

"Kerri. Jordan," she repeated, pointing to the door.

"Yes, but first we'd better leave mommy a note so she doesn't wake up and freak because we're not here," he said, setting her down.

And mini-she-devil returned.

"Bye-bye!"

Grabbing the first things he could find so the *bye-bye rant* didn't wake up mommy, Kevin scribbled a quick note on the back of an envelope…with a green crayon. At least it wasn't pink.

"All right, pumpkin, let's go." He scooped her into his arms, grabbed the diaper bag and rushed out the door.

Cripes. If he thought he was tired before, now he was dragging. But Kerri would help with that, provided he got down there before the kitchen closed. Booking it as fast as his Italian leather shoes and his bum foot would allow, he made it downstairs and into the back door of the kitchen in under a minute.

"Kevin?"

"Wow."

Jordan and Cole sat at the table in the back of the Texas-Pub kitchen and blinked at him. Mouths open. Jaws dropped. Gapping.

He laughed. "Ah, yeah. Is there a problem?"

"No." Jordan smiled while her husband shook his head and grinned.

"Not at all, buddy," Cole assured. "Don't take this the wrong way, but…that's a good look for you."

Kevin reeled back slightly, trying to discern if his friend was serious or blowing smoke up his ass. Caught off guard, he'd slipped up a little. Allowed feelings to show. His friend's innocent remark brought buried *secret* hurts to the surface. Hurts no one knew except his sister and cousin. Even after all these years, the pain was sharp enough to steel his breath at times. But he was the master of masking pain behind humor.

"What's a good look? Mermaids? I don't think the coat comes in my size, buddy."

"Not the coat, you as-s-goof." His boss quickly back pedaled, gaze darting to Amelia then back. "I'm serious. But you know that. You're trying to shift the focus."

Bossman had some killer mind reading skills.

"Jordan," Amelia squealed, opening and closing her fists as she reached for the rising deputy, and got his ass off the hook from having to address his buddy's comment further.

"Hey there, cutie pie." Jordan took the squirming bundle from him and he promptly removed her mermaid encrusted coat.

Hooking the jacket and the diaper bag on the back of a chair, Kevin flexed his arm and sat down. "I hope the kitchen hasn't closed yet. I'm starved."

"Nope. Still a few minutes left," Jordan informed. "What do you want? I'll go tell Kerri. She's out in the dining room turning the last of the steaks."

"Kerri," Amelia chanted while she clapped.

He smiled and leaned back in his chair. "One of those steaks would be great."

"You got it, cowboy." She hugged the little girl closer. "Let's go get Kerri."

102

Kevin was still smiling as he watched the deputy carry the little angel through the busy kitchen.

"So…" Cole's voice brought his gaze back to his boss. "How was the seminar?"

"Good," he replied, knowing full well his friend dropped one subject and was working his way to what he really wanted to know—how the hell he'd ended up with Amelia, *and* with his gonads attached since he was still in his suit. Everyone knew Shayla had a strong…*negative* reaction to suits.

He cocked his head and shrugged. "The seminar went well. We're definitely on the right track with our latest graphics card development, and our film editing software is going to kick ass, too. No one has one even close to production."

Kevin was proud of how the software was progressing. He'd put in a ton of research and interviews with test subjects to discover exactly what the industry was looking for before he even began to write his code. Cole had done the financials on the project, allowing him to take lead on programming.

The film editing software was his baby.

Not that he didn't feel the same about all his programs, but there was something special about this one. He was close. Very close to figuring out a way to combine the editing software with their new graphics card to produce what he knew would be a 3-D rendering so picture perfect, the industry would pay top dollar for, consumers would pay top dollar for, and most important, many hospitals would benefit from the program. Possibly making certain undetectable cancers, blood clots and blockages visible before it was too late.

Like it had been for his mom…

"We're back and we brought the cook," Jordan said, hefting a high chair while Kerri followed with a smiling Amelia in her arms.

Kevin rose to his feet to help settle the little girl into the chair Jordan placed at the head of the table. Ignoring the others, he bent to look the cutie pie in the eyes. "Who did you find?"

Amelia immediately turned and pointed to the cook. "Kerri."

"Yes she did." The grinning woman ruffled Amelia's hair, then glanced at him. "You want the usual?"

"Yes, ma'am."

"Okay, one medium steak with all the fixin's coming right up." Kerri nodded, then turned and moved about her kitchen, preparing his dish with practiced ease.

It was nice to see his sweet friend happy and relaxed. She'd really come a long way since last winter. Retaking his seat, he acknowledged he had to give *McMoose* some credit. The big lug was certainly treating his woman right, and it showed.

"Okay, so, what'd I miss?" Jordan asked, sitting down, gaze bouncing from him to her husband and back again.

"Not much." He shrugged. "Just talking shop."

She turned to Cole and narrowed her gaze. "You didn't ask him how he ended up down here with Amelia...without her mother?"

His bossman played it cool. Drank his beer and shrugged. "I knew better than to ask without you present. No sense in repeating answers. Isn't that right, buddy?"

Maybe if he ignored them, they'd go away, and take their questions with them. Fishing in the diaper bag, he pulled out a book and handed it to the fussing toddler. "There you go, pumpkin."

Kerri appeared with his salad and glass of water, and after she left, he glanced up to find two sets of brown eyes zeroed in on him. He knew how to play it cool, too. He was the king of cool. Mr. and Mrs. *Nosey* McCall were going to have to wait. He was hungry.

"Well?" Jordan raised a brow at him.

He raised one back. "Well, what?"

This brought a smile to her lips. "Well, how about you explain to us exactly where Shayla is?"

"Oh, that." He waved a hand at her and went back to stabbing lettuce with his fork. "She's in bed, where I left her."

Cole began to choke on his beer while his wife stared at Kevin, mouth open, eyes wide. Victory was sweet. He managed to shock them both speechless with one sentence.

A twofer.

Before the couple recovered enough to continue questioning, Kerri dropped off his steak and potatoes, and set a bowl of cereal in front of a smiling Amelia. "Here you go, sweetie," she said, handing the little girl a small spoon.

"She's a southpaw," he exclaimed, watching the little girl eat cereal with the spoon in her left hand. "Good girl." He smiled, holding up his fork in his left hand. "We're the only ones in our right minds, pumpkin."

"Oh, man, that one's getting old, Kev," Cole said with a shake of his head, while his wife pulled Kevin's plateful of steak away.

"Hey, that one's mine, darlin'. If you want one, I'm sure you're sister will be happy to get you your own."

"I don't want any steak, *darlin'*. I want answers."

"You're seriously holding my steak hostage?"

"Nope," she replied. "Using it as leverage, so start talking."

"Yes, Deputy McCall." He blinked rapidly at her.

She smiled and shook her head. "Not going to work on me, dreamboat. Save your energy for your answers."

"I don't have any energy. Someone took my steak away."

"So, start talking," the deputy repeated.

"I am. These are words coming out of my mouth."

"Okay," Cole said, holding up his hand. "You are both too stubborn, so this could go on all night. For the sake of sanity and sleep, just tell us why you have Amelia?"

"Oh, is that what you wanted to know?" He stared at Jordan and watched her nod as she pushed his plate back to him. "You should've just asked."

She balled up a napkin and lobbed it. "Come on, already."

He laughed. "All right. Jeez, you're so impatient." He stared at Amelia while pointing to Jordan. "Don't be like that when you grow up, pumpkin—ouch," he exclaimed when the deputy grabbed his finger and twisted. "Okay, fine. I stopped in to see Shayla because Mrs. Avery wants us to represent her charity in the Spring Dance-a-Thon."

"Why with Shayla?" Cole shook his head. "Did someone tell her about your New Year's Eve dance off?"

So—his gaze bounced from bossman to bossman's wife—apparently they hadn't seen the video. Good. Last thing he needed was the McCall brothers to get wind of that footage. Images of him and Shayla would start to pop up everywhere. At work. In the car. In the barn. He wasn't stupid. No way would he tell them. He shrugged. "I guess."

"Bet that went over well." Cole snickered.

"I haven't told her yet. She answered the door looking like death, all pale and shivering. Foolish woman is throwing up, running a fever and trying to watch this energetic little pumpkin." He pointed to the toddler preoccupied with her cereal. "So, I sent her to bed and brought Amelia down here because I hadn't eaten since lunch." He drew in a breath. "That about covers it."

"You do know if she wakes up and Amelia isn't there, she's going to freak," Cole pointed out.

"True." His wife nodded. "So hurry. Eat up."

"Really? You're going to be like that?" He stared at the smiling deputy.

"Seriously, though. You look beat, Kevin," Jordan said. "My shift is over at midnight. I'd be happy to relieve you so you can go home."

The woman was giving him an out. Giving him the opportunity to go home and sleep in his own bed, not an uncomfortable couch.

Take it, his mind screamed.

His gaze fell onto the little girl humming while she ate, and his thoughts turned to her momma.

Don't mess with Shayla, Kade had said. But he'd promised the woman he'd look after Amelia. And that was what he was going to do. *Dammit*. He didn't often make promises, but when he did, he kept them.

"Thanks, darlin', but that won't be necessary," he replied with a wink. "I got this. I still have to talk to her about the dance thing, anyway."

And hope he made it out of her apartment with both fellas still attached.

Chapter Six

Opening her eyes, Shayla sat up in bed with a start. Something hit her lap. She glanced down. A dried washcloth.

Kevin.

It wasn't a dream. *Shoot.*

Amelia...

Scrambling out of the bed, she fought off a dizzy spell and rushed through the apartment. What the hell had she been thinking to leave her daughter with that Casanova cowboy? *Cripes.* Hadn't she learned her lesson? You can't trust them to be responsible. That's what had drawn her to Amelia's dad.

A gorgeous, sweet-talking cowboy, Brandon had been looking for a good time, and she had looked right back. In a bout of weakness, after several weeks of running and relocating, Shayla had thrown caution to the wind and gave herself permission to enjoy the man's company for one night. To feel wanted, needed, desired, if only for a few hours. They'd had a hell of a time and both walked away happy, but a few weeks later, when she confronted the cowboy with the good news, he said he wasn't daddy material, shoved money in her hand and told her to take care of it.

After punching him in the jaw, twice, she tossed the money in his bloody face and walked out. To this day, her blood pressure still rose when she thought about it.

Yeah, sweet-talking, good-looking cowboys were nice from afar, but ugly up close. She knew this. Had gone through some rough times because of this, and yet, once again, in a moment of weakness, she'd trusted another Casanova. But this time, it was much worse. It was with her daughter.

Shayla's heart was in her throat as she rushed into the living room and stopped dead. All evidence of chaos and disorder from her daughter's free rein while she'd laid on the couch yesterday was completely gone. Erased. Deleted. The place was spotless. But that wasn't what tripped her heart and squeezed her chest so tight she had to suck in a breath.

Fingers pressed to her mouth, she fought to keep her reaction inside. *God*, they were so sweet. Leaning against the wall, she stared at the cowboy slumbering on her couch in an unbuttoned blue flannel shirt, well-worn jeans with his bare feet sticking over one end, while Amelia slept on his bare chest.

He'd changed out of his suit since last night. Probably Amelia's doing. Her lips twitched. They looked so cute. So relaxed. So…perfect.

Careful not to wake the pair, she reached for her phone on an end table, and without giving it much thought, snapped their picture should she need to remind herself that the Casanova had actually done something nice.

Okay, he'd done more than one nice thing. She inhaled and let it out slow. When Shayla had answered Kevin's knocking last night, she'd expected him to run away and wouldn't have blamed him. She'd looked like she'd felt. Horrible. But Kevin had come in, then held her hair while she threw up. *Who does that?* No guy she'd ever known. Not even Bobby. But the fun-loving cowboy had, and then he went on to take care of her, made her get in bed, brought her crushed ice and a cool washcloth.

Her heart softened toward the cowboy without her permission. *Damn*. She did not want to like him. *Lusting* him was fine. It made sense. She was a healthy female. He was a healthy man. Her gaze ran down the length of him then slowly scoured every inch of his bared torso. A *very* healthy man. The cowboy had more ridges than she'd expected. And the sprinkling of dark hair across his chest had been a surprise, too. A nice one. She ventured closer for a better look because Amelia's body was blocking the side view.

Ah, hell. He had a happy trail.

Her knees started to buckle. Blaming it on her weakened state, she bent to steady herself on the coffee table, then closed her eyes and drew in a breath. *Nope*. Didn't help. She drew in a few more. *Idiot*. Wasn't like she hadn't seen a handsome man naked before, and this one was far from naked. She was acting like a twit.

"What are you doing out of bed?"

Heaven help her, his low, sleep-coated voice was so damn sexy all the strength returning to her legs disappeared again.

"Whoa. I got you," he said, suddenly at her side, pulling her close while Amelia remained sleeping in his arms.

How in the world did he manage to stand without waking her daughter? *Cripes*. She could tip-toe on cotton balls and the little stinker would stir.

"Come on, back to bed with you," he whispered, guiding goose bumps down her body, then her *goose-bump-ridden* body to her room. "It's barely six am. You need more sleep."

The protest ready on her lips died an instant death when, instead of tucking her in bed and placing Amelia in her crib, the sleepy cowboy laid down next her, and drew her close. *Well, hell.* Now she had a problem. A big one. With herself. He should go home and take his rock hard, sexy body with him. This was bad. She should definitely protest. Her mind certainly did.

She shut her mind off.

He was warm and hard…and he was wearing flannel. Damn, she loved a cowboy in flannel. His body felt so…welcoming. Shayla burrowed into him, closed her eyes, and sighed when his arm tightened around her. She was tired, he was toasty and comfortable. End of story.

O pening her eyes in what seemed like minutes, Shayla sat up in bed with a start. Alone.

Kevin.

Was it a dream?

She glanced next to her. *No.* The pillow where he'd laid his head was still indented. It wasn't a dream.

Amelia…

Her gaze shot to the crib. Empty.

Scrambling out of the bed, she fought off another dizzy spell and rushed through the apartment. Now where had the cowboy gone? *Jesus*, he didn't leave the apartment with her daughter, did he? What the hell had she been thinking to leave Amelia with that Casanova cowboy? *Cripes.* Hadn't she learned her lesson? You can't trust—

She froze in the doorway at the sight of the cowboy sitting on the floor with her daughter, putting a puzzle together. He glanced up and smiled, showing off dimples dusted with sexy-as-sin scruff. Her pulse did a strange hiccup thing while her heart fluttered out of control in her chest.

111

"Mommy!" Amelia pushed to her feet then ran to her, arms out.

Shayla scooped up her baby girl and held tight. "Hi, sweetheart. Whatcha doing?"

Her daughter twisted in her arms then pointed to the rising cowboy. "Puz. Kebie."

Kebie? A smile tugged her lips hard. "A puzzle with *Kebie*. Sounds like fun."

"Fun," Amelia repeated with a smile of her own and pushed to get down.

The rambunctious bundle never could stand still for long. Shayla set her daughter on her feet then straightened, still smiling when she met the cowboy's friendly gaze.

"Good morning, or should I say afternoon?"

She glanced into the kitchen at the clock on the microwave. *One thirteen.* Damn. It was early afternoon. Her attention returned to the cowboy. "I'm sorry, Kevin. Why didn't you wake me? You don't need to be wasting your time here."

"No worries, darlin'. Amelia and I have had a great time," he stated.

She tried, really hard, to keep her gaze on his face and not the wide expanse of chest and abs and happy trail gapping at her through his opened shirt.

Why didn't he button the damn thing up?

"Well, thank you." Her voice came out a little hoarse. *Dammit.* She cleared her throat, proud she had at least kept her gaze level. "I feel much better. All that sleep has helped."

"Good, I'm glad."

He stared at her for a beat, then two and appeared as if he wanted to say something. But keeping her gaze north and her legs steady was eating up all her energy. She had none to spare in the thought department.

"Come on, you need to sit," he said, leading her to a stool at the island. "You're still warm. Do you think you can keep some medicine down now?"

She nodded. "The nausea has passed, but I still have that da-rn headache."

"Where do you keep the Tylenol?"

"In the medicine cabinet in my bathroom," she replied, and before she had the chance to tell him she'd get it, he was halfway down the hall, with Amelia following him chanting, "Kebie."

Kebie. A smile returned to her lips. She was not ever going to get that out of her head now.

He returned with the pills in one hand and her daughter in the other. "Here you go, darlin'." He placed the medicine on the counter then grabbed a bottled water from the fridge and set it along side. "Now, how about some toast?"

What was he up to? Why was he being so nice?

"I can get it," she said, making to stand.

A large hand clamped around her shoulder as he gently but firmly pushed her back down. "But you're going to appease me and remain seated until you've eaten. I don't want you to fall or faint in front of your daughter, okay?"

She glanced over her shoulder at Amelia happily babbling to her teddy bear as she worked on her puzzle. Shayla had been through that first hand, having watched her mom drop dead right in front of her and her sister in their kitchen while the three of them had been washing dishes. Tightness squeezing her chest, she forced herself to breathe through the sudden onslaught of pain. At sixteen, it had been horrific. Caitlin had been twelve and scarred. Shayla couldn't even imagine what would go through her young daughter's mind, not understanding why mommy didn't wake up. A fierce shudder wracked her body. *No.* She would never deliberately risk scaring her baby girl.

"Okay," she replied, turning back to face the kitchen. "Thank you."

"My pleasure." He removed his hand, but not before squeezing her shoulder.

The man vexed. Why was he being so nice? Better yet, why was he even here? Sipping her water, she watched the handsome man moved about her kitchen like he owned it, and contemplated the answer.

Was he trying to put the moves on her?

No. She mentally shook her head. At no time during this visit had any of his actions been sexual.

Was he after her daughter?

No. The cowboy had plenty of opportunity to take off with her daughter while she'd been asleep.

Shayla scratched her temple and pushed a strand of hair behind her ear, noting her hair felt limp and gross. *Great.* She must look absolutely horrid. Her chin rose. So what? She was not out to turn the man's head.

But she did want to know what was in it.

Kevin set a plate in front of her with a slice of lightly buttered toast cut in half, then sat across from her and dug into his own.

"Thanks."

"You're welcome, darlin'." A broad smile dimpled his cheeks.

"You know, I never did ask why you stopped by last night."

His gaze turned serious. "Yeah, about that…" He fiddled with his toast.

Uh oh. Her spine instantly stiffened. So he *had* wanted something. She knew it. There was no reason for him to come over.

"When I was younger, my mom had me take dance lessons from my former English teacher, Mrs. Avery," he said, completely throwing her off guard. "She's a great lady. Very funny, full of energy. You'd like her."

Having no idea where this conversation was leading or what he expected her to say, Shayla nodded and waited for the confusing cowboy to continue.

"I stop by her house every week to check on her, and this week she asked me if you and I would consider representing her quilting circle in an upcoming dance-a-thon. The winner's charity gets ten thousand dollars, but more importantly, exposure to their cause."

Dancing?

Yeah, she definitely hadn't expected the reason for his visit to be tied to dancing. For his former teacher. And for charity.

Well, he stopped by for nothing.

"I have to pass. I haven't danced in years."

"You haven't? What was the other night?"

"A fluke." She laughed. "I haven't competed since I was a teen, and after I…injured my knee, that part of my life became history."

A deep frown marred his handsome features. "Did your leg hurt real bad the other night?"

She shook her head. "No. It was just sore. Why?"

"Good, then it shouldn't give you a problem during our practices."

"Wait…our what?"

And when the hell had she said yes?

115

"Our practices. Mrs. Avery said we need to condition because stamina is key to winning the marathon."

The word stamina never *ever* should come out of that man's mouth. *Damn.* The naughty thoughts those words conjured made her whole body tingle. She blew out a breath and shook her head.

"Look, Kevin, I don't think so. It's just not my thing anymore. I'm sorry."

"I am, too," he replied, disappointment dulling his gaze. "I don't want to dance any more than you do, but this isn't about me or you, darlin'. This is about the underprivileged children, the *foster* children and winning so their plight gains the coverage needed to keep them off the streets and in school."

Her heavy heart rocked in her chest. No one knew that plight better than Shayla. *She'd* been on the streets. *She'd* dropped out of school her junior year. Maybe if there'd been more funding, there would've been more families willing to take in someone like her. And maybe that family would've been nice.

"You're right." She closed her eyes and sighed.

If there was any way she could help a teenager in her former shoes, she just had to try. A different house could've made a huge difference; one that didn't take in the maximum allowed just to collect the money, and yet hardly ever spend the money on the kids. One that would never allow some of the older kids to hit and bully the others.

She opened her eyes and stared at the silent cowboy with a slight grin tugging his lips. Kevin Dalton had played her. He had played her well. But she owed him, so, even knowing her desire to help was somehow going to backfire, she caved anyway.

"What do I need to do?"

Tuesday evening, as he parked his truck in front of Mrs. Avery's garage, Kevin had no explanation for the funny feeling in his gut. Unless he was catching that stomach thing Shayla had last week. Not a pleasant thought. However, he did wonder how the single mom was doing.

Before leaving her apartment last Saturday, he'd filled the woman in on Mrs. Avery's Tuesday/Thursday six-thirty schedule, along with the address. He glanced around the quiet residential street. No sign of Shayla's red SUV. Would she even bother to show up tonight?

Before that thought finished in his mind, the SUV pulled next to him in the driveway. Question answered. Now he wondered who he was going to deal with tonight. The sexy single mother? Or pain-in-the-ass redhead?

A smile twitched his lips. Maybe a combination of both. His ideal woman.

Slipping from his truck, Kevin waited for Shayla to join him on the driveway and silently cursed the rush of anticipation heating his veins. *Damn*, she looked great. Cheeks, rosy from the wind, had a nice healthy glow, complimenting her mesmerizing blue eyes even though apprehension was clouding their brilliance. He straightened and nodded as she approached. "You look great. I take it you're feeling better?"

"Yes. Thanks," she replied, ponytail swaying in the wind. "Sorry if I'm late. I dropped Amelia off at Brandi's."

"You're not late," he assured, turning slightly to walk with her toward the porch. Kade had mentioned something to him about watching Amelia and Cody that night with his fiancée.

117

Donna Michaels

A brilliant smile lit her pretty features and
momentarily robbed him of speech.

"You should've seen her face light up when she saw
your nephew."

He got the impression he was seeing the grown-up
version that very moment. And it was breathtaking.

"There you are, Kevin." His former teacher stood in
the doorway dressed in a long black skirt, blinding white
running shoes and a turtleneck that matched the
blue/gray tint of her hair. She opened the screen door,
and her brow rose in a sarcastic arch. "Well? Are you
going to jaw on the porch all night, or are you going to
come in and introduce me to your pretty girlfriend?"

Ah, hell...

The urge to step back as a precautionary measure to
the *fellas* was strong, but a quick glance at his
girlfriend's parted lips and wide-eyed stare had him
laughing instead. "Now, Mrs. Avery, you know I told
you Shayla and I are just friends."

"So?" The older woman shrugged. "She's a girl and
your friend, therefore she's your girl*friend*."

Guess there was no fighting that logic. He didn't
even try, just nodded and waited for redheaded fallout.

To his surprise, Shayla chuckled and extended her
hand to his teacher. "Well, when you put it like that,
you're right. Hello, Mrs. Avery, I'm Shayla Ryan. It's
nice to meet you."

"Hello, dear," his teacher replied, shaking Shayla's
hand as she drew his girl*friend* into her home. "Please,
call me Betty."

Betty?

Really? He'd known the woman practically his
whole damn life, took out her garbage, mowed her lawn,
shoveled her driveway and sidewalks, tilled her garden,

even fixed her damn toilet once, and she never invited him to call her Betty.

"You know, dear, you look very familiar. Have we met?" Mrs. Avery asked, gaze narrowed as she stared at his girl*friend*.

Chapter Seven

"N-no. I don't think so," Shayla stammered, pulling her hand free, suddenly a little pale and a lot nervous. "I'm from north Texas. I only just moved down here a few months ago."

"Maybe you saw her at The Creamery. She goes there with Brandi once in awhile," he suggested.

For some unexplainable reason, Kevin felt the need to jump in and help, and was glad when she turned to him and smiled bright. His gut took an invisible blow and his chest felt funny.

Yeah, he was definitely coming down with something.

"That's probably it."

Even Mrs. Avery nodded. "Could be. I go there to pick up cream for my babies." She motioned to the two big babies staring at them from across the room.

"Oh, what beautiful cats," Mrs. Avery's new best friend exclaimed, walking toward the kings sitting on their thrones in what he liked to call *submarine mode*, with their front paws curled under their chests.

"The one on the left is Davy and the other is Crockett." His former teacher beamed. "I rescued them six years ago. They're good boys."

Yeah, good boys who could eat more than him at one sitting. They weren't fat, just big cats.

"Watch out. Here come the new additions. Daniel and Boone," Mrs. Avery warned a little late.

The two rambunctious kittens were already climbing up Shayla's navy wool coat as she knelt between the thrones.

"What darlings." She chuckled, glancing up at him while hugging the terrors close.

Kevin's heart stopped for the briefest of moments, then rocked hard in his chest. With her hair pulled back and no makeup on, the woman was so damn beautiful she stole his breath and annihilated half his brain cells. And he had many. Or, at least, he used to, until she came to town.

Clearing his throat, he attempted to ease the lump that had mysteriously formed. These dance practices were going to be pure hell. He was going to need a required daily reminder. *No messing with the single mother, or remembering her sweet taste.*

Memories rushed to the surface and interfered with his pulse. She had tasted sweet with a whole helping of hot. He stiffened. *Ah, hell.*

Twice a day. Make that a *twice* daily reminder.

"Well, what do you say we go out to the studio in the garage and get started?" their instructor suggested before turning around and heading for the back door.

Let the torture begin.

As Kevin followed the two women through the house, across the well-manicured yard he maintained, and into the garage, he contemplated just what the hell was wrong with him. After all the years, and women who tried to coax more than a night of sex from him, he'd actually felt a tremor in the force.

Why? What was so special about Shayla?

They hadn't even had sex. Only shared two kisses. Okay, two incredible kisses, but still, a kiss couldn't be that life-altering, no matter what his buddies claimed.

Sure, he'd sensed the single mother was different, and dangerous to his peace of mind, but life altering?

Nah. *Hogwash*, as Mrs. Avery would say.

Of course, sleeping with the tempting redhead had been a dumb move. Even though it was all slumber and no sex, it was still stupid. He shouldn't have been in that bed. *Hell no.* He should've tucked the sick woman in, set her sleeping daughter in the mermaid decorated crib, and ran back to the damn couch. But *no.* Weakness had prevailed, and for the first time in over a decade, he'd felt *and* given into a long buried emotion.

Need.

Heaven help him, it hadn't solely been his weakness for soft and supple Shayla, melting into him with sighs rippling over his damn flesh in a light caress. He was in trouble. Big trouble.

But she wasn't his only problem.

Somehow, her cute little baby girl managed to reach deep inside and curl her tiny fingers around his heart. How? When? He had no idea, but at the time, he couldn't bear to release the sleeping angel. Amelia had been so sweet and tiny in his arms. So innocent. Buried paternal needs and *if onlys* had surfaced. He couldn't do it. Hadn't been able to let her go. So he'd held on to the sweet little pumpkin a little longer.

His actions were forcing him to take a good, hard look at his life.

Over the past ten years, he'd been with a handful of women…or two, even slept next to a few the whole night, but that hadn't prepared him for the likes of Shayla and Amelia Ryan. Now, his brain was scrambling through his *mind-palace* to see if there was a way to backtrack, to reverse the affect the single mom and her baby girl seemed to have on him. He wasn't what they needed or deserved.

He wasn't a permanent guy.

Or a responsible guy.

Hell, he was nothing but a *Good Time Charlie* and they were a pretty package of *white picket fence*.

Didn't mean he didn't want them, or want to be around them. Get to know them better. Because he did. And that scared the shit out of him. If it weren't for his admiration and devotion to his former teacher—the woman who had been there for him when his father had died, and again when his mother had passed—Kevin would not be about to voluntarily endure hell for the next two months.

Practicing twice a week, holding the sexy redhead in his arms *twice a week* while they danced whatever the hell kind of dances Mrs. Avery was going to put them through, was not going to help his plight. *Hell no*. Brushing against her soft curves was going to drive him insane.

Just watching the sashay of Shayla's sweet denim-covered ass while she walked in front of him into the studio heated his blood to unreasonable levels.

Yeah, he was a dead man walking. Or stumbling. His jeans had suddenly tightened. They already admitted they were combustible, and all his musings and thought processes boiled down to one honest fact.

Before the two months of practices were up, they were going to end up in bed.

"Well now, why don't you two hang up your coats while I pick out a few songs," Mrs. Avery said as she turned on the lights.

"Oh, wow," Shayla exclaimed, placing her coat on a metal hook by the door, excitement shining in her eyes, replacing her earlier apprehension. "This is great."

"Thank you, Shayla," their instructor replied.

Kevin hung up his coat and glanced around the familiar studio-converted garage. Stepping through the door had been like stepping back to his youth. The place hadn't changed much. Wide open with florescent lighting, the space had white, commercial tiling, a heating/cooling unit in the corner, a bathroom/changing room in the back and a seating area in the front for small recitals. Red checkered curtains covered a side window and window in the door, and mirrored walls paralleled one another with a hand rail along one side for ballet students.

A small smile tugged his lips. When he had been ten, after only a few months of lessons, his mom and Mrs. Avery tried to talk him into learning ballet.

The redhead walked to the closest mirrored wall and lightly caressed the rail. "You teach ballet?"

Her strokes mesmerized and his *mind-palace* immediately shut down. *Except for the basement.* Now his mind was full of images of the woman fondling an entirely different type of wood.

"Yes," their instructor was saying, nodding in his direction. "Tried my darndest to get him to give it a whirl. The boy was a natural, I tell ya. Fluid, strong, perfect for partnering a ballerina."

"Really?" The beauty released the rail, and his palace reopened.

With his mind no longer stuck in the basement, he remembered a time when his mom had even tried the *'it's a good way to meet girls'* card to get him to practice ballet, but it hadn't worked.

No way in hell were they going to get him to wear tights.

"Wasn't happening. Not to this cowboy." He jabbed a thumb toward his chest. "Ballet was not part of the deal with my mother."

Line dancing and ballroom dancing, sure, but nothing else. Thank God the women never forced the issue, because truth was, he would've done whatever his mother had wanted. She had been through so much. He just wanted her to be happy.

Shayla chuckled. "Let me guess, severe allergy to tights?"

"You got it, darlin'," he said with a smile.

The guys would've had a field day at his expense. Especially, Connor. *Yeah*, good 'ole *McJollyRancher* would've busted a gut at the sight of Kevin in tights. And he wouldn't have blamed the cowboy one damn bit.

"All right. Let's get down to it, shall we?" Mrs. Avery commanded without looking at them as she fiddled with the music system. "I'm going to play a group of songs of mixed genre, and watch the two of you dance. It'll give me an idea of what to work on, if you two even need work." She glanced up at them and smiled.

Why was the woman smiling? Maybe old age was actually catching up to his teacher.

"Bring it." He nodded, and returned the smile, even though he knew dancing with Shayla was a bad idea.

"You got it," Mrs. Avery said. "How about we start out with a little of Maroon Five?"

Shayla's eyes widened. Holding back a grin, he'd wager she thought pop, rock and hip-hop were out of Mrs. Avery's reach. *Wrong*. He knew first hand his teacher was well versed in all music genres and dance styles. And if he wasn't worried she'd break a hip, he'd coax the older woman onto the floor for a demonstration.

"Sounds good," he said. "'Cause 'I've got the moves like Jagger.'"

His girl*friend* laughed. "I just bet you do."

By the time they danced through Maroon Five, Enrique, Brookes and Dunn and Rascal Flatts, he noticed a change in Shayla. She was relaxed, smiling, gave herself over to the music. The woman was having fun. So was he. So much so, he forgot to be leery.

Just like at his New Years Eve party, when they danced, they connected on a different level, their bodies anticipated and moved like one. Shayla was a joy to accompany. When Usher came on, Kevin upped the game, pushed the envelope, mimicked the moves he'd seen in the video, and his beautiful partner kept up, hitting the marks, kick steps, moonwalking, whatever he threw at her, she threw back and volleyed a few of her own, challenging him. And *oh, hell yeah*, he loved challenges. Thrived on them. She pushed him to dig deep. To bring his A game.

And he loved it.

"Well now, that was fantastic." Mrs. Avery clapped from her perch on a stool near the stereo when the music ended. "I'm beginning to think you two could teach me a few moves."

He smiled. "Never. You'll always be the master."

The older woman chuckled, waving a hand at him. "And you'll always be a charmer, Kevin Dalton." She slipped off her stool to walk to the fridge. "Let me get you some water to cool off." She opened the door and clicked her tongue. "Except, stupid ninny that I am, I left the bottles in the house."

"No problem. I'll get them." He headed to the door.

"No, you two stay here and practice some more. Work on the slow songs. They'll be playing them at the competition, too." She flipped a switch and a ballad began to play. "I'll get the drinks. I need to make a phone call anyway."

And before he could reply, the woman was gone.

He was supposed to dance to a slow song. With Shayla. Unchaperoned.

This wasn't good.

Turning to his partner, he found her staring at him, gaze round and leery while she chewed on her lower lip. *Ah hell*, he wanted to nibble on it, and sooth with his tongue.

Instead, he held out his hands and led her in a dance, keeping their moves respectable and safe.

"M-maybe we should sit this one out," she said, body stiff but trembling.

Kevin knew the reasoning behind her words, but could not stop the question from leaving his mouth. "Why?"

She swallowed, took a deep breath, then transferred her gaze from his throat to his eyes. "Because I want to wrap myself around you like a pretzel and kiss you long and deep."

Son-of-a...

He stumbled to a stop and blinked at the woman who just stopped his heart. Her chest was still heaving, but he didn't know if it was from the past fifteen minutes of lively dancing, or the hunger smoldering in her blue eyes.

To hell with it.

He yanked her close and brought his mouth down on hers, molding her ass with his hands as he ground his throbbing erection against the heat emanating between her legs. She moaned, opening up to him, allowing his tongue access, and he took advantage, plundering inside as she practically climbed up him and did her pretzel thing. The woman tasted hot and desperate and so hungry he momentarily wondered if he'd be able to keep up with her demands. But then his own hunger kicked in, grew, intensified until his blood burned in his veins and the need to get them both naked shook through him.

"I know, that's what I told him," Mrs. Avery said from right outside the garage.

Shayla stiffened, then unwrapped herself just as their teacher opened the door, phone to her ear and six pack of water in her other arm. Kevin rushed forward to grab the bottles, giving his body time to cool off. Both their bodies. If that were even possible.

He'd been hungry and in lust many times, but he'd never felt a passion this strong before. Need shook through his body, and he literally ached to be inside the woman. That was new.

And alarming.

And exhilarating.

Placing the water in the fridge, he drew in a breath then blew it out slow. Now was not the time to act on that hunger. But, oh, they would definitely be acting on it. All these weeks he'd been fooling himself into believing he could resist the sexy redhead. He'd been wrong. The need, the want...the passion they'd just experienced was too strong to be denied. If he learned anything the past ten years, it was desire and hunger that strong won't just go away. You need to act on them to put out the fire.

Carrying two bottles across the floor, he silently handed one to Shayla before draining the other. His thirst was nowhere near close to being quenched. And by the heat still emanating from her gaze, she felt the same.

"Okay, I'll call you back later. Bye." Mrs. Avery hung up and sighed. "Sorry I took so long, but I just couldn't shake the feeling I'd seen you before, Shayla, and I was right."

His partner stiffened and pulled the bottle away from her mouth, only half-gone. "W-what do you mean?"

"I skimmed through some of the video I had of past competitions of my students and found one from more than a decade ago that you were in, but I don't think your name was Shayla back then."

What? Kevin's gaze shot to the redhead who was turning white as a ghost before his eyes, almost resembling zombie Shayla from last weekend.

She shook her head. "No, you must be mistaken."

Judging by her strong reaction, he'd say his teacher was spot on.

"That's what I thought," Mrs. Avery said. "Until I spotted a Garth Brooks routine from regional's where the dancer did the same incredible moves you did with Kevin on Youtube."

"Youtube?" Shayla's sharp inhaled echoed through the garage, and before his teacher could blink, the redhead was in front of her, holding the older woman's shoulders. "What was on Youtube?"

"Why, th-the dance-off between the two of you at Kevin's party."

She released the teacher and turned to him. "When? When did you post that?"

"I didn't. Mr. McCall did," he said, grabbing her by the shoulders this time. "Calm down."

"No, you don't understand. I need to know." She twisted to face the older woman, even as he held onto one of her arms. "Please, tell me what you meant, Mrs. Avery. Is it on the internet or not?"

"Yes, dear. But it's okay. You are fantastic."

She began to shake in his grasp. "When? When was it up?"

"I-I don't know. I saw it last week."

"Oh my God," she said, this time with panic thick in her voice. "I-I have to go." She yanked free and ran for the door.

"Shayla, wait." Kevin rushed after her, but reached the driveway in time to see her peel out down the street.

"Kevin, what in the world just happened?" Mrs. Avery was pale and shaking.

Shit. He calmed his voice and placed a hand on her shoulder. "I don't know, but I'll find out. It'll be okay. I promise. Don't worry."

Chapter Eight

Panic had a vile taste, similar to disgust and fury. Shayla hated them all. The last time she'd experienced the emotion, her father's goon had been chasing her through Dallas. But she'd kept her cool and managed to get away.

Just like now.

"Keep your cool," she said into the quiet car. "It'll be okay. He's not here. Maybe he hasn't seen the video yet. You have time to pack and leave."

She should call the sheriff. Shayla had promised Kade she would the minute there was trouble. But what could he do? Probably nothing. Still, she'd given her word and that was one of the few traits her mother had always insisted on. Honesty and keeping your word.

And she'd keep it.

Fishing in her purse for her phone, she stilled. Kade was with Brandi, watching Amelia.

She could just stop there...

No. Kids were very perceptive. She did not want her daughter or Cody to pick up on her panic. Besides, it would be quicker to pack without her daughter's help. A smile found her lips despite her dire circumstances.

Since her daughter couldn't be in safer hands with Kade, she could leave her at Brandi's while she talked to the next best thing to the sheriff—Deputy Jordan McCall, Harland County's future sheriff. Provided the woman won the election.

By the time Shayla came to this conclusion, she was pulling into the Texas Republic parking lot and spotted the deputy's SUV. *Thank God*. Now she didn't have to call her friend.

She parked around back, barely pulling her key from the ignition as she shot from the vehicle. She had no idea how much time she had before Lyle found them. And *dammit*, she hated this. Hated the panic and rushing, and uprooting her daughter and sister. It wasn't fair.

Fighting back a round of frustration-motivated tears, she rushed through the back door of the kitchen to find the deputy sitting at the corner table, but not alone.

Cole and Connor were there, too.

Shoot.

"Shayla?"

"What is it?"

"What's wrong, darlin'?"

The three of them stood at once, concern wiping the smiles from their faces. She pulled in a breath, fought back more tears, *dammit*, and shook her head. It was too late to try to talk to her friend alone. One of the McCall brothers shoved a drink in her hand while the other forced her to sit.

"I'm on the internet," she blurted. "I don't know how much time I have, Jordan." She sucked in a breath. "I should go pack." Then made to stand, but a giant hand clamped around her shoulder and gently held her in place.

"No, darlin', you need to sip your drink and then tell us what's wrong," Connor gently insisted. "Did Kevin do something to you?"

"Kevin?" She frowned, glancing up...and up at the cowboy. "No."

Other than turn her into a hot, trembling body of need with his incredible kiss. But she had bigger problems at the moment.

Cole placed a hand over her shaky one as the others retook their seats. "Then what's wrong, Shayla?"

He was sweet, but she didn't need to sit, she needed to pack.

"That's what I'd like to know, *Shayla*, if that's really your name," Kevin said, suddenly standing in the doorway, arms folded across his chest, expression hovering between angry and confused. "You nearly gave Mrs. Avery a heart attack, and over what? A stupid video of us dancing on Youtube?"

"Youtube?" Jordan jumped to her feet. "When?"

"Ah, not you, too," Kevin grumbled. "What the hell is going on?"

Her friend ignored the men, grabbed her hand and squeezed. "Shayla, are you saying there's a video of you and Kevin dancing on the internet?"

Finally!

"Yes. Mr. McCall posted it. And I don't know how long it's been on there. Could be since New Years. That's almost a whole week, Jordan. A whole *week*." Tears heated her damn throat again. She lifted her drink to her lips and gulped a good portion, welcoming the burn as it went down.

Enough with the panicking. She could and *would* handle this logically. Setting the glass down, she exhaled then stood. "It's too public here. Let's go to my apartment."

"Yes," Jordan said, whipping out her phone.

Brushing past Kevin, Shayla opened the door and forced her feet to walk at a normal pace as she headed across the lot and up the stairs. If she only took essentials, she'd be out of here in less than fifteen minutes, and with Amelia in less than twenty.

133

Then she'd call her sister…*God,* she hated to have to do this to Caitlin. The poor girl just found a nice guy and was enjoying college life. It wasn't fair.

When she reached her door, she turned to ask Jordan her thoughts about Caitlin, but the words died in her throat at the sight of the three cowboys standing behind the deputy.

Shoot. Who invited them? She hadn't. Not intentionally. "You all didn't need to come."

"Yes, we did," Kevin said, voice as stern as she'd ever heard.

No matter. She needed to keep moving. And since her father hadn't found her yet, she could risk coming back to the apartment for a few things. She pulled out her key, but Jordan took it from her.

"We need to check the apartment just in case."

And before Shayla could ask who Jordan had meant by *we,* the off-duty sheriff joined the chorus, rushing toward them down the hall.

"You okay, Shayla?" Kade stared down at her through concerned gray eyes, warm hands on her shoulders, strong and reassuring.

No. "Yes." She nodded, trying not to think about her daughter with Brandi and Cody unguarded.

"It's going to be okay." He squeezed before releasing her to nod at the cowboys. "You three stay out here and watch Shayla."

Then he nodded to his deputy who unhooked the strap from over her gun, but didn't pull the weapon. Shayla's heart began to pound. And pound nearly clean out of her chest as Jordan and Kade disappeared into her apartment.

Please don't let him be in there.

"Shayla, what is going on?" Kevin grasped her arm and turned her to face him. "Why are the sheriff and deputy searching your apartment? Who are you running from?" His grip tightened, and she shivered at the fierce expression darkening his face.

Hysterical laughter bubbled up her throat. "Life."

Gorgeous blue eyes clouded over in a frown. She knew he was confused. Her gaze shifted to the McCall brothers. *Yeah*, them, too. *Hell*, so was she.

How could this happen?

"It's all my fault." She sighed, knowing she'd screwed up. Big time. "All because I gave into the temptation to be normal and have a little fun at a party."

And now she was paying the price. Was going to have to hit the road. Leave a great job, great apartment. Great friends. Great kisser.

Had it really been worth it?

Yes.

For those three minutes, she'd reconnected with life. Remembered what it had felt like to have fun. To laugh. To live. Remembered what it was she wanted for her sister and daughter. Shayla wanted them to *live*.

"Well now, darlin'," Connor said, stepping closer. "No harm done."

"Yeah," Cole agreed. "It's perfectly normal to want to have some fun in your life."

She snorted. "Except my life isn't normal."

"You're not making any sense." Kevin released her and shook his head.

"Now *that* is my normal."

Jordan appeared in the doorway. "Okay, it's all clear. Come in."

Rushing into her apartment, she headed straight for her room.

135

"Oh no you don't. Hold on there, Shayla. I want answers," Kevin said, catching up to grab her by the elbow. "Who is after you?"

God, she didn't want to get into this now.

"Let her go, Kevin." Kade blocked the hall and stared at his cousin, who let out a curse.

"Fine." He released his hold. "But can I at least know why you freaked out enough to almost cause Mrs. Avery a heart attack?"

"Wait," she frowned at him. "You're serious?" Her heart hit the floor. She thought he'd been exaggerating in order to guilt her into talking. "Is she all right?"

"She's a little shaken. A little frightened, and a lot confused. But she'll be all right," Kevin said, his gaze a little less angry. "I called Jace. He's checking her out."

"Oh my God." The tears she'd held at bay finally cut loose. She hiccupped. "I'm sorry." Staggering to the island in the kitchen, she swiped the wetness from her face and sank onto the nearest stool. She almost killed Mrs. Avery. "I'm sorry," she repeated.

What had she done? Her gaze took in Jordan and the four men, standing around the counter, staring at her with concern. She'd just put them all at risk.

"Hey, it's not your fault," Jordan insisted, dropping onto a stool beside her, placing a hand on her arm. "You did nothing wrong."

She hiccupped again. "Yes, I did. I made friends." Stupid mistake. She blew out a breath. "I shouldn't have friends. I shouldn't be around people. This is why I need to go."

"No, it's exactly why you need to stay," her friend stated, grip on her arm increasing. "You need to stay because you made friends. We care about you."

Hot tears splashed down her face again. "Don't. It's too dangerous."

"What is?" Cole asked.

"Yeah, what's going on, Kade?" Kevin stared at his cousin who leaned against the wall, arms crossed.

The sheriff shrugged. "It's not my tale to tell."

"*Jesus*, really? You're going to be like that?" Kevin tossed his hands in the air. "Why can't I get a straight answer?"

All gazes shifted to her. She could feel them, like the sun through a magnifying glass in mid June. It stung. Shayla lifted her gaze until it clashed with an aggravated blue one.

"The less you know, the safer you are. I don't want anyone hurt because of me."

"Yeah, well, it's too late."

His words and his tone hurt, although she knew they weren't meant to.

"It's like Jordan said. We're your friends." He pushed his way in, grabbed her hand and squeezed. "Let us help. We care about you and your daughter and your sister. Level with us, Shayla."

Her heart was beating so loud and hard her body shook. What should she do? His blue gaze was so open, welcoming, and warm her chest ached. She wanted to tell him. *God*, she wanted to, but wouldn't that put him in danger?

"You don't need to be involved in my mess. None of you do."

A smile spread across his face and lit his eyes. "Too late for that, too, darlin'. We're already invested. You're our friend."

He was the last person she ever thought she'd hear say that.

"He's right," Cole agreed, slapping a hand on Kevin's shoulder. "You're our friend and we're going to help."

"Yeah, darlin', friends help friends around these parts, so you're stuck with us and our help."

"See?" Kevin winked. "Even *McJollyRancher* gets it."

She laughed, despite the vice squeezing her heart. These people were so nice. So was the town. Heck, the whole county. She didn't want to leave. Harland County was ideal. The perfect environment to raise her daughter. Good people who worked hard for a living and helped each other out.

All eyes were on her again. She just hated to air her dirty laundry. Especially to them. It was so embarrassing. But, if they could help...she rubbed her tattoo. If she truly wanted to stay and raise Amelia in such a wonderful town, then she had to take them up on their offer. Had to at least try.

For Amelia.

She cleared her throat, not looking anyone in the eye, and instead gazed at her thumb as she continued to rub her wrist. Just staring at the dragonfly gave her strength. "It's my deadbeat dad. He's out of prison. Greedy. Has connections. No morals. Bastard wants the death benefit money I received when Bobby died." He made her sick. She shot to her feet, pushed through the wall of McCall and began to pace. "We constantly move. I changed our names, but I know it's only a matter of time before he figures that out. I was just hoping Caitlin would have her degree by then and I'd have my..." She swallowed a curse. It wasn't fair; she could kiss her GED goodbye this time. And she'd already started the first week of classes.

Dammit.

"You're what?" Kevin prompted.

She shook her head. "Doesn't matter. But do you see now? It's better that I go."

"No, it isn't," the cowboy said, walking right up to her and pulling her into his arms. "Let us help you."

She closed her eyes and pretending—just for a second, that he was right—she sighed and hugged him close. He was warm, and welcoming, and smelled really, really good. All woodsy and male. She inhaled deeply. Yeah, so good. But it wasn't his warmth or great scent that got to Shayla. *No.* It was the fact that, for the first time since her father was released after her mother had testified against the bastard and put him away, Shayla felt safe.

Never in a million years did she ever expect to feel that in Kevin Dalton's arms. Lust, a deep wracking need, yes. And she had. But *safe*? She didn't see that coming.

He hugged her tight and kissed the top of her head. "It'll be all right. You'll see."

It already was all right. *Too* all right. And because she enjoyed the safe, warm cocoon of his arms, she pushed out and stood tall. Way too dangerous to become dependent on someone now. Maybe once her dad left her alone. Or was back in prison.

Like that was going to happen.

"So, Kade, what's our next move?" Kevin asked, facing his cousin.

"Yeah, buddy," Connor stepped close. "What do you need us to do?"

Cole slipped his arm around his wife and nodded. "We're very resourceful. Whatever you need, it's done."

"Well, first thing is to get that video off the net."

"Already done," Jordan said, raising her phone. "Called Mr. McCall and asked him to remove it."

The sheriff nodded. "We have no way of knowing if Lyle saw it, so we're going to go on the assumption he did. That means you need to lay low, Shayla." Gray eyes bore deep. "But not here. We're going to move you for a few days. Jordan and I will keep watch on the place and see if anyone suspicious turns up."

Her stomach knotted. She hated to put people out. Hated the not knowing. Hated that she had to put her life on hold for that bastard. But she'd do what she must to keep her family safe.

She nodded. "What about Caitlin?"

The deputy exchanged a look with the sheriff then turned to face Shayla. "Let her be. We don't know anything yet. No sense in upsetting her routine. I'll alert campus security. It's up to you if you want to alert Caitlin."

"Yes." She didn't hesitate. Not knowing was a one-way ticket to trouble. And her sister sure didn't need trouble. "I'll tell her about the video and to keep her eyes peeled."

She inhaled, feeling a little better, knowing her sister could stay in school and with protection. Her gaze shifted to the sheriff. "So, what about me and Amelia? Do you want us to go to a hotel or something?"

"Actually, I'm thinking you need to leave town." The sheriff's gaze bounced to his cousin. "Maybe lay low in Houston for a few days."

Kevin nodded. "Good idea, cuz. We can be there in an hour."

"Wait." She placed a hand on the cowboy's chest and narrowed her gaze on him. "What do you mean *we*?"

"*We* as in you, me and Amelia," he clarified, but did a piss-poor job. "I have a penthouse in Houston. You'll be safe there."

A penthouse? *Jesus*, what had she gotten herself into?

"Perfect." Jordan nodded, touching her arm. "It'll only be for a few days, right, Sheriff?"

Kade nodded. "Yes. No more than a week. I'll give you a call, Shayla, when I think it's safe."

A week.

Alone with Kevin.

In a penthouse.

Who was going to keep her safe from herself?

Chapter Nine

The next morning, Kevin stood in his kitchen cooking his famous bacon, mac and cheese omelet when he heard stirrings from his female guests. Good. He'd hoped the delicious smells weren't only enticing his growling gut. His guests needed to come from behind their locked door.

And he knew it was locked because he'd tried it last night when he'd heard Shayla quietly crying. She'd insisted on sleeping on the twin bed in the room where he'd had the concierge set up a crib. With two other bedrooms in the penthouse, she had more comfortable choices, but given the day's events, he wasn't surprised when she'd chosen to stay with her daughter.

The thought of what she must've gone through rippled his gut. Things had to be bad if the woman legally changed her and her sister's names. His mind had latched on to the mystery of her name, but knew he had no chance of ever finding out. And, really, what did it matter? He gave himself a mental shake. They were barely friends. She certainly didn't need to reveal that to him. Still, he did wonder. Kind of like a missing puzzle piece.

He hated missing puzzle pieces.

As the beauties emerged from down the hall, he did the mental shake thing again, and slid the omelets on three plates, then set them on the table.

"Kebie!" Amelia squealed, then released her mother's hand to rush through the open living room, straight into his arms.

He scooped up the smiling bundle of sunshine in a
pretty purple jumper. "Good morning, pumpkin. Don't
you look pretty today."

"Kebie," she repeated, laying another of her
wonderful, wet kisses on his cheek.

Wonder if he could get one from her pretty momma?
He glanced at the approaching woman wearing hip-
hugging jeans, emerald T-shirt and a frown.

"Why are you here?" she asked, sliding into a chair,
blue gaze direct, and just a little bit annoyed.

"That's the funny thing, darlin'." He winked,
deciding to keep things light. "I own the place," he
replied, hooking her daughter in the highchair they'd
hauled from Harland County.

Last night, Shayla had insisted they take enough
'familiar' things so her daughter wasn't freaked out by
the change of scenery. Seemed to work. He studied the
little sweetheart. Amelia sat babbling while she pounded
the tray with her fork. In her left hand. A smile tugged
his lips.

Southpaws rule.

"I know that, you goof," her mom said, leaning
toward her daughter to tie a yellow bib around the little
angel's neck. "I mean, why aren't you at work?"

"Oh." He shrugged. "*Bossman* told me to take the
day off."

She settled back in her seat with a humph. "Look,
Kevin. It's bad enough my life is turned upside down. I
don't want you to be put out, too."

Enough with the kid gloves. He reached across the
table and grabbed her knotted hands. "Look at me,
Shayla." He waited for her blue gaze to rise, then
continued. "If I had something pressing to do today, I
would've gone in to work. I promise."

143

She studied him a moment, then seemed satisfied with whatever she saw, because she nodded and relaxed under his touch. "Okay."

"Okay," he repeated, giving her a light squeeze before releasing her to dig into his steaming omelet. "Now, eat up. Melted cheese is always best eaten while warm."

She put a forkful in her mouth, closed her eyes and moaned.

Ah, hell. His body tightened in response. He wasn't getting up anytime soon. Jeans were cutting off the circulation to his brain. He swallowed. Hard. Then forced his gaze away from the ecstasy lining her face. *Damn.* If that's how she looked with a mouthful of bacon, egg and cheese, how the hell would she look if he was buried deep inside her?

The image those words conjured shot his blood pressure to unsafe, and need rushed through his body in a fierce, unrelenting wave. *Son-of-a-bitch.* He gripped the edge of the table, clenched his jaw and concentrated on opening doors and window in his *mind-palace.* He needed to relieve the pressure before it relieved itself in an unwelcomed, messy way.

Cripes. He hadn't had a mess in his pants since the seventh grade when Missy Phelps shoved his hand under her bra in the barn. That was his first, and last, mishap. But if he wasn't careful, he was going to up that number to two.

The redhead was potent. He reached for his glass of water and downed every last drop.

"You okay?" Baby blues blinked at him from across the table.

"Yep." He nodded, picking up his fork and stabbing his eggs. Best to focus on breakfast. Not dessert. And if she could just not moan again, he'd be able to get through the meal without incident. *Yeah*, that would help.

"How's Mrs. Avery?"

A good subject. A safe subject. He stared straight at the woman and sent her a reassuring smile. "She's good. I talked to Jace an hour ago, and he said she hasn't had any problems. Then, of course, she had to grab his phone and proceed to interrogate me about you."

"Me?" Shayla inhaled. "You mean she doesn't hate me?"

"Of course not. It'll take a h…ole lot more than that to upset the ole' gal." He glanced at Amelia, glad to see she hadn't picked up on his almost slip of the tongue. He could hear Mrs. Avery now. 'Mustn't cuss near the baby.' His gaze bounced back to Shayla. "She is worried about you, though. Made me promise to tell you not to worry, and that your secret is safe with her."

Anxiety pinched her face. She set her fork down and leaned back in her chair. "Do you think she'll tell her quilting buddies? Because the more who know, the better chance he'll find me."

"Mrs. Avery won't tell a soul. I promise," he replied. "That woman is a rock. Impenetrable and strong. Your secret is more than safe with her."

The single mother stared at him a moment, then apparently satisfied with what she saw in his eyes again, she released a breath and nodded. "Okay. Good."

"Yes, it is. So, eat up." He glanced at his watch, then back at his pretty guest. "I have the car picking us up out front in a half-hour."

"Car? What for?"

"To take us to Sea World, of course."

"Sea World?" She balked. "But that's hours away."

"Three hours and eight minutes, depending on traffic."

"But...I...it's early January. It'll be too cold."

He smiled. "It's supposed to hit sixty-two degrees there today. Stop your stalling. We'll be there by lunch, and back here by sundown. Let's go have some fun."

Fun.

They'd had fun all right. So much so, Shayla could honestly say it had been the best day of her life.

Stepping out of the shower later that night, she dried off and had to admit Kevin had been his usual charming self, and then some. He'd been sweet and attentive, never letting her or Amelia out of his sight. And even when women had hit on him, and there had been plenty, he'd always been polite but firm, telling them he was with her.

A big shock. She towel dried her hair, then combed it out before slipping into her terry robe. Sure, Kevin had been at the *park* and she had been at the *park*. They were *there* together, but she hadn't known he was *with* her. That shouldn't make her feel so good. *Dammit*. But it did. Even now, as she double-checked Amelia tuckered out in her crib with the stuffed penguin Kevin bought, which the sweetie insisted on calling a *goggy*, the euphoria of the whole day spent under *his* care, in *his* attention, still had the ability to steel her breath.

She was being foolish. She knew. Knew it well. The guy had been glued to her because of her situation. Not because he wanted to be with her. And yet, she was good at pretending, which she had done the whole day. Pretended they were together, like any normal couple, having a fun outing.

A smile still tugged her lips. It had been fun.

Tip-toeing to the nightstand to grab the monitor receiver, Shayla glanced at the photo a professional photographer had taken of the three of them. It had happened near a picnic area, right after the cute little three-year-old girl Amelia had been playing with saw her father and ran to him yelling *daddy*. Of course, this prompted her daughter to run to Kevin yelling the same endearment.

Bless him. He'd scooped her up, not missing a beat, but Shayla could've sworn she'd seen a flash of pain and longing darken his eyes, but in a blink it was gone and had her questioning if the emotions had been present at all.

She slipped the monitor in the pocket of her robe and sighed. None of it made any sense. Now *panic*, yes, that emotion she could understand going through the Casanova's eyes. But pain and longing? *No*, that was crazy. She must've misread his expression.

With a shake of her head, she quietly slipped from the room, hoping to grab something cold to drink and watch a little television without disturbing her host. He'd disappeared into his room when they'd gotten back. Amelia no doubt tuckered the guy out. Shayla wished she was tired. For some reason, she was all keyed up.

Probably the business with her deadbeat dad.

Her gaze scanned the living room she approached. So inviting and warm. She had to admit, she was a bit stunned by Kevin's penthouse. Having expected cold, modern, black and white, sleek furniture and decor, Shayla had been pleasantly surprised last night to walk into an apartment done in rich, warm earth tones. Beautiful, polished, mahogany wood floors ran throughout the penthouse with taupe walls, rich mahogany furniture in the bedrooms and living room, including an ornate coffee table with matching end tables, and a gorgeous six-foot credenza against a wall.

Floor to ceiling windows ran along the east side, capturing a breathtaking sunrise earlier that morning. She'd come out for a glass of water and stood, transfixed, watching the golden mass rise and illuminate the Houston skyline. Truly amazing.

Like Kevin's couch.

In the middle of the room sat the biggest, softest looking couch she'd ever seen, and it had a chaise built right in. Shayla was itching to sprawl out on the piece with a good book. Too bad she didn't have one with her. But there was a giant sixty-inch television above a stunning stone fireplace.

That would do.

She glanced behind her at the closed bedroom doors. The television appeared to be far enough away from them. She didn't think she'd disturb Amelia or Kevin if she sat down and watched a show or two.

Flipping on the baby monitor in her pocket, happiness lightened her steps, and rounding the corner to the living room, she let out a startled squeak as she smacked into a hard, warm…naked wall.

"Sorry, darlin'. Are you okay?" asked the naked wall, grasping her arms, nothing but a towel covering his lower half.

She nodded, because thanks to her reflexes, her palms were flat on some incredible pecs, and the feel of warm, wet skin and sprinkling of hair did funny things to her insides. Like steal her voice, and breath, and made her dizzy, and perked her nipples.

She had a hankering to drizzle him in chocolate sauce and lick him clean. Twice.

Stifling a moan, she hoped to goodness her robe was thick enough to camouflage her suddenly, heavy, needy breasts, reaching out, yearning to press into the hot, hard, sexy sinew that was Kevin. His gaze dropped right to them. *Guess not.* He clenched his jaw, tightened his grasp, then lifted his gaze. A deep, navy, hungry gaze.

Holy cowboys…

"Shayla?"

She swallowed, despite her suddenly dry throat. "Yeah?"

"Are you wearing anything under that robe?"

Funny how she was parched up north and wet down south. She slowly shook her head. "N-no."

"I didn't think so."

He continued to stare at her, through eyes that held a similar delicious promise his kisses had held in the past. Shayla knew she should run. She should release his tantalizing flesh, step out of his grasp, and turn and run like a little girl to her room.

But she didn't. In fact, she didn't move. Didn't breathe. Mostly because she couldn't feel her legs and something was squeezing her chest real tight.

"You need to stop looking at me like that," he breathed, voice rough, and sexy as hell. "You're making it very hard for me to be a gentleman."

Her need for him was too damn strong. She was so done. No more fighting this physical attraction.

"Maybe I don't want you to be." She cocked her head and skimmed her hands down his ridges, delighting in the way his flesh quivered under her touch.

He released her arms to clamp her wrists with his hands. "Be very careful, darlin'. We've already established we're combustible."

"I know," she said, fingering his happy trail.

"Shayla." He groaned. "You're killing me."

"That's not my intention."

Uttering an oath, he plastered her against the nearest wall and lifted her hands above her head. "What kind of game are you playing?"

"It's no game, Kevin," she said, need rushing through her body so fast she shook. "I want you. You want me. It's a matter of fulfilling each other's need."

He released her wrists, but didn't step back. "Are you sure, Shayla? I'm not a forever kind of guy. If that's what you're looking for, then you need to go back to your room."

She smiled, and reached up to caress the delicious scruff on his chin. "I'm not looking for forever either, Kevin. You know my situation. I can't stay in one place too long." She dropped her hand and sighed. "And as much as I love Harland County, we both know I'm going to eventually have to leave. There's no room in my live for forever. Just right now."

A small smile twitched his lips. "Just right now?"

"Yep."

"While we're in Houston?"

She smiled broadly. "Yes, I like that. While we're in Houston."

"Well then," he said, tugging the tie on her robe. "I do believe you have a need for me to take care of?"

She stepped away from the wall and let her robe fall to the floor, monitor thudding in the soft material.

He inhaled and ran his gaze down her body then back up. "Gorgeous."

A thrill like no other shot through her. She lifted her chin and sent him a grin. "You're right, I do have a need. A big one," she said, reaching for the knot in his towel. "Can you handle it?"

Never had Shayla ever been this brazen. But there was something about this cowboy that just went to her head.

"Only you can answer that, darlin'," he replied, stepping closer, filling her hand with the towel.

She loosened the knot, then watched, heart hammering in her chest as the white terry fell to the floor, revealing the biggest, mouthwatering erection she'd ever seen. Kevin Dalton truly was beautiful, head to toe. Muscular and ripped, with a sexy sprinkling of hair across his pecs and down his abs in a happy trail that led to a true treasure.

Of course his penis would be perfect, too. Not small or thin or a monster too painful to look at. No. She reached out and took him in her hand. He pulsed, and her body responded in kind. *Sweet mercy*. He had to be a good nine inches of thick, throbbing heat.

"Well?" He shook, but didn't make a move to touch her.

She released him and a breath, then met his heated gaze. "I've the feeling you're going to take care of me real good, cowboy."

A wicked smile crossed his face. "That's a promise, darlin'."

They stared for a beat, then lunged at each other, hands caressing every inch in a frenzy of moves, like they wanted to touch everywhere at once. She sure did. His mouth was hot and demanding on hers, drawing a response clear up from her toes.

He tasted of heat and desire, and in a swift move, cupped her ass to lift her up. Shayla immediately wrapped her legs around his hips and moaned at the sheer pleasure of brushing his erection where she ached the most. A second later, he began to walk, and the

Donna Michaels

friction nearly sent her over the edge. The man was delicious. Truly delicious, but before she could fall off that cliff, he set her on the credenza.

She broke the kiss and squeaked. "Cold."

"No worries, darlin', I'll warm you up," he said against her neck. "But I must apologize. This first time is going to be fast. I'm too far gone. This combustible thing is new to me."

"Good," she said, cupping his face, forcing him to meet her gaze. "Because I can't wait, Kevin. I'm about ready to burst."

He smiled into her palm. "Hold that thought, darlin'. I'll be right back."

Back?

He disappeared through the door on her left. The half-bath, her memory supplied from the tour he'd given the night before. He left her sitting on the credenza. Naked. But before her mind could formulate any addition thought, he returned with a foil packet in his hand.

"Sorry. Did you start without me?"

She laughed. "No, you goof."

"It's okay. I don't mind. Just maybe not this time," he said, before kissing her long and deep.

Deliciously deep.

Holy smokes, the guy could kiss. Decadent, drugging kisses. Shayla was just about to lean into him, when he stepped back and ripped the packet open. Apparently, they were on the same page. She needed to get to the next level. Fast.

"Let me help," she said, taking the condom from him to roll, and roll down his hard length.

He squeezed his eyes closed and inhaled. "Dammit, woman. You're killing me."

She laughed, and added another hand.

152

His eyes snapped open, and the need darkening his gaze clogged the breath in her throat and stilled her strokes.

He ran his hands up her body, over her breasts as his mouth came down on hers in a fierce, greedy kiss. The heat the man generated engulfed her senses. She needed to touch him, all of him.

Leaning forward, she ran her hands up his chest and shoulders to lock behind his neck where she caressed with her thumb. A sexy groan sounded in his throat and a wicked hand travelled down her curves to stroke between her thighs. He ripped his mouth away and sucked in a breath. "So wet," he said, stroking again. And again.

She whimpered. "I need you in me...now." Her body was tight and shaking, ready to snap. "But, what if the credenza breaks?"

He curled his hands around her hips and tugged her to the edge. "I'll buy another," he replied as the tip of his erection poked at the most perfect place.

"Yes," she said, shifting wider to take him in. Hell, *she'd* buy him another.

Needing no further instruction, Kevin thrust inside her in one sweet move and captured her satisfied cry with his mouth. Heaven help her, she'd never felt anything so intense, so achingly incredible as this man. He filled her completely. Deliciously full. The perfect fit.

He broke the kiss and pressed his forehead to hers. "You feel so damn good," he said, standing there, breathing heavy, letting her adjust to his size.

But she was already shaking.

"Cowboy, if you *move* it, I promise I'll *lose* it."

A big grin crossed his face. "Yes, ma'am."

And tightening his grip on her hips, he began to move, driving her out of her ever-loving mind with stroke after incredible stroke. Long and sure, with an angle that hit all her good spots. At once.

Her whole body was on fire and quivering. And she loved it.

Bending down, he sucked her nipple into his mouth, propelling her to that wonderful edge. Shayla moaned and arched closer. He upped his pace, driving into her with his deep, hard strokes. That was it. That's all it took. She clutched at his shoulders and cried out as she burst into a million and one pieces. He released her nipple, threw his head back and thrust in hard, letting go of one of those sinfully sexy sounds as he followed her with his own release.

Unsure how long they stayed that way, Shayla only knew it took a while for the world to come back into view. Heaven only knew where he'd sent her, but the cowboy had taken her right out of herself.

Hot breath rustled her hair as his chin rested on her head. "I think I like combustible," she said against his collar bone and felt him chuckle.

He drew back, and out, and smiled down at her. "Me, too, darlin'. Stay put."

As if she could walk at the moment. She couldn't even feel her legs. He reappeared, all cleaned up...with another packet in his hand.

Her stomach fluttered. *Holy Casanova*, he was ready for more?

"Miss me?" He scooped her up in his arms and carried her over to the couch. "Now that we got combustible out of the way, it's time for round two."

"Already? I've barely recovered from round one." She blinked up at him as he laid her out on the chaise. And she had been right about the couch. It was comfortable. She sank into an invisible hug. Of course, she never expected to be sprawled out on the cushions buck naked.

"Good," he said, kneeling down. "Now, close your eyes."

Her heart rocked in her chest. "Why?" She really wasn't into kinky things. At least she didn't think so.

A wicked smile dimpled his cheeks. "It's a surprise. Trust me. You'll enjoy it."

Digging deep, Shayla nodded and closed her eyes, letting go of the last of her inhibitions and doubts. The man had been with a lot of women. *Which was a good thing*, her mind insisted, because now, she could reap the rewards.

At the first feather-light touch of his hands, she jumped.

"Easy, darlin'."

She exhaled and reclosed her eyes. *Give up control. Have fun*, she told herself, and slowly began to enjoy the sensations his fingers created, skimming, caressing every inch of her body, except the tip of all her good spots. Damn him.

"I love freckles," he said against her ear and little shivers washed over her skin.

Never the same. The unknowing, the unexpected, all added to the titillation, and before long, her body was humming, and hungry, and needed more. Needed him to stroke her and take her. Now.

As if knowing, Kevin's touch grew stronger, bolder, and soon his mouth got in on the game. He kissed her over and over, then down her throat, as he slipped a finger between her legs. Shayla cried out at the unexpected pleasure and touch. With her eyes still closed, she rocked up to meet his strokes, and soon he had her panting, ready to take that dive again.

Then he did the unthinkable. Stopped kissing. Stopped touching. And she'd been so close. Fighting desperately to resist the urge to open her eyes, she clutched the cushions and listened for the sound of him opening the packet.

Yes, open the packet, she silently urged.

But the sound never met her ears, and just when she didn't think she could stand the suspense anymore, his hands skimmed up her legs and pushed them wider as she felt the delicious tickle of his breath on her thighs.

Then he licked her.

Shayla's eyes snapped open and hips lifted off the cushion, but the man was wise. He used the opportunity to grasp her tight and his mouth burrowed deep. *Holy*... Breath hitched in her throat and her eyes rolled back in her head. He was a master. The cowboy was a master. She wasn't going to last long.

"Kevin." She forced her eyes open. "I...can't...hold..."

He lifted his head and the most sinful smile crossed his handsome face. "Then don't."

The image she'd once had of the Casanova going down between her legs did not do the man justice. He was breathtaking. Blue eyes blazing wild, and dark and hungry. Exactly how she felt.

"Don't hold back, Shayla. You're delicious. I want to taste all of you." He put his mouth back on her, and did something incredible with his lips, or tongue, she couldn't be sure, but she settled back and closed her eyes, lost in the delectable sensations.

And when he added a finger and began to stroke while his mouth continued to lap, the tight band building and building inside her snapped. Her deep moan filled the room as he prolonged her orgasm with skillful precision. Then he slowed his strokes and licked one last time before he drew back and met her gaze.

"You're exquisite. I can't wait to do that again."

"Me either," she said between breathes. "Except I have nothing left to give."

A lopsided grin tugged his talented mouth. "You are so wrong," he said, ripping open the foil packet and sheathing his erection. "And I'm going to prove it.

Crawling up her body, Kevin kissed and stroked every curve, paying extra attention to each breast. Much to Shayla's surprise, heat returned to her belly in a delicious, all-consuming warmth and sparked her good parts back to life.

Damn, he was good.

She writhed underneath him, quivering and trembling, in desperate search of release. As if knowing exactly what she needed, he shoved that glorious erection deep inside, and this time, they both cried out at the sheer pleasure.

"So damn good," he said, lifting up, muscles bulging in his arms as he began to thrust, over and over again.

The band of desire returned, and at *explosion imminent* stage. No building required. She was there in one-point-two seconds. As sensations wracked her body, her gaze remained glued on the man. Eyes closed, mouth open, tightness worked across his face as he propelled them closer and closer to climax.

Magnificent.

And that was her last thought as her third orgasm ripped through her with such unexpected force she gripped the cushions, wrapped her legs around his hips and took him farther inside.

"Hell yeah," he said, voice rough before he drove into her in one deep thrust and shuddered with his own release.

Chapter Ten

"Okay, Kev. I'll bite. What gives?" Cole asked the following day, tossing his pen on his desk before leaning back in his chair. "Your mouth has been curved upward the whole morning. How come? Hot date last night?"

Kevin shook his head and held his friend's stare. "Nope. Haven't had a date since…well…last year." His *constant* smile broadened.

Technically, his day with Shayla and Amelia at Sea World yesterday hadn't been a date. Neither had their alone time last night. More of a mutual coming together of sorts.

Multiple times.

"Being that it's early January, I won't alert Kade's unit just yet."

He glanced up from his laptop and snickered. "Oh, you are just a riot today, *bossman*."

"And you are full of shit, Kevin." Cole laughed. "What exactly is going on between you and Shayla? You've had, what, two nights together now?"

"What exactly are you fishing at, Cole?"

No way was he about to discuss the numerous orgasms he gave the woman last night, although he knew the number and it made him stand a little taller today. And that wasn't even counting the one in his bed this morning.

In his bed.

No woman had ever been to his penthouse before, let alone slept in his bed. Until now. Until Shayla. This fact should freak his ass out, but for the moment, he was still

159

living on the high from the incredible release he'd achieved at daybreak surrounded by her warm, wet, pulsing walls.

Shit.

He shifted in his seat in front of his boss' desk. Now he was hot and hard, ready to break open the new box of condoms he'd purchased on his way into work that morning.

"You've slept with her," Cole stated, gaze neutral, voice devoid of judgment. "I hope you know what you're doing."

"What are you talking about?" Okay, so he hadn't exactly copped to the fact. And it was always best to deflect a taboo subject with a question.

His buddy sat back in his seat, elbows on the armrest, fingers steepled. "You know exactly what I'm talking about, buddy. I'm not stupid. The two of you have chemistry. Hell, I certainly wouldn't have lasted two nights cooped up with Jordan that first spring."

Kevin nodded. "You two were electric. Lots of sparks flew when she'd first returned. Still do."

A warm smile stole across Cole's face as his gaze appeared lost in thought. "Yeah, she was a spitfire, all right."

Kevin nodded again. It had been such a treat to watch the woman knock his friend back into the land of the living. And Cole hadn't returned quietly.

"And spitfires are hard to resist, especially when there's chemistry involved." A firm, direct gaze bore into him from across the desk. "Isn't that right, buddy?"

Busted.

Whatever. He shrugged, still not verbally copping to anything.

His boss' chuckle drifted through the room. "You might as well give it up, pal. You've been walking around today with such a satisfied look on your face, even the janitor noticed."

He stilled, wondering briefly if his friend was pulling his leg. "Bullshit. I'm smiling. So what? I always smile."

"True." Cole nodded. "But this time, it's different. This time it's more."

"More what?"

His friend shrugged, lifting his hands. "I don't know. More complete, I guess."

More complete…

Maybe. He certainly felt it. And he wasn't exactly sure what to do about it, or if the feeling was a good thing or not. Bachelors don't normally need a woman to make them complete. Just for physical relief. Which was what he and Shayla had agreed on. Maybe the *more complete* feeling stemmed from achieving that physical relief.

Several times.

"So, as I said. I hope you know what you're doing, Kev. Shayla's got it tough."

"I know." Kade had already pointed that out when he'd warned him off.

Shit. Kade.

He sat back in his chair and rubbed his jaw. He'd fully intended to heed his cousin's warning and not mess with Shayla, but when the beauty had stood naked under that damn robe, fingers stroking a trail of fire down his torso, succulent mouth confessing she wanted him, too, he was a goner. And when she tossed out the *Just Right Now* proposition…he'd grabbed on with both hands. The perfect solution, perfect fit to the *Sex with Shayla* puzzle

Donna Michaels

burning in his head for weeks, interrupting his sleep and thought process. Dropping his hand, he blew out a breath. He'd deal with Kade when they got back. For now—*Just Right Now*—satisfying Shayla was his priority.

Noting the concern in Cole's eyes, yet determined to keep the particulars to himself, he decided to give his friend a crumb. "We both agreed to act on the chemistry thing while we're here in Houston. No big deal."

His buddy blinked. Face deadpan serious. "I see. You both agreed to just have sex. No relationship, and only while you are here in Houston."

"Yes."

Cole snorted. "I give you a week."

"What the hell are you talking about now?"

"Once you're both back in Harland County, going about your own life, you aren't going to last one week without falling into bed with her again."

"Bullshit. You forget who you're talking to." What was up with Cole? His tie knotted too tight? Not enough oxygen to the brain? "If I want sex, there are plenty of women I can approach and not worry about them crying relationship to me."

"Of that I have no doubt, buddy. But I'm not talking about sex."

Kevin shook his head, then pressed a knuckle to his suddenly throbbing temple. "You aren't making sense, *bossman*. I think you may need more coffee." He released his head and pointed to the door. "Want me to buzz Stella?"

Cole's secretary would be in there with fresh, steaming brews in under a minute. The woman was efficient with a capital whip.

162

"No." His buddy chuckled. "I'm not the one with a problem. You are." Cole pointed at him. "You are in denial, my friend. All it's going to take is some cowboy sniffing around Shayla and you're going to go into stupid mode. Testosterone is going to take over and you're going to want to toss her over your shoulder and cart her off to your cave so she'll only have sex with you. It happens to all of us, buddy. I'm just trying to warn you."

Kevin leaned around his laptop and hit the intercom switch on the desk phone. "Stella, can you bring in some coffee? Better make that the whole pot. *Bossman* is operating on only half his brain cells today." He released the switch and sat back, holding Cole's amused stare as the secretary acknowledged the request.

Going all *caveman* because of Shayla.

Ridiculous.

The woman was free to do whatever and whoever she wanted.

His gut unexpectedly knotted. Probably because he'd skipped breakfast that morning. He'd had Shayla instead. Heat skittered down his spine. And she'd tasted better than any damn omelet.

Stella walked in carrying a tray with two mugs and a pot of coffee and set it on the desk between him and his boss. "Here you go, Mr. McCall." The older woman glanced at Kevin and nodded. "Mr. Smiley." Then pivoted on her heels and strode from the room.

What was with everyone and his smile? He poured two mugs, adding milk and sugar to his coffee. Didn't they have something better to do than contemplate his happiness? He always smiled. It meant nothing.

Cole lifted his mug and stared at him through the steam. "One week."

Saturday, Shayla was sitting next to her daughter on the couch, fiddling with her Rubick's cube while Amelia watched a Disney DVD of Cody's, when her boss sent her a text asking if they could Skype. Setting her puzzle aside, she smiled, happy for contact from the outside world. *Grown up* contact. She was beginning to hear animals sing in her sleep. Three days of doing nothing but watch children's shows was taking its toll. She grabbed her laptop and set up in the kitchen, far enough away to hear her boss, yet close enough to keep an eye on her daughter.

"I'm really sorry to make you work today, Shayla," Brandi exclaimed, thirty-minutes later, after outlining two out of three new jobs. Her boss sat in her cottage kitchen where they normally held their morning meetings, only this time, a webcam centered the pretty woman in the middle of Shayla's computer. "But, as you can see, since I signed up three jobs this week, I'm in desperate need of organization."

Secretly envious of her friend's gorgeous sun-kissed wavy brown hair, big brown eyes and traffic-stopping curves, Shayla smiled and waved a dismissive hand at the camera on top of her laptop. "No worries."

Oblivious as to her appeal to the opposite sex, Brandi was more focused on her fight with hypothyroidism and constant battle with weight. Not that guys cared. No. Her boss' fiancé was living proof. Kade was completely besotted with the beauty and her Marilyn Monroe-like figure. It was sweet.

Heck, there were times Shayla felt invisible standing next to the woman. Construction workers tripped over their tongues when Brandi was around. Sure, a few heads turned her way, just not at the volume of her voluptuous friend. Shayla was more like a toothpick with mosquito

164

bites. Okay, *that* was an exaggeration. She had an hour glass figure with a healthy C cup, but there were times she felt flat next to Brandi. Thankfully, the woman wasn't a bitch or Shayla just might have to hate her.

"I feel bad," her boss was saying.

"It's fine. Really," she reassured. "I'm grateful. Believe me, I was going stir crazy here."

Keeping busy was key. No time to dwell on the possibility of her dad showing up in Harland County, or here. Or going after Caitlin. Work was a welcomed distraction.

Otherwise, she'd be forced to think about her other problem. Kevin. And his sexy body and sinfully delicious lovemaking that would end when she left Houston.

Lyle or Kevin. Both dangerous subjects for two very different reasons.

Since that incredible night on the chaise, she'd taken to sleeping in the Casanova's bed. Her body was achingly in tune with the man. It was weird. She could sense his whereabouts in the room without the aid of sight. And the minute he was close, her need for the guy increased tenfold and she couldn't keep her hands off him. And if by some miracle she did, then he was all over her as if he couldn't get enough.

Cripes. By the amount of sex they'd been having the past few days, you'd think they would've gotten each other out of their systems. *Nope.* They were like cats in heat. She feared her body was going to become dependent on the cowboy. Not good. In fact, it was bad. *Very* bad. Every damn night, her intentions of sleeping in the room with Amelia would fly out the window with one touch, one glance, one single syllable. She was such a nymph when it came to that cowboy. It ticked her off.

165

"Well, I can understand you needing to keep busy. I really hate that you and your sister have to go through this, Shayla." Brandi sighed, concern etched in her face. "How's Caitlin? Do you want Kade to fetch her?"

She shook her head. "No, I talk to her daily, and just checked with her an hour ago. Things have been good all week. Normal. No strange occurrences, so she wants to stay put."

Brandi nodded. "If you change your mind and want her picked up, you know Kade will be there in a flash."

"Thanks." She smiled, trying not to open that box of worry.

Her sister was fine.

She was fine.

Everything was fine.

"And your GED classes? What did the center have to say?"

Brandi was the only other one beside Caitlin who knew about the classes because Shayla had needed the time off in the mornings to attend Monday through Friday for two weeks. Her boss, as always, was a huge supporter and promised to keep it quiet.

"I called the center on Wednesday and explained I had an out-of-town emergency," she replied, having tried to keep her excuse to them as truthful as possible. "They were very understanding." *Thank God.* "I'm enrolled in the next set of classes that start two weeks from now."

Surely Kade would give them the okay to go back by then. Shayla was sick over the fact she'd come so close to her diploma. So damn close. Her father always found a way to interfere. Ruin her joy. Kill her dreams. She'd be damned if she allowed him take this one away from her too.

"Oh, that's super, honey. I'm so glad. I know how much it means to you."

"Thanks." She shrugged, and wanting to get off the subject of *Shayla*, she turned the conversation back to work. "So, you told me about the McCaffrey addition and The Creamery's expansion. What's the third project you have on your plate now?"

"That would be the humane stables."

Shayla blinked. "What humane stables?"

"Kade's, on Shadow Rock Ranch." Brandi smiled, a beautiful, thousand watt smile, and a sheen of tears appeared in her eyes. "It's been his dream. You know how good he is with the abused and neglected horses."

Shayla nodded. She sure did. The man was a natural. She'd seen some 'before and after' photos of a few of his charges, courtesy of Connor's phone. The big cowboy said everyone in the county knew his friend was the *go-to* man if there was an animal in need. *People* should be added to that mix. And she was one of them. The National Guardsman helped anyone who needed helping. No questions asked. He'd certainly taken her under his wing.

"What a wonderful project." Her throat burned with emotion. "There's going to be a lot of happy horses."

Brandi nodded, a single tear running down her face. "I know. And animals. We're going to build one stable, and remodel the existing one that's off on its own.. One for the horses, the other for dogs, cats, goats, cows...whatever needs shelter and healing. Kade has already talked to the humane society to see what was needed, and the local vet is on board. Based on their information, I've already come up with a preliminary plan. I'll email it to you now."

And for the next two hours, they mapped out a pecking order, and who and what was needed for all three jobs. After disconnecting from their session, Shayla worked on her lists for each project as Amelia colored next to her in a book Kevin bought at Sea World. Her daughter had been excited to find a *goggy* and was coloring it special for *daddy*.

A frustrated sigh escaped her lips. No matter how many times she corrected Amelia, she couldn't get the bugger to call him Kevin/Kebie anymore. Suppressing her irritation, she focused on the welcomed boatload of work her boss just unloaded. Since it was the weekend, and she couldn't contact the people and county offices needed to get any of the balls rolling, her 'to do' list for Monday morning was quite extensive.

"Hello, honey. I'm home," Kevin called out with a grin as he walked in the door.

"Daddy!" Amelia scrambled from her seat and ran to the grinning cowboy who scooped her daughter up in his arms.

Arms her body had no trouble recalling how warm and welcoming they were or how strong as he leaned over her thrusting...

Shaking her head to dispel the memory, she ignored her tingling parts and smiled at the man she planned on resisting that night. Starting now. She was not going to get up, under any circumstances, until her list was complete.

"How was your day, dear?" she volleyed back, remaining in her seat, staring at him from across the room.

"Better now," he replied, dropping his coat and briefcase on the couch before he kissed her daughter's head. "How about you, pumpkin? Did you have a good day?"

Amelia's laughter filled the penthouse and Shayla's heart swelled at the sound. There was nothing better in life than to see and hear her daughter happy.

"Horsie," Ameila cried, pushing to get out of Kevin's arms.

She glanced at the picture her daughter had been coloring. It was the penguin, not a horse, so she had no idea what the little girl wanted.

"You have a one track mind. Wonder who you take after?" Kevin set her daughter down and glanced directly at Shayla, gaze wickedly sinful.

Heat skittered down her body to pool low in her belly. *Stupid body.*

"Okay, we'll play horsie for just a little bit," he said, sitting on the couch. "But then we have to be quiet so mommy can finish working before dinner arrives."

Dinner? *What* dinner? And what exactly was *horsie*?

"'Kay," Amelia said, climbing on Kevin's shin, big smile on her face. "Horsie."

The cowboy held her daughter's hands and began to lift his leg up and down. Her daughter giggled, and laughed and cackled. And whenever the cowboy stopped, the demanding toddler cried for more. Watching the two interact did funny things to her heart. It swelled so much it hurt to breath, and her stupid eyes burned.

Shayla had to swallow and blink a few times in order to focus on her list. Yes, much better to tune them out. Safer. Because in a few short days, Kevin wouldn't be living under the same roof or walking in at suppertime with smiles and kisses for Amelia to count on. Let her daughter enjoy the cowboy now, while she concentrated on working to keep that roof over their heads.

Fifteen minutes later, she closed her laptop and sighed, proud of herself for tuning everyone out long enough to finish her work. She glanced into the living room, shocked to find her daughter settled on the couch, clutching her *goggy* while watching some kind of educational program on TV—and Kevin setting her Rubick's cube back on the coffee table.

Finished.

Done.

Each colored side *friggin'* matching.

"Hey." She shot to her feet, then rushed forward, pulse hammering in her head. "What did you do?" She swiped the puzzle from the table and stared at the perfect cube for a moment before transferring her gaze to the frowning cowboy.

"I finished it for you. Why?" He rose to his feet and lightly touched her cheek with the back of his hand. "Was I not supposed to?"

No. He wasn't, and she'd tell him, just as soon her stupid body gave back control of her vocal cords. Those fingers caressing her face were soft and gentle, kind of like the expression in his blue eyes. Darn him. How was she supposed to stay mad at him when he was being sweet?

"I…" She cleared her throat. "I've been working on it for months now. Helps me relieve stress. But, it's okay. I can start over."

Yeah, big wuss when it came to him. That was not at all what she'd planned to say. And when a smile consumed his face, her whole thought pattern disintegrated into a warm haze.

"No problem, darlin'," he said, easing the cube from her fist, then turned it this way and that, and before she knew it, he handed her the cube *exactly* as she had left it that morning.

Shayla blinked at the puzzle, then glanced at him, shaking her head as if that would make things clearer. "How did you do that?"

His grin broadened as he shrugged. "I don't know. It's a gift. I see a flowchart or pattern clear as day."

"Really?" She shoved the cube into his chest. "Do it again. Show me."

"Sure." He took the cube, turned it this way and that, and in less than a minute he solved the puzzle.

Amazing.

She grabbed the cube, turned it over twenty times then shoved it back into his chest and smiled.

Without a word, just his sexy lopsided grin, the cowboy solved the cube yet again. For five whole minutes, Shayla messed the puzzle and Kevin solved. In total and complete awe of the man, she was only just starting to realize the cowboy's true brilliance.

He twisted the puzzle back to how he'd found it, then set the cube on the table. "You know," he said, stepping right into her personal space, mischief twitching his dimples to life. "I can't help but feel I'm being taken advantage of here. Shouldn't I get some kind of reward?"

"Reward?" She played dumb, fingering his collar while his hands trailed down her arms to settle deliciously on her hips.

"Yeah, darlin'. Even circus animals get treats after their performances."

She laughed. "So, if I throw you a fish, you'll catch it in your mouth?"

"Absolutely. And clap, too." His gaze sparkled with mirth, and something far hotter, as he drew her hips close.

"Well, then." She wrapped her hand around his tie and winked. "I guess I do have a little something for you."

And because she was such a Kevin nymph, she tugged his mouth right down on hers.

He was addicted to Shayla.

Kevin could deny it all he wanted to Cole, but the honest truth was evident as the gorgeous redhead in his bed. Sure, he could talk a good game. Convince just about anyone to do anything, but at the end of the day, trying to convince himself he'd rather lay on the couch with Amelia asleep in his arms than join her naked...wet momma in the shower, he had some hard truths to face.

He loved his time with Amelia, coloring, watching TV, holding the little pumpkin while she slept in his arms. She'd ridden her *horsie* right into his heart. He was going to miss her once they were back in Harland County. So, the fact he'd eagerly tucked the little angel in her crib so he could race to be with her momma when he knew their time together was quickly coming to an end, only proved how strong a pull the attraction was between him and Shayla.

The single mother gripped his attention, captivated his thoughts and tantalized his body. Yeah, he was addicted to Shayla.

Addicted to her mouth-watering curves, wicked lips, decadent taste, sinful touch, uninhibited and insatiable hunger. He stifled a groan and tried to talk his heating body out of needing the woman again. They'd just had incredible against the wall shower sex. His legs were still trying to find their bones, and yet he was quickly recovering for another round.

So? What the hell was wrong with that?

He should take whatever the woman wanted to give. And, *oh hell yeah*, she was very, very giving. And demanding. Heaven help him, the combination rocked his world.

As if of its own accord, his hand snaked under the covers to gently glide down her bare back, drawing circle after circle across her supple flesh. God, she was silky smooth and so damn soft.

"Mmm…" she uttered into the mattress before scooting close to toss a leg over him and burrow into his side.

The feel of her generous breasts mashed against him and wet heat between her legs curving around his hip had his dick twitching to life. He curled a palm around her sweet ass and forced his other to remain on the hand she used to stroke his chest. Keep it *simple*. Keep it *safe*.

"You're nice and warm." She snuggled closer, causing his eyes to cross.

Safe. Keeping it safe.

He lifted her wrist and kissed her tattoo. She stared up at him, mass of emotions fluttering through her eyes.

Don't do it. Don't ask.

"For your mom?"

Damn mouth wasn't good at following orders.

"Yes."

A one word answer. Good. The woman didn't want to answer any more than he wanted to know. And he didn't want to know, because knowing made sex personal. Which would be a mistake. A stupid one. Why ruin a good thing? They had four days of raw, passionate, crazy sex without hardly any words involved.

Don't mess it the fuck up.

It was still walk-away-able.

"Your mom liked dragonflies?"

173

Duct tape. Where the hell was the duct tape? He needed a big ass piece for his big mouth. Or maybe he could put it over hers should she feel inclined to answer. But this was Shayla. Surely, she'd tell him to mind his own damn business. *Yeah*, any second now. Any second now she was going to shut him down hard.

He held his breath, partly in anticipation, but mostly so he didn't ask another damn question.

"Yes. My mom used to say they were resilient and represented hope."

A bubble of some sort rippled through Kevin's chest, causing his heart to catch. Lack of oxygen, no doubt. He released his breath, kissed her palm, then set her hand back on his pecs.

"Smart woman."

Now she nodded. "Yep. The best. My hero."

Sweet. And informative. *Leave it at that*. No need to ask anything else.

Don't ask anything else.

Jesus, he was going to ask more. The hazards of mind-blowing sex. He was brainless. No cells left to form enough thought to keep his damn mouth shut.

"What do you mean?"

Yep, brainless.

"My mom saved my life."

Chapter Eleven

Damn. He hadn't expected that. He tightened his grip on her and frowned. "What do you mean?" he repeated, this time with his brain's consent.

She laid her head on his chest and the breath of her sigh goose-fleshed his skin. "My dad liked to possess. Dominate. Control. Punish. Hit. Beat into submission."

Anger, so sharp and fierce, sliced through Kevin in such a painful rush he stilled and clenched his jaw to keep in the slew of expletives. Never had he experienced fury so strong in his entire life.

"You're probably wondering why my mom stayed with him, but that's the thing. She didn't. She packed us up and left many times, but he'd always find us, bring us back and beat us bad. Well, not Caitlin. Never Caitlin. I made sure of that."

His heart caught again and the unspoken meaning in that sentence hit him hard. She'd taken beatings for her younger sister. *Son-of-a-fuckin'-bitch*. The urge to hit something—preferably her father's face—curled his hands into fists.

Shayla paused, and although he was past caring about the need to keep her quiet, he remained silent, forced his hands to open and stroked her arm as he waited for her to continue. Somehow, he sensed…he *knew* she needed to get this out. And *dammit*, he needed to hear, even though he was certain he wasn't going to like it.

"The last time was the worst," she said, voice low and devoid of all emotion. "I'd just competed and won regional's, and my mom, Caitlin and I were celebrating in our little apartment when he showed up with a baseball bat."

Son-of-a-bitch.

Kevin tried, really hard, to keep his body from stiffening and his breathing even. Any change in him and she was liable to clam up.

"He went to swing at me, and my mom stepped in the way and got hit in the head. She flew backwards, and when he went to hit her again, I jumped on his back. That pissed him off even more. He knocked me to the floor and deliberately whacked my leg just below the knee. When he reeled back to swing at my head, my mom stood up behind him and clobbered him with a cast iron pan. The police arrived then. Caitlin had hid in the closet and dialed 911."

"I'm sorry, Shayla." His words sounded feeble and stupid to his ears, but he had to say something. She'd been through hell. He could hardly stand it. No wonder the woman was closed off and cautious. Her demeanor made a lot of sense now. "Did your dad wear suits?"

"Yes. All the time. His goons, too."

That explained the *poling* incident last year. She must've caught him approaching from the corner of her eye and instinct, survival instinct had set in.

"I'm sorry," he said again, feeling guilty that he'd had such a loving, happy childhood while his father had been alive.

"Don't be." She turned to meet his gaze and did the most remarkable thing.

She smiled.

His heart caught again. How could she go through something like that, recant something like that, and smile?

"My mom and I pressed charges, and we sent him a way for a long, long time. Life was good, Kevin. The constant fear and suppressing, suffocating pressure in my chest was gone. Sure, my aspirations of dancing were shot, but it was so worth it. My mom found us a great house to rent, had a great job. My sister and I went to a good school. For the first time in all my life, I was happy."

"I'm glad," he said, tightening his hold, and knew she was waiting for him to ask. "What happened to your mom?"

She closed her eyes and laid her head back down on him. "Four years later, a few weeks after I passed my driver's test, we were all doing dishes after supper when my mom dropped a plate and grabbed her head. She was dead before she hit the floor."

"*Jesus*, Shayla. I'm so sorry."

The incredible woman nodded against him and drew in a breath so ragged he felt it clear to his toes.

"Me, too. She'd had one too many blows to the head, I guess. Even though my dad was in prison, he still managed to murder my mom."

Kevin held her close, and his heart squeezed at the emotion heavy in her voice and the hot tears dripping onto his chest.

So much for keeping their sex just sex.

After a revelation like that, they'd rounded the corner to personal, and there was no going back. He couldn't unhear what he'd heard. Or unfeel what he felt. Angry. Disgusted and so damn furious he could spit fire. And protective. He stroked her hair as she quietly cried.

Shayla Ryan was a good woman. He admired the hell out of her. A brave woman who'd been through so damn much she deserved nothing but happiness and smiles. Although he couldn't supply her with a lifetime of any of those, he could make her happy right then. That night.

"Dammit, Kevin." She sniffed, punching his shoulder. "I didn't mean to tell you all that. Jeez, you boffed my brains out and I have nothing but mush left in my head now." Lifting up on her elbow, she smiled at him, amusement returning to light her face. "It's all your fault."

"Me? You're the one who ravaged me and left my brains with my bones on the bathroom floor."

"Oh, really?" Bold and wicked, her hand trailed down his abs to stroke his favorite body part back to life. "Looks like I missed one," she said, before taking him in her warm, wet mouth, making him swallow his tongue.

He knew what she was doing, besides *him*. She was trying to get them away from that personal business and back on track with the hot sex. That worked for him. *Yeah.* He was much better at the hot sex thing than the personal thing and open feelings. Time to get them back on the good-time track and show her some of his famous fun.

A little while later, after he silently vowed to make her forget everything, including her real name, he watched as she rode him hard and fast, and at that moment, he didn't care about the name she was born with—only Shayla—the incredible, sexy woman who fogged his mind. Long, beautiful hair fell past her shoulders in soft, auburn waves, brushing her glorious, bouncing breasts, and her breathtaking, euphoric expression completely wiped the sadness from her face.

Good. That was his goal. Make her happy. Give her everything she wanted.

"Look at me, Shayla." Blue eyes, wild and full of heat and need, so much need, stared down at him, nearly snapping his control. He knew what she wanted. And he was going to give it to her. "I want to watch you burst."

She nodded. "Make...me...."

Wicked, incorrigible woman.

He knew every inch of her gorgeous body and all her special spots. Running his hands down her breasts, he tweaked her mouthwatering, silver-dollar nipples and upped their rhythm.

The little mewling sounds coming from her parted lips sent heat down his spine and the tell-tale tightening in his groin. They were both close now. Gripping her hip with one hand, he brushed her center with the thumb of his other, applying just the right amount of pressure exactly where she liked it the most. A second later, Shayla let out the sexiest damn moan as her walls clamped around him. Tight.

"Hell yeah..."

She felt good. So damn good.

Kevin thrust hard and deep and completely lost his breath as her orgasm milked the fiercest climax he'd ever had. When the ringing subsided in his head, and vision returned, he removed his thumb from her center, and watched her come back to herself, with the best satisfied expression to date on her face.

And as Shayla fell forward and landed on his chest panting and spent, Kevin knew he'd caught the extraordinary, resilient, single mother with his heart. No amount of denial could delete the fact they would never have *just* sex again.

Best sex of her life.

Not that the whole week had been shabby. *Hell no.* The things Kevin Dalton had done to her last night, the responses the Casanova cowboy had pulled from her were just this side of epic. The need, the burning, fierce drive to have him inside her was mind boggling. A puzzle she'd never solve. Shayla wasn't even going to try. Just chalk it up to that combustible chemistry.

But last night had been different. More. And she knew why. Because she'd opened up and shared part of her past. Part of her soul. Although it was a dumb, stupid slipup, she couldn't bring herself to be mad or upset. The resulting sex had been too exhilarating and brain cell-zapping to care.

Smiling, she made the bed, half of her happy, the other half sad that he'd gone into work again today. In fact, he'd been up at dawn working on some sort of code—after he'd worked on her. The man had an insatiable appetite. Which matched the one he'd created in her. *Damn him.* It was as if he reached in and rewrote her code. She was never going to be the same.

But, she'd worry about that when she was back in Harland County. Not now. Not tonight. No. Tonight she planned to ask him about his parents. Make *him* open up. In between rounds of hot sex, of course. Asking after they'd had an incredible climax was key. Defenses would be down. Mind and body too relaxed to stop the tongue from waggling.

Exactly what had happened to her last night.

"Goggy."

The sound of Amelia talking in her crib emanated from the monitor on Kevin's gorgeous nightstand. With the décor of the penthouse continuing into the master bedroom, the cowboy's furniture was that beautiful, heavy mahogany, and the king-size bed they'd used at every angle was just as magnificent for sex as it was for sleeping. Damn man was spoiling her. Good thing Kerri had had a king-size bed in the apartment Shayla rented. At least going back to Harland County wouldn't require her to downsize the mattress.

Just give up one occupant.

Her chest tightened at the thought, but she ignored the sensation, and the reason for the hiccup, and went to fetch her daughter. Keep it simple. They'd gone from having sex to friends having sex. That was okay. Normal. Sort of. Wasn't exactly like when she and Bobby had had sex. But then again, that combustible chemistry hadn't been a factor, either.

Yeah, that was the difference. It was still okay. No harm done. No heart involved.

But even as she went through the morning routine of dressing, feeding and playing with her daughter, Shayla knew, deep down, after last night, things had changed.

Two hours later, mug of coffee in hand, she stared out at the Houston skyline, marveling at the height of some of the buildings, including the one she stood in. The view below was amazing. From the high angle, she could see forever.

If only her life, her future was so attainable. Would Lyle ever leave her alone? Would Caitlin graduate and live happily with Greg? Would Amelia grow up to be happy and strong? Would Kevin be in her life?

Whoa. She blinked and shook her head. Where the hell had that question come from? Of course the cowboy wouldn't be in her life, at least, not in a forever kind of way. He was a player. Not bankable in a relationship. Yet, her gut told her this was untrue. Her eyes had even witnessed the guy doing things a Casanova would not do. He was not as irresponsible as she'd first believed.

He was sweet to her daughter. A player would've run like a baby in the opposite direction once he discovered she had a child.

He took care of her when she'd had the flu. A player would've turned around and raced down the hall when she'd first opened her door that night, not hold her hair back while she'd been sick, put her to bed and taken care of her daughter the whole night.

Then there was Mrs. Avery. He stopped in and looked after his former English teacher. A player wouldn't give a damn about an old lady and her cats.

Even now, the cowboy stepped up to the plate. He took her and her daughter in, let them invade his space while her crazed father was on the loose. A player would've turned his back and left her to fend for herself, like Amelia's father.

Kevin was nothing like Brandon. Nothing like a player. *Hell*, he wasn't a Casanova at all.

Her heart caught in her chest, then rocked hard.

Kevin was every bit of a good man, a responsible man like Kade, Cole and Connor. So, why did he pretend to be the opposite? What deep-seeded pain, guilt, was eating at him?

The ringing of her cell phone startled her from her thoughts. Maybe it was Kade. Her pulse thundered in her ears. Maybe there was a problem. Or maybe it was just her boss with a job update. Shayla rushed to the counter where she set her mug before digging the phone from her snug jeans.

That cheesecake she'd eaten off of Kevin last night wasn't helping her hips. But, she should be burning off a trillion calories with all the *sexercize* she'd been getting. The smile twitching her lips grew when she glanced at the screen and saw Kevin's name.

"Hey," she answered, her brain suddenly empty. *Hey? Really?*

Idiot.

"Hi, darlin'." His rich, sexy voice reached through the phone and tickled her spine with an invisible caress. "How's my favorite houseguest?"

Houseguest. Right. That's really all she was. A guest in his house. Nothing more. She'd do well to keep that in mind.

"I'm good. A little sore, but it had been worth it." *Shoot.* Why was she telling him that? She rummaged through the closest drawer. Duct tape. She needed some duct tape to stop her trap from upping her mortification meter.

His soft chuckle warmed her inside. "Hot damn, darlin'. You got that right. I'd contemplated sitting in the elevator on the ride down to the garage this morning, but was reluctant to go through the third degree with Hoffman. He is a very thorough bodyguard/driver. But you're thorough, too."

She leaned her back against the counter and laughed. "I was just returning the favor, cowboy."

"Mmm...you have great return, darlin'."

Her smile broadened.

"I hate to intrude into your day, but I need you to go into my office."

"Okay," she said, heading out of the kitchen to take a left and enter the room where she'd experienced her second orgasm trifecta Thursday night. His home office.

Luxurious leather furniture, huge mahogany desk, equally big matching credenza, floor to wall window. Just remembering their rigorous sex stole her breath. She cleared her throat. "I'm here."

"See the folder that this idiot forgot in his haste to exit while his legs would barely carry him this morning?" he asked, smile evident in his tone.

Her own mouth curved in a smile. "Yes. It's red."

"That it is, darlin'," he replied. "I need you to bring it to me here at McCall Enterprises."

Her smile disappeared. "What?"

"Sorry, Shayla. I hate to ask you to leave the penthouse, but I need that folder for a phone conference marketing has in an hour. And I don't have the information on my computer here at work. I prefer to safeguard it at home."

A small thrill shot through her, cancelling her insecurity of navigating through a strange city. No big deal. She'd manage. For him. The man was entrusting her with something he guarded as valuable. She would damn well be sure to deliver it to him in time.

"No worries," she reassured, grabbing the file before exiting the room. "Just tell me how to get there."

"You don't have to worry none about that. Hoffman is on his way. He'll drive you in, and no, I don't want you to hand the file to him. I'd prefer you bring it to me. I trust the man with my life, not my code," Kevin informed.

With her heart hammering in her suddenly dry throat, she nodded as if the man could see her. *Idiot.* She swallowed past the lump his confidence in her had created, and forced herself to speak. "No problem."

"Thanks, darlin'. I owe you."

A wave of sensual heat washed down her body, dampening her thong as she shoved the file in Amelia's diaper bag. "Oh, cowboy. That is a dangerous statement," she said, restacking the books her daughter had spread out across the coffee table, as she worked to regain part of her composure.

Amelia quickly pitched in, adding a book to the teetering pile.

She could relate. Her restraint was eerily similar at that moment.

"I know it's dangerous. Please, make me pay," he teased, effectively knocking over her teetering pile of self-control from within.

Shayla laughed. "Count on it." Then hung up to finish getting ready.

The man was incorrigible.

She was just placing Amelia's empty sippy cup in the diaper bag along with an unopened juice box when a knock sounded on the door. Her heart hit the floor, but then common sense kicked in. Hoffman.

Her daughter pushed up from the floor and smiled. "Daddy."

Shoot. Little bugger turned and ran to the door. Another knock sounded, louder this time. Shayla scooped up the redheaded roadrunner and peeked through the peephole. Just to be careful.

A woman. Pretty. And blonde. In a blue flight attendant uniform.

Her racing heart sank. *Ah hell.* Had to be one of Kevin's lovers. Wiping all emotion from her features, Shayla answered the door.

Chapter Twelve

"Surprise, Ke—"

The woman's smile and voice disappeared as she blinked at Shayla and Amelia.

"Kevin's not here," she said, proud to note her voice was even and strong.

"Oh." The Barbie wannabe glanced past them, no doubt horrified at the toy disaster strewn all over the living room.

"He's at work," she added. "Was he expecting you?"

"Not really. We sort of have an arrangement when I have a layover." The woman studied her and the unusually quiet Amelia. "Cute kid. And I'm sure Kevin thinks so, too, but I wouldn't get too comfortable playing house. That cowboy likes to keep things simple. No responsibility and that sort of thing."

The flight attendant's words reminded Shayla that even though *she* knew Kevin was not a player, the cowboy didn't realize it yet. He had a carefree, thriving social life. And as soon as she was out of Houston, he'd go back to playing in that very broad field.

Tipping her chin, she held the woman's gaze. "I know. We're not a thing. Kevin was kind enough to let my daughter and I stay here a few days while we're in Houston."

There. That should be enough information to not ruin things for him with the blonde in the future. And why Shayla's stomach knotted at the thought, she refused to analyze.

"Oh. I see." The woman smiled and warmth returned to her eyes. "He is a sweetheart. Will you please tell him Amber stopped by?"

Amber? Shayla blinked. *Really?* The woman had blonde hair and blue eyes.

"Sure. Of course. Do you want me to have him call you?"

Blonde Amber with blue eyes shook her head and grinned. "No. I'm only here 'til three. You all enjoy. I'll catch him next time." And with that, the woman got in the elevator and disappeared.

Next time.

Just how many times had Amber *enjoyed* Kevin?

Whoa. That was twice now she'd had to stop a crazy thought train that morning. The cowboy's love life was none of her business. She had no stake. No claim on the man. And because she was beginning to want to, Shayla decided then and there, her plans for the night had just drastically changed.

Tonight she was sleeping in Amelia's room.

A half-hour later, Shayla was holding Amelia and balancing the diaper bag, speeding toward the top floor of McCall Enterprises with Hoffman and a vaguely familiar pretty woman.

"Is this your first time here?" the woman asked with a smile.

Shayla nodded. "Is it that obvious?"

"No, but this building can be a bit overwhelming."

Understatement. Why she'd thought it would've been some kind of warehouse was a mystery. Shayla had certainly never pictured the company the two cowboys ran to be a massive, impressive skyscraper with more than forty floors.

"I'm, Nadine. I just started working here after the New Year." The friendly woman held out her hand.

"Shayla. And this is Amelia." She studied the woman smiling at her daughter, then it dawned on her why the pretty brunette seemed so familiar. Nadine had been at the Texas-Pub last month. Dancing with Kevin.

"Kevin said you'd be coming to bring him the file he'd forgotten."

Kevin? Just how friendly where they?

Damn. She did it again. Crossing the just-sex zone.

Back off, she told herself. The man's love-life was his business. It was just a little surprising he'd mix business with pleasure.

"Yeah. I have it my bag."

"I'm sorry we had to pull him away from you today."

"Oh, you didn't pull him away," she rushed to say. "I mean, we're just friends. We had nothing planned."

Other than avoiding the immanent wild sex. Hopefully he'd work late. That would help her to keep her resolve to sleep in Amelia's room tonight.

"That's too bad. He's a great guy," Nadine exclaimed, glancing at Hoffman who stood with his gaze straight ahead, and arms folded across his massive chest before the woman's brown gaze shifted back to Shayla.

A small smile tugged her lips. Now those were the kind of eyes that went with the name Amber.

"Kevin was a sweetheart to me last year when my well-meaning brother asked him to take me to my college formal. I was well past mortified, especially when he'd told Kevin no sex. Right in front of me."

Okay, yeah, see, she didn't want to hear this. Her gaze shot to Hoffman. Still no emotion. Damn man was a rock.

"Anyhow, it wasn't like that. We played video games all night. I kicked his ass half the time. And well, he made me understand that being a nerd was all right. You can imagine my shock when I realized who he was. I mean, some of the games he's designed are legend. And yet, you'd never know the guy was vice president to such a prestigious company, or named programmer of the year several times, or had a net worth that exceeded eight digits. Kevin is just a nice, fun-loving, down to earth cowboy."

Wasn't that the plain truth?

Shayla never considered any of that. In fact, the realization was beginning to hit her like a steamroller. The man she considered a fun-seeking, irresponsible player, the very man whose body she'd been seeking fun with all week, was a well-known and respected businessman.

A billionaire.

Her stomach began to knot. "Yes, he's been very kind," she said, knowing the talkative woman was waiting for a response, and held in a sigh of relief when the elevator stopped at the top floor and the doors opened.

Nadine was nice, but Shayla wasn't used to being open with her feelings, especially concerning the blue-eyed cowboy...programmer...businessman....billionaire. Just what was she supposed to call him now? Casanova cowboy didn't seem to fit anymore.

It didn't compute.

"This is Mrs. Dixon." Nadine drew her forward to the secretary sitting behind the tall desk in a spacious reception area.

A large picture of Mr. McCall, one of Cole McCall and one of Kevin covered the back wall, while plaques and awards lined the other two surrounding reception. *Holy awards*. There had to be more than twenty.

"Please, call me Stella," the stylish, middle-aged woman in a light blue power suit insisted as she stood. "It's nice to finally meet you, Shayla. And this must be Amelia." The secretary approached with a no-nonsense, graceful gait, her arm extended.

"Nice to meet you, Stella," she said, shaking the woman's hand, her gaze going back to the multitude of plagues. "I hadn't realized McCall Enterprises had so many awards."

"Not all of them are for the company," the woman stated, ending the hand shake. "Many are for Cole and Kevin, although, these aren't even half of them. Those two guys hate the pomp and circumstance. I had to dig these from their desk drawer. And even the garbage. They don't do it for the fame."

Shayla's chest tightened as she began to realize just how smart Kevin was, and what he'd accomplished with his life. High school. College. Part owner of thriving horse ranch. Vice president to prestigious, world renown company. World famous programmer. While she was a single mother who constantly moved around and never made it past the eleventh grade. He was friendly, brilliant with a ton of friends. She was closed up, diploma-less with a couple of friends she could count on one hand. Compared to the cowboy, she was lacking. Big time.

"Yeah," Nadine stepped close, gaze alive with excitement. "They don't create the programs for fame. They do it for the challenge."

A familiar tingling skittered down Shayla's spine, and she knew without turning Kevin had appeared. Was this how Cole knew Jordan was near?

"Exactly," the cowboy said, and her daughter immediately pushed to get down.

Turning with a ready smile on her lips, she was determined to squash the excitement his nearness created. The past twenty-four hours had certainly been eye-opening. If she'd thought them worlds apart before, they were universes apart now.

Smile still firmly in place, she nodded at Cole and Kevin.

"Daddy," Amelia yelled, running full speed at the smiling, blue-eyed executive while everyone else stilled to the point of not breathing.

If the floor found it within itself to open up and swallow Shayla she'd be forever grateful. But *no*. Seemed her daughter decided the top floor of McCall Enterprises was a great place for public humiliation.

"Hey, pumpkin," Kevin said, scooping her daughter in his arms to receive his routine sloppy kiss.

When Shayla's pulse slowed down to warp speed, she swallowed and forced a laugh. "She saw a little girl do that at Sea World, and we can't seem to get her to stop." The need to explain her daughter's behavior was strong enough for Shayla to risk further embarrassment.

"You three went to Sea World?" Cole asked, huge grin consuming the man's handsome face.

"Yeah," Kevin replied, shifting Amelia to sit on his shoulders. "On Wednesday. We had a great time watching the penguins, didn't we, angel?" He smiled at Shayla and winked.

She wasn't sure if the cowboy had been asking her or Amelia. After all, the man had only ever called her Shayla or darlin', except for a few sexy, erotic endearments when he was buried deep inside her. Heat rushed to her face, and since she hadn't been embarrassed enough, she friggin' went and blushed.

She was so out of her element.

Still unsure if he'd been talking to her or not, Shayla nodded and fumbled with the diaper bag, trying to pull out the folder so she could leave. A sippy cup, juice box, wallet, strip of condoms...*Shit*. How'd that get in there? She shoved the packets back in, hoping to God no one had seen them. The intake of breath and soft snicker filling reception pretty much laid that hope to rest. *Dammit*. Digging deeper, she finally managed to wrestle the red folder from the damn bag.

"Here's the file," she said, walking to a dimple-glaring Kevin.

She was going to kill him later.

When she stopped in front of him, he bent slightly and said, "God, you're adorable."

Mortified was more like it. She shoved the folder into his gut and smiled back when he grunted. "And you're a dead man."

And because his open, happy expression drew her in and warmed her from purple toenails to the roots of her tingling scalp, Shayla stepped back.

Keep it simple.

She inhaled and chanced a glance at the others. Smiling and friendly, except for Hoffman. He had that dead pan stare. Wonder if he gave lessons?

Mrs. Dixon waved at Amelia babbling in Kevin's arms. "Don't worry any about your daughter. Kids have a mind of their own. I remember one Fourth of July when my son was four, he was so excited, jumping up and down, pointing at the fire engines, screaming at the top of his lungs. *'Look at the fire trucks! Look at the fire trucks!'* Too bad his TR's came out like F's."

Shayla's hand flew to her mouth, but it didn't stop the giggle from escaping and joining the others.

"Yeah, that was one parade I'll never forget," Stella stated. "Neither would Reverend Moore or his wife or his eighty-eight-year old mother, rest her soul. They were all standing to my right."

Even Hoffman cracked a smile on that one.

"Well, I don't know if that makes me feel better or worse," she said, glancing at her chortling daughter, banging on Kevin's head.

"That's it, sweetheart," Cole said, smiling up at Amelia. "Knock some sense into him."

Shayla snorted. "Fat chance."

"Hey." Kevin tried to scowl at her, but the expression ended up somewhere between sexy-as-hell and sexier-than-he-had-the-right-to-be.

Stella chuckled and patted Shayla on the shoulder. "I like you," the secretary stated before returning to her perch behind her desk.

"So do I," the brilliant, executive, billionaire cowboy stated with a grin.

"You like a lot of women." That might have come out a wee bit bitter as the image of the blue-eyed, blonde flight attendant flashed in her head.

Kevin's brow creased with his confusion. "Where'd that come from?"

Her chin lifted. "You had a visitor before I left."

Confusion was instantly replaced by concern. "Who?" His fingers closed around her upper arm as he gently but firmly tugged her out of earshot from the others. "I told the front desk no visitors."

"I guess he figured in Amber's case you'd make an exception."

She waited and watched, curious to see if he remembered the woman.

Confusion returned. He released her, but didn't move away. "The flight attendant?"

"Bingo." Guess that answered that. "She said she only had a short layover today, but would look you up on the next one."

"Sorry. She'd never been upstairs. We meet in the lobby." He clenched his jaw, apparently not as happy as she'd thought about the unexpected visit. "Excuse me. I need to call concierge to see why they allowed her on an elevator." He fished the phone out of his pocket and walked away.

Shayla still hadn't figured out what his feelings were for the blonde and was mulling it over when Nadine approached.

"It was nice meeting you."

"You, too."

The pretty brunette lowered her voice. "You're mistaken if you think you and Kevin are just friends. You two do not look at each other like just friends or act like just friends. There is definitely more. Much more. But that's a good thing." She squeezed Shayla's arm. "Embrace it. You're a lucky woman. He's a good man."

And with that, the pretty woman with amber eyes twisted on her heels, walked over to Kevin for the red folder, then disappeared down the hall, leaving Shayla's mind in a whirl.

Kevin didn't look at her like a friend? Then how did he look at her?

She glanced at the man, talking on the phone, frown creasing his normally smooth brow, while he held her daughter's legs. *Shoot.* Amelia still sat on his shoulders. She'd forgotten about the little cutie. Rushing forward, she silently scolded herself and promised to get her head out of her backside.

He finished his call and slipped his phone back in his pocket. "You didn't have any other visitors, did you?"

"No." She stopped, plight momentary forgotten. "Why? Were you expecting other girls?"

Okay, now she was sounding jealous. *Idiot.* She had no claim to him. What was her problem? Of course he had other women.

He laughed and shook his head. "Nope. You're the only woman allowed in my space."

She cocked her head, reveling in that statement. "You really don't bring any of your...of them to your penthouse?"

"No. Never." He shook his head, gaze open and honest. "I like my privacy."

She could certainly see where it could become an issue. That had to suck. Apparently, Amelia agreed because she nodded and slapped Kevin's head again.

"Sorry. Here, let me take her," she said, reaching for her daughter.

Amelia screamed and kicked in protest.

Great. She didn't need this.

"Hey, pumpkin, now that's enough," Kevin said, pulling her screaming daughter off his shoulders to cradle her in his arms. "You don't tell your momma no. Understand?"

Miraculously, the little bugger cut the waterworks and smiled up at the man. "Ya."

"Now, you go with Mommy, while I talk to Uncle Cole about work, then we can all go to lunch, okay?"

"'Kay," Amelia said, but the minute he went to hand her daughter over, the screaming recommenced. "Daddy! No. Want daddy!"

Shayla's heart squeezed tight. Not from embarrassment. No. It was from pain. Somehow, even though they'd been living with Kevin less than a week, her daughter had gotten very attached to the man. The last thing she'd ever wanted was for her daughter to be hurt.

And now it was unavoidable.

It wasn't anyone's fault but her own. Not Kevin's. Not Amelia's.

Mine.

If she had access to even one tenth of her damn brain cells this week, she would've realized her daughter was becoming attached to the friendly man.

So was she.

Hell, she and Amelia had both been partially smitten before she'd even discovered the existence of that damn video. But Shayla would deal with the separation. She understood. She had made a deal with the cowboy to return to their own lives back in Harland County.

Her daughter didn't. She was innocent. Vulnerable. Impressionable.

Dammit. Amelia was Shayla's responsibility to keep safe and happy, and she was screwing up royally.

"Come on, baby girl. Let Kevin finish his conversation," she said, carrying the squirming banshee to the seating area, keeping her tone steady through her daughter's tantrum. Setting the bag on an adjacent chair, she sat down with her daughter who stiffened her body and threw herself backward. "How about you have your juice while we wait?"

Once again, the tears disappeared, and Amelia sat up and sniffed. "Juice."

Yeah, miracle in a box.

After filling the sippy cup, Shayla handed the juice to her daughter and let out a sigh a second before her phone rang. Heart dropping to her knees, she fished out the cell and stopped breathing for a beat when she read the caller ID.

"Kade?" she answered, and Kevin's concerned gaze snapped to her from across the room.

Was there a problem? Was Caitlin okay? Could she go home?

All three questions bounced through her mind at once as she watched the cowboy rush forward with Cole on his heels.

"Hi, Shayla. How's my cousin treating you?"

Relief flooded her veins in a wave of warmth. If there had been a problem, the sheriff would've stated it right off. "Good, thanks."

"You ready to come home?"

What a question. A simple one really. A question she thought she knew the answer to, until the blue-eyed cowboy had reminded her what it felt like to be alive. Pampered her with incredible, mind-blowing sex. Treated her and her daughter like...family.

Did she want to leave that behind? No. *Hell* no.

She dropped the cowboy's gaze and stared at Amelia.

Staying would only delay the inevitable. Make it that much harder to leave. And her daughter was already too attached to the man.

"Is it safe?"

"I'll be honest. I don't know," Kade replied. "I wish I had a definite answer, but all I can tell you is that there hasn't been anyone new in town. No one looking or asking for you. Same goes for Caitlin at school. Things seem to be fine. But that doesn't mean it can't change overnight. Doesn't mean your father won't run into someone who had seen the video and tells him about it, and he tracks you down." Frustration rumbled in the sheriff's tone. "I'm really sorry, but there's just no way to know."

Shayla let out a breath and nodded. "I understand."

But she didn't know what to do.

Whether she stayed in Houston or went back to Harland County, she and her daughter were in danger. Still, she had to make a decision. Immediately.

Go back to Harland County and keep looking over her shoulder, risking being found by her father. Or stay in Houston, live with Kevin. Sleep with Kevin. Have crazy monkey sex with Kevin. Risk her daughter becoming even more attached to Kevin.

"So, what's it going to be?" Kade asked again.

The choice was actually very simple. She had to do what was best for Amelia.

She straightened her spine and met the cowboy's troubled blue eyes. "We're coming back to Harland County."

"Okay, give me a shout when you're clo—"

Kevin swiped the phone from her ear, deep frown creasing his brow. "Kade, what's going on? Is it safe or not?" he asked, striding a few feet away.

No sense in getting angry, or trying to regain custody of her phone. The cowboy was just concerned. He was a good friend.

She stood and faced Cole. "Kade said there haven't been any signs of my dad. It's up to me whether to wait longer." Shayla glanced at her daughter who set her cup on the chair and climbed down to run to Kevin and wrap her arms around his legs. "It's time to go back."

"If you want to go back tonight, I'll take you," Cole said, regaining her attention. "Kevin has to stay and take the information our marketing team is gathering from their meeting right now, and give a presentation to stock holders in the morning. But you're more than welcome to stay and wait to drive back with him tomorrow. It's up to you."

A big, friggin' invisible elephant seemed to have parked its butt on her chest. Breathing was a chore. Thinking was even harder. Shayla rubbed the ache, watching the cowboy approach with her daughter smiling in his arms.

"Tonight."

Chapter Thirteen

Wednesday evening, Kevin pulled up at Shadow Rock, noting Brandi's crew had broken ground on Kade's animal sanctuary that day. Silent equipment dotted the far landscape where the new stable would stand. With a plan to remodel the existing sanctuary stable, his cousin wanted to add a new one to shelter non-equine breeds.

Kade was a saint.

His cousin was certainly a savior to many neglected horses in the past. Now, Sgt. *Saint* was spreading out to help dogs, cats, pigs, cows…flying monkeys, unicorns, whatever needed rescuing. And Kevin had gladly signed on to lend a hand. He hated to see anyone, or anything unhappy.

Dalton DNA.

The sun was setting as he got out of his truck and the construction crew slid into theirs to leave for the day. It wasn't all that late, but until the spring, daylight ended early. He walked around several cars, including Shayla's SUV. His pulse picked up speed. He hadn't seen the woman since she left McCall Enterprises Sunday afternoon.

Foolishly assuming she'd wait a day and go back with him Monday, he'd felt a sucker-punch to the gut when she drove back with Cole instead. Determined to brush it off, he'd arrived at the penthouse Sunday night to find it spotless. Quiet. Empty. No sign that the single mother who'd willingly and thoroughly shared her body with him all week, or her little angel who swiftly wormed her way into his heart, had ever been present.

Weird. He'd never minded the quiet solitude before, he'd actually welcomed it, took pains to maintain his privacy at the penthouse. He never brought a woman there, preferring to go to a hotel or their place. It was of his experience that a woman favored having sex in her own bed, anyway. So why he'd suddenly found the silence deafening, and the place cold, made no sense. Even sleeping, which was never a problem before, turned into a chore. He'd been restless and tossed all night. After a few hours, he got up and tried playing video games, then writing code. Nothing helped. Still restless. It was crazy. Lonely.

And that's when he'd realized the problem. His body was going through withdrawal. Having had incredible marathons of sex with the tantalizing redhead, he'd suddenly gone cold turkey. His favorite body part had gotten use to being used. Rising to the redhead's demands. But, there were other women out there, and last night, he'd headed to a bar for some fun. His snort blew away with the wind. Waste of time. This weekend, though, he was going to get back into the swing of things and return to the field, instead of isolating himself with just one.

Feeling better, he entered the ranch and snuck down to his room to shower and change before supper. It was a jeans and T-shirt kind of evening. Besides, he'd distinctively heard Amelia in the kitchen. The desire to rush in there and see the little pumpkin had been strong. *Too strong*. So strong he'd forced his feet in the opposite direction.

She's not your daughter, he reminded himself as he entered his room. *Stay away. Keep it simple.*

Thirty minutes later, dressed in his favorite jeans, old boots and worn-out college T-shirt, he slipped on a gray flannel shirt calculating he'd stalled long enough. Shayla should've had enough time to finish work, grab her kid and leave.

His heart grew heavy. *Tough.* They were back in Harland County. Back to normal. Time his heart got over it. Damn thing wasn't supposed to be involved, anyhow.

Pushing through the kitchen door, he entered with a smile on his face, ready to bullshit his way through another supper of well-meaning, but *getting-damned-annoying* questions.

Work was fine.

He was fine.

Everything was fine.

Two nights of it was enough. Today had better be different. And it was. He'd immediately sensed it. *Yep.* The addition of Connor, Kerri, Brandi, and of course, Shayla sitting at the table with Amelia on her lap was definitely a different Shadow Rock occurrence.

Damn.

Since several gazes were on him, it was too late to retreat. He'd just have to up the bullshit factor and pretend things were peachy.

And that pissed him off more.

Things *should* be just fine. He never had a problem with seeing a lover in a non-lover environment. Eating with Shayla should be no different.

Except it was.

The redheaded temptress was in his *home*. His other private domain that had always been lover-free.

Of course she'd be welcomed at Shadow Rock. The woman had been at the ranch plenty of times before they'd become lovers. He was an idiot. He should've taken that into account before he'd taken her to bed. Seeing a former lover in a grocery store was a hell of a lot different than running into her at his house, on his property, in his fucking kitchen.

And did she have to look so damn good? Auburn hair all lose and wavy around her pretty face, showcasing the deep, mesmerizing blue of her eyes. His body was acting strange, with a weird fluttering going on.

Ah, hell, he needed a damn time out.

Apparently, a few days away weren't enough. At least the temptress hadn't shown up at Mrs. Avery's last night, claiming Amelia had the sniffles. His gaze settled on the little girl too busy slapping the table to notice him. She appeared fine. A miraculous recovery.

Whatever the case, he had been relieved. His body was still too in tuned to the single mother. As if to confirm that hypothesis, damn awareness suddenly skittered down his spine while his blood turned up the volume in his ears.

"Hey, Kevin. Have a seat. We saved you some pot roast," his sister Jen said, motioning to a vacant chair, surprisingly not next to Shayla.

Maybe fate was on his side.

"I'm sure Connor and Kade will move over so you can squeeze in."

Or laughing her ass off.

Play it *cool*. Keep it *simple*.

"Great. Thanks," he replied, smile still in place.

"Daddy!" Amelia scrambled from her mother and barreled right to him.

A thrill he refused to dissect raced through his veins. He knew he should probably correct the little darlin', but his heart always belayed the order.

"I didn't know Ukewl Kevin was Amelia's daddy," his nephew Cody said, amazement coating his high-pitched tone.

"He's not, honey," Shayla quickly responded.

Ignoring the myriad of shocked faces, he bent to scoop up the little angel and held her close. "Hey, pumpkin." He received a combination of butterfly and sloppy kisses while her momma went on to explain why the little girl showered him with the endearment. Kevin never took offense. The title was an honor. Although, he understood Shayla's concern.

He was *not* Amelia's dad.

He had no right to her.

And no real role in her future.

What he did have was a heart slowly warming for the first time in days. Always the one to bring other's pleasure, Kevin found it strange to have the tables turned. The little pumpkin made *him* smile. Made *him* happy. Made *him* feel alive.

So did her momma.

Damn. Where the hell had that thought come from?

Didn't matter, it was true. The thought was unwelcomed until he got his routine back on track. Started dating again. Last night's fiasco with the redhead from a local honky tonk didn't count. Disgust soured his palate. He hadn't been ready, was all. The mood wasn't there. The attraction wasn't there. His head hadn't been in it. Either of them.

Dammit.

No life. Not a spark.

Limp city.

"Sorry," Shayla said, gaze apologetic as she approached to remove her daughter from his grasp.

And oh, look at that. Spring city. Damn dick sprang to life now. *All systems go.* His favorite body part was pumping up good and thick the longer she stood there brushing against him.

"Daddy," Amelia cried, clinging to him, crying, on the verge of one of her tantrums.

"It's okay," he told the frustrated redhead, shifting the little pumpkin in his arms. "I got her." Then, without waiting for a reply, he turned and walked straight to his chair and sat down, all eyes still on him. "Looks like you made some progress today," he said to Brandi, and the conversation about the new stable lasted clean through dessert.

"Damn, Kerri," Kade said, digging into his second strawberry shortcake. "Nobody makes a strawberry taste better than you. Unless I'm sharing it with Brandi."

A blush seeped into Kerri's face, matching the designer's, as she smiled at the happy couple. "Thanks."

"Everything my wife makes is delicious," Connor stated, reaching for her hand to bring to his mouth.

Strawberry sharing...

Kevin's body heated just thinking about the strawberry he'd shared with Shayla last year.

Their first kiss.

Delicious. Decadent. Damn near perfect. Shayla and strawberries went well together. He'd eaten several off her delectable body last week. Covered her sexy freckles with Redi whip and slowly licked them clean.

Heat skittered down his spine. Not exactly appropriate considering the woman's daughter was in his arms. Pushing images of sex with Shayla out of his mind, Kevin kept his mouth shut, his gaze downcast and let the others dominate the conversation. And before he knew it, dessert was done, the table was cleared and Cody approached.

"Come on, Amelia," his nephew said. "Let's go play."

She smiled. "'Kay." Then scooted off Kevin's lap. "Play."

"Yeah, maybe *wiff* the *bwocks* this time," the four-year-old said, holding Amelia's hand as they rushed from the room.

"Well, if I know my son, that means everything that's on the coffee table is going to hit the floor. I'd better make sure he doesn't break anything," Jen said, getting up from the table.

"I'll help," Shayla offered.

No surprise. The redhead was good at running. That wasn't fair. He grimaced inwardly at his meanness. Damn woman was smart, though. She knew when to leave to avoid confrontations.

Why was he complaining? He didn't want her near. She made things throb.

"I'll watch," Kerri said.

"Me, too," Brandi added, and soon only the men were left in the room.

His brother-in-law rose to his feet. "And I have paperwork waiting for me." Brock nodded at them before exiting out the back door.

"Well now," Connor said, getting up, but he didn't leave, he headed to the fridge to grab three beers. "At least the tension has subsided. I was plumb afraid to breathe there for a while." Moose tossed a beer to Kade, then set one down in front of him before retaking his seat. "You look like you need that."

JD would've been better, but he popped the cap and took a long pull. The ice-cold brew slid down his throat in a welcomed chug.

"Well?" Connor stared at him.

Kevin glanced from Moose to Kade then back again. "Well what?"

"Is there something you want to tell us, *Daddy*?" McJollyRancher sat back in his chair and laughed.

"Nope." He shook his head. "Shayla already explained all that to you, Moose. Sorry if she used big words."

The giant chuckled while Kade sat back and drank his beer. Watching. Quietly. *Damn.* Sgt. Observation was in the house. Which meant trouble. When his cousin was in the *all-seeing/all-knowing* mode, no one was safe. He'd much rather deal with McQuestions on his right.

Kevin wasn't stupid. He glanced away, drank his beer, biding his time until he could leave without appearing to run.

"Nearly a week together," Connor continued, shaking his head. "You were brave, man. I would've never been able to do that in the early days with Kerri. No way could I have kept my hands off her."

"He didn't," Kade stated, gaze glued to Kevin's, direct. Spot on.

Dammit.

"Ah, hell, Kevin." Moose set his bottle on the table with a thud. "What'd you go and do that for? Now you're screwed."

Kevin snorted. "Seemed like a good idea at the time."

The big cowboy nodded and lifted his beer in a toast. "Ain't that always the case?"

"You couldn't just leave her be?" Kade shook his head, disappointment clouding his gaze.

"I hate to break this to you, cuz, but it was mutual, you know," he defended, but declined to mention it was actually Shayla who had initiated sex the first time. She'd propositioned *him*. Not that it had taken much. In fact, it had taken very little—the fact she'd had very little on under her robe.

He downed the rest of his beer then got up and grabbed another. Definitely a multiple kind of night. *Ah, hell*. Stupid word choice.

"You're right," his cousin said. "And I wouldn't have been able to last cooped up with Brandi like that, either. I'd just hoped you were stronger."

"Nope. Human like the rest of you," he said, dropping back into his chair.

"Then let me guess…" Connor leaned forward. "You probably agreed to a friends having sex thing."

"Yeah, with no relationship," his cousin added.

Kevin pulled the bottle from his mouth and shook his head. "Not exactly. Ours was a Houston thing."

Moose frowned. Must've been an adult word in there the big guy hadn't understood. Kevin glanced at Kade. *Damn*, his cousin was frowning, too.

"We agreed to have sex only while we were in Houston," he clarified before he tipped back his beer, feeling a little better at having explained his dilemma.

"Well, hell."

"Damn."

He held up his bottle in mock salute to their responses. "Exactly."

"So, when are you going back?"

"What?"

"If you two can only have sex in Houston, when are you going back?" Connor asked.

Kevin laughed. "We're not, you idiot."

"Oh, so you're just not going to have sex anymore."

"What? No. I mean, yes…I mean no." He shot to his feet, a fierce restlessness rushing through him.

"Ah shit," Moose grumbled. "Kade, your cousin is going through withdrawals."

"Yeah, but as soon as I figure out how to fix things, I'll be fine."

"Fix what things?"

"My body."

"What the hell's wrong with your body?"

"She broke it."

Moose pounded on his chest as he choked on his beer. "She broke your body?"

"Yeah. It doesn't work anymore. Nada. Zip. Not even a twitch," he stated, pointing to his crotch.

McGiant turned a little green as reluctance dulled his eyes. "Do I want to know how you know this?"

"I was out with this smokin' hot redhead last night—"

"You mean Shayla?" Connor interrupted.

"No, a dental hygienist at a honky tonk in Galveston."

"So, what happened?"

"Nothing. Not a damn thing, that's just it." Shoving a hand through his hair, Kevin blew out a breath in an attempt to relieve the pressure in his chest. "We were dancing, having a great time, when she pushed me against the wall and kissed me long and deep."

"And nothing happened," Kade said.

"Exactly." Kevin slapped the counter. "Nothing. No spark, no twinge. The one-eyed monster is on strike. No lead in the pipe. Limp biscuits 'r' us. But oh..." He reeled back, lifting his hands. "One little look from Shayla, one innocent brush of the hand and *bammo*. Hello Houston we now have liftoff. All systems are a go-go!"

The guys just stared at him. And blinked. Smiling. *Dammit.* It wasn't funny.

He dropped back down in the chair with a curse. "It's not right. It's like she rewrote…" pausing, he sat up straight and blinked at the two chuckleheads. "Son-of-a-bitch. She did. Somehow she rewired my libido so it only responds to her touch."

"Sorry, cuz." Kade chuckled. "You know that's not possible."

"Sure it is. I'm living proof. It's like a signature on a gun. You program it only to fire with a certain palm print around the handle."

"Oh." Connor nodded. "So, your limp biscuit will only work if Shayla's palm—"

"I think we get the picture," Kade interrupted.

"Yes." McGiant nodded. "Kevin here has entered the girl vortex."

His cousin grunted, tipping his beer.

"Exactly my problem," Kevin agreed. "Now there's no movement below the belt unless I'm near Shayla's vortex."

A grinning Connor rose to his feet and slapped him on the back. "Well, good luck with that, Dalton."

"Really?" Kevin frowned up at the giant. "That's all you've got to say?"

"Yeah, except we've all been through it, man. Every last one of us. Including your brother-in-law Brock. You'll figure it out. We all did and lived to tell about it."

"He's right," Kade agreed.

"Yeah, but you and Connor and Cole and Brock are all in relationships now." He glanced from one smiling man to the other. "You know that's not for me. Besides, Shayla isn't staying. If it weren't for committing to the

Dance-a-thon and helping the charity, she would've split Sunday night."

"You think so?" McCall's brows disappeared under his hair.

"I know so, and I'm betting once the contest is over, she's gone. So, that means no relationship."

"Seems to me that should work well for you, then." Connor slapped his back again. "You're a smart guy. I'm sure you'll figure something out." And with a two finger salute, the cowboy sauntered out of the kitchen.

The big guy had a point. If Shayla wasn't staying, there was no danger of having a relationship. But, she wasn't the only one who sparked his concern.

"You're worried about Amelia." Kade stared at him from across the table, gaze direct and intense.

"Yeah. She's kind of grown attached to me."

"Just her?"

"Yeah, her mom seems fine leaving things in Houston."

"I wasn't talking about Shayla."

He blinked. Trying to clear his head. He probably shouldn't have finished that second beer so fast. "I don't think Caitlin is attached to me."

"Not Caitlin, you screwball. I'm talking about you."

"Me? I'm very attached to me."

"Kevin."

Uh oh. Sgt. Hardass was back in the building.

"I'm talking about you being attached to Amelia."

He scoffed and waved a hand at his cousin. "No worries. I'm not attached to—" Kevin stopped. Whether he finished the sentence with daughter or mother, it would be a lie. And he hated lies. And secrets. Like the one his college girlfriend had kept from him.

"Kevin, how are you really doing?"

"I'm fine," he automatically replied.

"So, this business with Amelia calling you Daddy and hugging you like you're her whole life hasn't brought back memories? Hasn't stirred up the loss of your child?"

"It wasn't a loss. It was murder. Tina shouldn't have kept that news from me. She should've told me she was pregnant. Not get an abortion without my knowledge." With the road paved by alcohol, long suppressed emotions rose to the surface. "I would've been a good dad. I would've stepped up to the plate."

"I know."

And Tina should've known that, too. Granted, they'd gone out all through high school and then college and he hadn't put a ring on her finger. But he'd figured they'd had time. He'd been busy helping keep the ranch afloat, building his career, taking care of his sister and mom. All things that needed to be accomplished before he could concentrate on his future. But apparently, she got tired of waiting. And he didn't blame her for that. Really, he didn't. He'd waited too long.

But she never told him she was pregnant.

She just gave an ultimatum—make a commitment or she was walking. Kevin had asked her to give him some more time. The program he was working on was going to be huge, he just knew it, and that would solve the ranch's debt problems, then he could shift his focus. But she'd just shook her head, kissed his cheek with tears in her eyes and said good-bye. Not, *oh by the way, I'm carrying your baby.*

"I just want you to be clear on your feelings now," Kade said.

Kevin frowned, his head beginning to pound. "What do you mean?"

212

"Make sure you're not using Shayla and her daughter as a substitute for your loss."

Well damn.

Kevin blinked, and sat in stunned silence. Was he doing that? He didn't think so. The attraction between him and the single mother was real. Combustible. Can't fake that. And he really did enjoy playing with Amelia and taking care of the little angel. Her sloppy wet kisses and uncontrollable giggles.

Sure, he thought about his own unborn child. Whether the baby would've been a boy or a girl. A southpaw like him. A puzzle solver. Aptitude for math. But, he'd thought about those things long before he'd ever meet Shayla and her daughter.

Were they a substitute?

No.

Were they dangerous?

Yes.

His heart was way too close to the surface in their presence. Which at times, made him feel great. But others, like now, not so great. Vulnerable.

The best thing for him to do was follow Shayla's lead. Keep it simple. Uncomplicated. Straightforward. Sooner or later his lower extremities would fire up without her help.

He'd just have to hunker down. Firm his resolve, and wait it out.

Shayla had dodged the bullet the last few nights. Not tonight. Thursday night.

Dance lesson night.

She'd already used the cowardly 'my daughter has the sniffles I can't make it' excuse on Tuesday. Guilt had soured her stomach. She hated lying. Hated using her daughter for that lie. Vowed never to do it again.

So, here she was, pulling into Mrs. Avery's driveway, relief slumping her shoulders at the sight of Kevin's missing truck. He hadn't arrived yet. Maybe he couldn't make it. Hope sparked a light in her heart. She really wasn't up to dancing with the cowboy just yet.

At the sound of a car backfiring, she jumped in her seat and set a palm over her racing heart. *God*, she hated this. Hated the not-knowing, the fear, always looking over her shoulder. Ever since she got back a few days ago, she'd been double-checking her doors, watching in her rearview mirror to see if she was being followed. In time, things would settle, but right now, she was jittery. Bless Kade. The sheriff made her call in a SITREP—situation report—every morning at eight, and promised to have a patrol car drive by every few hours. Both eased the tight grip fear had on her throat.

She was feeling flushed. Her hand left her thudding chest to settle over her forehead. Fever? That would certainly get her out of tonight. But, her forehead was cool. *Dammit*. No excuse. She had to do this…had to go in the studio and dance with the sexy man who'd had her body in ways that would make a porn star blush. And Shayla want more.

No. That was Houston. This was Harland County. *No sex with Kevin Dalton in Harland County.*

Dancing, talking, laughing, eating, all perfectly acceptable.

No kissing, groping, nibbling, or sucking, because it would undoubtedly lead to sex. *Definitely no sex*. Sex with the cowboy was bad. Heat flooded her belly and simmered in all her good parts. *No*…sex with the cowboy was good. Very, very good. Ecstasy, rapturous, life-affirming good.

Which was bad.

He didn't want a relationship. Heck, *she* didn't want a relationship, yet the more Shayla was around the guy, the more she wanted to *be* around the guy. And if they kept having sex, then didn't that make it a relationship of sorts?

Not going to happen.

She sucked in a breath and got out of her car. No reason to poke that bear. All she had to do was curb her hunger and get her stupid libido under control. Simple. She blew out the breath and headed for the garage. And doable. After all, she wasn't staying.

Once the Dance-a-thon was over, Shayla was out of Harland for good. After she helped the foster children's charity get as much money and recognition as possible, she would hit the road. Take her stupid drama away from the good people of Harland County. Nausea flooded her stomach, as it always did, when thoughts about leaving entered her mind. But, with her father still out there, and the threat of someone telling him about the video, she had no choice. She had to leave.

With a light rap on the side door to the garage, Shayla entered the studio, hoping Mrs. Avery would tell her Kevin was stuck in traffic so practice was cancelled.

"Shayla!" The older woman rushed forward to draw her into a hug. "I'm so sorry, dear. Are you okay?"

It was like déjà vu from Monday morning when she'd dropped Amelia off at Mrs. McCall's for her routine babysitting. The lovely woman and her husband had taken turns hugging and apologizing for posting the video online. She reassured the anxious couple things were fine. But, she was too fearful to stay in town past

Donna Michaels

the dance-a-thon. That would be tempting fate. As it was, she was figuratively sticking her middle finger at it right now. Living in the county on borrowed time.

"I'm fine, Mrs. Avery. How are you?" She drew back to look into the older woman's eyes. Clear, but anxious. "I didn't mean to scare you last week, but I nearly had a heart attack."

The instructor smiled and patted her arm. "Understandable, dear. I'm just glad things have worked out. And you don't have to worry about me saying anything. As far as anyone needs to know, you're Shayla Ryan from north Texas."

She nodded, returning the woman's smile. "Thank you. I'd rather forget the other name. It's too dangerous and carries a lot of bad memories. I like Shayla Ryan now."

Much better memories associated with her new name, mainly thanks to a certain blue-eyed cowboy.

"I like her, too," Mrs. Avery said with another pat to her arm. "Oh, Kevin called, said he was going to be fifteen minutes late."

Trying not to look too hopeful, Shayla waited for the woman to tell her what exactly that meant as far as their practice that night. *Please let her cancel...*

"So, while we wait, I hope you don't mind, but I called one of my younger students and asked her to come over. She's dancing in the local competition at the end of the month, and I could use your help."

Shayla's heart rocked hard in her chest. *Her help?* Shoot. How could she help? Especially since she couldn't disclose much about her dancing past.

"Don't worry, dear," Mrs. Avery said, patting her arm again. "I just told Macy and her mom that you danced in a few competitions when you were a child."

All true.

"And that you would take a look at her three minute routine. We've choreographed all the required technical and free dance moves. But I just want to make sure there's enough wow factor. You know what I mean?"

Shayla nodded. She knew all too well nailing a routine wasn't enough. Talent. Precision. Pizzazz, costuming, all played key roles. Tell a story through performance. Make the judges believe it. Feel it.

God, she missed it.

But, that was a lifetime ago. When dancing was her whole life. Now, she had a different one. Amelia was her whole life.

A knock sounded on the door a second before it opened to a pretty little girl with her brown hair pulled back in a pony tail and an eager expression on her face, followed by an older version with a hint of sacrifice and exhaustion rounding her shoulders.

It was as if she caught a glimpse of the past, and her thumb brushed over her tattoo. Memories of her and her mom rushed through her mind. The preparations. Practices. Last minute adjustments.

"Aw, Macy, Clair, so glad you could come on such short notice," Mrs. Avery said.

"My goodness, no problem. We appreciate it," the mother said, turning to send her a smile. "You must be Shayla. Thank you for agreeing to help. My daughter has worked so hard. We just want everything to be right."

"Of course. I understand." When she was Macy's age, dancing was an escape. Competing was a challenge of her dream. She threw herself into her routine, thriving on the freedom. The happy and safe world she'd created in order to cope with her crappy reality.

"Oh, thank you, Ms. Ryan," Macy said, shaking her hand. "I know the routine inside and out, and it has all the artistic and technical qualifications, but, I don't know. I just feel like there's something missing. You've competed. You know. Maybe if you watch it, you'll see what I mean."

"Sure. Of course. Go ahead. Show me," she said, moving off the floor to stand by Mrs. Avery and the little girl's mother.

For the next seventeen minutes, Macy danced and Shayla made suggestions and demonstrated those suggestions, then danced side by side with the talented girl, until the wonderful routine turn outstanding. Exuding confidence and poise, the girl had talent and grace, and such control of her movements Shayla knew the child was special. Macy had a bright future, and she felt honored and blessed to have helped.

She was so caught up in the adrenaline and rush of excitement, her mind hadn't registered what her body had noted for the past five minutes. Mistaking the flush of her skin and increased pulse as elements from the dancing, she hadn't made the connection to Kevin having walked in. The cowboy leaned against the wall, knee bent, smiling.

"Well done, Macy," he said, clapping as he moved from the wall. "You nailed it."

The little girl beamed from ear to ear. "Thanks, Kevin. Did you see the move Ms. Ryan had added? Isn't it perfect?"

"Sure is," he replied, something unnamable passing through his warm gaze.

Heat flooded her body and raced to her face. Shayla got the impression he wasn't referring to the dance.

She patted the girl's shoulder. "Macy's a natural. We only tweaked just a little."

"Thank you so much." The preteen hugged her tight, then drew back, big smile still residing on her face. "Will you come to my competition?"

Mrs. Avery stepped closer. "It's at the rec center next Saturday."

Indecision squeezed Shayla's chest. It would be tough to step back into that environment. To the place she'd loved and always thought she'd succeed.

"Yes," Clair smiled, handing her daughter a coat before slipping into her own. "It would be so nice having you there to help cheer Macy on."

"I'd be honored," she said and meant it. She did not take being on the other side of that coin lightly.

"Sweet!" Macy hugged her again. "Thank you so, so much. I can't wait. Bye, Mrs. Avery. Bye, Kevin."

Ten seconds later, the little girl and her mother were gone.

The older lady, eyes a little misty, came over and squeezed Shayla's hands. "That was a nice thing you did. As you could tell, it meant the world to that little girl. And I have a few others that could benefit from your knowledge and experience. Ever think about teaching dance?"

Swallowing past a hot throat, Shayla refused to glance at Kevin who stood silently watching. "Not with the way I move around. The kids would never be able to count on me," she said, squeezing back.

"I understand." Mrs. Avery smiled, then released her to walk over to her old stereo.

The eighties called, they want their boom box back...

The system was a bit dated, but put out the desired results.

219

Donna Michaels

"Now," their instructor continued, glancing at them as she tapped the stereo. "I've got a good hour of ballroom classics on this tape. The contest is sure to have a few, so let me pop it in and you can get started while I heat up some supper. Busy day. I didn't have the chance to eat yet."

"Oh, please, go eat," Shayla said.

"Would you all like some?"

"No," Kevin rushed to say. "Thank you, Mrs. Avery. I ate late today."

The older woman glanced at her, but judging by the way her dance partner was quick to refuse...and the way he adamantly shook his head behind the sweet woman, she decided to heed his warning. "No, thanks, I've already eaten." Which was true, so she didn't feel so bad refusing.

"Okay, then. Get to it." The woman pushed a button and the music of a waltz began to play. "Just remember, when waltzing, no spaghetti arms. Resistance is essential so your body can sense which direction to move. Other than that, you don't really need me around. These sessions are mainly for you to get used to dancing for long periods of time."

Weird. If Shayla didn't know better, she'd swear the woman was leaving them alone on purpose.

"We'll be fine," Kevin said, opening the door for Mrs. Avery. "I can assure you there won't be anything limp."

As he closed the door and turned to face her, Shayla realized she was alone, for the first time since Sunday, with the man who had her moaning his name in ecstasy all last week. *Limp* body parts were never an issue.

"Shall we dance, darlin'?"

220

Chapter Fourteen

Gaze open and friendly, Kevin held out his hands and waited for her to lock in their *closed* dance position. With a nod, she placed her right hand in his, set the other on his shoulder, her arm resting lightly on his arm, while he cupped her body just below her shoulder blade. Deploying the resistance Mrs. Avery mentioned, Shayla felt the slight pressure from the heel of Kevin's hand on her back and immediately followed his lead.

Grateful the dance required a 1/8 turn of her head to the left, she gazed over his shoulder, and after a few minutes and several turns around the dance floor, relaxed enough to approach the subject of apologizing. Something she should've done yesterday, but the cowboy had been a bit stiff and tightlipped, and, well, she'd chickened out.

Not today. No matter what, she would apologize and thank him.

"So, how's your week going?" he asked.

The sight of his dimple hit her peripheral vision and warmed the fluttering in her stomach. "Okay."

"Just okay? You haven't had problems, have you?"

"No." She shook her head. "Not like you think. Just with my conscience. I-I need to apologize to you. I'm sorry, Kevin."

"Me?" His footing stumbled slightly. "What for?"

"For leaving with Cole on Sunday." She paused, waiting for input from him, but he remained silent, so she continued. "I needed to get Amelia back to our apartment environment. She's growing too attached to you, and I just don't want her hurt."

Focused on doing the right thing, she ignored the little voice in her head that asked, *Just Amelia*? Her attachment and wants weren't the issue. And after mistakenly overhearing his conversation with Kade in their kitchen yesterday, about his former girlfriend leaving him and aborting their child without his knowledge, she loathed to hurt Kevin, too. Her heart ached for the man, and the pain and loss evident in his tone last night still twisted her gut. But even though the cowboy told his cousin he was not using her and Amelia as a substitute, she would always wonder.

Good thing they were not in a relationship.

He nodded. "No worries. I understand. And I'm sorry I put you in that position."

"That's sweet." She chanced a glance at him. "It's not your fault you have that effect on women."

A big smiled spread across his face and lit his gaze to spine-melting results. This time, *she* stumbled. *Dammit*. She couldn't feel her legs. Well, she could. They were like rubber.

"Oh really?" The smile turned deliciously wicked, stealing her already thin breath. "Do I have that effect on you?"

"You know you do, cowboy."

And he did. *Bastard*. So, when he drew her up flush against him, she was powerless to protest.

"And what effect would that be, darlin'?"

She smacked him on the shoulder and stumbled backward until her legs got their bearings. "This isn't about me. We're talking about my daughter," she said, drawing in a deep breath, a little relieved to see some of the playfulness leave his gaze, because, *dammit,* she lost control when he was fun-loving. "Amelia likes you." She softened her tone and shrugged. "Okay, we both do, but since neither you nor I want a relationship, it's foolish to let my daughter get attached to you when you won't always be around."

The cowboy shoved a hand through his hair, and blew out a breath. "Yeah, I know."

"Then I hope you also know I consider you a friend."

His gaze snapped to hers. "You do?"

"Yes." She nodded, trying not to smile. "One of the few I have. Actually, you're a good friend, Kevin Dalton. And don't think for one minute I don't appreciate all you did for me last week. Because I do. Very much." Lightly cupping his chin, she lifted up on tiptoe and kissed his cheek, fighting off the fierce urge to wrap around him like a pretzel again. "Thank you, for all you did for me."

And to me.

Strong fingers curled around her elbows and held her immobile as he cocked his head and grinned. "Well now, darlin', I know you can do better."

She fought a battle with a burgeoning laugh and lost. "Yes, I could, but that's the problem."

"You and I have two very different definitions of the word *problem*."

"I bet." She sobered and held his gaze. "Seriously, Kevin, thank you for all you did for me last week."

Trailing a finger down her arm then back up again, he stared at her, blue eyes smoldering to a deep, delicious cobalt. "Trust me, Shayla, I enjoyed every damn minute."

Between his shiver-inducing finger, low, sexy voice and brain cell-zapping presence, she could barely think past her last breath. Other than she wanted to touch him.

To rewind back to last week and stall the hours so she could get her fill. Because she couldn't have him now. And, *dammit,* she wanted him. Bad.

"Come to Houston with me this weekend."

Oh, God. She drew in a shaky breath. "I want to, Kevin. So much."

"But?"

She exhaled and shook her head while he watched and waited. "But it's not smart. You and I both know it."

They stared at each other a beat, and when an imminent pounce shook through her, Shayla, being the pounce-ee, took a step back, then another, until control returned.

"Let's keep things simple."

His gaze narrowed a moment, before a smile twitched his lips. "And straightforward."

"Yes." She nodded, relief melting the stiffness from her spine. "Friends?"

He scratched the bridge of his nose and chuckled. "What the hell. Friends." His smile reflected his ever-dependable fun-loving nature. "So, what do you say we get back to dancing?"

For two hours, they danced and laughed, and completely ignored the fact their bodies wanted more. Much more. And she knew Kevin wanted more, too. *Felt* the unmistakable evidence first hand.

Every brush, every pass, every connection only intensified the burn. Shayla was on fire, body humming, needing, thirsting for all the intimate dance moves they'd practiced in Houston.

By the time the session was over and she drove away, she was a tingling mass of erogenous need. Waltzes and quick-steps weren't bad, but the tangos? Murder. Pure murder on her poor, deprived body. The night air and quick drive home helped her regain enough composure to face Mrs. Masters. Her friend's mother was sweet enough to agree to watch Amelia at the apartment so the little girl's bedtime routine wasn't interrupted.

"Hello, Shayla. How was your practice?" the lovely woman greeted, beautiful as ever in jeans and a white, long-sleeved shirt, not a should-length hair out of place.

How could Jordan's mom wear white and still remain unmarked after nearly three hours with Amelia? Shayla never wore white anymore. White was just a beacon, an empty canvas waiting for stains to happen.

She shrugged out of her coat and set it on the back of a chair. "Good, thanks. Any problems tonight?" she countered, smiling at her daughter curled up with *goggy* on the couch, watching one of her favorite educational cartoons, already dressed in her penguin pajamas.

"No, not at all. She had her bath, and her snack, and now she's winding down."

As if just realizing someone else had entered the room, her daughter's attention turned to her and she smiled. "Mommy." Pushing from the couch, Amelia waddled to her in a sleep-relaxed state.

Shayla scooped up the tired tot and hugged her close. "Hi, honey. Did you have a good time?"

"Ya." Amelia nodded, big yawn taking over, then apparently tuckered out by the yawn, she set her head on Shayla's shoulder and closed her eyes.

Nothing in the world felt better than holding her sleeping baby girl. Nothing. It was the recharge, the reset her psyche needed to tip her world back on its axis. And one glance at her friend's mother and she could tell the woman wholeheartedly agreed.

"I'll see myself out," the smiling wannabe grandma whispered, slipping into her coat, then out of the apartment.

Mrs. Masters wore the same longing and hopeful expression as Mrs. McCall. It was evident in the way both women cared for Amelia and stared at times. Walking into her room to place her daughter in her crib, Shayla smiled. With the virile McCall brothers so besotted with their wives, she suspected it was only a matter of time before one or both sisters became pregnant.

Standing in front of the crib, she swayed back and forth for a few minutes, enjoying the feel of her sweet, innocent baby girl, while contemplating motherhood for her friends.

With Jordan running for Sheriff, would the woman be allowed to be pregnant and sheriff? Not really her field of expertise.

She set her daughter down in her crib and covered her before sneaking out of the room. It was too early for bed, besides, she was way too keyed up from all that 'dancing' with Kevin. *Again.* The cowboy put the sex in sexy, and she needed something cold to help simmer down.

Shayla was just spooning the last of The Creamery's Death By Chocolate into her mouth when a lit rap sounded at the door.

She froze, heart suddenly pounding in her ears, via her throat. Armed with her empty spoon, she hurried to peek through the keyhole. Dark hair, blue eyes, worn jeans hugging a lean, trim…

The pounding in her ears skipped loud and shot straight to deafening, while a flood of heat washed through her body in a delicious wave. *Kevin.* Why was he there? She unlocked then opened the door.

"Are you okay? Is something wrong?" She stood there, frowning at him with a spoon in her hand.

Idiot.

"Yeah, well, no," he said, glancing behind her into the apartment. "Is Amelia asleep?"

She nodded. "Yes, why?"

"Because I was trying to respect your wishes to help with her attachment, but I needed to see you." Troubled blue eyes stared unblinkingly at her. "There was one more thing we forgot to discuss tonight."

"Oh? What?" She asked, mind fogged by his unexpected visit and potent presence.

"This."

Before she could reply, he was in the apartment, door closed, pressing her against the wall with his deliciously, hot, hard body, sure hands thrust deep into her hair, holding her head immobile as his mouth caught her startled breath.

Damn, he moved quick. And the delectable nature of his swift, sure, deliberate movements reawakened the heat in her belly. *Oh Lordy* did she *like* this discussion.

The floor caught the spoon that slipped from her hand as she reached out to grip his collar and hold on tight. Hot and full of desire, the cowboy tasted way better than ice cream. She was open to discussing this all night long, and would've told him, but her tongue was currently down his throat.

Without releasing her mouth, he lifted her up, and she happily wrapped her legs around his hips. A grunt sounded in his throat, then repeated when he pressed his erection against her center.

He broke the kiss. "I've missed this," he said, trailing hot kisses down her neck, stopping to nibble behind her ear.

She sucked in a breath and crushed him closer, kissing a path across the only flesh available to her, his temple. "We shouldn't be doing this."

There, she managed to say it out loud. Whatever happened, happened. At least she had the clear conscience of stating the obvious.

"I know." His warm breath tickled her ear as his teeth nipped her earlobe and sent goosebumbs down her body. Then his hand slid under her sweater, skimming over her ribs to cup her bra and brush a thumb across her lace-covered nipple.

The heat pooling in her belly spread to every pore north and south. At once. Things were getting real.

Yeah, *real* good.

Shayla grabbed Kevin's head and pulled his face to hers, gaze full of so much heat and longing it was nearly his undoing.

"Please tell me you have a condom," she said, voice breathy with need before kissing the corner of his mouth and running her tongue over his lower lip.

Jesus, she was killing him.

"Yes, ma'am," he replied, returning the favor, then slid his tongue into her mouth for a very thorough sparring match that had need spiking through him and her gorgeous prone body shaking in his arms. Breaking the kiss, he sucked in a breath. "What room?"

"Guest room," she replied, kissing his jaw. "Amelia's asleep in mine."

He pushed them from the wall and headed down the hall, two hands full of a world-class ass he'd never tire of touching. Or kissing. Or biting. Or licking. Heat skittered down his spine. He only came by for a kiss, to satisfy the fierce ache the damn dancing had created. An ache only her lips could assuage. But somewhere between assuaging and drawing back, the lines blurred, resolve shifted, and the next thing he knew, her legs were around his hips and he was hard. Hell, he'd been hard since that damn tango at Mrs. Avery's.

This was a bad idea, but he was past caring. Especially when she nipped at his chin, then bottom lip and sucked it into her mouth. *Damn*, she was potent.

Kevin carried her to the bed, then let her slide slowly down, enjoying every single soft curve brushing his body. Groaning, he drew her in closer, kissing her long and deep and... *Oh Jesus,* her hands slipped under his shirt and skimmed his abs as she unbuttoned his jeans.

Sneaky little minx.

Desire flamed through his body. He released her mouth and ran his hands down her sides to rest on her hips. "We need to lose the clothes. Fast."

"I agree, cowboy," she said, stepping back to pull off her sweater, then unbutton and unzip before she shrugged out of her jeans.

With his coat and shirt already on the floor, he nearly lost his balance and fell on top of them as he shucked his boots, socks and jeans while she stood before him in a lacey black bra and matching panties.

"Nice."

The gorgeous woman had no idea what she did to him. He removed his boxers, stepped close and fell with her onto the bed, vaguely thinking that Cole was right. He hadn't lasted a week.

He pushed the thought to the back of his mind and grinned down at the beauty beneath him. "What'll it be?" He brushed the hair from her face. "Top or bottom?"

A wicked smile curved the lips she pressed to his palm. "Both." Then a second later, she rolled them until she was on top. "Okay?"

"Absolutely, darlin'." His voice was low and rough to his ears, but considering he was hard and throbbing, he wasn't surprised. He skimmed his hands up her thighs and ribs on his way to her back. God, she was so soft. Silky. With a quick flick, he unhooked her bra and tossed it over the side of the bed. Freed, her beautiful breasts bounced, those silver-dollar nipples bared and begging for his attention.

He obliged.

Cupping and tweaking, he brushed his thumbs over both peaks, and she closed her eyes and moaned while she rocked on his erection. *Stars.* Kevin saw stars and clamped down hard on his control. She was magnificent, and so damn responsive he wanted to hear her scream his name. Stroking a finger over the black lace covering her mound, he was rewarded with a long, low moan.

"I need you in me," she said.

He grabbed her upper arms and tugged her down, temperature nearing inferno at the feel of her soft, full breasts brushing his chest. She opened her mouth, but he didn't wait for her words, he kissed her hard and deep, needing so much. She trembled and touched her tongue to his. That's what he needed. Her hunger, her heat. He needed to know he wasn't in the crazy firestorm of need alone.

Running his hands down the curve of her back, he released her mouth to kiss a path down her throat and sink his teeth in her neck just behind her ear. She sucked in a breath and rocked against him. Heat ricocheted down his body. He ripped off her panties then flipped them over so he was on top. "My turn," he said against her collar bone as he brushed his lips down her breast and sucked a nipple into his mouth.

"Kevin," she said in a breathy whisper, her fingers thrusting into his hair to hold him there.

But he had plans.

He released her gorgeous peak in exchange for the other where he tugged until her squirming had him fighting to keep from exploding. The woman was a gift. She gave without even knowing. He kissed a path down her quivering belly straight to the part he longed to taste and explore the most. Shayla trembled and opened her legs as if she needed his mouth on her there, too.

Well, he was not about to disappoint. Kissing a trail down her inner thigh, he spread her farther, holding her open with his shoulders as he brushed a finger over her center. "You're wet," he said before pressing his mouth to her glistening folds.

A sweet, sexy whimper met his ears as her fingers returned to tangle in his hair and hold him in place. Glancing up, intent on telling her he wasn't going anywhere, he stilled, heart rocking hard in his chest at the sight of her caught up in the fiery passion. Lips parted, eyes half-closed, glazed over and dark with need. She was every man's fantasy.

She was his tonight.

Empowered by the knowledge, he watched her face as he pressed his mouth back on her and didn't let up until he commanded the scream he'd yearned to hear. When her shuddering finally stopped, he brought her down slowly, enjoying every last bit of her succulent taste, before pulling his mouth away.

She was so sweet.

So beautiful.

So hot.

"Damn, cowboy," she said, lifting up on her elbows to stare down at him. "I needed that."

A chuckle broke from his dry throat. "Me too, darlin." He kissed one thigh, then the other before leaving the bed to fish the condom from his jeans. Foil packet in hand, he returned and brushed her hand aside when she went to help.

"Thanks, darlin', but if you touch me now, we'll be done before we start."

A killer smile crossed her face. "Well, we don't want that," she said, laying back down while he covered himself.

"No, we don't." He bent to kiss her hip, brushing his hands up her body until he filled them with two glorious breasts.

She moaned, arching into him, tight nipples poking his palms while he nipped at the sexy curve of her waist, kissing a path to her belly button where his tongue slipped out to explore.

She inhaled and squirmed. *Damn*, the woman had great squirm. And hunger, because she grasped his head and tugged him up to her mouth and kissed him wet and hot and deep.

Ah hell, he was done.

"I need you in me, now, Kevin," she said against his lips. "Please."

Burnt bagel done. Without the salsa. Shayla's gorgeous spread was hot enough. "Anything you want," he said, voice low and raspy.

Lifting up, he positioned his erection against her hot, wet heat and pushed in. His moan mingled with hers in a matching proclamation of pleasure.

"I wish you knew how exquisite you feel around me," he told her, watching her eyes glaze over as he slid in and out of her slick, silky warmth. "Exquisite," he repeated.

Soft hands skimmed up his abs and pecs, as her desire laden gaze held his stare. "I was thinking more like magnificent."

She thought he was magnificent?

More of that power went to Kevin's head, and puffed out his chest. The sexy, erotic creature thrusting beneath him with lush curves, beautiful red hair and mesmerizing blue eyes thought he was magnificent. *Yeah*, he could live with that.

He'd been with a lot of women and prided himself on putting a pleased smile on their faces after a mutually satisfying romp. But none had ever made him feel ten feet tall, or want to pound on his chest. Or just plain *feel*.

Shayla did.

The others all kind of blurred together. Not Shayla Ryan. *Hell no*. The gorgeous, sexy woman stood out. Her hot kisses, charged touch, sensual scent, sweet, exquisite taste.

God, he loved her taste.

Grabbing her hands, he held them by her head, pressing into the mattress as he lowered his mouth to hers to sample more of her hot, addicting sweetness. He swept his tongue into her mouth, and she moaned and bucked against him. Heat shot down his spine and his body began to tighten.

With the edge close, he released her lips to kiss a tight peak and received a moan of approval. When she arched, inviting, begging him for more, he drew her farther into his mouth and sucked hard.

"Kevin."

He released her nipple and lifted up to lock his elbows. "What? Anything," he said as he thrust deeper inside.

"That," she replied.

The rapturous look on her face took him to the very edge. Another deep thrust, then another was all it took, and as he watched her burst, hard, she took him with her.

When the world stopped spinning and Shayla came back down into her body, she was surprised to find herself alone. Did Kevin leave? She sat up, still on top of the covers, and refused to consider the reason why relief flooded her body at the sight of his clothes still piled on the floor.

He didn't leave.

And since he returned with a glass of water, before thoughts on why his sticking around made her happy, she pushed the subject to the back of her mind and smiled at the gloriously naked cowboy.

"I thought you left," she told him, taking the glass he offered, warmed by the gesture and the smile crossing his face.

He waited while she drank. "No, darlin'. Despite what you might think of me, I never kiss and run."

Smiling, she handed him the glass and nodded. *Good to know.* She hadn't particularly liked how hollow her stomach had felt that split second before she'd spotted his clothes. Which made no sense, because they shouldn't be doing this, had agreed back in Houston to *not* do this in Harland County.

And yet, here they were.

In bed.

In Harland County.

"Besides, we're not done," he said, placing the glass on the nightstand before peeling back the covers and settling against the pillows, holding the covers open in an invitation for her to join him.

The moment of truth.

Indecision rippled through Shayla, messing with her pulse. He looked incredible all hard and ripped. *What to do?* Join him under the covers and commit to hot, uncommitted sex, or refuse and send him on his merry way, chalking the sex they'd just had as a moment of weakness.

Trouble was, she *was* weak, and hungry, and really wanted to ask him a few personal questions. Now was the perfect time. Guard down, softened by orgasmic interference. *Perfect time.*

Curiosity winning out, she crawled up and snuggled against his warm body, sighing when he lowered the covers and two strong arms surrounded her and pulled her in close.

"That's my girl," he said, kissing the top of her head.

The thrill bursting through her body was probably not a smart thing. *So what?* She didn't have to be smart tonight. No. Tonight, she was content. Happy. Tomorrow she could be practical and smart.

Body still tingling with a post-orgasmic high, she pressed her ear against the side of his chest, palmed his ribs and sighed. "I figure the feeling should return to my legs any minute now."

"Good luck." His chuckle rippled through her, warming her heart. "I'm still struggling, darlin'. It's a miracle I made it to the kitchen and back." He kissed her head again. "But don't worry. I'll be out of here before Amelia wakes up."

"Thanks for understanding," she said, brushing her thumb back and forth across his ribs.

"So, when were you going to tell me about your GED?"

She stiffened. *How the hell...?*

"I saw the envelope on the counter just now. Sorry, wasn't snooping, darlin'. It was just there. I think it's great."

"You do?" She lifted up to stare at him, embarrassment heating her face. "I feel like such a loser."

"Hey, no. Don't ever say that." He frowned. "Circumstances were out of your control. But now you're taking action. That really is something. *You're* something," he said, finger grazing her cheekbone, sending a strange, gooey feeling through her body.

"Thanks," she said, laying her head back down, heart suddenly feeling two sizes too big for her chest. She continued to stroke his ribs. He was too dangerous. "Even though you're really good for my ego, we really can't do this again, Kevin."

The hand cupping her right shoulder squeezed. "I know. No worries, darlin'. My momma raised a smart boy."

Her lead in.

"Yes, she did," she said, careful to keep emotion from her tone. "You are a lot more kind and considerate than I gave you credit for when we first met. I'm sorry."

"No harm done," he replied smoothly. "I thought you were an uptight bi—abe."

She laughed. "Yeah, I was a bit uptight." She tipped her head to stare at him. "But you seemed to have loosened me up a little."

"Well now, it's been my pleasure. Believe me." He tugged her closer and kissed her sweetly.

When he drew back, she settled against him again, and continued her caressing. "I would've liked to have met your mom. And your dad."

His hold tightened for a split second. "They would've liked you and Amelia."

Without stopping her strokes, she squeezed her eyes shut and took a chance. "What happened to them?"

When he didn't immediately respond, she figured she'd pushed too much, but was surprised by his admission a few seconds later.

"I let them down and they died."

Her eyes flew open and heart clutched tight. "What?" Turning in his arms, she lifted up and stared hard into his troubled gaze. "I'm sure that isn't true."

God, just the thought of him thinking he was to blame for his parents' deaths made her ache. Physically ache. And that, coupled with the pain she'd heard in his voice when he'd talked about his unborn child to Kade last night, she could barely breathe. The desire to take away his pain shook through her body.

"But it is true, darlin'," he insisted, twisting a piece of her hair around his finger. "My dad died when he fell off a horse I forgot to exercise, and my mom died from cancer before I was able to finish creating the software that now helps aid in early detection."

She cupped his hand and squeezed. "Kevin, honey, none of that is your fault."

He released her hair to put his finger to her lips. "Yes, it is, but I don't want to talk about it. I'd much rather discuss your next orgasm."

To press his point, he flipped her onto her back and traced a light circle around her breast, brushing her puckering nipple back and forth with his thumb. The heat simmering in her belly stoked into a delicious flame only he knew how to fan. And he knew how so well. *Dammit.*

Mind hazing over with lingering desire, she let the subject drop. Didn't want to push too hard. Now that the door was open, she'd broach the subject again in the future. Right now, she wanted to broach him.

Arching into his touch, she gazed up, a grin tugging her lips. "Yes, cowboy. It's been fifteen minutes. You're slipping."

"Exactly my plan," he said, blue eyes suddenly smoldering. His hand skimmed down to settle between her legs, long finger brushing her folds.

With the subject of his parents pushed aside, and dawn slowly approaching, she wanted to enjoy every minute, every second, with the man before their time was up. Preferably without talking. Kevin Dalton communicated best when his lips were put to other uses.

That was how she wanted to remember their time together.

Because this was *not* going to happen again.

Chapter Fifteen

The next morning, a little tired and a lot satisfied, Shayla answered a knock on the door Kevin had exited an hour earlier. Thank goodness he'd left without being seen, not only by Amelia, but by any of their friends. She wasn't in the mood for twenty questions, although, she was feeling a bit mellow.

Morning sex will do that to you.

The thought flashed through her mind as she looked through the peephole before opening the door to a smiling deputy.

"Hi, Shayla." Jordan stepped inside, holding up a bag her nose detected contained some of Kerri's mouthwatering blueberry muffins.

Her weakness.

"Hi." She turned and followed her friend into the kitchen. Great sex topped off with a decadent Kerri McCall blueberry muffin. Didn't get much better than that. Smiling, she poured out two mugs of fresh brewed coffee and joined her friend at the breakfast bar.

"Thanks," Jordan said. "Did you sleep well?"

What did the deputy mean by that? She narrowed her eyes. Had her friend seen Kevin leave? Shayla's stomach dropped to her feet. She hoped not.

"Ah…yeah." She glanced around for any sign of the guy. None. She breathed an inner sigh of relief. Secret was safe.

"You just missed him."

"Missed who?" She frowned, attempting to play stupid. Not much of a stretch this past week.

Her friend's smile widened. "The good-looking, blue-eyed cowboy that was warming your bed." *Damn.* Jordan had seen him leave? But how?

"When you missed the morning SITREP with Kade, I volunteered to come over," the deputy answered as if reading her mind.

Shoot. Her gaze shot to the clock. She completely forgot to check in as scheduled.

Damn, sexy cowboy really had her mind all out of wack. And body quivering half the night. She stifled a yawn and faced her friend. "So, how did you know…"

"That Kevin was in your bed? I didn't, until now." Her friend smiled. "He was downstairs guzzling some coffee, keeping Kerri in stitches while he ate two helpings of steak and eggs."

The man certainly had an appetite. She ought to know. Heat flooded her belly and overflowed right to her face.

"Well, it won't happen again. It was just a…thing." Yeah, a thing left over from Houston. Now that they got it out of their system—all night—life would go back to normal.

"Why?" Jordan frowned, setting her cup on the counter. "Kevin isn't an irresponsible guy. You seem to be getting him confused with someone else."

Maybe. She blew out a breath. "I know." That was no longer a concern. But the fact he might use her daughter as a substitute to his loss simply twisted her gut. What if he realized a few weeks from now that Amelia wasn't a substitute and just left? Her daughter would be devastated. *Hell*, she'd be…

She forced the thought to stop. They were just friends. *Keep it simple.* No more benefits.

A soft, yet firm hand settled on hers and squeezed. "Talk to me. What are your concerns about him?"

Concerns? Where did she start? His lack of commitment? Unfounded guilt? Loss? Shayla got the impression from the cowboy's conversation with Kade the other night that no one, not even Cole, was aware of the unborn child, so she kept her mouth shut. Not her business to share.

But she did worry.

"He's a good man. Trust me. And he really cares about you and Amelia." Jordan squeezed her hand again before releasing to grab her mug. "You should've seen him the night you were sick, Shayla. Suave businessman, dressed in Armani with an aqua diaper bag draped over one shoulder, while he carried a cute little mermaid into the kitchen. I tell you, if he'd gone into the dining room, every female in our restaurant would've swooned."

Shayla laughed because she didn't know what else to do. She understood the swooning. *Hell*, she was guilty of it herself. But, this wasn't about her. Or Kevin. It was about Amelia. And trying to keep her baby from being hurt.

"I know he's a good man. And I appreciate all he's done for me. Us," she corrected. "But that's the problem. Amelia is very attached to him." She pushed off the stool and began to pace. "Have you heard what she calls him? Daddy."

"I heard. It's cute."

"No, no, it's not." She stopped and frowned. "He's not her daddy and won't ever be, so I need to help my daughter ease away from her attachment to the guy." She shoved her hands in her back pockets and blew out a breath. "And I can't stop her. No matter what I say, she doesn't listen. Keeps calling him Daddy."

"What do you mean he won't ever be?"

"He doesn't do relationships, Jordan."

"People change."

She laughed, a bitter sound echoing through the kitchen. "Kevin's not people. He's a drop-dead gorgeous cowboy billionaire with his pick of woman. Why would he give that all up to saddle himself with a single mom and her daughter who can't stay in one town too long because of her deadbeat dad?"

"Oh, hun, you're asking the wrong question."

She blinked at the deputy, then gave her head a little shake. *Nope*. Her friend's statement still didn't make sense. "You'll have to tell me, because I'm clueless. What question?"

"Why *wouldn't* he give that all up?" Jordan replied. "You are worth loving, Shayla. Kevin would be damn lucky to have you."

Two weeks.

Two long weeks since Kevin had lost control and succumbed to his need for Shayla that unforgettable Thursday night. Three times. A smile found its way to his lips and tugged hard. What a night. Incredible. Bone shifting. Back breaking. One hell of an invigorating night.

But the sexy single mother had started to cross the line. Asked questions. They may have shared bodies in every way imaginable, but that didn't mean he wanted to get personal with the woman.

Actually, he did. And wasn't that just the problem.

The thought of opening up and sharing that side with her held, of all things, appeal. How stupid was that? *Damn stupid*. Luckily, he'd caught himself just in time and redirected her...energy.

As he walked across the driveway to meet Kade, Cole and Connor to pitch in with revamping the existing humane stable to house other animals, Kevin thought about the new stable.

Construction was set to start on Monday. Created from scratch, the beauty would consist of state of the art equipment, heating and cooling, fifteen stalls, lounge, gorgeous tack room, bath/utility room, examination room, and a huge indoor riding arena with cedar mulch footing. Perfect for healing horses. The designer had really outdone herself. Brandi rocked the design, incorporating all the requirements his cousin had brought to the table. With her construction and Kade's kind heart, Shadow Rock was going to help many animals from Houston on down to Harland County. Kevin was happy to be a part of it right from the start.

Passing several vehicles, he noted Brandi's regular crew had arrived. According to his soon-to-be-cousin-in-law, Saturday was just an extension of the week in the construction and design business.

Did that include Shayla?

He stopped dead and glanced around. No red SUV in sight. Kevin let out a breath and continued toward the group of cowboys gathered by the empty humane stable, grateful the single mother wasn't there. She was more a planner, organizer, producer, not hands on physical.

Although, *damn*, the woman sure did excel in that department. He groaned. Not wise to revisit those memories. Avoiding her on all days that didn't rhyme with Tuesday and Thursday was his best defense against a libido gone rogue. Dancing with the temptress during their practices, holding her close, brushing that exquisite body of hers was enough to put him in a *sexually frustrated* coma.

Dribbling and drooling—not a good look for him.

So, Kevin made a point to steer clear of her on non-dancing days whenever possible. Now that he'd had time to cool down since that night in her apartment, things were a bit clearer. His vow not to have sex with her again was a little easier to keep when he reminded himself they were getting too personal. Continued sex with Shayla would lead to more opening up. It was inevitable.

Abstinence. Yeah, that was the key. Abstaining and taking *matters* into his own hands was his only defense. *Hell*, he wasn't even sure if the pipes still worked with other women. Hadn't tried since Galveston.

Hadn't wanted to.

Shit. He halted again, the crunch of gravel diminishing with his steps. Where the hell had that thought come from? More importantly, was it true?

Before he could form an honest answer, his cell phone rang. Happy for the interruption, Kevin pulled the phone out of his pocket and stared at the caller ID.

Amber.

Decision time. If he answered, he'd be making a date. But could he deliver what the flight attendant had come to expect?

Did he want to?

Shit. There goes that damn inner voice again. Because he was frustrated and more than a little ticked off for being weak, he took the call and made the date.

Houston at five pm.

It was time to get back on that damn horse. And if anyone could help him in the saddle it was Amber. The uninhibited woman always brought something interesting with her from her travels.

The familiar thrill associated with that fact never arrived.

Dammit.

Now his thrill meter was busted? *Cripes*, was that tied to Shayla, too? What the hell didn't that woman have her fingers on? *Damn*. No. Not going there. Not thinking about her talented, wicked hands, or her hot, erotic stroking.

He thought about it.

Even visualized.

And now he was hard. As hard as the corner fence post he passed, zipper of his jeans cutting into his favorite body part, slowing his stride. *Great*, now she affected his swagger.

Was nothing safe from that woman?

"What happened? Forget to put sugar in your coffee this morning?" Connor McCall asked, leaning against the outside of the stable, watching his approach with the others.

"I did, but apparently not enough," he lied, and didn't care. The truth would give his buddies way too much joy. And he wasn't exactly in a joyous mood.

Cole's gaze narrowed. "You sure that's all it is?"

"Yeah, why? What did you think it was?" he asked, bringing the travel mug to his lips.

"Shayla."

Kevin choked while Connor chuckled and Kade and Cole studied him closely. The single mother's list of ownership was growing. He just added *swallowing* to the list. The woman affected the way he walked, talked, screwed, swallowed, breathed, thought...*Shit.*

She was everywhere.

When the hell had he given her access to everything?
And how had she gotten in? Under his skin. A virus?
They'd been having sex. Not a relationship.

He didn't talk to her unless it was sex related.

Except he did.

Well, he didn't know about her past.

Yes, he did. And her future goals, too. *Damn.*

He certainly didn't do non-sexual nice things for her.

Ah, hell. He did that, too. When she was sick. In
danger. Hungry. Tired. He leaned back against the fence
post and cursed.

"Let me guess, the girl vortex?"

"Yeah." He nodded to Moose. "Got it on the first
try."

His cousin studied him over his to go mug. "You
know, Kev, it's easier if you don't fight it."

Yeah, that didn't work for him. "Have to, cuz. Can't
let the woman control me."

All three men laughed. *Great.* The chuckleheads
were back.

"What's so damn funny?"

Moose sobered and cupped Kade's shoulder. "Aw,
isn't that cute? Your cousin thinks we have a choice."

"I'm right here, *McHiliarious*," Kevin stated,
pounding his chest. "And of course we have a choice."

Cole shook his head. "No, we don't. Not if we want
to be included in their lives."

Ah hell. He didn't sign up for this. "How do you stop
it?" He bounced his gaze between his friends. "How do
you get out before it's too late?"

"Oh, buddy. I'm sorry. If you're asking these
questions, it means it's *already* too late."

All three cowboys were nodding. And smiling.
Damn. Not good.

"He's right, Dalton," Connor said, making a pucker motion with his lips. "Kiss your Casanova days goodbye."

Shit no. "I'm not kissing anything goodbye, *McPessimist.* For your information, I'm heading up to Houston this afternoon to rendezvous with a flight attendant."

A very attentive flight attendant.

"You sure that's wise, Kevin?" Kade asked quietly.

"Wise? Who knows? Necessary? *Hell ya.* If anyone could get me over this slump it's Amber."

"Let me save you the trouble, and the time. It's not going to work," Connor told him. "I had the same stupid idea while I was in denial about Kerri. In my infinite wisdom, I took out the Fletcher twins."

"*Flexible* Fletchers?" His brows rose. *Damn.* The sisters were record holding gymnasts. And flexible. He'd *flexed* with them a few years back. The positions those girls could hold while he... A sinking feeling settled in the pit of his stomach. "Wait. Are you saying things didn't go well?"

Moose snorted. "That's exactly what I'm saying, *genius.* Things didn't go at all."

Kevin blinked. It didn't compute. "But the sisters are willing, and inventive, and...flexible."

"True, but they weren't the most important thing," the tall cowboy said, gaze suddenly serious.

It was never a good thing when Connor McCall was series. Kevin swallowed hard. "What?"

"They weren't Kerri."

Cole nodded. "Just as Amber is not Shayla."

He knew that. The blonde was carefree, unattached, uninterested in a relationship, shallow, self-centered...*Shit.* He halted that train of thought before it

247

completely derailed. Wasn't helping his resolve to quite sniffing around Shayla.

The redhead was warm and caring, passionate and compassionate. A deadly combination Kevin usually ran away from like a little girl. So, why was he contemplating doing the opposite?

Oh, right, because he was an idiot.

"I know," he finally replied. "But Amber doesn't have a daughter who's growing attached to me."

There, he said it. His biggest reason for staying away from the redhead. Amelia.

"You sure it's not the other way around?" Kade asked in that calm, commanding tone.

Kevin blew out a breath. "No, I'm not sure. And that's another big reason to stay out of Shayla's life."

The three men nodded. *Finally*, they got a clue.

"Then I guess there's no reason to tell you about the surprise party my fiancée and Kerri and Jordan are throwing for her this afternoon."

Surprise party for Shayla? "Why?"

"Because you just said you want to stay away."

"No, you jerk." He shoulder checked the guy. "I mean, why are they throwing her a party? Is it her birthday?"

He realized with a start, the fact he didn't know that was proof maybe they hadn't gotten as personal as he'd first feared.

"No."

Great. A one word answer. His cousin was really pushing it.

"Then what is it?"

"Can't tell you. Might be too personal."

"Dammit, Kade, quit pissing around and just tell me."

A slight tugging pulled Sgt. Hardass' lips into a grin. "She's graduating."

Had she already finished her two weeks of classes? His mind computed their time since Houston. Three weeks, going on four, and no sign of her father, either. He smiled. "She got her GED?"

"Ah, so you do know about it." Cole nodded from his quiet perch near the fence, and Connor cocked his head. "Doesn't that make things a little personal, Dalton?"

"Stuff it, Moose." He turned back to Kade. "So? Did she?"

His cousin shook his head. "Not yet. According to Brandi, Shayla's taking the last of her tests from 8-4 today."

Right now.

Kevin's heart squeezed. *Bet she's nervous*. Damn, he wished she had said something on Thursday. He would've…what? Wished her well? Helped her study? Actually*, yes*, he would've done both. Happily. He knew this was a huge dream for Shayla.

But, well, she didn't need him. Didn't need anyone. The woman had proven time and again she could take care of herself.

"She's got this." He nodded, mouth curving into a grin. Happiness and a feeling akin to pride washed through him in a wave of warmth. Her resilience was something else. "Good for her."

"Yep, and we'll be sure to tell her for you while we help her celebrate the accomplishment. You go ahead." Bastard slapped him on the back with a giant paw. "Go to Houston. Don't worry your pretty head about it none."

And he didn't. Much.

For most of the morning and half of the afternoon, Kevin focused on renovating the existing stable which would serve to shelter the neglected and abused smaller animals. Assigned to assemble metal shelving that would hold numerous medical supplies because none of his friends could figure out the instructions, he constructed eight towers and secured them into place in the new supply room Connor and Kade had fashioned from two stalls. He was just screwing the last bolt into place when his cousin called it a day. The McCall brothers had left a half-hour ago, but Kevin had wanted to finish the last shelf.

"It's not too late to change your mind, you know. You can still come to the party," Kade said as they put tools away in a battered, red, four-drawer tool box situated against the wall in the walkway.

He stowed the drill in the bottom and straightened. "Nah, I'm good. You enjoy," he replied, determined to stick to his plans.

Leave Shayla alone. Don't encourage Amelia.
Keep it simple.

"Any news on how she did?" Kevin couldn't help it. He had to know. All afternoon he'd wondered despite his attempt to focus on work. At one point, he'd stopped, stomped out of the storage room, intent on sitting in his truck at the rec center to wait for the redhead to emerge. Someone should've been with her. Been there for support, to congratulate, or console, which ever was required.

He hated the thought of her being alone. She'd gone through life that way for far too long.

"Yeah, Brandi said she'd talked to Caitlin who was at the center."

Relief eased the stiffness from his shoulders. Her sister had been with her.

"Shayla passed. With honors."

Kevin let out a breath and smiled. "Well, of course she did. Damn woman is smart."

God, she must be so happy. He could visualize the relief in her eyes and dazzling smile on her beautiful face. The urge to see her, to celebrate with her, to give her a congratulatory kiss rushed through him.

"I think she'd like it if you were at her party." Kade studied him, waiting, watching.

He rubbed at the tightness in his chest. Not an easy decision. He wanted to go, but if he did, that meant he'd taken a huge step into foreign territory. "No. I think it's best if I stay away. Just tell her congratulations for me."

"All right." His cousin nodded, cupping his shoulder as they exited the stable. "Have a safe drive. Don't forget to call Jen when you get there. You know she worries like a mother hen."

Kevin laughed. His younger sister worried about everyone. "I will."

"If you change your mind, the party's at the McCall's at four," Kade informed. "They're watching Amelia, so it'll be easy to spring the surprise when Shayla goes to pick up her daughter."

"Makes sense." He nodded as they scurried around vehicles leaving the ranch, some, no doubt, going to the party. But he was heading to Houston, not Wild Creek Ranch.

A fact Kevin reminded himself an hour later as he drove through town, determination tightening his jaw. Stopped at a light, he glanced at the clock on the dash. An hour and a half before rendezvous in Houston. He had time. Amber's flight wasn't touching down for another hour yet. He'd get to their usual hotel and have everything waiting for her for when she arrived.

Movement out of the corner of his eye caught Kevin's attention. A red SUV pulled in front of Brandi's beach cottage, and Shayla and Caitlin got out as Brandi's door flew open and the smiling designer rushed outside. Even with his windows closed, he could hear the happy cheers that matched the three women's smiling expression and jumping embraces. With the light still red, he continued to watch, sucked in, pulse kicking a hard beat against his ribs.

Big blue eyes bright with joy. Wide smile, opened and unrestrained. Shayla stole his breath. But when she drew back and wiped her face, something inside him cracked. Split wide open. Feelings he hadn't felt in years seeped out and the ache in his chest increased.

No doubt about it. The woman made him feel.
Too much.

The short beep of a horn alerted him the light had turned green. With a strange heaviness squeezing straight down to his ribs, he drove through the intersection and forced air into his lungs.

Driving past the turnoff to the interstate, Kevin continued down Main Street until he pulled into the first vacant spot he could find and parked the truck. Was he making a mistake leaving? Or was it a bigger mistake to stay? He didn't want to screw up Shayla's life. Or Amelia's.

Which decision would cause more harm?

Rubbing his temples to relieve the pressure, because his *mind-palace* was brimming with answers and he had no damn idea which ones were correct, he acknowledged the overwhelming, out-of-control feelings had been buried for a reason. He didn't like not having control. Not having a plan.

Not having a clear-cut idea of how to proceed.

The reason for keeping his feelings locked up tight since Tina. He didn't want to feel. Didn't want to rely on someone else for his happiness. Or worse.

Didn't want someone else to rely on *him* for theirs.

Taking everything in, his mind worked on solutions to his dilemma. There were three:

1. Get on the interstate and meet Amber as planned.

2. Attend Shayla's party and take a small, tentative step toward a monogamist relationship.

3. Drive over to the pub and get drunk.

He voted for number three.

Releasing his temples, he opened his eyes and focused on his surroundings.

"Son-of-a-bitch..."

There it was. The answer to his problem stared at him with glinting precision from the store window. What were the chances he would've pulled in that exact spot at that exact store with that exact item in the window?

He'd never really believed in fate until Jordan and Cole were reunited. Especially since they'd both married other people. Then Connor was systematically, and quite comically, taken down by sweet, gifted Kerri. And after that, he'd witnessed how a tiny ad placed online had brought a special, understanding woman from up north and set her in his cousin's path when Kade had returned from deployment in need of that understanding.

Fate? *Hell yeah. You bet your ass he believed in it.*

Pulling the phone out of his pocket, he eyed the eclectic storefront of the little gift shop, and left a voice mail to one soon-to-be pissed off flight attendant. He was not going to be able to make their rendezvous or any in the future. There was someone—*two* someones—far more important in Harland County.

Kevin got out of the truck, checked the time, then slipped the phone back into his pocket. He might be a little late for the party, but he wasn't going empty handed.

He had a graduation present to buy.

She did it.

She got her GED.

For the first time in a long time, pride and happiness swirled in Shayla's chest. After all these years of living with the knowledge she was a high school dropout, she could now hold her head high with new knowledge she'd gotten her GED. An accomplishment she'd thought, for a while there, would never happen. Especially this month, when she finally signed up to take the classes only to have to 'drop out' of them because of Lyle.

But this time, she didn't let him control her life, or control how she lived her life. She'd caught the next scheduled classes and finished them this week. And yesterday and today, she was able to take the actual tests. No interruptions. No stupid Lyle rearing his ugly head. She was calm. Relaxed. Took the tests and passed. Finally. *Finally*, she had her high school education and could legitimately state that on applications.

Her stomach flopped. Okay, she wasn't going to think about job applications today. Or her father showing up. Or leaving the county. People she'd grown to care about. Kevin. *Nope.* Not thinking sad thoughts. For the moment, she had a fantastic job, sweetheart of a daughter, and a terrific sister who sat the whole day today and waited until Shayla had finished. Caitlin was the first person she told about passing. The pride and happiness shining in her sister's eyes was something she'd never forget. She felt lighter. Like a heavy, concrete barrier had been lifted off her shoulders.

She also had wonderful friends.

Especially Brandi, Jordan and Kerri who kept taking turns congratulating. Sniffing back another round of tears, *dammit*, she hugged one of her hosts, again. "I can't believe you did this for me."

Dozens of people had yelled surprise when she'd walked into Wild Creek Ranch to pick up her daughter. She had no idea where all the cars were parked. But, a bunch of good folks were there laughing and smiling and eating Kerri's wonderful food, helping her celebrate her special day. People from town, the Masters and McCalls, of course, her friends and their husbands and fiancé, some of Kade's guard buddies. Doc Turner. Her sister and Greg, Jen and Brock and Cody. Mrs. Avery, and even Macy and her mom.

"You deserve it," Jordan said, hugging her back.

"Yes." Brandi changed places with the deputy. "We are all so proud of you, Shayla."

The thought of her friends going through all this trouble and that it could've been for nothing, cramped her stomach. "What if I had failed?"

"Not a chance," Kerri said, pulling her in for a hug when Brandi finished. "You got your GED with honors. That rocks."

"Yeah, I was surprised. But I don't technically have my GED yet. I have to wait for them to mail it to me," she explained, drawing back. She'd only gotten the verbal results.

"Well, at least they told you today and you don't have to wait to find out."

"I know. I don't think I could've waited."

255

Donna Michaels

Waiting was always tough. For Kerri's blueberry muffins to finish baking. Winter to end. Her dad to show up. The other shoe to drop. Kevin to walk in. Yeah, waiting was tough, especially when you already knew the outcome.

Her sexy dance partner wasn't coming.

She'd overheard Jen telling Mrs. McCall that her brother was on his way to see some flight attendant in Houston. Shayla tried to ignore the stab of pain that had pierced her heart at the news. And still remained.

They weren't a *thing*. He had no reason to show. Yet, it was weird. The first person she'd wanted to share her news with had been Kevin. Not her sister, or Jordan, or Brandi, or Kade. But Kevin. It was his handsome face that had come to mind when the instructor said the words *'passed with honors.'* Silly. Stupid, actually. But it was the truth.

A truth she'd deal with as always. On her own. In the quiet confines of her room later that night. Right now, she'd focus on the happiness of nailing her GED.

"Here's Mommy."

She turned to find Connor approaching with a chortling Amelia in his arms. Jeez, the cowboy was big. Her daughter looked like a doll in his hands. It was actually really cute. "Hi, baby."

"Mommy!" The little tornado launched at her, all smiles. "Hi, Mommy."

Her laughter echoed with the others. "Hi, baby. Did you have fun with Uncle Connor?"

"Yes," Amelia replied, hugging her neck and kissing her cheek. "Mommy."

The little girl was on a roll today, hugging and kissing everyone in sight. No one was safe. And no one seemed to mind.

"We went to see the bulls," the cowboy said, slipping an arm around Kerri, lopsided grin dimpling his cheeks. "And she got to pet one."

Knowing the cowboy would never have put her daughter in harm's way, Shayla squeezed the little girl and smiled. "You got to pet a bull? Did you like it?"

Amelia nodded, then wrinkled her nose and shook her head. "Stinky."

Again, her laughter mixed with the others and her mood lightened.

"You sure she's not talking about Connor?"

Heart suddenly in her throat, Shayla turned to watch Kevin approach, gaze friendly, smile warm and his stride sure and damn sexy.

He was *here*. Not Houston.

He came. To see *her*. Not Amber.

Shayla's glee was short-lived when common sense returned. The cowboy was just stopping in on his way. Despite their pact to not have sex, they had formed a bond, and she felt safe to consider him a friend. So, that was probably all this was…one friend stopping in to share an achievement with the other before leaving for a date.

Swallowing the bitter-sweet pill, she forced the smile to remain on her face and her heart to get over itself. The man was free to do what and *who* he wanted. She needed to get a clue.

Still, she was touched that he made time for her in his weekend plans.

Her "Hi, Kevin," mingled with the others, and she noted a few of their friends wore surprised expressions on their faces.

Except for Cole and Kade.

"Nice of you to join us," his cousin said, lip twitching into a grin.

Cole cupped his shoulder. "Stopped for a gift, I'm guessing."

Before the smiling cowboy could answer, Amelia twisted in her arms and spotted him. "Daddy!" Delight lit her daughter's eyes like the stars in the Texas sky, then her face puckered and she burst into tears. "My, daddy...daddy," the little girl sobbed, reaching out to the frowning cowboy with both arms.

"Hey, pumpkin, don't cry," he soothed, taking her daughter to cradle against his chest, tenderness and concern softening his gaze as he stared down at the now sniffling little girl. "It's okay. I got you."

"Okay," Jordan spoke up, making a shooing motion to the others with her hands. "Let's go eat and give them some privacy."

And just like that, the three of them were alone. Amelia lifted a hand to tenderly touch Kevin's face with such love and joy in her little heart, Shayla's chest ached.

"My daddy," her daughter repeated, smile once again in place.

Yeah, her daughter was definitely besotted with the cowboy. Shayla, too. *Dammit.* And she'd been so careful, for them both. Fat lot of good it did. The cowboy still had them wrapped around his finger.

Clearing her throat in an attempt to remove the lump lodged there, she stepped closer and touched her daughter's head. "Sorry, I guess she was missing you more than we'd realized."

At least Shayla had gotten to see him at dance practices, but her daughter hadn't seen him since they'd eaten dinner at the Dalton's over three weeks ago.

"No worries, darlin'," he said, glancing up, blue gaze so affectionate and sweet that ache in her heart increased. "I missed her, too."

By the tone in his voice, and way he stared at her with open longing, Shayla got the impression she was included in that remark. She nodded, and forced her racing pulse to slow.

"Thanks for coming. Jen had said something about you going to Houston to see Amber."

He nodded, and she waited for him to explain he was just stopping on his way out of town.

"I was. Figured it was best to stick with our original plan, but I'd actually like to talk to you about that," he said instead, sending that simmering pulse back into orbit.

He wanted to talk? About their no sex plan? *Oh Lordy*, she didn't think she could just have sex with him anymore. She wanted to. So very much, but she had to be truthful…

Her heart was no longer out of the equation.

Chapter Sixteen

"Sorry to interrupt," Kerri said, face flushing as she came to a stop. "But I thought maybe Amelia would want to see the doggy and give you some time alone." The considerate cook turned her warm gaze on Shayla's daughter. "What do you say, cutie? Want to see Bullet?"

"Goggy." Amelia perked up. "See Bullet. See Bullet." Then reached for Kerri and happily went with her friend in search of Jordan's retired police dog.

She turned to Kevin, surprised to find him staring at her. "You were saying?"

"First, I want to say congratulations."

He stepped close and wrapped his arms around her tight. Unable to resist, she slid her arms around his back and fought off more tears.

"I'm so damn proud of you," he said against her ear and hell, the tears spilled over. He kissed her head then drew back and gently swiped the wetness with his thumb. "I wish you would've told me you were taking your tests. I would've been there for you. Waited for you to come out."

"You would've?" She hiccupped.

He nodded. "Yes. This is a milestone. A huge achievement, Shayla. I hate the thought of you going through it alone."

She swallowed and forced words past her hot throat. "Caitlin was there today."

Relief softened his features. "I know. I heard. I'm glad."

"And I'm glad you're here," she said, reaching up to touch his chin, enjoying the feel of stubble scraping her palm. "And not on your way to Houston."

"Yeah, about that," he said, grabbing her hand to twine their fingers together. "Let's go somewhere a little less crowded."

She nodded without even attempting to respond because his touch was causing a crazy fluttering in her chest and drying her throat. His hand was firm and strong, and she was happy when he led her to the McCall's gathering room, sat with her on the sofa but didn't release his hold. Her heart beat wildly in her chest, and she tried desperately to find her voice while he stared at their hands.

"My sister was right," he finally said, but didn't glance up. "I was heading to Houston to see Amber. I'd already made the date with her before I found out about your party."

Her thundering heart nosedived into her ribs. "I see," she managed to say, but didn't mean it. She was completely confused.

"But, on my way out of town, I realized something important."

"What?"

He smiled, a secret smile as if it held some kind of meaning or shared joke. "She's not you."

"Oh?" Now her pulse was back to thundering in her ears again.

"She doesn't make me feel, but you do."

"I do?"

"Yes."

She blinked as the meaning set in.

"What I'm trying to say is, if you're willing to take a chance, I'd love to see you in a sexually monogamist way."

"Like...in a relationship?" Her heart rocked in her chest.

He blew out a breath and nodded. "Yes. That."

"I'd like that, too."

She was going with her heart on this, not her head. No thoughts of how brilliant and rich the man was, or the number of girlfriends he had, or the possibility of her and Amelia being a substitute. Screw it. Her heart wanted to be with him. Her body sure as hell wanted to be with him, so her mind could either get on the same damn page or shut up.

"Yeah?" A smile reached his eyes for the first time in ten minutes. "So, you'll be gentle with me? Because I haven't been in a relationship in over ten years. And that one ended badly. Mostly because of me."

His admission on top of another admission took her by surprise. She blinked and squeezed his hand. "I haven't been in one either," she admitted, and when confusion wrinkled his brow, she smiled weakly. Since he thought Bobby was Amelia's father, he was no doubt confused as to how she could've been engaged without having a relationship. "Long story. I'll tell you about it someday, but right now, I'd rather just take it one step at a time."

"Deal, darlin'." A brilliant smile crossed his face as he released her hand to caress her cheek. "I'm so damn proud of you, Shayla."

She was too busy trying to keep her tears in check to respond. But he didn't seem to care. He just leaned in and brushed her lips with his. Twice. Nipping and nibbling, soft kisses that drove her wild. Powerless and hungry for more, she leaned into him and kissed him back. Cupping his face, she enjoyed the feel of rough stubble on her palms, and smiled at his groan.

Or was that her?

When they drew apart, he rested his forehead against hers and sucked in air. "God, I've missed that."

She nodded, still finding her breath. "Me, too. I can't believe you're here." And he wanted a relationship.

"No more running." He pulled back and stared deep into her eyes while he grabbed her hands and squeezed. "For either of us. We'll face your dad together if he shows."

Once again, tears blurred her vision as she nodded. "Okay."

She wasn't leaving Harland County. And if everything worked out, she was...*home*.

He gently kissed both of her hands, then released them to draw a square box from his shirt pocket. "This is for you. For getting your GED. When I saw it, I knew it was meant for you. To commemorate your special day."

Today was special, but it had nothing to do with her testing and everything to do with the gorgeous cowboy handing her a gift. No man ever bought her a gift before.

Her hands were trembling as she lifted the lid, and a split second before the tears returned to her eyes, she'd caught a glimpse of a metal and turquoise dragonfly necklace.

So achingly perfect.

"It's beautiful," she whispered, fingering the precious gift, tears rolling unchecked down her face, again. "I love it. Thank you." She couldn't take her gaze off the necklace, even though her vision was all blurry.

He lifted her right hand, turned it over and kissed her dragonfly tattoo. "Beautiful. Like you. Resilient. Like you," he said, kissing her wrist after each word.

Shayla's chest hurt. In a good way. And when he placed the necklace around her neck, he said the words that were in her heart.

"I think your mother guided me to this necklace."

She inhaled and nodded, fat tears dripping down her cheeks. "Me, too," she choked out, feeling so close to her mother at that moment. "Thank you."

"Come here," he said, drawing her against his chest, holding her tight as she made an idiot out of herself and cried like a baby.

She finally got her GED. Her mom was here with her. This wonderful, incredibly sweet, incredibly good-looking cowboy holding her tight, stroking her hair, wanted *her* in his life. What a perfect day. Shayla didn't have many. The only other one had been the birth of her daughter.

When she finally regained some composure, she drew back and wiped her face. "Sorry." She sniffed. "I had a moment of weakness."

"No, darlin', no. That wasn't weakness. That was emotion. You're like me. You bottle it up too much."

Another admission. She didn't think her heart could expand anymore, but the trust the cowboy was showing by opening up to her was huge. The monumental step wasn't lost on her.

Shayla held his face with both hands and smiled. "Then we'll work on *un*bottling together."

"Deal." His mouth curved and he leaned forward and kissed her. But instead of deepening the kiss, he broke it and drew them both to their feet. "We'd better get back to the party. If I stay in here any longer with you, we'll be testing the integrity of the sofa, and I don't think the McCalls' bought it with that in mind."

Shayla laughed, and as Kevin grabbed the empty gift box and tucked it back in his shirt pocket, she dared to believe that maybe, just maybe, her life was going to be full of good things for a change.

Two weeks after Shayla had taken the tests, her GED arrived in the mail, along with a print out of her scores. Kevin ran right out and had everything framed, including a picture he had insisted on taking of her holding the items. She deserved something special. Now they all resided on the wall where the woman could see her achievement every day.

That was three weeks ago, and every time he entered the apartment, like now, his gaze was drawn to the pictures, and his mind slipped back to the day of her party. Nervous excitement had ruled his pulse because of the huge step he wanted to take with her. He never planned to travel the relationship road again, but Shayla was different. *Special.* A kind, caring woman with a tough backbone and will to survive. She was intoxicating, and he loved being around her. She made him feel good. She made him happy.

The night of the party, after they'd moved Amelia into her own room and the little angel had fallen asleep, Kevin took his time showing Shayla exactly how happy he was to be in her life. And she showed him right back. With much enthusiasm.

He smiled. They'd been *enthusiastic* for over a month now. And he really couldn't ever remember being happier. He wanted to know things about her, personal things like her birth date, favorite band, flower, color, all things he'd shied away from in the past. It was different

265

with Shayla, a *good* different. He already knew her favorite spot, rhythm and position. Now, he was ready to go beyond the basics. This past week, he'd been at a conference in Seattle. It was the first time since the party he'd been away from his girls for more than one night. It sucked.

"Kevin, you're back early," Shayla said, rushing out of the bedroom, hair wet, navy towel wrapped around her delectable curves, giving him a glimpse of the promise land as she rushed to him. "I didn't hear you come in."

Damn, she looked good enough to eat.

He dropped his briefcase and overcoat on a chair in time to crush her close and taste the woman he'd missed to within an inch of his life. The strong, powerful feelings Shayla invoked in him were definitely scary, but he had to credit Moose with some good advice. *It's easier if you don't fight it.* The big guy was right. Kevin was beginning to understand his friend's logic worked well, and following that advice reaped incredible reward.

Just like following the seam of her mouth with his tongue opened up a whole lot of rewards. She moaned and fisted his shirt, practically crawling up him. He liked that. A lot.

Sneaking his hands under the towel, he cupped her gorgeous, bare ass and ground his heavy erection into the sweetness he'd been without for far too long. He needed to put his lips on her, taster her, be in her...

Shit.

He ripped his mouth away and rested his cheek on her head. "Where's Amelia?" His voice was rough and low. The libido train was out of control, and a crash was eminent if he didn't slow things down.

She stepped back, smiled up at him, gaze heated, and *oh hell yeah*, deliciously wicked as she dropped the towel. "At Mrs. Masters'."

God bless Jordan and Kerri's mom. She was getting something extra for Christmas.

In seconds, his suit coat and tie hit the chair, then slid off onto the floor. He stepped over them and reached for his beautiful redhead, kissing her deep and desperate, running his hands over her beautiful curves while she unbutton his shirt. Wicked fingers skimmed over his chest, down his abs, and heaven help him, stroked his ridges until they quivered under her touch. It took his breath. *She* took his breath, and her fingers moved lower, to the band of his pants.

He released her mouth and sucked in a breath. "Shayla."

"I need you now," she murmured, unbuckling his belt.

He lifted her, pressing her to the wall near her photos, dipping to taste each perfect peak. They demanded attention. She shudder and he release her nipple to kiss a path to her shoulder where he nipped and soothed with his tongue.

"I missed you. Missed us. Missed this," he said, trailing a hand down between her quivering thighs to dip inside, finding her hot and wet. "Oh, yeah," he muttered, biting her shoulder.

She grabbed his face and tugged until they were eye to eye. "I missed you, too. I need you." Her lips brushed his with each word.

"Yeah?"

"So much, Kevin. So much," she whispered, mouth kissing and drinking.

But he needed more. Much more. Everything. All of her. He deepened the kiss, taking, demanding and she gave and demanded until he was at the verge. She unzipped his pants, and before they could fall, he rescued a condom from his pocket.

"Allow me," she said, ripping the packet open, freeing his erection and rolling the condom down excruciatingly slow.

"Killing me," he ground out hoarsely against her collarbone.

"Good. Then we're even."

He choked out a laugh and drew back. Beneath the smoldering heat in her eyes was a sparkle of humor.

God, he missed her. He missed *her* most of all. Sure, the heat and the desire were incredible, but he missed Shayla's wit and timing and heart. But he wasn't ready to tell her. Not with words, anyway.

Capturing her mouth for another rough, hot, deep kiss, he lifted her higher and shoved into her, their gasps of pleasure echoing in the room. Heat skittered down his spine then burst in all directions as he drove in and out, barely hanging on. She came on the third thrust, and he followed her, fighting his damndest to remain upright until her shuddering subsided. Still embedded deep inside her, he slid to the floor and held her tight, face buried in her hair.

When his breathing settled and mind returned to its palace, Kevin recognized something was different. More.

"I missed that," she said against his shoulder. "Next time you go away, please take me with you."

He drew back and stroked a wet strand of hair from her face. "Okay, but I'm not going anywhere for a long, long, time."

"Good. This week was tough," she said. "Everywhere I turned, someone was making out. Connor and Kerri, Cole and Jordan, Kade and Brandi, Jen and Brock, even Caitlin and Greg were visiting and I caught them kissing in the kitchen."

"Ah, poor baby," he cooed, trailing a finger down her nose. "Is that all I'm good for? Is that all you missed is my kissing?"

Frowning, she shook her head. "No, of course not. I missed the back scratching and neck rubs, too."

A little flutter of disappointment settled in Kevin's gut. He knew how hard it was to open up. Sometimes she had a harder time than him. But he wished she'd give him a little more. He'd seen the emotion in Shayla's eyes, felt it in her touch, yet, she kept it to herself.

Since he was guilty of it, too, he had no right to get upset. Not wanting to rock the boat, especially since he'd only just gotten back from his trip, he shook it off and picked up on her playfulness. Reaching out, he stroked a finger down her breast to the puckering tip. "I'm going to get a shower, and since you stated you wanted me to take you wherever I went, I guess that means you have to go, too."

"I just got out of one," she said, shuddering, spark of heat returning to her gaze.

"But not with *me*."

An hour later, after giving the woman back scratching, body rubbing and more kisses, Kevin was driving them to the Masters' to pick up Amelia. He missed the little pumpkin and hoped Shayla would let him put her daughter to sleep that night. Reading to Amelia, rocking her in the chair, tucking her into her bed with her *goggy*, their time together was unbelievably special to him.

"Thanks, Kevin," Shayla said, causing him to turn to her.

"For what?"

"For taking good care of me." Her grin was both sweet and wicked and had his blood heating in seconds.

He cocked his head and grinned. "You do have one of those incredibly satisfied expressions on your face."

It was true. Her mouth was relaxed, face was flushed, gaze was lazy and warm.

"So do you, cowboy."

Kevin glanced in the rearview mirror and laughed. "You're right. I do. Because I am satisfied. Big time." He reached for her hand and squeezed. "Thank you, Shayla, for taking care of me, too."

She opened her mouth as if she wanted to say more. Possibly open up. His heart rocked in his chest. But they arrived at the Masters' to find Mr. and Mrs. McCall getting out of their car. Whatever Shayla had been about to say remained a secret.

"You're welcome," she said instead, squeezing his hand back in response.

With the older couple smiling from the driveway, he nodded to them before turning to Shayla. "I'd prefer you to thank me later," he said, then slipped out of the truck and walked around to meet her at the passenger door. "You're supposed to let me open it for you."

"Sorry." Her face flushed, turning her eyes a brilliant blue. "I keep forgetting."

He smiled, saddened and strangely warmed by the knowledge he was the first guy to ever open doors for the beautiful woman. "No worries, darlin'. You'll remember eventually."

"Nice job, son," Mr. McCall said, nodding approval.

Mrs. McCall reached up to pat his face. "You were always a gentleman, Kevin."

"Yes, ma'am," he replied, grabbing Shayla's hand to hold tight as they followed the older couple inside.

"Mommy! Daddy!" Amelia ran across the great room the second she'd spotted them.

Still holding Shayla's hand, he scooped down and lifted her daughter up with the other. "Hi, pumpkin.

"Hi, Shayla. Hi, Kevin. Nice to see you back," Mr. Masters said, getting up off the floor where he'd been sitting building a very impression house of blocks.

"I thought you were due in tomorrow. What a nice surprise," Mrs. Masters added, lifting up on tip-toe to kiss his cheek.

"One of the lecturers got sick, so they cut it a day early." *Thank God.* He wouldn't have lasted through another boring lecture without hanging himself with his tie.

"I'm glad," Shayla said, surprising him by showing her feelings in front of others. Then she blushed. "Not that the guy got sick. I mean, I'm glad that you're back early."

God, she was adorable.

"Thank you." He leaned over and kissed the freckle on her nose. So adorable.

"Daddy." The little girl in his arms grabbed his face and gave him the butterfly kisses he'd missed all week long.

"What are you going to do about Amelia's second birthday? It's in two weeks, right?" Mrs. McCall asked, smiling sweetly at the little girl in his arms.

She was going to be two already? Why didn't he know this? He was seeing her mom. His chest tightened with some unknown emotion. They were in a relationship. Some of these things he should know. Kevin glanced from daughter to mother who lifted her gaze to him and smiled.

"Actually, last night, Cody happened to generously offer to have it at his house." Shayla informed, turning her attention to the others. "So, as soon as he gives me more details, I shall pass them along. But thank you so much for asking."

The other couples laughed.

"That Cody is a pickle." Mr. McCall chuckled.

"You've no idea," he said, finding it hard not to smile. His almost five-year-old nephew was a treat. "Takes after his Uncle Kade."

Mrs. McCall shook her head and waved a hand at him. "Ah, I'd say he's more like you."

True. At times. The little boy was mischievous like him, but also kindhearted like Kade.

"We'd better let you go," Mrs. Masters said, carrying Amelia's diaper bag as she walked with them toward the door. "You have a busy two weeks between the big Dance-a-Thon next Saturday and then Amelia's party the following week."

"Yes, I can't believe it's almost here," Shayla replied, squeezing his hand.

He glanced down at her and smiled. Hard to believe the event that pulled them together back in January was nearly upon them. "I look forward to winning with you."

The redhead leaned into him, body warm and soft. "Me, too, cowboy. The others don't stand a chance."

Hell, *he* didn't stand a chance. Not of keeping his heart safe from her. She already ruled it. Owned it. And he was all right with that.

He just wondered if he owned any piece of hers at all.

Chapter Seventeen

All those weeks of practicing had paid off.

Shayla couldn't believe it. More than half-way through the Dance-a-Thon and she wasn't the least bit tired. Her gaze raked over her partner, smiling as they quick-stepped around the floor. *Nope.* He wasn't tired either.

Held in a college gymnasium the next town over, the thirty-six hour Dance-a-Thon had over a hundred couples representing many wonderful charities. Each couple had to raise an entrance fee that was automatically catalogued for their charity. McCall Enterprises sponsored four couples, her and Kevin, Jordan and Cole, Kerri and Connor and Brandi and Kade, paying their entrance fees, matching the fee each hour the couple stayed on the floor. The Foster Children's Charity was going to benefit whether any of the couples won or not.

If the contestants weren't dancing, they had to stand, but with the amount of wonderful food the Texas-Republic had donated, bottomless cups of sweet tea, coffee and water, they were set.

"How are you feeling?" Kevin asked as they slow danced to a George Straight song.

She lifted her head and smiled. "Great, although, alone, with you, naked would be better."

His gaze darkened and jaw flexed with his groan. "You are killing me. You know we still have ten more hours to go, even if we're the only ones left."

She nodded, recalling the rules that were read to everyone before the first song was played and the large digital stop watch began running, displaying the time in red numbers. The winning couple both had to be standing/dancing the full thirty-six hours, and in the event of a tie, the clock would keep running. Special prizes would be awarded to couples who showed skill and perseverance. They had both.

"I know," she replied. "I'm hoping it'll be the incentive to keep you going."

He pulled her close, smiling sexy and naughty, ramping her pulse to full throttle in the middle of the crowd. "How about I write a check to the charity and we go find the nearest hotel?"

Shayla laughed, enjoying the dancing. Enjoying the man. She was lighthearted and happy, a feeling she often felt over the whole six weeks she'd been in a relationship with the handsome man. He didn't push, but he supported. Didn't dig, but he listened. Didn't dictate, but he followed, except for sex, he did take lead a lot. Mostly because she enjoyed whatever he dished.

"I love the idea, but I don't think Mrs. Avery would." She nodded toward their die-hard instructor, reclining in a lounge chair the woman brought, propped with a pillow and covered with a blanket.

"Killjoy," he muttered, but his gaze held too much mirth to be taken serious. "But Kade and Cole got to leave. It's not fair."

She chuckled, patting his shoulder. "They left because both the sheriff and deputy got a call."

"They probably bribed someone to call so they could leave." He snorted.

"Connor doesn't seem to have a problem dancing with Kerri. Don't you want to dance with me?"

"You know I love to dance with you," he said, twirling her around as a waltz began to play. "You also know what happened after practices when we got back to your apartment, or almost back."

And just like that, she was wet. *Dammit*. Rigorous practices always led to hot, fast, vigorous sex with the incorrigible man. He deliberately mentioned them.

"Hey, I know," he continued to tease, holding her in the closed position they knew so well. "What if we had sex up against the wall in the bathroom?"

Her heart rocked in her chest while liquid heat pooled low in her belly.

"If we're still standing, we won't get disqualified, right?"

She laughed. "I'm not sure, but we could get arrested for indecent exposure."

"Killjoy."

Shayla was still smiling over the conversation and Kevin's fun-loving nature when the clock signaled they'd danced for over thirty-four and a half hours. Limbs were aching and heavy, but her spirit was still high, thanks to her wonderful, funny partner.

"Well, we're down to just one other couple now," Kevin said as the third remaining couple stumbled off the floor to sit down, near Mrs. Avery.

The woman gave them a thumbs up.

"It was a good night."

"I agree." She squeezed his hand. "Thanks for making it fun."

"Any time, darlin'."

Suppressing a yawn, she fought to think of something, anything to keep her mind going. "I'm surprised Kerri and Connor had lasted thirty hours," she said. "And they didn't even practice."

"That you know of," her partner said. "*McMoose* is very competitive. I wouldn't put it past him to have worked in a few sessions with Kerri the past few weeks."

Shayla smiled. Totally seeing the big cowboy doing just that to prepare. "Well, it paid off. They raised some great funds tonight…today. Whatever it is."

With no windows to look outside, she wasn't sure.

"It's six-thirty Sunday evening, my little sleepy head." He led her to a dessert table. "You won't fall down if I let go of you, will you?"

She laughed. "No, I'm not that tired."

"Okay, then will you hold me so I don't fall down?" he asked with a grin, before letting her go to fill up two coffees with lots of sugar, no cream, to keep them going.

They had just finished their coffee and dessert when the McCalls and Masters walked in and gathered by Mrs. Avery. Shayla glanced around. There were a lot of people in the building again. Not on the dance floor, but crowding the other areas, waiting to see who would win.

Her and Kevin.

When a Charlie Daniels song came on, one she'd enjoyed hearing Brandi play many times, Shayla grabbed her partner's hand. "Let's take 'em."

Heat sparked in his eyes and a deep grin spread across his face. "You got it, darlin'."

Forty-seven minutes later, as they danced to one of her favorite ZZ Top songs, it became obvious they had when the female from the other couple slid to the floor. Automatically disqualifying them.

Cheers went up around the room. Connor's hoots and Cole's hollers echoed the crowd.

Kevin picked her up and twirled her around. "We did it," he said, tone happy and sure. "It's ours to lose now, and darlin', that isn't going to happen."

"Folks, settle down. Settle down," the announcer said, trying to quiet the crowd and keep people from rushing the floor. "We only have one couple, you're right, but they still have," the man paused to glance at the clock, "Forty-three minutes to go. Let's give them some space and cheer them on!"

Two waltzes, a tango, jitterbug, a rock ballad, a polka and an Irish jig later, Shayla had her second wind and enjoyed creating some fancy moves with her partner as they danced to an Usher tune. Damn, she loved how her cowboy moved. Heat rushed through her veins and she danced around the guy very close. His moves inspired a need best left for privacy.

Or that bathroom, *up against the wall* scenario.

"Darlin', if you don't stop looking at me like that, I'm going to blow our winning in the final minutes just to get inside you."

Her intake of breath was lost to the cheering around them. "Then stop dancing so sexy."

A lop-sided grin tugged his lips. "I can't. Don't know any other way."

With a little less than eight minutes left, the crowd went wild when *their* Garth Brooks song came on. Everyone was on their feet, clapping, whistling, cheering. Shayla exchanged an excited glance with Kevin.

"Well, darlin', what do you say we give them what they want?"

Feeding off the adrenaline of the crowd, Shayla danced her heart out, and feet off, and even had enough to see her through the final, appropriate song about champions by Queen.

They won. They did it.

And an hour later, after several awards, a big postcard check to the charity head, photos and congratulations from a teary-eyed, grateful Mrs. Avery and all her quilting buddies, their friends and relatives and complete strangers, Shayla was ready to drop. But she sucked it up and managed to walk to Kevin's truck without assistant.

"Well, darlin' I think we earned a sleep in tomorrow," he said, starting his truck.

"I agree." She yawned. "It was nice of your sister to take Amelia tonight for a sleepover with Cody."

He nodded and pulled onto the road, his hand reaching for her thigh. "Yes, because we have one final dance of the night to do to take care of my damn two-day hard on."

Friday afternoon, Amelia's birthday party/barbecue was in full swing at Shadow Rock Ranch. With unseasonably warm temperatures, Cody's request for an outdoor party was granted and Shayla was happy to see the little boy enjoying the party as much as the guest of honor.

"Thank you so much, Cody, for helping me throw Amelia such a great party," she told the little boy.

His chest puffed out and shoulders straightened. "You're welcome. My pleasure," he said with a finger to the tiny black Stetson on his head.

Fighting a grin, she nodded and moved on before her amusement won out.

"You look absolutely beautiful today, Shayla," Kevin said, sneaking up from behind to pull her in close and kiss her neck. "What are my chances of getting you alone to stargaze in my truck later?"

She turned sideways to grin at him. "Is that what they call it now?"

He chuckled. "No, but sometimes it does lead to that."

"Does it? I wouldn't know. I've never stargazed."

Kevin stilled, then twisted her around to face him. "That's not right. We're going to amend that later."

She wrapped her arms around his neck and her heart beats increased when his hands slid to her hips. "I look forward to *stargazing* with you." Leaning in, she kissed him, lingering, enjoying the freedom of not having to worry about offending the others with a public display of affection. Jordan, Kerri, Brandi and Jen all kissed their men plenty of times today. Even the older McCalls and Masters stole a few kisses.

"Mommy, daddy," Amelia chanted, squeezing her way between their legs.

She broke the kiss and laughed with Kevin who bent to lift her daughter.

"What do you want, birthday girl?" he asked, fixing Amelia's frilly, purple dress he'd bought.

How the heck he knew what size to buy, was a mystery. But the man was spot on.

"Horsie," her daughter yelled, pushing to get down, but not before grabbing Kevin's hand. "Horsie!"

Amelia led him to the nearest chair, right between Connor and Cole, and was straddling his leg before he'd even had the chance to fully sit. Shayla bit her lip, but her chuckle must've escaped because he glanced up and narrowed his eyes.

"Laugh it up. You're the one who'll have to rub my knee later."

As serious as possible, Shayla nodded and held his gaze. "No problem. I like rubbing you."

The McCall brother's snorted, while Kevin stilled and his mouth fell open.

"That's a good look on you," she said.

Two for two. She was on a roll.

His opened mouth turned into a lopsided grin as he continued Amelia's horsie ride. "Just remember what they say about payback, Shayla. I'm going to take care of you real good."

Tipping her head, she ignored the snickering brothers watching them like a tennis match and concentrated on Kevin. "I'm counting on it, cowboy."

Sparring was fun. The cowboy challenged, and she said and did some pretty daring things. Relaxing a little more every day, she was opening up, and he seemed to like it. She'd exchanged birthdates, favorite foods, colors, and had a heated discussion about basketball teams, which led to a heated discussion of another kind. A smile tugged her lips at the memory. *Damn*, her man sure could *discuss*.

Desire glittered in his gaze, along with something more. Her pulse kicked up. She liked the *something more*. He made her feel things, and not just physical things or needs with her body, but *heart* needs and wants. The man had touched her everywhere, and in many ways, and her heart was not excluded.

Kevin Dalton was the only one with a key card to her heart. The only one with complete access. So, it was time. Later on, when they were stargazing, she had some truths to share with him.

With one last glance, she turned to find Jordan smiling behind her. Shayla lifted her chin. "Did that about cover it?"

The woman nodded. "Yep. I'd say so. Come on. Brandi, Jen and Kerri are doing jello shots. I think it's time we joined them."

For the next hour, she had a lime and raspberry jello shot and two hallowed out strawberries, rimmed with salt that Kerri filled with a margarita jello mixture. A third one would've been much welcomed, but Shayla didn't want to be too tipsy for her stargazing adventure with Kevin. Wouldn't do for the stars to be spinning overhead. That'd only make her sick, and she wanted to have a heart to heart with him, preferably not from the ground.

After cake, and ice cream and presents, she finally sat down and watched her daughter having the time of her life, playing with the big stuffed moose from Connor and Kerri. Climbing in and out of the outdoor playhouse castle built by Kade and Brandi, which was now a permanent fixture at the Dalton's. It made Shayla feel like maybe she and Amelia were permanent fixtures at the ranch, too.

It was a wonderful feeling.

"She's having a blast," Kevin said, settling onto the bench with her, draping his arm across her shoulder and tugging her in close. "Good thing she's staying over with Cody again tonight. I'm not sure you'd get her to leave."

She was so grateful to Jen and Brock. Her daughter really enjoyed her time with Cody. "Yeah, I think you're right," she admitted, snuggling closer, exactly where she wanted to be. With this man. Loving this man. Forever.

Her heart rocked so hard in her chest she stopped breathing.

She was *in love* with Kevin Dalton.

Breathing returned, but kept catching in her throat. What did she know about love? What if he didn't feel the same? He could have anyone. Why would he love her? Shayla halted the negative thinking. She was worthy of love, and he'd be the first person to tell her that, so there was no room in her head for depressing thoughts.

His grip tightened and warm breath washed over her cheek as he kissed her temple.

"You ready for some of that gazing?"

Shayla glanced up at the sun slowly setting in the sky, then into Kevin's eager gaze. "Whenever you are."

Chapter Eighteen

After the yard was cleaned up and the party proclaimed a success by Cody, Shayla sat next to Kevin in his truck as it bounced over Shadow Rock Ranch. Having only been on the land near the house and stables, she was curious to glimpse some of the raw acreage that made up the property.

"We're almost there," he said, caressing her thigh, drawing little circles with his thumb, the simple movement played havoc with her pulse. "I haven't been out here in the truck in ages."

Her mind immediately wondered how many girls he'd taken to *stargaze*.

"When I was a teenager, there were only three girls I brought out here," he said as if reading her mind.

"Tina?"

He nodded. "But I never brought anyone to this spot." He slowed the truck to a stop then parked near several live oak trees clustered in the middle of an open field. "You're the first," he said, turning in his seat to caress her cheek. "And the last."

Hope beat loud and strong in her ears. She drew in a breath and smiled. "I'm glad," she said, covering his hand on her cheek.

Slowly, he lowered his mouth to hers and kissed her so achingly sweet her heart was full to bursting with all the emotion in the embrace. When he pulled back, he placed soft kisses from her mouth to her temple. She returned the caress.

"If we hurry, we can still catch the sunset." Grabbing her hand, he kissed her knuckles. "Wait here while I fix the back." Then he was out of the cab and in the back, moving blankets and unrolling sleeping bags and stacking pillows.

Her heart raced at how romantic everything was, and she longed to lay down and open up her heart to him under the vast night sky.

"Okay," he said, reappearing to take her hand and walk with her to the back of the truck.

She sat on the tailgate and removed her shoes with him, then she crawled on all fours onto the sleeping bag, smiling at his soft curse and low groan about killing him. A second later, he was behind her, settled his back against the cab and her against his side.

"What do you think?"

Breath caught in her throat as the sun slowly set, streaking the horizon with a blaze of orange before eventually fading into pink, purple then dark blue. "Perfect," she whispered.

His arms tightened around her a second before he shifted and she found herself flat on her back staring up into his eyes as he leaned on an elbow. "Agreed." He lightly brushed the hair off her forehead, then lowered his mouth to her temple and placed more of those killer soft kisses over her eyes, her nose, her cheek, as if kissing her freckles before finding the corner of her mouth.

She sighed, lifting a hand to cup his face, brushing his temple with her thumb as his lips conveyed such sweet emotion her throat burned. There was a lot she wanted to say, to reveal, to share, but his lips were drugging, and need was beginning to take over. His kiss was changing, heating, deepening while he slipped a hand under her shirt to stroke her belly, ribs, over her bra, then yes, peeled back the lace and brushed over her nipple. Shayla moaned, and arched up into his hand, needing more, feeling more.

He broke the kiss and pressed his lips to her throat, zeroing in on the hot spot behind her ear. She gasped and clutch at him, lost in sensations and racing pulse and building need. Her hands went to his shirt and began to unbutton. "Too much clothes."

"Agreed," he said against her collarbone, then sat back on his knees to shed his shirt, heat blazing in his eyes as he watched her rip hers over her head. Then he stood, and with economical movements, removed his jeans, boxer briefs and socks.

Trying to keep up, she unbuttoned and unzipped her jeans, then stilled at the sight of him standing naked above her, a possessive, heated expression etched on his face, the setting sun bronzing his skin, casting shadows over the ridges she longed to lick and explore. He was magnificent. Her whole body heated at once, and she went to stand to finish undressing, but he shook his head and dropped to his knees.

"No," he said, pressing her onto her back with a hand before he moved to kneel between her legs. "Let me." He grasped her waistband and tugged her jeans, sucking in a breath when he saw her baby blue thong. "Gorgeous," he murmured, putting his mouth on her, his lips and heated breath tickling her center. Her eyes fluttered closed as she clutched the blankets and moaned.

Then he was tugging them down, along with her jeans, and she opened her eyes and lifted up on her elbows to watch him finish pulling them off before removing her socks. A lacey blue bra the only scrap of clothing between them, she sat up and reached behind to unhook the barrier. Despite the diminishing daylight, her gaze remained glued to his, heartbeats rocking hard in her chest at the hunger she could still see smoldering in his eyes as he watched her breasts bounce free.

He inhaled. "So beautiful," he said, crawling up her body, nudging her down on the blankets, pinning her with his weight. *Heaven was Kevin Dalton on top of her*. Shayla was sure of it. Everything was so clear out in the peaceful wide open space. She could hear her heart speak. Hear her heart yearn, and it yearned for Kevin to yearn for hers back. He already owned it.

With the moon rising in the sky, illuminating their little love nest, she lifted her hand to trace his jaw. "I'm yours, Kevin," she said, as he hovered near her mouth, gaze inches from hers. "All yours."

Joy and satisfaction mixed to brighten his gaze. "Good, because I love you, Shayla," he said, brushing her cheek with the back of his knuckles as he stared deep into her eyes that were suddenly burning with unshed tears.

She blinked and stared at him, hardly daring to breathe. "You do?"

"Yes." He smiled, so tender, so sweet, more tears appeared and slid down the side of her face.

"I love you, too, Kevin. I never dreamed y—"

He stilled. "You do?"

"Yes. So much."

A brilliant smile crossed his face, and he leaned down and kissed her lips with all the feelings he's just professed. Shayla kissed him back, showing him, telling him she felt the same. This time, they weren't going to have sex. This time, they were going to make love.

But as his hands slipped into her hair, and she gripped his back, she realized they'd been making love for a long time now. When exactly the sex had stopped, she wasn't sure, only that it had been before the Dance-a-Thon, before he'd gone to Seattle, before they agreed to try a relationship.

He broke the kiss and buried his face in her neck. "So beautiful," he murmured, brushing the spot behind her ear again. She sucked in a breath, dug her fingers into his back and ground helplessly against him.

His attention shifted to her collarbone, both breasts, then lingered on her nipples. She pressed closer to him, the mounting pressure making her desperate for relief.

"I'm going to take care of you real good," he said, reminding her of their sparring earlier. He lifted his gaze to her, and heaven help her, it was hot and mischievous and almost did her in.

Lowering back down, he kissed her belly button, nipped at her hip, then pushed her thighs up. "*Real* good," he murmured again, breath tickling her sensitive skin.

She gripped the blanket and squeezed her eyes closed at the heat and need rushing through her body. He grasped her hips and kissed an inner thigh, rough stubble scraping her skin in exquisite torture. She could barely breathe.

"I need…"

"I know," he said against the other thigh, kissing and scraping until she moaned. Then he kissed in between. And traced with a finger. Shayla cried out his name.

"I got you," he said against her.

Her heart was pounding hard in her chest as she rocked up to meet his light kisses. She was hot and shuddering, and he was right at her core. Then he took her into his mouth and added two fingers, sending her to a shattering climax that had her seeing stars. As she slowly came back down, she realized the stars were real, her eyes were open and she was staring up at the brilliant night sky.

"Your taste is addicting," he muttered with one last lap, then she watched him sit back and roll on a condom.

Sweat glistened off his skin, and his blue eyes were deliciously hot and needy and fierce. She shivered in anticipation as he held her gaze, entwined their fingers near her head and slid into her in one long, deep thrust. Their murmurs of approval mingled in the air as their bodies connected. Hearts connected. Souls connected.

He lowered himself onto his forearms, and Shayla had never been so close, so linked, so bonded to anyone before. She felt his heart beating. Felt him breathe. Felt him loving her with each slow, pulling movement. He gently kissed her eyes, cheek and mouth as if she was his world.

He was everything to her. All she'd dared to dream of. Desired. Hope for.

And all the hardships she'd ever faced, faded to the background. She was blessed.

Blessed with Kevin.

He lifted his head, gaze dark with hunger and emotion, and as he drew nearly all the way out then pushed in to the hilt, she fought to keep her eyes open. She wanted to hold his smoldering gaze, see everything revealed in his eyes, and reveal all she felt in hers.

She gasped, squeezing his hands, rocking her hips to meet his increased thrusts. Their breathing mingled, hard and ragged, and everything began to fade as the need and hunger took over.

Nothing mattered. The world didn't matter. Their past didn't matter. Only the here and now. "I love you,

Kevin," she whispered, empowered by the fierce emotion lighting his eyes.

"I love you, too," he said, dipping down to kiss her long and deep, his tongue mimicking their thrusting bodies, driving her wild.

She wrapped her legs around his hips, forcing him in deliciously deeper.

Releasing her mouth, he let out a low, sexy sound and drove in and out of her in a rhythm that had her calling out his name as she spiraled and burst into a million stars, and he followed with her name on his lips.

The next day, Shayla was pitching in to help with the renovations on the stable at Shadow Rock Ranch, stealing glances at a certain blue-eyed cowboy working, shirtless, *hello*, putting in posts for a new corral. Side-by-side with the other cowboys, the man captured her attention and tripped her pulse with his black hair, trim muscles, lean hips and long legs.

Their time under the stars had been eye-opening, incredible, memorable, and continued back at the ranch, when they'd snuck into his room and made love well into the early morning hours. Shayla felt new, whole, *complete* for the first time in her life. It was amazing, and she couldn't keep from smiling.

"There she goes again, Brandi. What'd you do, give her a raise?" Jordan joked as the women painted a new break room area for future volunteers.

No, but Kevin did. She snickered and her friends smiled as if knowing.

"I think that expression is courtesy of my soon-to-be cousin-in-law over there," her boss replied, motioning out the window toward the Daltons, McCalls and Kade's guard buddies. Brandi blinked then straightened, her intake of breath echoing around them. "Damn."

Yeah, damn. Over ten hard-bodied cowboys and National Guardsmen all shirtless, all swinging hammers, sledge hammers or lifting posts. It was muscle-flexing heaven.

"Okay, I'm ordering a break. Right now. At the window," Brandi stated, walking across the room for a better look.

Shayla set her brush down on a lid and eagerly joined the smiling women. "Pass the popcorn."

Her boss chuckled. "Amen."

"Pass the hose," Jordan said, and they fell into a companionable silence, each, no doubt, lost in a fantasy involving hoses and their hot cowboy. "Damn, now I need that hose," her friend said.

"Amen," Brandi repeated and Shayla echoed, glancing at her phone for the time.

Still another hour to go. She eyed the half-painted wall. Doable. And a goal. Finish the wall, then she can concentrate on Kevin.

Two hours later, after enjoying leftovers from Amelia's birthday barbecue, Shayla sat with Kevin on the porch swing at Shadow Rock, contentment washing over her again. She never thought she could be this happy. And she'd probably feel even better once she told him about Amelia's father.

"Care to share the reason behind that sigh?" he asked, arm around her, pulling her in close.

She lifted her head off his shoulder and turned to gaze into his eyes, loving the affection and heat that always seem to be there. He was no longer holding back either. It felt good. She hoped the truth didn't ruin anything. Hoped he didn't think less of her for her dishonesty. She knew how it cut him to the bone with Tina. "I'm just happy."

"Me, too." He smiled and kissed her lips, running his tongue over her bottom one, making her moan.

The familiar haze began to cloud her mind, but she wanted to get this off her chest. She drew back and blinked at him. "Hold on there, cowboy. I'd like to talk to you about something, and I get sidetracked when you kiss me." Yesterday was proof positive of that.

Reluctance and a little bit of apprehension furrowed his brow when he nodded. "Okay. What about?"

She blew out a breath, and tried to decide the right words. *So, about Amelia's dad.* No. *Amelia's dad is a Casanova cowboy.* Nope. Her chest rose and fell with another sigh.

A warm hand settled over her knotted fingers resting on her lap. "Hey, it's okay, darlin'. Whatever it is, you know you can tell me anything."

With her pulse pounding in her ears, she nodded and forced herself to talk. "Remember when I overheard you talking to Kade about Tina and your baby?"

Pain flittered through his gaze as he stiffened. "No... You heard that?"

Complete confusion and worry darkened his eyes. He withdrew his hand and vaulted to his feet.

Dammit, she was screwing this up big time. *Idiot.* She jumped up and raised a hand to touch his stiff back, but slowly lowered it instead. "Yeah, I did. Sorry...I just didn't know how to bring it up."

He twisted around to face her, anger darkening his gaze. "You just open your mouth and talk. Say something like, oh, I don't know...*Hey, Kevin, I heard you and Kade talking about Tina and your baby.*"

Her chin lifted. "Well, I did hear, and I…felt bad for you. So bad, Kevin."

His jaw clenched and eyes momentarily closed. When they opened, they held a little less anger. "Did you hear Kade ask me if I was using you and Amelia as substitutes?"

She swallowed and nodded.

"And…?" His dark gaze was intense. No softening, no warmth. Nothing.

"You said no, and I believed you. Trusted you," she answered. "I would never have gotten involved with you otherwise. Surely you see that?"

He ran a hand through his hair and exhaled. "Right now, I don't know what to believe. What else haven't you told me? What else haven't you been honest about?"

"Bobby wasn't Amelia's father," she blurted.

He reeled back, brows raised as he stared at her. "He's not?"

"No. Her father is a Casanova cowboy. A jerk I was with one time, right after Lyle…" she let out another breath and shook her head. "Doesn't matter. His name is Brandon. I tracked him down after I found out I was pregnant. He shoved money in my hand, told me he wasn't daddy material and to take care of it."

Kevin's jaw cracked so loud it echoed around them. "Bastard."

She nodded.

"Is that why you didn't want anything to do with me at first?"

She nodded again. "Yeah. I was completely cured of gorgeous, self-centered cowboys. But it soon became obvious you weren't one." She grabbed his hand and squeezed.

He didn't squeeze back. "Did Bobby know?"

She let go of his hand and frowned. "Yes. Of course. I…Oh, hey, no, I didn't try to trap him if that's what you're getting at."

Kevin shrugged, gaze no longer open. She had no idea what he was thinking now.

"Bobby already had me down as his beneficiary because he didn't have any family. And when he found out I was pregnant, he insisted we claimed he was the father—that way the birth would be covered under his guard healthcare, and then the baby would be too once she was born." Memories of that conversation, as plain as day, brought back with it the loss of her friend. "He was always looking out for me." She blinked back a round of tears.

"You need to tell Kade." Kevin grabbed her arm and pulled her toward the empty stable where Brandi and Kade disappeared after supper.

Halting at the edge of the porch, Shayla tugged him to a stop. "Wait. I already did."

Kevin blinked at her. "You did?"

"Of course." She released him and folded her arms across her chest. "Once I realized the trouble Kade was having over Bobby's death, I told him."

"Oh," he said, face not quite as pinched.

"He's the only one who knows, besides you and Caitlin." She reached out to lightly touch his arm, testing the waters. He moved away to lean against a post and stare out at…anything that wasn't her. "I'm sorry, Kevin. I didn't want you to be hurt." She wasn't sure why this would hurt him, except for showing her dishonest side. "Amelia's dad was the only thing I've ever been dishonest to you about."

He glanced at her then, gaze narrowing. "Unless you're being dishonest now. Hell, I don't even know your actual name."

Closing her eyes, she fought back more tears. This was what she'd been afraid of. That he would never believe anything she said again. Opening her eyes, she held his gaze and swallowed past the lump in her throat.

"It's Shannon. My mom's name was Kayla. I combined the two."

His chin lifted slightly, acknowledging he'd heard her, but he remained silent, waiting.

"Shannon is dead. Too dangerous; has too many bad memories. It's not me. I'm Shayla. The same Shayla you said you loved," she reminded, voice tight and low, pinched with pain. "And I'm not lying now. It's one of those things you'd have to trust me on, Kevin. Like *me* trusting *you* when you told Kade you're not using Amelia and I as substitutes."

His jaw cracked again and he ground out, "I'm not."

She nodded. "And I believe you."

Why couldn't he believe her? Shayla held his gaze, begging him, imploring him to say something. Do something. Show her it was going to be okay.

Tell her he believed her, too.

He shoved a hand through his hair again, and did neither. "I hate dishonesty, Shayla. I hate it," he said, voice low and rough, full of all the hurt and pain she'd never intended. "I'm going for a ride. I need to think. Go home. I don't know when I'll be back."

And without waiting for a reply, the blue-eyed cowboy strode to the barn, back ramrod straight, gait stiff, carrying the weight of the world on his shoulders and her broken, bleeding heart in his hand.

It was Sunday morning, and after forcing herself to get out of bed, Shayla somehow ended up walking the beach near Brandi's cottage, shoes in hand, reaching for her phone for the bazillionth time. She pulled the cell from her jeans. No messages. No missed calls. *Super*.

Since Jen, bless her, had sensed something was wrong and suggested she let Amelia stay there another night, she was free to mope at will. The urge to just stay in bed, staring at the ceiling as she had most of the night—interrupted by bouts of crying and exhausted sleep—had been strong, but she was stubborn.

She hadn't really done anything wrong to Kevin. *Dammit*. And she had told him the truth about Ameila's dad before he found out from someone else. Plus, she hadn't done anything wrong where Amelia's dad was concerned, either—she'd contacted Brandon to let him know he was going to be a father, which was a hell of a lot more than Tina had done with Kevin. Those were all good things, very good things, she reasoned, picking her way through the dunes and sea grass back to the path that lead to the boardwalk near The Creamery.

If she just gave him a little time, she was fairly certain Kevin would come around. He would see she was nothing like Tina. He would remember how she'd shown him trust and would show her the same courtesy.

God she hoped so.

The empty, desolate, heavy feeling squeezing her chest was too unbearable. It hurt to think. So she didn't. To eat. So she didn't. To breathe. *Okay*, that she had no choice. But it still hurt.

Coming off the path and onto the boardwalk, she stomped the sand off her feet. Even dried, it stuck to her toes. Wouldn't let go. Kind of like the dire feeling in her gut. But she refused to think about it. Everything was going to be okay. It had to.

Kneeling, she brushed the sand away with her hand, feeling a little more optimistic. Today was a good day to set things straight. To get everything out in the open. To resolve issues. If he just gave her a chance.

She slipped her feet back into her running shoes when a shadow fell across her path. Her heart rocked in her chest. *Kevin.* He came to talk.

Straightening, her euphoria died an instant death as icy cold fingers of fear gripped every molecule in her body at once.

"Hello, Shannon. Or should I call you *Shayla*?"

Frozen in the mid-March sun, she fought to keep her scream inside.

Chapter Nineteen

Kevin felt like shit.

Lost. Confused. Hurt. And knowing he caused Shayla to suffer the same only made him feel worse. Working with his cousin and Cole on the south section of the corral for the old barn, he thought the physical labor would help alleviate frustration and pave the way for clear thinking.

Bullshit.

Now he was hot, tired and dirty. And his head and muscles ached. All right, lack of sleep probably didn't help, but nothing was working. His *mind-palace* was still a damn mess.

His chest hurt. Even breathing hurt.

And breakfast that morning with Amelia asking for her mommy? *Pure hell.* Kevin had never experienced a pain so consuming and deep, he'd even gone into the bathroom to glance in the mirror to make sure nothing was lodged in his chest.

He didn't like it. The pain, the feeling, it had to stop.

That's the reason he was at the corral whacking the shit out of a post with a sledgehammer, the percussion rippling up his arms, vibrating through his aching shoulders.

"I think it's in far enough," Cole said, then chuckled at his own joke. "I seem to recall my brother saying that to me when I was having trouble two years ago with the *girl vortex* as he puts it."

Since there wasn't much he could say to that statement, Kevin kept quiet and whacked the post again.

He knew his buddy sensed a problem. *Hell*, so did Kade. His cousin gave him the *First Sergeant* stare all morning. Detecting. Dissecting, whatever the hell the Guardsman did with his recruits to keep them happy and on an even keel.

Kevin *was* off keel. So far off keel his damn ship was sinking and fast. But he didn't see how the guys could help.

"It helps to talk, buddy."

Apparently, Cole thought different.

"Yeah, keeping things bottled up is bad, trust me, cuz."

And so did Kade.

His cousin cupped his shoulder while his buddy removed the sledgehammer from his other hand. Apparently, they were going to talk.

Fine.

"I don't like dishonesty."

The guys exchanged a look then glanced back at him.

"Okay," Cole said slowly. "What does it have to do with Shayla?"

"That's not even her real name."

"It is her legal one," Kade said, voice as stern as his gaze. "You know the reason she changed it."

Yeah, he did. And he was being stupid.

Kade's phone rang. "Yeah? I'll send him over." He hung up and glanced at Cole. "Your brother needs some help with the drill you brought today and said something about more lumber. He's at the empty stable."

Nodding, his buddy set the post-hole digger against the last post they'd secured, then stepped to him. "Nobody is perfect, Kevin. And we all make mistakes. Even geniuses. This is a good time for me to recite the advice you gave me two years ago." Making a production of clearing his throat, Cole placed a hand on his shoulder and cocked his head. "Get the fuck over yourself."

Kade chuckled.

"Remember telling me that?"

He smiled. "Yeah. I do. It was good advice, too. Once you got over yourself and your fears, your preconceived ideas, you saw things clearly and ended up getting the girl."

"All good reasons to take your own advice." His buddy patted his shoulder, nodded to a smiling Kade, then headed for the stable.

Kevin shook his head, watching his friend make his way across the corral. "That man is seriously too happy."

"Beats how he was before the advice."

His cousin's simple statement sobered Kevin real fast. True. Cole hadn't been pleasant. Yeah, he definitely didn't miss that Cole. He'd been a bitch to work for, too.

"So, now that we're alone. You want to tell me what's really bothering you?"

He glanced at Kade and he shrugged. "Shayla told me about Amelia's dad."

Dawning filtered through his cousin's gray eyes and his chin lifted. "She must trust you."

Ah hell.

Kevin's gut twisted. Not the response he'd expected. His guilt intensified and gnawed like frenzy of cockroaches on a stack of wood.

Kade frowned at him, gaze troubled. "Ah, Kev, what did you say?"

"Not much. Just that I needed to think."

"About what? She's not Tina."

He winced.

"What's that look for? Did you tell her about Tina?"

"Not really." He shook his head. "But apparently, she overheard us talking in the kitchen that time she had dinner here after Houston."

Houston. Hot. Decadent. Mind-blowing. *Cripes*, that seemed like a lifetime ago.

"What did she overhear? My concern about you using them as substitutes?"

"Yeah." He nodded.

"Does she think you are?"

He shook his head again. "No."

His cousin tipped his head and studied him. "And why does she think that?"

"Because I told her I wasn't."

"And she believed you."

"Yeah."

"But you don't believe her."

"Yeah…I mean, no. I mean. *Ah hell*, Kade. I don't know what the hell I mean anymore." Kevin tossed his hands up and began to pace. He was antsy and apprehensive and out of whack.

His cousin leaned back against the finished fence and folded his arms. "How did you two even get on the subject of Amelia's father?"

"She just came right out and told me."

Kade whistled and ran a hand through his short hair. "Oh, man."

Yeah, now that he thought about it, that admission was a huge step for her…and he just pulled the proverbial rug out from under her feet.

Shit.

"I'm not sure you understand just how much she trusted you, Kevin."

"What do you mean?"

"What she did, lying about Bobby being the father was wrong. And she could get in a lot of trouble if anyone found out. Arrested for fraud. Put in jail. Have her daughter taken away."

With each word his cousin uttered, Kevin's stomach tightened.

"Kev, she risked everything to tell me last year. She didn't have to. No one made her, but she did it on her own because she hated the thought of me thinking..." Kade paused to shove another hand through his hair and blew out a breath. "Anyway, point is, I could've turned her ass in."

He snorted. "You'd never do that."

"But she had no idea. She risked it. For me."

Kevin's throat was hot and tight and something large was smack in the middle making swallowing damn hard.

"She's a good person, cuz. One who has been through *hell*. But you know all this," Kade said. "Don't use her two times at dishonesty—which, I might add, were *both* in order to keep people she loved, safe—don't use those as an excuse to walk away because you're in uncharted waters, vulnerable. I nearly made that stupid mistake with Brandi. But I realized it's okay to give up control once in awhile, let someone help you, walk beside you. Trust me, you'll enjoy the journey much more. So, I'll ask you again. What is really bothering you?"

Never could pull one over on the guy. Especially when *Sgt. Hardass* was in the building. Or in this case. The corral.

Taking a deep breath, he shared his deepest fear. "What if I let her down, too?"

"Kevin, you've never let anyone down."

"Oh, you are so wrong, cuz." He laughed without mirth. "I've let *everyone* down that has counted on me. I let them down, and now they're dead."

Kade sucked in a deep breath, held it a few beats then released it slowly as his hands clamped around Kevin's shoulders, two five-fingered vises. "In no way, shape or form did you let your mom or dad down."

"Wrong." He shook his head. Hell, his whole body shook. "I didn't finish the puzzle," he said, knocking his fisted knuckles off his temple. "I didn't get the code completed for the machine before she died."

"Kevin, she developed the problem when you were just a baby. The scanner would've had to have been created back then."

He knew this to be true, but it still cut deep. The medical scanner he helped create could've saved his mother's life three decades ago. Nothing he could do about it now, not without a time machine. Maybe he'd work on that next. He tried to smile at his attempt at humor, but not even a spark appeared.

"I know," he replied, moving out of his cousin's grip. "But I am responsible for my dad's death. I was the one who neglected to exercise the horse that morning. *I* should've been thrown. Not dad. He picked up *my* slack and died for it. Don't tell me it wasn't my fault, Kade, 'cause we both know it was."

Not something he'd ever forget or forgive, and his cousin needed to realize this and drop it.

"Look, Kev, I understand. I do. I understand your guilt. I don't agree with it, but I do understand it," Kade acknowledged. "I know I didn't kill Sgt. Nylan. But, he died under my command."

A tough pill for anyone to swallow. It killed Kevin to know his compassionate cousin struggled with this issue daily.

"I'm responsible for all my soldiers," Kade continued. "I gave out orders. He followed them and got killed. I didn't kill him, but it's my fault he's dead, because I ordered him to do that duty. You see?" He stepped close, gaze haunted, yet resolute. "I feel the guilt, too, Kevin. I will always live with it, but I won't let it rule me. I won't let it stop me from living. Don't let it stop you."

If his cousin could use that advice to move on, to live life and be happy, then maybe he could, too.

Throat hot and tight, he cleared it. "I won't." He hugged his cousin and slapped him on the back. "I promise."

"Then maybe you have a phone call you need to make?"

Feeling foolish and remorseful, he blew out a breath and nodded. "Yeah. Hope she doesn't hate me."

"Nah, that woman loves you," Kade said, picking up the sledgehammer to whack the last post they'd placed. "We can all see it, just as we can see you love her, have for a while now."

It was on the tip of Kevin's tongue to deny it, but then he realized Kade was right. His feelings for the woman were deep, going back before he first proposed they try making it a go at their relationship. His love for the redhead was what planted the idea in his head in the first place. That, and the fact he couldn't live without her.

Cripes, he was such an idiot.

Unsure what he'd even say to her, he pulled out his phone anyway and called her, knowing to at least start with an apology. But he didn't get the chance to tell her because she didn't answer. Could she still be sleeping? He glanced at the time. No. It was one in the afternoon. Unless she tossed all night like him. Probably.

Just in case she had the phone off so she could sleep, he sent her a quick text.

SORRY. I'M AN IDIOT. PLEASE CALL ME.

After a few seconds went by and there was no answer, his heart started to feel squished. He tried a few more. And called again.

Nothing.

Damn, she didn't skip town, did she?

His head snapped up and he glanced at Kade. "Amelia's still here, right?"

"What?" His cousin frowned. "Yeah, I think so, why? What's wrong?" He dropped the hammer and was in front of him in a second.

"I've called and texted several times, and there's no response." He dragged air into his lungs and asked a tough question, "Do you think she's so mad at me she's not answering, or do you think there's a problem?"

"One way to find out." Kade pulled out his phone, called, texted.

No response.

In a flash, Kevin hopped the fence and ran like hell to his truck. His cousin was right behind him, phone to his ear, giving orders to his deputy, then he made another call. "Caitlin? It's Sheriff Dalton. I'm calling to check in with you. Good. Is Shayla there with you? No?"

Shit.

Kevin's heart felt as if pinched in the jaws of life. Shayla was his life. Why hadn't he realized it before his *idiot of the year* entry? When he reached his truck with Kade in tow, the McCall brother's dropped the wood they'd been carrying and rushed over, concern darkening their gazes.

"I'm not sure," his cousin told Caitlin. "No. Kevin is right here. She's not answering her phone. I need you to go to wherever your designated safe place is right now and wait for my call. Okay? Good. I will. Okay. Bye."

"What's going on?" Cole bounced his gaze between them.

"Shayla's not answering our calls or texts." Kevin grabbed his friend's shoulders. "You don't know where she is, do you?"

"No. Sorry."

He released him and glanced at Connor.

"No clue," the giant replied. "Do you want me to call Kerri and ask her to go up to the apartment?"

"No," Kade rushed to say. "No. I'm not sure it's safe. Jordan's on her way there now."

Feeling as if someone was ripping the heart out of his chest with a barbecue tong, Kevin stared at his cousin. "Did *she* try calling?"

Kade swallowed and nodded. "No response."

Muttering a curse, he willed the pounding in his head to cease until he realized his pulse was thundering, making the racket. "That son-of-a-bitch is in town."

"You don't know for sure," Cole tried to reassure, but his gaze was full of the apprehension prickling Kevin's spine.

"He's here. And Shayla's in danger." Because of him. *Dammit.* "I shouldn't have been such an idiot. She would've been here if I hadn't—"

"Cut it. You have no control over her dad," Kade barked. "Thoughts like that will not help you right now."

Connor stepped close. "What will?"

"Yeah, name it," Cole stated.

"I need you both to stay here and guard Amelia. At the first sign of trouble get her out of here."

"What about everyone else?" Connor asked.

"I'm going to take care of that now," Kade said and rushed to his guard buddies working near the old stable.

Through all of it, Kevin kept texting. No response.

Once again, he screwed up. Let someone he loved down. But *dammit,* Shayla was not going to die as a result. He couldn't stand…air funneled into his lungs as he inhaled deep.

"It'll be all right, buddy. Jordan and Kade know what they're doing," his friend reassured, and Kevin marveled at how calm Cole was considered his wife might have to put herself in harm's way in order to help Shayla.

He had a new appreciation for the hell Brandi and Cole went through whenever their significant other was on duty, or the phone rang, or a siren went off.

Growing impatient by the second, Kevin watched his cousin, willing him to hurry the hell up so they could leave. He needed to get to Shayla. To find her. Make sure she was safe.

The designer walked out of the stable, brow creasing as she headed for the workers gathered around Kade. Kevin noted how the crowd broke apart and his cousin stepped to Brandi and said something before opening his arms and holding the frightened woman tight.

That's all he wanted to do. He just wanted to hold Shayla. Wanted another chance. *Please God let her be safe…*

Kevin's insides were already so knotted it was a miracle he wasn't stooped over. He needed to go. Time was wasting. He had to find Shayla. Help her. His stomach pitched. *If anything happened to her…*

Grimacing, he sucked in a mouthful of air and fought off the bout of nausea.

Kade approached at a fast clip with Brandi following with equal speed. She stopped to stand with the McCalls, face pale and worried. Cole draped an arm around her and gave Kevin a reassuring nod.

"Ready, Kev?" his cousin asked.

"Yes." He fell into step. "I was just about to leave without you."

Kade stopped and turned to face him. "If you're going to go off half-cocked then stay here. You'll do Shayla more harm than good." Two hands clamped on Kevin's shoulders as a set of steel gray eyes held his gaze. "What's it going to be?"

"Let's go."

"My vehicle," Kade stated, motioning to his SUV.

Muttering a curse, he turned and rushed around to the passenger side then climbed in. "This isn't the time to play who's the better driver."

"It's not that," his cousin stated, starting the car, nodding toward the glove compartment. "My gun's not in your truck."

Kevin's already nauseous stomach lurched at the thought of guns involved anywhere near Shayla.

Kade glanced at him before racing down the drive. "How you holding up?"

"I'm good," he lied through his teeth, willing the five mile drive to be over in ten seconds.

His cousin nodded, then reached into his pocket to pull out his ringing phone. "What'd you find?"

Breathing through a tight chest, while not impossible, wasn't easy. Kevin found if he took short breathes the tightness loosened a little. And the ringing in his ears subsided enough for him to hear the rest of his cousin's conversation.

"Wait for me. Okay." Kade ended the call and glanced at him again. "That was Jordan. Shayla wasn't home."

"And?"

"What do you mean?"

"Look, I might be freaking out over the fact the woman I love is in harm's way, but I'm not stupid, Kade. Your tone dropped several octaves and your grip is a lot whiter on the wheel."

His cousin studied him a second, then nodded. "The apartment was ransacked."

The son-of-a-bitch does have her.

Chapter Twenty

It was taking all of Shayla's control to keep from running. She knew that would not help. Her priorities were clear. Keep everyone safe. Her daughter, her sister, friends, strangers, everyone. She eyed her father. He'd lost weight since their last encounter a year ago. Actually, he hadn't looked too good then either. But he was worse now. Gaunt features, sunken eyes. Hard living had caught up to him. Or karma. But probably cancer. He'd always been a chain-smoker. Yeah, he would be easy to outrun. As long as he wasn't packin. But the brick wall with legs, striped suit, dark glasses? Paid muscle. She did not need to be body-checked by that guy.

Instead of panicking, Shayla was going to do this smart. Amelia was safe. From what she could tell by her father's chatter the past ten minutes as they sat at an outdoor table at The Creamery and ate ice cream as if everything was normal, he had no clue where Caitlin was either. Two huge weights off her shoulders. If it was just herself she needed to worry about, this was a no-brainer.

There were several people at the window ordering ice cream, three tables were taken, plus theirs, leaving two empty as well as several benches. A few families sat on blankets under the trees at the small park to her right and the boardwalk behind her was busy with foot traffic from people enjoying the warm spring morning.

For now, her father was playing nice, throwing the bull, trying to blend in and not draw attention to himself, but what he didn't realize was the brick wall in a suit with dark glasses stood out like a sore thumb. Several people were giving their table some strange looks.

God, she hoped someone dialed 911.

The owner's niece, Holly, kept glancing her way as she waited on customers, but with the two men constantly watching Shayla's every move, she had yet to signal for help. She was also trying to figure how to get her hand on her phone in her jeans without Lyle or *the Wall* noticing. It was on silent, but kept vibrating. In her heart, she knew it was Kevin. *Oh, how she wished she was with him now.* She wanted so bad to answer, but knew her phone would end up in the trash if it saw daylight. Hopefully, whoever it was figured out something was wrong and called Kade. And Caitlin. And would alert Jen to keep Amelia safe.

"That was some dancing you did with that cowboy for charity, Shannon. It made the news," her father said between spoonfuls of ice cream. "Shame you couldn't do that for a living."

"Go to hell."

From her right, a large hand clamped around her wrist and squeezed. "Show your father some respect," The Wall threatened.

The longer she remained silent, the harder he squeezed. Pain shot out in all directions, but she clenched her jaw and refused to give either of them the satisfaction of crying out.

"I'd do what Bruno says, or he's liable to snap your arm like a twig," her father warned between mouthfuls.

"Hi, Shayla. How is everything?" Holly asked, stopping at the table, polite expression on her face.

Bruno immediately released her wrist, and she casually dropped her hands to her lap. The pain lessened to a dull throbbing, enough for her to fish out her phone and redial the last caller. She hoped. With luck, whoever it had been would hear the conversation and call the sheriff.

"Everything is fine, thanks," she finally replied, bringing her hands back up to the table.

"I noticed you haven't touched much of your ice cream. Was there something wrong with it?"

She shook her head. "No. Just busy talking," she said, noticing the woman glance at her red wrist. The one she usually ate with, that was starting to really throb. Using her left hand, she grabbed the spoon and managed to get some ice cream in her mouth without dripping any. "Mmm...delicious as always."

Holly smiled, then bounced her gaze between the men. "How about you gentlemen, is everything all right?"

"Yes, very good. Thank you," her father replied, cordial smile on his face, the one right before he did something awful.

"All right, well if there's anything else I can get for you, just let me know," Holly said before walking back inside the building.

Shayla released a silent sigh of relief. The last thing she wanted was to bring Holly into the mess. She had no doubt, if it had been less crowded, that's exactly what would've happened.

"Glad to see you play that smart, Shannon." Lyle nodded. "I would hate to see anyone get hurt because of you."

Relief flooded her body when she saw the woman dialing a phone. She had no idea of knowing if her redial attempt had worked. This way, she just doubled the odds of finding help. Now she just needed to keep the men from noticing, and pray Holly had dialed the sheriff.

"Look, Lyle," she said, pushing her barely touched, triple chocolate delight out of the way with her left hand. "Let's cut the crap. Why are you here?"

"What? Can't a father see his daughter and granddaughter?"

"Sure, but you're no father."

He held a hand over his heart and grimaced. "Oh, you wound me."

She'd liked to wound him. Up over the head with a chair, grab her baby girl and her sister and never look back. Her heart lurched at the image of a certain blue-eyed cowboy. She couldn't leave him.

"What do you want?"

"What I always want, money."

"Then get a job like everyone else."

She didn't see the backhand coming, but she felt it, teeth rattling from the forceful blow to the side of her face. A hot stinging spread out above her left eye, from his stupid gold pinky ring, no doubt.

Bastard.

He pushed a napkin in her hand. "Take care of that. Can't have you bleeding and drawing attention to yourself."

Yeah, because hitting her in public certainly hadn't.

Shayla dabbed at her eye, telling herself to hang in there a few more minutes. The sheriff was coming. Someone was coming. She could feel it.

"I don't have money."

"Sure you do," he replied, pointing his spoon at her. "You've been holding out on me."

"The death benefit is paying for my sister's college and eventually for my daughter's, too."

A sly smile slicked across his mouth. "Oh, I'm not talking about that, honey. That's nothing. Why settle for a tomato when you can have the whole vine."

Her heart slammed in her throat. "What are you talking about?"

But she knew. She knew by the devious glint in his eyes.

"Your billionaire boyfriend, of course."

She forced her features to remain calm and her voice to remain cool. "I don't have a boyfriend."

Which was sort of true. After yesterday, she wasn't sure. She just hoped, after today, she had the chance to find out.

"Don't lie to me," he hissed. "You're no better than your bitch of a mother."

Before her mind had the chance to tell her it was a bad idea, Shayla hauled off and kicked him square in the shin. He cried out, and several people glanced in their direction. The Wall grabbed her sore arm again, and this time she couldn't stop the painful gasp from escaping her throat.

Things were getting out of hand. Her family might not directly be in harm's way, but she still didn't want to see anyone else get hurt. Lyle knew this, the bastard, and would definitely use one of the innocent people of Harland County as leverage to make her do what he wanted. That's why he'd chosen this spot.

"Now, behave and we might return you to your boyfriend in one piece," her father threatened, bending down to rub his leg. "*After* he pays a hefty sum, of course."

Shayla wrenched her arm free and shook her head, disgust souring her stomach. "Was I adopted?"

It made no sense. The man had no heart. How could they be related?

His gaze hardened to a cold, hard stare and she shivered despite the hot sun beating down.

"Not exactly," he said, lips twisting into an ugly expression. "You're the product of an affair your slut mother had with my cousin when I was away on business."

"What?"

Shock rang down her body in uncontrollable waves. Lyle wasn't her father?

"You heard me. You're not my daughter, but I raised you, so you'll show me some respect or you will end up like your parents. Dead."

Between her stinging head and throbbing arm, she had trouble trying to comprehend the bomb Lyle just dropped. The bastard wasn't really her dad. It was starting to make sense. All the beatings and snide comments. The stark hatred she'd seen in his eyes when he looked at her. *Yeah*, it made a lot of sense.

Going on the assumption she'd actually redialed someone and they were listening, Shayla decided to play the hand Lyle just dealt. "You killed your own cousin?"

The sly smile returned. "He got what was coming to him, and now I want mine. What do you say we give your boyfriend, Kevin Dalton a call?"

"No."

Despite her efforts to move her hand out of the way, Bruno caught it, pulling it under the table so others couldn't see and squeezed.

"He's not...my...boyfriend," she said between clenched teeth. "We...had a...fight."

No way in hell was she getting him involved, risking his life. No way. Bruno could break all her fingers, she wasn't going to do it.

"You stupid bitch. Fix it." Her father pushed his phone at her. "Now."

"No."

The pain was so bad her whole arm was going numb. Her mind registered stark concern on Holly's face and Shayla hoped the woman didn't act on it.

"I'd die before...calling him...for you."

The throbbing stole her breath and she struggled for air.

"Call him!"

Lyle was an idiot, and she longed to tell him, that thanks to Bruno, she couldn't yell or scream, let alone talk on a damn phone.

Fighting to remain conscious, she picked up the phone with her left hand, and right in front of the jerk, she dialed 911. He cursed and tried to grab it. Surely, out of her three attempts to call for help, one of them worked.

Then things got a little fuzzy. She saw a flash of movement behind *The Wall*, then heard Jordan's voice.

"No need to get up," the deputy said, a second before Bruno's head connected with the table.

Three times.

His hold slackened, and Shayla fought the pain-induced dizziness to scramble to her feet, cradling her throbbing arm.

A second later, Lyle rounded the table, fury adding color to his gaunt face. "You bitch!"

He raised his hand and Shayla braced for the blow she knew all too well.

It never came.

A hand caught the wrist, quickly twisted it behind Lyle's back and slammed him into the table across from Bruno. "You *ever* lay a hand on her again, and I swear I'll kill you," a familiar voice boomed, rough and full of so much venom even she flinched.

Kevin?

Shayla blinked, her fuzzy gaze clearing enough to see the man she loved handing Lyle off to Kade. When had they gotten there? She stumbled and would've fallen but for two strong arms coming around her. Soon, she was cradled against a warm, hard chest.

"It's okay, now, darlin'. I've got you. I've got you," Kevin repeated, kissing her head.

"Amelia? Caitlin?"

"Both safe and sound," he reassured, stroking her hair, his heart pounding a steady beat in her ear. "He won't hurt you again."

And because Shayla knew this to be true, and she was where she longed to be most in the whole world, she drew in a shuddering breath, burrowed into him and let go of her control.

A flurry of activity went on around her, but she closed her eyes and clung to Kevin. Completely drained and in pain, she let him take over. He sat down on the bench with her on his lap and held her tight.

Only he mattered. He was there.

After a few minutes, she recovered enough to draw back and manage a smile. "You came for me. H-how d-did...?"

A wide, proud smile claimed his face. "You called me."

Tears of relief filled her eyes and spilled down her cheeks. "It worked. I wasn't even sure what I was hitting."

316

"God, Shayla, I'm so sorry," he said, voice raw with emotion. "I should never have let you go yesterday. I love you. I was just scared. I've been burned before, and I guess my inner safety mechanism kicked in. Please forgive me for being such an idiot."

Throat too hot and swollen to speak, she nodded as a lone tear spilled down her face. He caught it with his thumb and brushed her cheek.

"I won't ever let anyone hurt you again." He leaned in to kiss her forehead, gently moving hair away from her stinging temple. His tone matched his gaze, full of fire and conviction. "I swear it."

"I love you, Kevin," she choked out, heart bursting at the seams, full of love and hope and happiness.

No more running. Or hiding. Or living in fear.

Lyle was done.

She was free to let herself care. Free to let herself feel. Free to let herself love. And she did. A gorgeous, fun-loving, kind-hearted man.

"I love you, too. So damn much." He pulled her close again, careful of her injuries, cradling her face against his chest as if she was the most precious thing in the world. He was to her. Kevin Dalton was her world. She held tight, the thundering of his heart a soothing sound she heard clear to her soul. It sounded like *home*.

No more running or longing. She finally found it.

Found home.

Home was her forever cowboy.

Epilogue

"We set a date."

Brandi's face was radiant as she made the announcement with Kade at Jordan's celebratory party for winning the Harland County Sheriff election.

Shayla stood cheering next to Kevin in a small crowd gathered away from the rest of the good citizens of Harland County. This announcement was just for the McCalls, Masters and Daltons. She was happy for her boss and his cousin, her *soon-to-be- cousin-in-law.* Her gaze fell to the diamond on her finger, heart light and happy at the prospect of marrying the man she loved in late October.

He grabbed her hand and brought it to his mouth, brushing his lips over the ring he'd placed there two weeks ago. On the one year anniversary of his *polling.* He was such a romantic.

"Happy?" he asked, gaze warm and affectionate.

"You know I am, cowboy," she replied, lightly tracing his jaw with her thumb.

"Well, Kade? Come on, man. Tell us. When are you getting your ball and chain?" Connor asked, receiving a well-placed elbow to his ribs by his wife.

These were good people and she was happy to call all of them her friends. And happy to have her sister around. Caitlin had moved back in with her for the summer after Greg received a duty station overseas and felt it best if they parted as friends rather than try to make a go of a long distance relationship. Her sister stepped

318

closer, flute of champagne in hand. Her third of the evening. *Yeah*, not taking the parting too well.

"We're getting married September twenty-seventh," Kade replied, glancing at the cheering crowd gathered around the smiling couple. "This is the tricky part, and I'm hoping Cole and Kevin can help me out."

"Sorry, cuz, I'm spoken for. You're going to have to handle your husbandly duties all on your own," Kevin said, lopsided grin dimpling his cheeks. "No offense, Brandi."

The couple laughed, and Shayla playfully elbowed his ribs.

"Behave."

He bent toward her ear. "Since when do you like when I behave?"

Her good parts tingled, confirming they loved his misbehavior.

"Thanks, Kev. Not what I need help with though," Kade said, his gaze turning serious. "We're getting married up in Pennsylvania. At the resort in the Poconos Brandi's brothers run. We'd like you all to come, so we were hoping the president and vice president of McCall Enterprises would offer up the jet."

"Of course," Cole said immediately, shaking Kade's hand. "It's at your service."

"Hopefully, I'll have a deputy by then so I can take a few days off," Jordan said, hugging Brandi and Kade.

"And hopefully I'm not too big by then," Kerri said, placing a hand over her stomach as she glanced up at her husband. Connor's eyes about fell out of his head, and a second later, the loudest whoop echoed in the room as the big cowboy lifted Kerri off the floor and spun her around.

When the congratulations subsided, and Mrs. McCall and Mrs. Masters wiped away happy tears, Shayla squeezed Kevin's hand and smiled up at him. "Hopefully, I'm not too big, either."

It took him a full three seconds to realize she'd just told him what Doc Turner confirmed with a phone call a half-hour ago. Kevin touched her belly, then glanced at her.

"Yeah?"

She smiled and nodded. "Yeah."

Unabashed joy and affection crossed his face, lighting his eyes with a brilliant light like she'd never seen as he flashed a dazzling smile. "God, I love you, Shayla Ryan. Just when I think you can't make me any happier, you done go and blow my *mind-palace* to smithereens."

As another round of cheers filled the Texas-pub, her fiancé cupped her face and kissed her soft and tender. The cowboy was so giving and so sweet, she was blessed to be creating a child with him and looked forward to filling their forever home.

♥

Holly's stay in Harland County, Texas is limited. She's only there to help run her uncle's ice cream business while he recuperates from an operation. Her home is in Colorado. Her life is in Denver. Her dream job is in Denver but won't be if she doesn't get back before her leave of absence runs out. Everybody knows this, but apparently her heart and body didn't get the memo because they spark to life whenever her uncle's smoking, hot doctor is around.

The cowboy isn't looking for a relationship. She isn't staying. Perfect set up for a fling. What harm could there be?

♥

Please visit the cowboys of Harland County

Her Healing Cowboy
Harland County Series: Book Five/Jace
Coming Soon

♥

***

**For announcements about upcoming releases
and exclusive contests:
Join Donna's Newsletter**
Visit me at: www.donnamichaelsauthor.com
***
Harland County Series

Visit my **Harland County Series Page** at my
website www.donnamichaelsauthor.com for release
information and updates!

**Book One: Her Fated Cowboy
Book Two: Her Unbridled Cowboy
Book Three: Her Uniform Cowboy
Book Four: Her Forever Cowboy**

Coming soon:
Book Five: Her Healing Cowboy

Become a *Cowboy Tamer!*

Drop me a line at donna_michaels@msn.com and
request some Cowboy-Tamer swag!

***

Harland County Series
Book One: _Her Fated Cowboy_

L.A. cop Jordan Masters Ryan has a problem. Her normal method of meeting a crisis head-on and taking it down won't work. Not this time. Not when fate is her adversary. Having kept her from the man she thought she'd always marry, the same fickle fate took away the man she eventually did. Thrown back into the path of her first love, she finds hers is not the only heart fate has damaged.

Widower and software CEO, Cole McCall fills his days with computer codes and his free time working the family's cattle ranch. Blaming himself for his wife's death, he's become hard and bitter. When his visiting former neighbor sets out to delete the firewall around his heart, he discovers there's no protection against the Jordan virus. Though she understands his pain and reawakens his soul, will it be enough for Cole to overcome his past and embrace their fated hearts?

***

Harland County Series
Book Two: *Her Unbridled Cowboy*

Homeless and unemployed thanks to an earthquake, divorced California chef Kerri Masters agrees to head back to her hometown to help plan her sister's Texas wedding. It must be her weakened state that has her eyeing the neighbor she used to follow around as a child. Her tastes tend towards gentlemen in suits, cultured, and neatly groomed— not a dimple-glaring, giant of a cowboy. He's big and virile, and makes her want things the inadequacies brought out during her divorce keep her from carrying out.

Connor McCall's brotherly feelings for the pesky former neighbor disappear when the grown up version steps on his ranch in her fancy clothes and shiny heels. Too bad she's a city girl, because he has no use for them. Three times he tried to marry one, and three times the engagements failed. He's not looking for number four no matter how much his body is all for jumping back in the saddle and showing the sexy chef just how it feels to be loved by a cowboy.

Turns out the earthquake was nothing compared to the passionate, force of nature of an unbridled cowboy, and Kerri learns far more about herself, and Connor, than she ever expected. But when events put his trust in her on the line, will he choose his heart or his pride?

***

Harland County Series
Book Three: *Her Uniform Cowboy*
Crowned Heart of Excellence – InD'tale Magazine
Voted BEST COWBOY in a Book/Readers' Choice-LRC

Desperate for change after a verbally abusive relationship, Brandi Wyne leaves a symphony career, her family, and the Poconos to fall back on a designing degree and a chance to renovate a restaurant/pub in Texas. Even though part of a National Guard family, she'd sworn off military men when the last one proved less than supportive of her thyroid condition and subsequent weight gain. Too bad her body seems to forget that fact whenever she's near the very hot, very military local sheriff.

Texas Army National Guard First Sergeant Kade Dalton never planned on becoming Harland County Sheriff or the attraction to a curvy, military-hating designer from Pennsylvania. Heavy with guilt from the death of a soldier under his command during a recent deployment, and dealing with his co-owned horse ranch and a bungling young deputy, it's hard most days just to keep his sanity. But it's the Yankee bombshell who threatens not only his sanity, but tempts his body...and his heart.

Fighting their attraction becomes a losing battle, and Kade soon finds sanctuary in the arms of the beautiful designer. Does he really have the right to saddle Brandi with his stress issues? And if so, can he take a chance on the town's newest resident not abandoning him like others in his past?

***

Time-shift Heroes Series
Book One: Captive Hero
2012 RONE Awards Nominee Best Time Travel

When Marine Corps test pilot, Captain Samantha Sheppard accidentally flies back in time and inadvertently saves the life of a WWII VMF Black Sheep pilot, she changes history and makes a crack decision to abduct him back to the present. With the timeline in jeopardy, she hides the handsome pilot at her secluded cabin in the Colorado wilderness.

But convincing her sexy, stubborn captive that he is now in another century proves harder than she anticipated— and soon it becomes difficult to tell who is captor and who is captive when the more he learns about the future, the more Sam discovers about the past, and the soul-deep connection between them.

As their flames of desire burn into overdrive, her flying Ace makes a historical discovery that threatens her family's very existence. Sam's fears are taken to new heights when she realizes the only way to fix the time-line is to sacrifice her captive hero...or is it?
Can love truly survive the test of time?

Time-shift Heroes Series
Visit my <u>Time-shift Heroes Series Page</u> for release information and updates!
Book One: Captive Hero
Book Two: Future Hero
Book Three: Unintended Hero

***
<u>Cowboy-Sexy</u>

Honky Tonk Hearts Series with The Wild Rose Press by <u>Donna Michaels</u>

4 Star RT Magazine Review*&*NOR Reviewer Top Pick

Finn Brennan was used to his brother playing practical jokes, but this time he'd gone too far--sending him a *woman* as a ranch hand, and not just a woman, but a Marine.

When Lt. Camilla Walker's CO asks her to help out at his family's dude ranch until he returns from deployment, she never expected to be thrust into a mistaken engagement to his sexy, cowboy twin--a former Navy SEAL who *hates* the Corps.

The Corps took Finn's father, his girlfriend and threatened his naval career. He's worked hard for another shot at getting back to active duty and won't let his brother's prank interfere. The last thing he needs is the temptation of a headstrong, unyielding, hot Marine getting in the way.

***

She Does Know Jack
A Romantic Comedy Suspense
by Donna Michaels

NOR Reviewer Top Pick

Former Army Ranger Capt. Jack 'Dodger' Anderson would rather run naked through a minefield in the Afghan desert than participate in a reality television show, but when his brother Matthew begins to receive threats, Jack quickly becomes Matthew's shadow. As if the investigation isn't baffling enough, he has to contend with the addition of a beautiful and vaguely familiar new contestant.

Security specialist, Brielle Chapman reluctantly agrees to help her uncle by going undercover as a contestant on the *Meet Your Mate* reality show. Having nearly failed on a similar assignment, she wants to prove she still has a future in this business. But when the brother of the *groom* turns out to be Dodger, the only one-nighter she ever had—while in disguise from a prior undercover case—her job becomes harder. Does he recognize her? And how can she investigate with their sizzling attraction fogging her brain? Determined to finish the job, she brings the case to a surprising climax, uncovers the culprit and *meets* her own *mate*.

***

Thanks for reading!

41907316R00211

Made in the USA
Lexington, KY
01 June 2015